A CROWN
OF LIGHTS

Phil Rickman

A Crown of Lights

MACMILLAN

First published 2001 by Macmillan
an imprint of Macmillan Publishers Ltd
25 Eccleston Place, London SW1W 9NF
Basingstoke and Oxford
Associated companies throughout the world
www.macmillan.com

ISBN 0 333 75174 4

1 3 5 7 9 8 6 4 2

A CIP catalogue record for this book is available from
the British Library.

Phototypeset by Intype London Ltd
Printed and bound in Great Britain by
Mackays of Chatham plc, Chatham, Kent

Part One

Goddess worshippers . . . are particularly concerned with creativity, intuition, compassion, beauty and cooperation. They see nature as the outward and visible expression of the divine, through which the goddess may be contacted. They have therefore more to do with ecology and conservationism than with orgies and are often gentle worshippers of the good in nature.

Deliverance (ed. Michael Perry)
The Christian Deliverance Study Group

ONE

The Local People

Betty was determined to keep the lid on the cauldron for as long as possible, which might just – the way she'd been feeling lately – mean for ever.

The arrival of the old box was no help.

It turned up on the back step at St Michael's only a few days after they had moved into the farmhouse and a week after Betty turned twenty-seven. It wasn't her kind of present. It seemed like a direct threat – or at least confirmation that their new life was unlikely to be the idyll that Robin expected.

For Betty, the first inkling of this – if you could call such experiences inklings – had already occurred only minutes before on that same weird evening.

The new year had been blown in, battered and dripping, and the wind and the rain still bullied the hills. Tonight, though, it looked like being clean and still and iron-hard with frost, and Robin had persuaded Betty to come with him to the top of the church tower – *their* church tower – to witness the brilliant winter sunset.

This was the first time she'd been up there, and the first time she'd ever been into the church out of daylight hours. It wasn't yet 5 p.m. but evening still came early to the Radnor Valley in late January – the dark side of Candlemas – and Robin was leaning over the cracked parapet to watch the final bloodrush over an otherwise unblemished sky.

'I guess what we oughta do,' he murmured playfully, 'is shake down that old moon.'

The Forest was laid out before them: darkening storybook hills, bearded with bracken. There were few trees – misleadingly, it had been named forest in the medieval sense of a place for hunting. Betty wondered how much of *that* still went on: the lamping of hares, the baiting of badgers. Maybe some night Robin would be standing up here and would see a party of silent men with guns and dogs. And then the shit would fly.

'So, uh, how would you . . .' Robin straightened up, slapping moss from his hands. ' . . . how would you feel about that?'

'You mean now, don't you?' With both hands, Betty pushed back her wild, blonde hair. She backed away from the edge, which had got her thinking about the death of Major Wilshire. Down below, about six feet out from the base of the tower, two flat tombstones had been exposed beneath a bush blasted back by the gales. That was probably where he'd fallen. She shivered. 'You actually mean *out here?*'

He shrugged. 'Why not?' He wore his orange fleece and his ludicrous flattened fez-thing with tiny mirrors around the side. The way Betty saw it, Robin Thorogood, having grown up in America, had yet to develop a functioning sense of the absurd.

'Why *not?*' Betty didn't remember exactly when 'shaking down the moon' had become his personal euphemism for sex, but she didn't altogether care for the term. 'Because this is, you know, January?'

'We could bring up blankets.' Robin did his abandoned puppy face.

Which no longer worked on Betty. 'Mother of God, I bet it's not even safe! Look at the floor . . . the walls! We wind up down in the bloody belfry, in a cloud of plaster dust, with multiple fractures, what happens *then?*'

'Aw, come *on*. It's been here for six . . . *eight* centuries. Just because—'

'And probably falling apart for most of the last hundred years!'

Betty gripped one of the battlements, then let go quickly in alarm, convinced for a second that a lump of mortar, or whatever medieval mixture those old masons used, was actually moving underneath it. The entire tower could be crumbling, for all they knew; their funds had run to only a cursory survey by a local bloke who'd said, 'Oh, just make sure it doesn't fall down on anybody, and you'll be all right.' They ought to bring in a reliable builder to give the place a going-over before they contemplated even having a picnic up here. If they could ever afford a builder, which seemed unlikely.

Robin stood warrior-like, with his back to the fallen sun, and she knew that in his mind he was wearing animal skins and there was a short, thick blade at his hip. Very like the figure dominating his painting-in-progress: Lord Madoc the intergalactic Celt, hero of Kirk Blackmore's *Sword of Twilight*. 700 pages of total bollocks, but it was misty cover designs for the likes of Blackmore that were going to have to meet the mortgage premiums until Betty dared come out locally as a herbalist and healer, or whatever was socially acceptable.

'Just I had a sensation of what it would be like afterwards,' the great visionary artist burbled on, unabashed, 'lying here on our backs, watching the swirl of the cosmos, from our own—'

'Whereas I'm getting a real sensation of watching the swirl of tomato soup with croutons.' Betty moved to the steps, took hold of the oily rope, feeling about with a trainered foot for the top step. 'Come on. We'll have years to do all that.'

Her words lingered in a void as hollow as these ruins. Betty could not lose the feeling that this time next year they would not even be here.

'You know your trouble?' Robin suddenly yelled. 'You're becoming sensible before your time.'

'What?' She spun at him, though knowing that he'd spoken without thinking . . . that it was just petulance . . . that she should let it go.

'Well . . .' He looked uneasy. 'You know . . .'

'No, I don't.'

'OK, OK . . .' Making placatory patting gestures with his hands, too late. 'Wrong word, maybe.'

'No, you've said it now. In normal life we're not supposed to be sensible because we're living *the fantasy*. Like we're really not supposed to bother about everyday stuff like falling to our deaths down these bloody crumbling steps, because—'

'There's a guy over there,' Robin said. 'In the field down by the creek.'

'It's a brook.' Betty paused on the top step.

'He's looking up.' Robin moved back to the rim of the tower. 'He's carrying something.'

'A spear of light, perhaps?' Betty said sarcastically. 'A glowing trident?'

'A bag, I think. A carrier bag. No, he's not in the field. I believe he's on the footway.'

'Which, of course, is a public footpath – which makes him entitled to be there.'

'Naw, he's checking us out.' The sunset made unearthly jewels out of the tiny round mirrors on Robin's fez. 'Hey!' he shouted down. 'Can I help you?'

'Stop it!' Sometimes Betty felt she was a lot older than Robin, instead of two years younger. Whole lifetimes older.

'He went away.'

'Of course he did. He went home to warm his bum by a roaring fire of dry, seasoned hardwood logs.'

'You're gonna throw that one at me all night, I can tell.'

'Probably. While we're sitting with our coats on in front of a lukewarm stove full of sizzling green pine.'

'Yeah, yeah, the wood guy ripped me off. He won't do it again.'

'Dead right he won't. First rule of country living: show them, from the very start, that you're not an urban innocent.'

Robin followed her down the narrow, broken stone steps. 'While being careful not to antagonize them, right?'

Betty stopped on the spiral, looked back up over her shoulder. It was too dark to see his face.

'Sooner or later,' she said, 'there *is* going to be antagonism – from some of them at least. It's a phase we're going to have to go through and come out the other side with some kind of mutual respect. This is not Islington. This is not even Shrewsbury. In Radnorshire, the wheels of change would grind exceeding slow, if they'd ever got around to inventing the wheel.'

'So what you're saying, making converts could take time?'

'We won't live that long. Tolerance is what we aspire to: the ultimate prize.'

'Jeez, you're soooo—*Oh, shit*—'

Betty whirled round. He'd stumbled on a loose piece of masonry, was hanging on to the hand-rope.

'You OK?'

'Third-degree rope burn, is all. I imagine the flesh will grow back within only weeks.'

She thought of Major Wilshire again and felt unsettled.

'I was born just twenty miles from here,' she said soberly. 'People *don't* change much in rural areas. I don't want to cause offence, and I don't think we need to.'

'*You* changed.'

'It's not the same. I'm not *from* yere, as they say.' Betty stepped out of the tower doorway and onto the frozen mud of what she supposed had once been the chancel. 'My parents just happened to be working here when I was born. They were from Off. I am, essentially, from Off.'

'Off what?'

'That's what they say. It's their word. If you're an immigrant you're "from Off". I'd forgotten that. I was not quite eleven when we left there. And then we were in Yorkshire, and Yorkshire flattens all the traces.'

Curtains of cold red light hung from the heavens into the roofless nave. When Robin emerged from the tower entrance, she took his cold hand in her even colder ones.

'Sorry to be a frigid bitch. It's been a heavy, heavy day.'

The church was mournful around her. It was like a huge, blackened sheep skeleton, with its ribs opened out. Incongruously, it actually came with the house. Robin had been ecstatic. For him, it had been *the* deciding factor.

Betty let go of Robin's hand. She was now facing where the altar must have been – the English side. And it was here, on this frigid January evening, that she had the flash.

A shivering sense of someone at prayer – a man in a long black garment, stained. His face unshaven, glowing with sweat and an unambiguous vivid fear. He'd discovered or identified or been told something he couldn't live with. In an instant, Betty felt she was suffocating in a miasma of body odour and anguish.

7

No! She hauled in a cold breath, pulling off her woollen hat, shaking out her sheaf of blond hair. *Go away. Don't want you.*

Cold. Damp. Nothing else. Shook herself like a wet dog. *Gone.*

This was how it happened. Always without warning, rarely even a change in the temperature.

'And it's not officially a church any more,' Robin was reminding her – he hadn't, of course, sensed a thing. 'So this is not about causing offence. Long as we don't knock it down, we can do what we like here. This is *so cool*. We get to reclaim an old, pagan sacred place!'

And Betty thought in cold dismay, What kind of sacred is this? But what she actually said, surprised at her own calmness, was, 'I just think we have to take it slowly. I know the place is decommissioned, but there're bound to be local people whose families worshipped here for centuries. And whose grandparents got married here and . . . and buried, of course.'

There were still about a dozen gravestones and tombs visible around the church and, although all the remains were supposed to have been taken away and reinterred after the diocese dumped the building itself, Betty knew that when they started to garden here they'd inevitably unearth bones.

'And maybe,' Robin said slyly, 'just maybe . . . there are people whose distant ancestors worshipped here *before* there was a Christian church.'

'You're pushing it there.'

'I like pushing it.'

'Yeah,' Betty agreed bitterly.

They moved out of the ruined church and across the winter-hard field and then over the yard to the back of the house. She'd left a light on in the hall. It was the only light they could see anywhere – although if they walked around to the front garden, they would find the meagre twinklings of the village of Old Hindwell dotted throughout the high, bare hedge.

She could hear the rushing of the Hindwell Brook, which almost islanded this place when, like now, it was swollen. There'd been weeks of hard rain, while they'd been making regular trips back and forth from their Shrewsbury flat in Robin's cousin's van, bringing all the books and stuff and wondering if they were doing the right thing.

Or at least Betty had. Robin had been obsessed from the moment he saw the ruined church and the old yew trees around it in a vague circle and the mighty Burfa Camp in the background and the enigmatic Four Stones less than a couple of miles away. And when he'd heard of the recent archaeological discoveries – the indications of a ritual palisade believed to be the second largest of its kind in Europe – it had blown him clean away. From then on, he *needed* to live here.

'There you go.' He bent down to the back doorstep. 'What'd I tell ya?' He lifted up something whitish.

'What's that?'

'It is a carrier bag – Tesco, looks like. The individual by the river had one with him. I'm guessing this is it.'

'He left it on our step?'

'House-warming present, maybe? It's kinda heavy.'

'Put it down,' Betty said quietly.

'Huh?'

'I'm serious. Put it back on the step, and go inside, put on the lights.'

'Jeeeeeeez!' Robin tossed back his head and howled at the newborn moon. 'I do not understand you! One minute I'm over-reacting – which, OK, I do, I overreact sometimes, I confess – and this is some harmless old guy making his weary way home to his humble fireside . . . and the next, he's like dumping ten pounds of Semtex or some shit—'

'Just put it down, Robin.'

Exasperated, Robin let the bag fall. It clumped solidly on the stone. Robin unlocked the back door.

Betty waited for him to enter first. She wouldn't touch the bag.

It was knotted at the top. She watched Robin wrench it open. A sheet of folded notepaper fell out. He spread it out on the table and she read the type over his shoulder.

Dear Mr and Mrs Thorogood,

In the course of renovation work by the previous occupants of your house, this receptacle was found in a cavity in the wall beside the fireplace. The previous occupants preferred not to keep it and gave it away. It has been suggested you may wish to restore it to its proper place.

With all good wishes,
The Local People

'"The Local People"?'
Robin let the typewritten note flutter to the tabletop. '*All* of them? The entire population of Old Hindwell got together to present the newcomers with a wooden box with. . . .' He lifted the hinged lid. ' . . . some paper in it.'
The box was of oak. It didn't look all that old. Maybe a century, Betty thought. It was the size of a pencil box she'd had as a kid – narrow, coffin-shaped. You could probably fit it in the space left by a single extracted brick.
She was glad there was only paper in there, not . . . well, bones or something. She'd never seriously thought of Semtex, only bones. Why would she think that? She found she was shivering slightly, so kept her red ski jacket on.
Robin was excited, naturally: a mysterious wooden box left by a shadowy stranger, a cryptic note . . . major, *major* turn-on for him. She knew that within the next hour or so he'd have found the original hiding place of that box, if he had to pull the entire fireplace to pieces. He'd taken off his fleece and his mirrored fez. The warrior on the battlements had been replaced by the big schoolboy innocent.
He flicked on all the kitchen lights – just dangling bulbs, as yet, which made the room look even starker than in daylight. They hadn't done anything with this room so far. There was a Belfast sink and a cranky old Rayburn and, under the window, their pine dining table and chairs from the flat. The table was much too small for this kitchen; up against the wall, under a window full of the day's end, it looked like . . . well, an altar. For which this was not the correct place – and anyway, Betty was not yet sure she wanted an altar in the house.

Part of the reason for finding a rural hideaway was to consider her own future, which – soon she'd have to confess to Robin – might not involve the Craft.

'The paper looks old,' Robin said. 'Well . . . the ink went brown.'

'Gosh, Rob, that must date it back to . . . oh, arguably pre-1980.'

He gave her one of those looks which said: Why have you no basic romance in you any more?

Which wasn't true. She simply felt you should distinguish between true insight and passing impressions, between fleeting sensations and real feelings.

The basic feeling she had – especially since her sense of the praying man in the church – was one of severe unease. She would rather the box had not been delivered. She wished she didn't have to know what was inside it.

Robin put the paper, still folded, on the table and just looked at it, not touching. Experiencing the moment, the *here*ness, the *now*ness.

And the disapproval of his lady.

All right, he'd happily concede that he loved all of this: the textures of twilight, those cuspy, numinous nearnesses. He'd agree that he didn't like things to be over-bright and clear cut; that he wanted a foot in two countries – to feel obliquely linked to the *old* worlds.

And what was so wrong with that? He looked at the wild and golden lady who should be Rhiannon or Artemis or Titania but insisted on being called the ultimately prosaic *Betty* (this perverse need to appear ordinary). *She* knew what he needed – that he didn't want too many mysteries explained, didn't care to *know* precisely what ghosts were. Nor did he want the parallel world of faerie all mapped out like the London Underground. It was the gossamer trappings and wrappings that had given him a profession and a good living. He was Robin Thorogood: illustrator, seducer of souls, guardian of the softly lit doorways.

The box, then . . . Well, sure, the box *had* been more interesting unopened. Unless the paper inside was a treasure map.

He pushed it toward Betty. '*You* wanna check this out?'

She shook her head. She wouldn't go near it. Robin rolled his eyes and picked up the paper. It fell open like a fan.

'Well, it's handwritten.' He spread it flat on the tabletop.

'Don't count on it,' Betty said. 'You can fake all kinds of stuff with computers and scanners and paintboxes. *You* do it all the time.'

'OK, so it's a scam. Kirk Blackmore rigged it.'

'If it was Kirk Blackmore,' Betty said, 'the box would have ludicrous runes carved all over it and when you opened it, there'd be clouds of dry ice.'

'I guess. Oh *no.*'

'What's up?'

'It's some goddamn religious crap. Like the Jehovah's Witnesses or one of those chain letters?'

'OK, let me see.' Betty came round and peered reluctantly at the browned ink. '"In the name of the Father, Son and Holy Ghost, amen, amen, amen . . ." Amen three times.'

'Dogmatic.'

'Hmmm.' Betty read on in silence, not touching the paper. She was standing directly under one of the dangling lightbulbs, so her hair was like a winter harvest. Robin loved that her hair seemed to have life of its own.

When she stepped away, she swallowed.

He said hoarsely, 'What?'

'Read.'

'Poison pen?'

She shook her head and walked away toward the rumbling old Rayburn stove.

Robin bent over the document. Some of it was in Latin, which he couldn't understand. But there was a row of symbols, which excited him at once.

$$\mathcal{XƆ4X}\text{:}\dot{\text{O}}\text{:}\ \mathcal{4X94A}\text{:}\dot{\text{O}}\text{:}\ \mathcal{ƆA44}$$

Underneath, the words in English began. Some of them he couldn't figure out. The meaning, however, was plain.

In the name of the Father Son and Holy Ghost Amen Amen
Amen . . .

O Lord, Jesus Christ Saviour Salvator I beseech the
salvation of all who dwell within from witchcraft and from
the power of all evil men or women or spirits or wizards or
hardness of heart Amen Amen Amen . . . Dei nunce . . . Amen
Amen Amen Amen Amen.

By Jehovah, Jehovah and by the Ineffable Names 17317 . . .
Lord Jehovah . . . and so by the virtue of these Names Holy
Names may all grief and dolor and all diseases depart from the
dwellers herein and their cows and their horses and their sheep
and their pigs and poultry without any molestation. By the
power of our Lord Jesus Christ Amen Amen . . . Elohim . . .
Emmanuel . . .

Finally my brethren be strong in the Lord and in the power
of His might that we may overcome all witches spells and
Inchantment or the power of Satan. Lord Jesus deliver them
this day – April, 1852.

Robin sat down. He tried to smile, for Betty's sake and because,
in one way, it was just so ironic.

But he couldn't manage a smile; he'd have to work on that.
Because this *was* a joke, wasn't it? It *could* actually be from Kirk
Blackmore or one of the other authors, or Al Delaney, the art director
at Talisman. They all knew he was moving house, and the new
address: St Michael's Farm, Old Hindwell, Radnorshire.

But this hadn't arrived in the mail. And also, as Betty had pointed
out, if it had been from any of those guys it would have been a whole
lot more extreme – creepier, more Gothic, less homespun. And dated
much further back than 1852.

No, it was more likely to be from those it said it was from.

The Local People – whatever that meant.

Truth was they hadn't yet encountered any *local* local people,
outside of the wood guy and Greg Starkey, the London-born landlord
at the pub where they used to lunch when they were bringing stuff
to the farm, and whose wife had come on to Robin one time.

Betty had her back to the Rayburn for warmth and comfort.

Robin moved over to join her. He also, for that moment, felt isolated and exposed.

'I don't get this,' he said. 'How could anyone here *possibly* know about us?'

TWO

Livenight

There were four of them in the hospital cubicle: Gomer and Minnie, and Merrily Watkins . . . and death.

Death with a small 'd'. No angel tonight.

Merrily was anguished and furious at the suddenness of this occurrence, and the timing – Gomer and Minnie's wedding anniversary, their sixth.

Cheap, black joke. *Unworthy of You.*

'Indigestion . . .' Gomer was squeezing his flat cap with both hands, as if wringing out a wet sponge, and staring in disbelief at the tubes and the monitor with that ominous wavy white line from a thousand overstressed hospital dramas. 'It's just indigestion, her says. Like, if she said it enough times that's what it'd be, see? Always works, my Min reckons. You *tells* the old body what's wrong, you don't take no shit – pardon me, vicar.'

The grey-curtained cubicle was attached to Intensive Care. Minnie's eyes were closed, her breathing hollow and somehow detached. Merrily had heard breathing like this before, and it made her mouth go dry with trepidation.

'It's rather a bad one,' the ward sister had murmured. *'You need to prepare him.'*

'Let's go for a walk.' Merrily plucked at the sleeve of Gomer's multi-patched tweed jacket.

She thought he glanced at her reproachfully as they left the room – as though she had the power to intercede with God, call in a favour.

15

And then, from out in the main ward, he looked back once at Minnie, and his expression made Merrily blink and turn away.

Gomer and Minnie: sixty-somethings when they got married, the Midlands widow and the little, wild Welsh-borderer. It was love, though Gomer would never have used the word. Equally, he'd never have given up the single life for mere companionship – he could get that from his JCB and his bulldozer.

He and Merrily walked out of the old county hospital and past the building site for a big new one – a mad place to put it, everyone was saying; there'd be next to no parking space except for consultants and administrators; even the nurses would have to hike all the way to the multi-storey at night. In pairs, presumably, with bricks in their bags.

Merrily felt angry at the crassness of everybody: the health authority and its inadequate bed quota, the city planners who seemed bent on gridlocking Hereford by 2005 – and God, for letting Minnie Parry succumb to a severe heart attack during the late afternoon of her sixth wedding anniversary.

It was probably the first time Gomer had ever phoned Merrily – their bungalow being only a few minutes' walk away. It had happened less than two hours ago, while Merrily was bending to light the fire in the vicarage sitting room, expecting Jane home soon. Gomer had already sent for an ambulance.

When Merrily arrived, Minnie was seated on the edge of the sofa, pale and sweating and breathless. *'Yow mustn't . . . go bothering about me, my duck, I've been through . . . worse than this.'* The TV guide lay next to her on a cushion. An iced sponge cake sat on a coffee table in front of the open fire. The fire was roaring with life. Two cups of tea had gone cold.

Merrily bit her lip, pushing her knuckles hard into the pockets of her coat – Jane's old school duffel, snatched from the newel post as Merrily was rushing out of the house.

They now crossed the bus station towards Commercial Road, where shops were closing for the night and most of the sky was a deep, blackening rust. Gomer's little round glasses were frantic with city light. He was urgently reminiscing, throwing up a wall of vivid memories against the encroaching dark – telling Merrily about the night he'd first courted Minnie while they were crunching through fields and woodland in his big JCB. Merrily wondered if he was fantasizing, because it was surely Minnie who'd forced Gomer's retirement from the plant hire business; she hated those diggers.

'. . . a few spare pounds on her, sure to be. Had the ole warning from the doc about that bloody collateral. But everybody gets that, isn't it?'

Gomer shuffled, panting, to a stop at the zebra crossing in Commercial Road. Merrily smiled faintly. 'Cholesterol. Yes, everybody gets that.'

Gomer snatched off his cap. His hair was standing up like a small white lavatory brush.

'Her's gonner die! Her's gonner bloody well snuff it on me!'

'Gomer, let's just keep praying.'

How trite did *that* sound? Merrily closed her eyes for a second and prayed also for credible words of comfort.

In the window of a nearby electrical shop, all the lights went out.

'Ar,' said Gomer dismally.

Through the hole-in-its-silencer roar of Eirion's departing car came the sound of the phone. Jane danced into Mum's grim scullery-office.

The light in here was meagre and cold, and a leafless climbing rose scraped at the small window like fingernails. But Jane was smiling, warm and light inside and, like, *up there.* Up there with the broken weathercock on the church steeple.

She had to sit down, a quivering in her chest. She remembered a tarot reader, called Angela, who had said to her, *'You will have two serious lovers before the age of twenty.'*

As she put out a hand for the phone, it stopped ringing. If Mum had gone out, why wasn't the answering machine on? Where *was* Mum? Jane switched on the desk lamp, to reveal a paperback New Testament beside a newspaper cutting about the rural drug trade. The sermon pad had scribbles and blobs and desperate doodles. But there was no note for her.

Jane shrugged then sat at the desk and conjured up Eirion. Who wasn't *conventionally* good-looking. Well, actually, he wasn't

17

good-looking at all, in some lights, and kind of stocky. And yet . . .
OK, it was the smile. You could get away with a lot if you had a
good smile, but it was important to ration it. Bring it out too often
and it became like totally inane and after a while it stopped reaching
the eyes, which showed insincerity. Jane sat and replayed Eirion's
smile in slow motion; it was a good one, it always *started* in the eyes.

Eirion? The name remained a problem. Basically, too much like
Irene. Didn't the Welsh have some totally stupid names for men?
Dilwyn – that was another. Welsh women's names, on the other hand,
were cool: Angharad, Sian, Rhiannon.

He was certainly trying hard, though. Like, no way had he 'just
happened to be passing' Jane's school at chucking-out time. He'd
obviously slipped away early from the Cathedral School in Hereford
– through some kind of upper-sixth privilege – and raced his ancient
heap nine or ten miles to Moorfield High before the buses got in.
Claiming he'd had to deliver an aunt's birthday present, and Ledwardine was on his way home. Total bullshit.

And the journey to Ledwardine . . . Eirion had really spun that
out. Having to go slow, he said, because he didn't want the hole in
his exhaust to get any bigger. In the end, the bus would've been
quicker.

But then, as Jane was climbing out of his car outside the vicarage,
he'd mumbled, 'Maybe I could call you sometime?'

Which, OK, Jane Austen could have scripted better.

'Yeah, OK,' she'd said, cool, understated. Managing to control
the burgeoning grin until she'd made it almost to the side door of the
vicarage and Eirion was driving away on his manky silencer.

The phone went again. Mum? Had to be. Jane grabbed at it.

'Ledwardine Vicarage, how may we help you? If you wish to book
a wedding, press three. To pledge a ten-thousand-pound donation
to the steeple fund, press six.'

'Is that the Reverend Watkins?'

Woman's voice, and not local. Not Sophie at the office. And not
Mum being smart. Uh-oh.

'I'm afraid she's not available right now,' Jane said. 'I'm sorry.'

'When *will* she be available?'

The woman sounding a touch querulous, but nothing threat-

18

ening: there was this deadly MOR computer music in the background, plus non-ecclesiastical office noise. Ten to one, some time-wasting double-glazing crap, or maybe the *Church Times* looking for next week's Page Three Clerical Temptress for dirty old canons to pin up in their vestries.

'I should try her secretary at the Bishpal tomorrow,' Jane said.

'I'm sorry?'

'The Bishop's Palace, in Hereford. If you ask for Sophie Hill . . .'

Most of the time it was a question of protecting Mum from herself. If you were a male vicar you could safely do lofty and remote – part of the tradition. But an uncooperative female priest was considered a snotty bitch.

'Look.' A bit ratty now, 'It *is* important.'

'Also important she doesn't die of some stress-related condition. I mean, like, important for me. Don't imagine *you'd* have to go off and live with your right-wing grandmother in Cheltenham. Who are you, anyway?'

Could almost hear the woman counting one . . . two . . . three . . . through gritted teeth.

'My name's Tania Beauman, from the *Livenight* television programme in Birmingham.'

Oh, hey! 'Seriously?'

'Seriously,' Tania Beauman said grimly.

Jane was, like, *horribly* impressed. Jane had seen *Livenight* four times. *Livenight* was such total crap and below the intelligence threshold of a cockroach, but compulsive viewing, oh yeah.

'*Livenight*?' Jane said.

'Correct.'

'Where you have the wife in the middle and the husband on one side and the toyboy lover on the other, and about three minutes to midnight one finally gets stirred up enough to call the other one a motherfucker, and then fights are breaking out in the audience, and the presenter looks really shocked although you know he's secretly delighted because it'll all be in the *Sun* again. That *Livenight*?'

'Yes,' Tania said tightly.

'You want her on the programme?'

'Yes, and as it involves next week's programme we don't have an awful lot of time to play with. Is she in?'

'No, but I'm Merrily Watkins's personal assistant, and I have to warn you she doesn't like to talk about the other stuff. Which is what this is about, right? The Rev. Spooky Watkins, from Deliverance?'

Tania didn't reply.

'I could do it, of course, if the money was OK. I know all her secrets. I'd be *very* good, and controversial. I'll call *anyone* a motherfucker.'

'Thank you very much,' Tania said drily. 'We will bear you in mind, when you turn twelve.'

'I'm sixteen!'

'Just tell her I called. Have a good night.'

Jane grinned. That was all Eirion's fault. Making her feel cool.

In the silence of the scullery, the phone went again.

'Jane?'

'Mum. Hey, guess wh—'

'Listen, flower,' Mum said, 'I've got bad news.'

THREE

Loved Like That

'So, like . . . how long will you be?'

'I just don't know, flower. We came here in Gomer's Land Rover. It was all a bit of a rush.'

'She was never ill, was she?' Jane said. 'Like really *never.*' The kid's voice was suddenly high and hoarse. 'You can't count on anything, can you? Not even *you.*'

Merrily sighed. Everybody thought she could pull strings. Gomer and Minnie's bungalow had become like the kid's second home in the village, Minnie the closest she'd ever had to an adopted granny.

'Flower, I'll have to go. I'm on the pay phone in the corridor, and I've no more change. As soon as I get to know something . . .'

'She's not even all that old. I mean, sixty-something . . . what's that? Nobody these days—'

Jane broke off. Remembering, perhaps, how young her own father had been when his life was sliced off on the motorway that night. But that was different. His girlfriend was in the car, too, and the hand of fate was involved there, in Jane's view.

'Minnie's strong. She'll fight it,' Merrily said.

'She isn't going to win, though, is she? I can tell by your voice. Where's Gomer?'

'Gone back in, to be with her.'

'How's he taking it?'

'Well, you know Gomer. You wouldn't want him prowling around in your sickroom.'

Gomer, in retirement, groomed the churchyard, cleared the

21

ditches, looked out for Merrily when Uncle Ted was doing devious, senior-churchwarden things behind her back. And dreamed of the old days – the great, rampaging days of Gomer Parry Plant Hire.

'He'll just smash the place up or something, if they let her die,' Jane concurred bleakly.

Meaning she herself would like to smash something up, possibly the church.

How many hours had they been here? Hospitals engendered their own time zones. Merrily hung up the phone and turned back into the ill-lit passage, teeming now: visiting hours. Once, she'd had a dream of purgatory, and it was like a big hospital, a brightly lit Brueghel kind of hospital, with all the punters helpless in operation gowns, and the staff scurrying around, feeding a central cauldron steaming with fear.

'Merrily?'

From a trio of nurses, one detached herself and came across.

'Eileen? I thought you were over at the other place.'

'You get moved around. We'll all end up in one place, anyway, if they ever finish building it, and won't that be a fockin' treat?' Eileen Cullen put out a forefinger, lifted Merrily's hair from her shoulder. 'You're not wearing your collar, Reverend. You finally dump the Auld Feller, or what?'

'We're still together,' Merrily said. 'And it's still hot.'

'Jesus, that's disgusting.'

'Actually, I had to leave home in a hurry.' Merrily spotted Gomer coming out of the ward, biting on an unlit cigarette, for comfort. 'I came with a friend. His wife's had a serious heart attack – unexpected. You won't say anything cynical, will you?'

'What's his name?' Sister Cullen was crop-haired and angular and claimed to have left Ulster to escape from 'bloody religion'.

'Gomer. Gomer Parry.'

'Well then, Mr Parry,' Cullen said briskly as Gomer came up, blinking dazedly behind his bottle glasses, 'you look to me to be in need of a cuppa – with a drop of something in there to take away the taste of machine tea, am I right?' She beckoned one of the nurses over. 'Kirsty, would you take Mr Parry to my office and make him a special tea? Stuff's in my desk, bottom drawer.'

Gomer glanced at Merrily. She moved to follow him, but Cullen put out a restraining hand. 'Not for you, Reverend. You've got your God to keep your spirits up. Spare me a minute?'

'A minute?'

'Pity you're out of the uniform . . . still, it's the inherent holiness that counts. All it is, we've got a poor feller in a state of some distress, and it'll take more than special tea to cope with him, you know what I'm saying.'

Merrily frowned, thinking, inevitably, of the first time she'd met Eileen Cullen, across town at Hereford General, which used to be a lunatic asylum and for one night had seemed in danger of reverting back.

'Ah no,' said Cullen, 'you only get one of those in a lifetime. This isn't even a patient. More like your man, Gomer, here – with the wife. And I don't know what side of the fence he's on, but I'd say he's very much a religious feller and would benefit from spiritual support.'

'For an atheist, you've got a lot of faith in priests.'

'No, I've got faith in *women* priests, which is not much at all to do with them being priests.'

'What would you have done if I hadn't been here?'

Cullen put her hands on her narrow hips. 'Well, y'*are* here, love, so where's the point in debating that one?'

The corridor had cracked walls and dim economy lighting.

'I'd be truly happy about leaving this dump behind,' Cullen said, 'if I didn't feel sure the bloody suits were building us a whole new nightmare.'

'What's his name, this bloke?'

'Mr Weal.'

'First name?'

'We don't know. He's not a man who's particularly forthcoming.'

'Terrific. He seen Paul Hutton?' The hospital chaplain.

'Maybe.' Cullen shrugged. 'I don't know. But you're on the spot and he isn't. What I thought was . . . you could perhaps say a prayer or two. He's Welsh, by the way.'

'What's that got to do with the price of eggs?'

'Well, he might be Chapel or something. They've got their own ways. You'll need to play it by ear on that.'

'You mean in case he refuses to speak to me in English?'

'Not Welsh like *that*. He's from Radnorshire. About half a mile over the border, if that.'

'Gosh. Almost normal, then.'

'Hmm.' Cullen smiled. Merrily followed her into a better lit area with compact, four-bed wards on either side, mainly elderly women in them. A small boy shuffled in a doorway, looking bored and aggressively crunching crisps.

'So what's the matter with Mrs Weal?'

'Stroke.'

'Bad one?'

'You might say that. Oh, and when you've said a wee prayer with him you could take him for a coffee.'

'Eileen—'

'It's surely the Christian thing to do,' Cullen said lightly.

They came to the end of the passage, where there was a closed door on their right. Cullen pushed it open and stepped back. She didn't come in with Merrily.

She was out of there fast, pulling the door shut behind her. She leaned against the partition wall. Her lips made the words, nothing audible came out.

She's dead.

Cullen shrugged. 'Seen one before, have you not?'

'You could've explained.'

'Could've sworn I did. Sorry.'

'And the rest of it?'

'Ah.'

'Quite.' What she'd seen replayed itself in blurred images, like a robbery captured on a security video: the bedclothes turned down, the white cotton nightdress slipped from the shoulders of the corpse.

The man beside the bed, leaning over his wife – heavy like a bear, some ungainly predator. He hadn't turned around as Merrily entered, nor when she backed out.

She moved quickly to shake off the shock, pulling Eileen Cullen a few yards down the passage. 'What in God's name was he *doing*?'

'Ah, well,' Cullen said. 'Would he have been cleaning her up, now?'

'On account of the NHS can't afford to pay people to take care of that sort of thing any more?'

Cullen tutted on seeing a tea trolley abandoned in the middle of the corridor.

'Yes?' Merrily said.

Cullen pushed the trolley tidily against a wall.

'There now,' she said. 'Well, the situation, Merrily, is that he's been doing that kind of thing for her ever since she came in, three days ago. Wouldn't let anyone else attend to her if he was around – and he's been around most of the time. He asks for a bowl and a cloth and he washes her. Very tenderly. Reverently, you might say.'

'I saw.'

'And then he'll wash himself: his face, his hands, in the same water. It looked awful touching at first. He'd also insist on trying to feed her, when it was still thought she might eat. And he'd be feeding himself the same food, like you do with babies, to encourage her.'

'How long's she been dead?'

'Half an hour, give or take. She was a bit young for a stroke, plainly, and he naturally couldn't come to terms with that. At his age, he was probably convinced she'd outlive him by a fair margin. But there you go: overattentive, overpossessive, what you will. And now maybe he can't accept she's actually dead.'

'I dunno. It looked . . . ritualistic almost, like an act of worship. Or did I imagine that?' Merrily instinctively felt in her bag for her cigarettes before remembering where she was. 'Eileen, what do you want to happen here?'

Cullen folded her arms. 'Well, on the practical side . . .'

'Which is all you're concerned about, naturally.'

'Absolutely. On the practical side, goes without saying we need the bed. So we need to get her down to the mortuary soon, and that means persuading your man out of there first. He'd stay with her all night, if we let him. The other night an auxiliary came in and found him lying right there on the floor beside the bed, fast asleep in his overcoat, for heaven's sake.'

'God.' Merrily pushed her hands deep down into the pockets of Jane's duffel. 'To be loved like that.' Not altogether sure what she meant.

Cullen sniffed. 'So you'll go back in and talk to him? Mumble a wee prayer or two? Apply a touch of Christian tenderness? And then – employing the tact and humanity for which you're renowned, and which we're not gonna have time for – just get him the fock out of there, yeah?'

'I don't know. If it's all helping him deal with his grief . . .'

'You're wimping out, right? Fair enough, no problem.'

Merrily put down her bag on the trolley. 'Just keep an eye on that.'

Well, she didn't know too much about rigor mortis, but she thought that soon it wouldn't be very easy to do what was so obviously needed.

'We should close her eyes,' Merrily said, 'don't you think?'

She put out a hesitant hand towards Mrs Weal, thumb and forefinger spread. The times she'd done this before were always in the moments right after death, when there was still that light-smoke sense of a departing spirit. But, oh God, what if the woman's eyelids were frozen fast?

'You will,' Mr Weal said slowly, 'leave her alone.'

Merrily froze. He was standing sentry-stiff. A very big man in every physical sense. His face was broad, and he had a ridged Roman nose and big cheeks, reddened by broken veins – a farmer's face. His greying hair was strong and pushed back stiffly.

Without looking at her, he said, 'What is your purpose in being here, madam?'

'My name's Merrily.' She let her hand fall to her side. 'I'm the . . . vicar of Ledwardine.'

'So?'

'I was just . . . I happened to be in the building, and the ward sister asked me to look in. She thought you might like to . . . talk.'

Could be a stupid thing to say. If there ever was a man who didn't like to talk, this was possibly him. Between them, his wife's eyes gazed nowhere, not even into the beyond. They were filmed over, colourless as the water in the metal bowl on the bedside table, and they seemed the stillest part of her. He'd pulled the bedclothes back up, so that only her face was on show. She looked young enough to be his daughter. She had light brown hair, and she was pretty. Merrily imagined him out on his tractor, thinking of her waiting for him at home. Wife number two, probably, a prize.

'Mr Weal – look, I'm sorry I don't know your first name . . .'

His eyes were downcast to the body. He wore a green suit of hairy, heavy tweed. 'Mister,' he said quietly.

'Oh.' She stepped away from the bed. 'Right. Well, I'm sorry. I didn't mean to upset you . . . any further.'

There was a long silence. The water bowl made her think of a font, of last rites, a baptism of the dying. Then he squinted at her across the corpse. He blinked once – which seemed, curiously, to release tension, and he grunted.

'J.W. Weal, my name.'

She nodded. It had obviously been a mistake to introduce herself just as Merrily, like some saleswoman cold-calling.

'How long had you been married, Mr Weal?'

Again, he didn't reply at once, as though he was carefully turning over her question to see if a subtext dropped out.

'Nine years, near enough.' *Yerrs*, he said. His voice was higher than you'd expect, given the size of him, and brushed soft.

Merrily said, 'We . . . never know what's going to come, do we?'

She looked down at Mrs Weal, whose face was somehow unrelaxed. Or maybe Merrily was transferring her own agitation to the dead woman. Who was perhaps her own age, mid to late thirties? Maybe a little older.

'She's . . . very pretty, Mr Weal.'

'Why wouldn't she be?'

Dull light had awoken in his eyes, like hot ashes raked over. People probably had been talking – J.W. Weal getting himself an attractive young wife like that. Merrily wondered if there were grown-up children from some first Mrs Weal, a certain sourness in the hills.

She swallowed. 'Do you, er . . . belong to a particular church?' Cullen was right; he looked like the kind of man who would do, if only out of tradition and a sense of rural protocol.

Mr Weal straightened up. She reckoned he must be close to six and a half feet tall, and built like a great stone barn. His eyebrows met, forming a stone-grey lintel.

'That, I think, is my personal business, thank you.'

'Right. Well . . .' She cleared her throat. 'Would you mind if I prayed for her? Perhaps we could—'

Pray together, she was about to say. But Mr Weal stopped her without raising his voice which, despite its pitch, had the even texture of authority.

'*I* shall pray for her.'

Merrily nodded, feeling limp. This was useless. There was no more she could say, nothing she could do here that Eileen Cullen couldn't do better.

'Well, I'm very sorry for the intrusion.'

He didn't react – just looked at his wife. For him, there was already nobody else in the room. Merrily nodded and bit her lip, and walked quietly out, badly needing a cigarette.

'No?' Eileen Culleen levered herself from the wall.

'Hopeless.'

Cullen led her up the corridor, well away from the door. 'I'd hoped to have him away before Menna's sister got here. I'm not in the best mood tonight for mopping up after tears and recriminations.'

'Sorry . . . whose sister?'

'Menna's – Mrs Weal's. The sister's Mrs Buckingham and she's from down south and a retired teacher, and there's no arguing with her. And no love lost between her and that man in there.'

'Oh.'

'Don't ask. I don't know. I don't want to know.'

'What was Menna like?'

'*I* don't know. Except for what I hear. She wasn't doing much chatting when they brought her in. But even if she'd been capable of speech, I doubt you'd have got much out of her. Lived in the sticks the whole of her life, looking after the ole father like a dutiful child's supposed to when her older and wiser sister's fled the coop. Father dies, she marries an obvious father figure. Sad story but not so unusual in a rural area.'

'Where's this exactly?'

'I forget. The Welsh side of Kington. Sheep-shagging country.'

'Charming.'

'They have their own ways and they keep closed up.'

The amiable, voluble Gomer Parry, of course, was originally from the Radnor Valley. But this was no time to debate the pitfalls of ethnic stereotyping.

'How did she come to have a stroke? Do you know?'

'You're not on the Pill yourself, Merrily?'

'Er . . . no.'

'That would be my first thought with Menna. Still on the Pill at thirty-nine. It does happen. Her doctor should've warned her.'

'Wouldn't Mr Weal have known the dangers?'

'He look like he would?' Cullen handed Merrily her bag. 'Thanks for trying – you did your best. Don't go having nightmares. He's just a poor feller loved his wife to excess.'

'I'll tell you one thing,' Merrily said. 'I think he's going to need help getting his life back on track. That's the kind of guy who goes back to his farm and hangs himself in the barn.'

'If he had a barn.'

'I thought he was a farmer.'

'I don't think I said that, did I?'

'What's he do, then? Not a copper?'

'Built like one, sure. No, he's a lawyer, as it happens. Listen, I'm gonna have a porter come up and we'll do it the hard way.'

'A solicitor?'

Cullen gave her a shrewd look. She knew Sean had been a lawyer, that Merrily herself had been studying the law until the untimely advent of Jane had pushed her out of university with no qualifications. The *difficult* years, pre-ordination.

'Man's not used to being argued with outside of a courthouse,'

Cullen said. 'You go back and find your wee friend. *We'll* sort this now.'

Walking back towards Intensive Care, shouldering her bag, she encountered Gomer Parry smoking under a red No Smoking sign in the main corridor. He probably hadn't even noticed it. He slouched towards her, hands in his pockets, ciggy winking between his teeth like a distant stop-light.

'Sorry about that, Gomer. I was—'

'May's well get off home, vicar. Keepin' you up all night.'

'Don't be daft. I'll stay as long as *you* stay.'

'Ar, well, no point, see.' Gomer said. He looked small and beaten hollow. 'No point now.'

The scene froze.

'Oh God.'

She'd left him barely half an hour to go off on a futile errand which she wasn't up to handling, and in her absence . . .

In the scruffy silence of the hospital corridor, she thought she heard Minnie Parry at her most comfortably Brummy: *'Yow don't go worrying about us, my duck. We're retired, got all the time in the world to worry about ourselves.'*

Instinctively she unslung her bag, plunged a hand in. But Gomer was there first.

'Have one o' mine, vicar. Extra-high tar, see.'

FOUR

Repaganization

Tuesday began with a brown fog over the windows like dirty lace curtains. The house was too quiet. They ought to get a dog. Two dogs, Robin had said after breakfast, before going off for a walk on his own.

He'd end up, inevitably, at the church, just to satisfy himself it hadn't disappeared in the mist. He would walk all around the ruins, and the ruins would look spectacularly eerie and Robin would think, *Yes!*

From the kitchen window, Betty watched him cross the yard between dank and oily puddles, then let himself into the old barn, where they'd stowed the oak box. Robin also thought it was seriously cool having a barn of your own. *Hey! How about I stash this in . . . the barn?*

When she was sure he wouldn't be coming back for a while, Betty brought out, from the bottom shelf of the dampest kitchen cupboard, the secret copy she'd managed to make of that awful witch charm. She'd done this on Robin's photocopier while he'd gone for a tour of Old Hindwell with George and Vivvie, their weekend visitors who – for several reasons – she could have done without.

Betty now took the copy over to the window sill. Produced in high contrast, for definition, it looked even more obscurely threatening than the original.

First the flash-vision of the praying man in the church, then this.

O Lord, Jesus Christ Saviour Salvator I beseech the salvation of

31

all who dwell within from witchcraft and from the power of all evil . . . Amen Amen Amen . . . Dei nunce . . . Amen Amen Amen Amen Amen.

Ritualistic repetition. A curious mixture of Catholic and Anglican. And also:

By Jehovah, Jehovah and by the Ineffable Names 17317 . . . Holy Names . . . Elohim . . . Emmanuel . . .

Jewish mysticism . . . the Kabbalah. A strong hint of ritual magic. And then those symbols – planetary, Betty thought, astrological.

It was bizarre and muddled, a nineteenth-century cobbling together of Christianity and the occult. And it seemed utterly genuine.

It was someone saying: *We know about you. We know what you are. And we know how to deal with you.*

Inside the barn, the mysterious box was still there, tucked down the side of a manger. All the hassle it was causing with Betty, Robin had been kind of hoping the Local People would somehow have spirited this item away again. It was cute, it was weird but it was, essentially, a crock of shit. A joke, right?

The Local People? He'd found he was beginning to think of 'the local people' the way the Irish thought of 'the little people': shadowy, mischievous, will o' the wispish. A different species.

Robin had established that the box did originally come from this house. Or, at least, there were signs of an old hiding place inside the living-room inglenook – new cement, where a brick had been replaced. So was this the reason Betty had resisted the consecration of their living room as a temple? Because it was there that the anti-witchcraft charm had been secreted?

Betty's behaviour had been altogether difficult most of the weekend. George Webster and his lady, the volatile Vivvie, Craft-buddies from Manchester, had come down on Saturday to help the Thorogoods get the place together, and hadn't left until Monday afternoon. It ought to have been a good weekend, with loud music, wine and the biggest fires you could make out of resinous green pine. But Betty had kept on complaining of headaches and tiredness.

Which wasn't like her at all. As a celebratory climax, Robin had wanted the four of them to gather at the top of the tower on Sunday night to welcome the new moon. But – wouldn't you know? – it was overcast, cold and raining. And Betty had kept on and on about safety. Like, would that old platform support as many as four people? What did she think, that he was planning an orgy?

Standing by the barn door, Robin could just about see the top of the tower, atmospherically wreathed in fog. One day soon, he would produce a painting of it in blurry watercolour, style of Turner, and mail it to his folks in New York. *This is a sketch of the church. Did I mention the ancient church we have out back?*

And *ancient* was right.

This was the real thing. The wedge of land overlooking the creek, the glorious plot on which the medieval church of St Michael at Old Hindwell had been built by the goddamn Christians, was most definitely an ancient pagan sacred site. George Webster had confirmed it. And George had expertise in this subject.

'Just take a look at these yew trees, Robin, still roughly forming a circle. That one and that one ... could be well over a thousand years old.'

Red-haired, beardy George running his hands down the ravines in those huge, twisting trunks and then cutting some forks of hazel, so he and Robin could do some exploratory dowsing. What you did, you asked questions – Were there standing stones here? Was this an old burial place, pre-Christianity? How many bodies are lying under here? – and you waited for the twig to twitch in response. Admittedly, a response didn't happen too often for Robin, but George was adept.

No, there'd been no stones but perhaps wooden poles – a woodhenge kind of arrangement – where the yews now grew. And yes, there had been pre-Christian burials here. George made it 300-plus bodies at one time. But the area had been excavated and skeletons taken away for reburial before the Church sold off the site, so there was the possibility that some pagan people been taken away for *Christian* burial. The arrogance of those bastards!

What happened, way back when the Christians were moving into

33

Britain, was some smart-ass pope had decreed that they should place their churches on existing sites of worship. This served two purposes: it would demonstrate the dominance of the new religion over the old and, if the site was the same, that might persuade the local tribes to keep on coming there to worship.

But that was all gonna be turned around at last. Boy, *was* it!

Robin stood down by the noisesome water, lining up the church with Burfa Hill, site of an Iron Age camp. He couldn't remember when – outside of a rite – he'd last felt so exalted. Sure, it only backed up what he'd already instinctively known from standing up top of the tower the other night. But, hell, confirmation was confirmation! He and Betty had been meant to come here, to revive a great tradition.

It was about repaganization.

They hadn't talked too much about long-term plans, but – especially after the weekend's discoveries – it was obvious these would revolve around in some way reinstating the temple which had stood here before there ever was a Christian church. Physically, this process had already begun: the church had fallen into ruins; if this continued, one day only the tower would remain . . . a single great standing stone.

Beautiful!

So why wasn't Betty similarly incandescent with excitement? Why so damn moody so much of the time? Was it that box? He'd wanted to tell George and Vivvie about the box and what it contained, but Betty had come on heavy, swearing him to silence. *'It's no one else's problem. It's between us and them. We have to find our own way of dealing with it.'*

Them? Like who? She was paranoid.

And also, he knew, still spooked about what had happened to Major Wilshire, from whose widow they'd bought this place.

The Major had died after a fall from a ladder he'd erected up the side of the tower. Hearing the story, George Webster – who'd drunk plenty wine by then – had begun speculating about the site having a guardian and maybe needing a sacrifice every so many years. Maybe they could find out if anyone *else* had died in accidents here . . .

At which point Robin had beckoned George behind the barn and told him to keep bullshit ideas like that to himself.

Besides, if there *was* any residual atmospheric stress resulting from that incident, Robin figured the best answer would be to do something positive on the tower itself to put things right, and as soon as possible.

Some kind of ritual. Betty would know.

Back in the house, he placed the oak box on the kitchen table. Betty's sea-green eyes narrowed in suspicion.

'We have to deal with this, Bets,' Robin told her. 'Then we forget about it for ever.'

'But not necessarily now,' Betty said irritably.

But Robin was already reading aloud the charm again, the parts of it he could decipher. He suspected Betty could interpret some of those symbols – as well as being more psychically developed, her esoteric knowledge was a good deal deeper and more comprehensive than his own – but she was not being overhelpful here, to say the fucking least.

'OK,' he conceded, 'so it's probably complete bullshit. I guess these things must've been real commonplace at one time – like hanging a horseshoe on your gate.'

'Yes,' Betty said with heavy patience. 'I'm sure, if we make enquiries, we'll find out that there was a local wise man – they called them conjurors in these parts. They were probably still going strong in the nineteenth century.'

'Like a shaman?'

'Something like that. Someone who dealt in spells and charms. If a couple of dozen lambs went down with sheep-scab or something, the farmer would start whingeing about being bewitched and call in the conjuror. It was usually a man – probably because farmers hereabouts didn't like dealing with women. The conjuror would probably write out a charm to keep in the fireplace, and everyone would be happy.'

'There you go. We just happened to be exposed to this one when we were overtired and stressed-out and ready to leap to gross conclusions.'

Betty nodded non-committally. Against the murk of the morning, she was looking a little more vital, in her big, red mohair sweater and her moon talisman. She'd already gotten sweating piles of pine logs stacked up both sides of the Rayburn. Yesterday, she and Vivvie had hung Chinese lanterns on the naked bulbs and called down blessings. But when George had suggested consecrating the temple in the living room itself, Betty had resisted that. Not something to be rushed into. Give the house spirits time to get to know them. Which had sounded unusually fey, for Betty.

'You know, if I'd followed my first instinct when I spotted that guy from the tower, I'd've run down directly and caught him dumping the carrier bag.'

Betty shook her head. 'If whoever it was had come face to face with you on the doorstep, he'd just have made some excuse – like seeing lights in the house, coming over to check everything was OK. He'd have pretended the bag was his shopping and just taken it away with him.'

He didn't argue; she was usually right. He put his hands on the box, closed his eyes, imagined other hands on the box – tried for a face.

'I did that already,' Betty said, offhand. 'Nothing obvious.'

Robin opened his eyes. If she'd tried it and gotten nothing then there was nothing to be had. He had no illusions about which of them was the most perceptive in *that* way. He didn't mind; he still had his creative vision.

'Put it back, now huh, Rob?'

'In the fireplace?'

'In the *barn*, dickhead! Let's not take any chances. Not till we know where it's been.'

'Ha!' He sprang back. 'You just have to know, dontcha?'

'I'd quite *like* to know,' Betty said casually.

'Bets . . .' He walked over, took her tenderly by the shoulders. 'Look at me . . . listen . . . What the fuck's it matter if someone *does* know we're pagans? What kind of big deal is that these days?'

'No problem at all,' Betty said, 'if you live in Islington or some-where. In a place like this—'

'*Still* no problem is my guess. Bets, this is *not you*. It's me does the overreacting. Me who won't leave the house if there's only one magpie out in the garden. I'm telling you, this is a *good* place. We're *meant* to be here. We came at the right time. Meant, right? Ordained. Making the church site into a sacred place again. All of that.'

Betty gently disengaged his hands. 'I thought I might go and see Mrs Wilshire. The note says, "The previous occupant preferred not to keep it and gave it away." So presumably they're talking about Mrs Wilshire. Or more likely her husband.'

'He was an old soldier. He'd have thought this was pure bullshit.'

'Before he died,' Betty said.

'Whooo!' Robin flung up his hands, backed away, as if from an apparition. 'Don't you start with that!'

'They didn't even get to live here, did they? They get the place half-renovated and then the poor old Major is gone, crash, bang.'

Robin spread his arms. 'Bets, it's like . . . it's an ill wind. It's a big pile of ifs. If the Wilshires had gotten all the renovation work done, everything smoothed out and shiny, and then put the place on the market, it'd've been way out of our price league. If people hereabouts hadn't been put off by the tragic reasons for the sale, there might've been some competition . . . If it hadn't gone on sale in November, all the holiday-home-seekers from London woulda been down here. If . . . if . . . if . . . What can I say? All the ifs were in our favour. But, if it makes you feel better, OK, let's go see her. When?'

'What?'

'The widow Wilshire.'

'Oh. No, actually, I thought I'd go alone. She struck me as a timid kind of person.'

'And I would spook her?'

'We don't want to look like a delegation. Anyway, you've work to do.'

'I do. I have work.'

The Kirk Blackmore artwork was complete, and would now be couriered, by special arrangement, not to the publishers but to Kirk himself. But the idea of producing a painting of the church, fog-swathed, had gotten hold of Robin, and if he mentioned it to Betty she'd be like: *If you've got time for that, you've got time to emulsion a wall.* But while she was gone, he could knock off a watercolour sketch of the church. He was already envisioning a seasonal series . . . a whatever you called a triptych when there were *four* of them.

'Besides . . .' Betty walked to the door then turned back with a swirl of her wild-corn hair. 'I'm sure there are lots of new things you want to play with, without me on your back.'

Robin managed a grin. With Betty around it was sometimes like your innermost thoughts were written in neon over your head. Sometimes, even for a high priestess, this broad was awesomely spooky.

And so beautiful.

Face it: if he really thought there was an element of risk here, any danger of it turning into an unhappy place, they would be out of here, no matter how much money they lost on the deal.

But that wasn't going to happen. That wasn't a part of the package. How they'd come to find this place was, in itself, too magical to ignore: the prophecy . . . the arrival of the house particulars within the same week, the offer of the Blackmore contract along with the possibility of a mega-deal for the backlist.

It was like the road to down here had been lit up for them, and if they let those lights go out, well that would really attract some bad karma.

The Local People?

Assholes. Forget them.

FIVE

Every Pillar in the Cloister

'Paganism.' The bishop spooned mustard on to his hot dog. 'What do we have to say about paganism?'

'As little as possible?' Merrily suggested.

The bishop put down his spoon on Sophie's desk. 'Exactly.' He nodded, and went on nodding like, she thought, one of those brushed-fabric boxer dogs motorists used to keep on their parcel shelves. 'Absolutely right.'

The email on the computer screen concluded:

> The programme will take the form of a live studio discussion and protagonists will probably include practising witches, possibly Druids, and 'fundamentalist' clergy. Would you please confirm asap with the programme researcher, Tania Beauman, in Birmingham?

'So, it's a "no", then. Fine.' Merrily stood up, relieved. 'I'll call them tonight. I'll say it's not a debate to which we feel we can make a meaningful contribution. And anyway, it's not something we encounter a particular problem with in this diocese. How does that sound?'

'Sounds eminently sensible, Merrily.' But the bishop's large, hairless face still looked worried.

'Good. Nobody comes out of an edition of *Livenight* with any dignity left. The pits of tabloid TV – Jerry Springer off the leash.'

'Who is Jerry Springer?' asked the bishop.

'You really don't want to know.'

'One finds oneself watching less and less television.' He brushed crumbs from his generously cut purple shirt. 'Which is wrong, I suppose. It is, after all, one's pastoral duty to monitor society's drab cavalcade . . . the excesses of the young . . . the latest jargon. The ubiquity of the word "shag" in a non-tobacco context.'

'I'll get my daughter Jane to compile a glossary for you.'

The bishop smiled, but still appeared strangely apprehensive. 'So this . . .' he peered at the screen ' . . . *Livenight* is not current affairs television?'

'Not as you know it. How would you describe *Livenight*, Sophie?'

'Like a rehearsal for Armageddon.' A shudder from the bishop's lay secretary, now permanently based in Merrily's gatehouse office. Sophie tucked a frond of white hair behind one ear and used a tissue to dab away a blob of English mustard which the bishop had let fall, appropriately, on the head of the burger-gobbling Homer Simpson on the computer's mouse mat. 'They begin with a specific topic, which is loosely based on a Sunday paper sort of news item.'

'Say you have a suburban husband who pimps for his wife,' Merrily said, 'is she being exploited, or is it a valid way of meeting the mortgage premiums?'

'Invariably,' Sophie said, 'they contrive to fill the studio with loud-mouthed bigots and professional cranks.'

Merrily nodded. 'And if you're insufficiently loud-mouthed, bigoted or cranky they just move on to the psycho sitting next to you who's invariably shaking at the bars to escape onto live television. Whole thing makes you despair for the future of the human race. I don't really think spreading despair is what we're about.'

'No,' the bishop said uncomfortably, 'quite. It's just that if you *don't* do it, we . . . we have a problem.'

Merrily stiffened. 'What are you saying exactly, Bernie?'

Bernie Dunmore had taken to wandering down to the Deliverance office on Tuesdays for a snack lunch with Merrily. He always seemed glad to get away from the Bishop's Palace.

Which was understandable. He was not actually the Bishop of

Hereford although, as suffragan Bishop of Ludlow, in the north of the diocese, the caretaker role had fallen to him in the controversial absence of the Right Reverend Michael Hunter.

In the end, though, Mick Hunter's disappearance had not detonated the media explosion the diocese had feared, coinciding as it had with the resignation of two other Church of England bishops and the suicide of a third – all of this following calls for an outside inquiry into their personal expenses exceeding £200,000 a year, and the acceptance of unorthodox perks.

Questions had also been asked about Hunter's purchase of a Land Rover and a Mercedes, used by his wife, and, as neither the press nor the police had been able to substantiate anything more damaging, the diocese had been happy to shelter behind any other minor scandal. Now the issue had been turned around: four bishops had spoken out in a *Sunday Times* feature – 'Keeping the Mitre on C of E Executive Stress' – about the trials of their job in an increasingly secular age. There was, inevitably, a picture of Mick Hunter in his jogging gear, 'escaping from the pressure'.

Was it better, under the circumstances, that the truth had not come out? Merrily wasn't sure. But she liked Bernie Dunmore, sixty-two years old and comfortably lazy. Prepared to hold the fort until such time as the search for a suitably uncontroversial replacement for Mick Hunter could begin. No one, in fact, could be less controversial than Bernie; the worst he'd ever said about Hunter was, 'One would have thought the Crown Appointments Commission would have been aware of Michael's personality problems.'

As Mick's appointee, Merrily had offered Bernie her resignation from his Deliverance role, citing the seasoned exorcist Huw Owen's warning that women priests had become a target for every psychotic grinder of the dark satanic mills who ever sacrificed a cockerel.

'All the more reason for you to remain, my dear,' Bernie had told her, though she couldn't quite follow his reasoning. She hoped it wasn't just because he enjoyed his Tuesday lunchtimes here sitting on the Deliverance desk with a couple of hot dogs and a can of lager.

*

'*You* explain, Sophie,' the bishop said.

His lay secretary sat up, spry and elegant in a grey business suit with fine black stripes, and consulted her memo pad.

'Well, as you know, this programme approached us some weeks ago, with a view to Merrily taking part in a general discussion on supernatural phenomena – which Merrily declined to do.'

'Because Merrily was afraid of what they might already know about recent events in Hereford,' added Merrily.

'Indeed. I then received a personal call from Ms Tania Beauman relating to this week's proposed paganism programme, again requesting Merrily.'

'They've obviously seen that understatedly sexy photo of you, my dear,' said Bernie.

Merrily sighed, looked at the clock: 1.35. She had to be back in Ledwardine by three for Minnie Parry's funeral.

Sophie said, 'You'll probably both recall the story in the papers last Thursday about the pagan parents in Somerset who demanded that their child be allowed to make her own religious observances at the village primary school.'

The bishop winced.

'*Livenight*'s programme peg for this week,' Sophie explained. 'It's now claimed there are over 100,000 active pagans in Britain. Either belonging to groups – covens – or nurturing their beliefs independently.'

'Complete nonsense, of course.' The bishop sniffed. 'But figures like that can't be proved one way or the other.'

'The programme will discuss the pagans' claim that they represent the traditional old religion of the British Isles and, as such, should be granted rights and privileges at least equivalent to those accorded to Islam, Buddhism and other non-indigenous faiths.'

Bernie snorted. 'Most of their so-called traditions date back no further than the '50s and sixties. They're a sham. These people are just annoyed because they've been refused charity status.'

'In a secular state,' Merrily said, 'it could be argued that their superstitions are just as valid as ours – I'm doing my devil's advocate bit here.'

The bishop jutted his chins and straightened his pectoral cross.

'My question, though, is should we be actively *encouraging* people to strip off and have sex with each other's wives under the full moon while pretending it's religion? I think not. But neither do I think we should be engaging them in open battle – boosting their collective ego by identifying them as representatives of the Antichrist.'

'However,' Sophie said, 'that *does* reflect the general approach of one of our more . . . outgoing rural rectors: the Reverend Nicholas Ellis.'

'Oh,' Merrily said.

'In his sermons and his parish magazine articles, he's tended to employ . . . quite colourful terminology. *Livenight*'s own kind of terminology, you might say.'

Sophie and the bishop both looked enquiringly at Merrily. She shook her head. 'I know of him only through the press cuttings. Loose-cannon priest who dumped his churches. Spent some years in the States. Charismatic. Direct intervention of the Holy Spirit . . . Prophecy . . . Tongues.'

'Split the community,' Bernie said, 'when he expressed disdain for actual churches and offered to conduct his charismatic services in community halls, barns, warehouses, whatever. So Mick Hunter agreed to appoint a regular priest-in-charge in the area, to appease the traditionalists, and let Ellis continue his roving brief.'

Merrily recalled that Ellis now belonged to a fast-growing Anglican anti-Church faction calling itself the Sea of Light.

'Awfully popular figure, this Nicholas, I'm afraid,' Bernie Dunmore said. 'Since we cut him loose, he's set up in some run-down village hall and he's packing it to the rafters with happy-clappies from miles around. Which makes him somewhat unassailable, and yet he's not a demonstrative bloke in himself. Quiet, almost reticent, apparently. But came back from America with a knowledge of agriculture and farming ways that seems to have rather endeared him to the Radnorshire people.'

Merrily grimaced, recalling what Eileen Cullen at the hospital had said about the piece of Wales just over the border: '*They have their own ways and they keep closed up.*'

Bernie flicked her a foxy smile. 'The man was after your job, did you know?'

Her eyebrows went up. 'Deliverance?'

'Wrongly assuming you'd be on the way out in the aftermath of Michael's, er, breakdown. Soon as I showed my face in Hereford, there was Nicholas requesting an audience.'

'Did he get one?'

'Showed him the door, of course, but tactfully. Good God, he's the last kind of chap you want as your exorcist. Sees the Devil behind every pillar in the cloister. Fortunately, Deliverance is rarely up for tender. Press-gang job, in my experience.' He beamed at Merrily. 'And all the better for that.'

'Is he currently doing any deliverance work?' she asked warily.

'Frankly, my dear . . . one doesn't like to enquire. Though if there are any complaints, I suppose we'll have to peer into the pond. Meanwhile . . . this *Livenight*.' The bishop snapped back the ringpull on his can of lager and accepted a tall glass from Sophie. 'Apparently, he *has* been mentioned as a possible – what do you call it? – front-row speaker.'

'Having already been approached by Ms Beauman,' Sophie said, 'and having apparently said yes.'

'But not on behalf of the diocese,' Merrily said. 'Just a lone maverick, surely?'

The bishop shrugged, spilling a little lager. 'One can't stop the man appearing on national television. And one can't be seen to try to stop him.'

'But if he starts shooting his mouth off about the invasion of sinister sects and child sacrifice and that kind of stuff, it's going to reflect on all of us.'

'In the wake of recent events here,' said the bishop, 'we were all rather looking for a quiet life for a while.'

Merrily looked into the big, generally honest face of the suffragan Bishop of Ludlow, a lovely old town in south Shropshire from which he was commuting and to which he clearly couldn't wait to get back.

'Well . . .' Sophie folded a square of green blotting paper into a beer mat for the bishop, giving herself an excuse not to look directly at Merrily. 'Ms Beauman did intimate to me that they might be prepared to consider rescinding their invitation to the Reverend Mr

Ellis . . . if they could recruit for their programme the person they originally had in mind.'

There was an uneasy silence. The bishop drank some lager and gazed out of the window, across Broad Street. It was starting to rain.

'Shit,' Merrily said under her breath.

SIX

Unkind Sky

'A box?' Lizzie Wilshire looked vaguely puzzled. But more vague than puzzled, Betty thought.

'Inside the fireplace.'

'I did rather *like* that fireplace,' Mrs Wilshire recalled. 'It had a wonderful old beam across the top. It was the one emphatic feature of a rather drab room.'

'Yes, the living room.'

'You thought there ought to be beams across the ceiling too. Bryan said there still must be, underneath all the plaster. But I did like the fireplace, if precious little else.'

The fireplace to which Mrs Wilshire's chair was presently pulled close was forlornly modern, made of brownish dressed stone. It surrounded a bronze-enamelled oil-fired stove – undernourished flames behind orange-tinted glass.

Mrs Wilshire frowned. 'It also had woodworm, though.'

'The box?'

'The beam, dear. That worried me a little, until Bryan said, "Lizzie, it will take about 300 years for the worms to eat through it." I would still have wanted it treated, though.' She blinked at Betty. 'Have you had it treated, yet?'

'Not yet. Er, Mrs Wilshire . . . there was a box. It was apparently found in the fireplace, while you were having some repairs done to the walls. It contained a paper with a sort of . . . prayer. I suppose you'd call it a prayer.'

'Oh!' Understanding came at last to the bulging eyes of frail

Lizzie Wilshire – big eyes which made her look like an extra-terrestrial or a wizened, expensive cat. 'You mean the *witch paper!*'

'Yes,' Betty said softly, 'the witch paper.'

It wasn't that she was particularly old, early seventies, Betty reckoned, but she had arthritis – obvious in her hands – and accepted her own helplessness. Clearly, she'd never been used to doing very much for herself or making decisions. 'It's so confusing now,' she said. 'So many things I know nothing about. Things I don't *want* to have to know about. Why should I?'

She was still living in this colonial-style bungalow on the edge of New Radnor, the tiny town, or big village, where she and the Major had lived for over fifteen years, since his retirement. Just a stopgap, the Major always said, until they found the right place... an interesting place, a place he could *play* with.

She told Betty how she thought he'd finally accepted that he was too old to take on something needing extensive refurbishment when, out on a Sunday drive, they'd found – not three miles away, at Old Hindwell – the house with which Major Bryan Wilshire, to the utter dismay of his wife, had fallen hopelessly in love.

'It was empty, of course, when we saw it. It had belonged to two reclusive bachelor farmers called Prosser. The last surviving one had finally been taken into a nursing home. So you can imagine the state it was in.'

Betty already knew all this from the estate agents, and from their own searches. Also she'd sensed a residual sourness and meanness in rooms left untouched by Major Wilshire. But she let his widow talk.

'And that awful old ruined church in the grounds. Some would say it was picturesque, but I hated it. Who could possibly want a disused church? Except Bryan, of course.'

The Major had found the church fascinating and had begun to delve into its history: when it had last been used as a place of worship, why it had been abandoned. Meanwhile, the house was to be auctioned and, because of its poor condition, the reserve price was surprisingly low. This was when the market was still at low ebb, just before the recent property boom, and there was no rush for second homes in the countryside.

'There was no arguing with Bryan. He put in an offer and it was accepted, so the auction was called off. Bryan was delighted. It was so cheap we didn't even have to consider selling this bungalow. He said he could renovate the place at his leisure.'

A reputable firm of contractors had been hired, but Major Wilshire insisted on supervising the work himself. The problem was that Bryan was always so hands-on, climbing ladders and scaffolding to demonstrate to the workmen exactly what he wanted doing. Lizzie couldn't bear to look up at him; it made her quite dizzy. But Bryan had always needed *that* element in his life, serving as he had with *that* regiment in Hereford. The SAS, Betty presumed, and she wondered how an all-action man like Major Wilshire had ended up with a wife who didn't like to look *up*.

At least that had spared Lizzie an eyewitness memory of the terrible accident. This had been brought about by the combination of a loose stone under a slit window in the tower, a lightweight aluminium ladder, and a freak blast of wind from the Forest.

At first they'd told her it was simply broken bones, and quite a number of them; so it would have taken Major Wilshire a long time to recover. Many months. But no internal injuries, so it could have been worse. He'd at least be home in a matter of weeks. Mrs Wilshire meanwhile had determined that he would never again go back to that awful place.

But Bryan had never come home again. The shock – or something – had brought on pneumonia. For this energetic, seemingly indestructible old soldier, it was all over in four days.

There was one photograph of the Major on the mantelpiece: a wiry man in a cap. He was not in uniform or anything, but in the garden, leaning on a spade, and his smile was only a half-smile.

'So quick. So bewilderingly *quick*. There was no time at all for preparations,' Mrs Wilshire said querulously. 'We'd always made time to prepare for things; Bryan was a great planner. Nothing was entirely unexpected, because he was always ready for it. Whenever he had to go away, my sister would come to stay and Bryan would always pay the bills in advance and order plenty of heating oil. He always thought ahead.'

How ironic, Betty thought, that a man whose career must have involved several life-or-death situations, and certainly some gruelling and risky training exercises, should have died after a simple fall from a ladder.

From a church? Was this ironic, too?

When it started to rain harder, Robin packed up his paints and folded the easel. A few stray drops on a watercolour could prove interesting; they made the kind of accidental blurs you could use, turned the painting into a *rain*colour. But if it came on harder, like now, and the wind got up, this was the elements saying to him: Uh-huh, try again.

He stood for a moment down below the church ruins, watching the creek rush down into a small gorge maybe fifteen feet deep, carrying branches and a blue plastic feed-sack. Wild! There was a narrow wooden footbridge which people used to cross to get to church. The bridge was a little rickety, which was also kind of quaint. Maybe this even explained why the church had become disused. Fine when the congregation came on foot from the village, but when the village population had gotten smaller, and the first automobiles had arrived in Radnorshire . . . well, not even country ladies liked to have to park in a field the wrong side of the Hindwell Brook and arrive in church with mud splashes up their Sunday stockings.

In the distance, over the sound of the hurrying water, Robin could hear a vehicle approaching. It was almost a mile along the track to reach the county road, so if you heard any traffic at all, it had to be heading this way. Most often it was Gareth Prosser in his Land Rover – biggest farmer hereabouts, a county councillor and also a nephew of the two old guys who used to own St Michael's. Robin would have liked if the man stopped one time, came in for a beer, but Gareth Prosser just nodded, never smiled to him, never slowed.

Country folk took time to get to know. Apparently.

But the noise wasn't rattly enough to be Prosser's Land Rover, or growly enough to be his kids' dirt bikes. It was a little early to be

Betty back from the widow Wilshire's, but – who knew? – maybe she at last had developed the hots again for her beloved husband, couldn't wait to get back to the hissing pine fires and into the sack in that wonderful damp-walled bedroom.

Sure.

Robin kicked a half-brick into the Hindwell Brook, lifting up his face to the squally rain. It would come right. The goddess would return to her. Just the wrong part of the cycle, was all. He offered a short, silent prayer to the spirits of the rushing water, that the flow might once again go their way. Winter was, after all, a stressful time to move house.

The vehicle appeared: it was a Cherokee jeep. When the driver parked in the yard and got out, Robin stared at him, and then closed his eyes and muttered, 'Holy shit.'

He didn't need this. He did not need this now.

'But we don't believe in those things any more, do we, my dear? Witches, I mean.'

How on earth had the wife of an SAS officer managed to preserve this childlike, glazed-eyed innocence? Betty smiled and lifted the bone china teacup and saucer from her knees in order to smooth her long skirt. Jeans would have been the wrong image entirely and, after the assault on the house over the past few days, she didn't have an entirely clean pair anyway.

Clean was paramount here. It was a museum of suburbia; it had actual trinkets. Betty guessed that the Major's wife had secretly been hoping that the renovation work at St Michael's would *never* be completed, that it would be simply a long-term hobby for him while they went on living here in New Radnor – which, although it was on the edge of the wilderness and still dominated by a huge castle-mound, was pleasant and open, with a wide main street, neat cottages, window boxes in the summer, a nice shop. Unlike Old Hindwell, it kept the Forest at arm's length.

Mrs Wilshire said, 'It was silly, it was slightly unpleasant. And, of course, it wasn't even terribly old.'

'About 1850, as I recall.'

'Oh,' said Mrs Wilshire. 'Have you found another one?'

'No, I think it's the same one,' Betty said patiently. 'Someone brought it back, you see.'

'Who in the world would do that?'

'We don't know. It was left on the doorstep.'

'What an odd thing to do.'

'Yes, it *was* odd, which is why we'd like to find out who did it. I was hoping you might be able to tell me who you gave the box to when you . . . gave it away. Do you remember, by any chance?'

'Well, Bryan saw to that, of course. Bryan always knew where to take things, you see.'

'Would there perhaps have been . . . I don't know, a local historian or someone like that who might have had an interest in old documents?'

'Hmmm.' Mrs Wilshire pursed her tiny lips. 'There's Mr Jenkins, at the bookshop in Kington. But he writes for the newspapers as well, and Bryan was always very suspicious of journalists. Perhaps it was the new rector he gave it to.'

'Oh.'

'Not that he was terribly fond of the rector either. We went to one of his services, but only once. So noisy! I've never seen so many people in a church – well, not for an ordinary evensong. They must have come from elsewhere, like football supporters. And there were people with guitars. And candles – so many candles. Well, I have nothing against all that, but it's not for the likes of us, is it? Are you a churchgoer, Mrs Thorogood?'

'Er . . . No. Not exactly.'

'And your husband? What is it your husband does for a living? I'm sure I *did* know . . .'

'He's an artist, an illustrator. He does book covers, mainly.'

'Bryan used to read,' Lizzie Wilshire said distantly. 'He'd go through periods when he'd read for days in his sanctum.' Her big eyes were moist; Betty thought of parboiled eggs.

'Look,' she said, 'is there anything I can do, while I'm here? Vacuum the carpet? Clean anything? Prepare you something for tea? Or is there anywhere you need to go? You don't drive, do you?'

'Bryan never wanted me to use the car. He always said rural roads were far more dangerous because of the tractors and trailers. And we have a local man, Mr Gibbins, who runs a sort of part-time taxi service. He takes me into Kington twice a week and carries my shopping for me. You mustn't worry about me, my dear, with all the work you must have on your hands, getting that old place ready to move into.'

'We moved in last week, actually.'

Mrs Wilshire's small mouth fell open. 'But it was an absolute hovel when—'

She stopped, possibly remembering that her own estate agent had preferred phrases like 'characterful and eccentric'.

'It's still got one or two problems,' Betty said, more cheerfully than she felt, 'but it doesn't let the rain in. Well, not in most of the rooms. Mrs Wilshire, is there anyone else apart from the rector that your husband might have handed that box to – or even told about it?'

Mrs Wilshire shook her head. 'He brought it back here to examine it, but he didn't keep it very long, I know that, because I wouldn't have it in the house – so dirty. I do rather remember something, but . . .'

Betty sighed. 'Look, let me wash up these cups and things, at least.'

'No dear, I can manage.' She fumbled her cup and saucer to the coffee table, but the cup fell over and spilled some tea, which began to trickle over the edge of the table onto the carpet. Betty snatched a handful of tissues from a box nearby and went down on her knees.

Mopping, she glanced up at Lizzie Wilshire and saw years of low-level pain there, solidified like rock strata. And then, as sometimes happened when observing someone from an oblique angle, she caught a momentary glimpse of Lizzie's aura. It was not intact and vibrated unevenly. This woman needed help.

Betty gathered up the cups and saucers. 'Are you having treatment for the . . . arthritis?'

'Oh, yes, Dr Coll. Do you know Dr Coll?' Betty shook her head. 'Dr Coll says I shall need a new hip, soon, and perhaps a new knee. But that may mean going all the way to Gobowen. Sixty miles or more! In the meantime, I'm on a course of tablets. Can't have new hands, unfortunately, but Dr Coll's been marvellous, of course. He—'

'Steroids?'

Mrs Wilshire looked vague again. 'Cortisone, I believe. And something else – some different pills. I have to take those *twice* a day. I haven't been taking them very long. Just since after Bryan died . . . It seems to have got so much worse since Bryan died. All the worry, I suppose.'

'Mrs Wilshire . . . I hope you don't mind me asking, but have you ever tried anything . . . alternative? Or complementary, as some people prefer to say.'

'You mean herbs and things?'

'Sort of.'

'I would be very wary, my dear. You never know quite what you're taking, do you?'

Betty carried the cups and saucers into a large kitchen – made pale, rather than bright, by wide windows, triple-glazed, with a limited view of a narrow garden, a steep, green hillside and a slice of unkind sky. At the bottom of the garden was a shed or summerhouse with a small verandah – like a miniature cricket pavilion.

Betty's compassion was veined with anger. Lizzie Wilshire was happily swallowing a cocktail of powerful drugs, with all kinds of side-effects. An unambitious woman who'd let her husband handle everything, make all her decisions for her, and was now willingly submitting to other people who didn't necessarily give a shit.

When Betty came back, Lizzie Wilshire was staring placidly into the red glow of the oil heater.

'Are you going to stay here?' Betty asked.

'Well, dear, the local people are so good, you see . . . You young-sters seem to flit about the country at whim. I don't think I could move. I'd be afraid to.' Mrs Wilshire looked down into her lap. 'Of course, I don't really like it at night – it's such a big bungalow. So quiet.'

'Couldn't you perhaps move into the centre of the village?'

'But I know Bryan's still here, you see. The churchyard's just around the hillside. I feel he's watching over me. Is that silly?'

'No.' Betty gave her an encouraging smile. 'It's not silly at all.'

*

She walked out to the car feeling troubled and anxious in a way she hadn't expected. That unexpected glimpse of the damaged aura suggested she was meant to come here today. Prodding the little Subaru out onto the long, straight bypass, under an already darkening sky, Betty decided to return soon with something herbal for Mrs Wilshire's arthritis.

It would be a start. And she was getting back that feeling of having come right round in a circle. It was as a child in Llandrindod Wells, fifteen or so miles from here, that she'd first become fascinated by herbs and alternative medicines – perhaps because the bottles and jars containing them always looked so much more interesting than those from the chemist. There was that alternative shop in Llandrindod into which she was always dragging her mother then – not that *she* was interested.

They were both teachers, her parents: her mother at the high school, her dad in line for becoming headmaster of one of the primary schools. Betty was only ten when he failed to get the job, and soon after that they moved to Yorkshire, where he'd been born.

Teaching? Until she left school, she didn't know there *was* any other kind of job. Her parents treated it like a calling to which they were both martyrs, and it was taken for granted that Betty would commit her life to the same kind of suffering. As for those 'flights of imagination' of hers . . . well, she'd grow out of all that soon enough. A teacher's job was to stimulate the imagination of others.

Her parents were unbelieving Anglicans. Their world was colourless. Odd, really, that neither of them was sensitive. If it was in Betty's genes, it must have been dormant for at least two generations. One of her earliest memories – from a holiday up north when she was about four – was her grandma's chuckled 'Go 'way wi' you' when she'd come up from the cellar of the big terraced house in Sheffield and asked her who the old man was who slept down there.

Betty drove slowly, *feeling* the countryside. The road from New Radnor cut through an ancient landscape – the historic church of Old Radnor prominent just below the skyline, like a guardian lighthouse without a light. Behind her, she felt the weight of the Radnor Forest hills – muscular, as though they were pushing her away. At Walton – a pub, farms, cottages – she turned left into the low-lying fertile bowl which archaeologists called the Walton Basin, suggesting that thousands of years ago it had been a lake. Now there was only the small Hindwell Pool, to which, according to legend, the Four Stones went secretly to drink at cockcrow – an indication that the Hindwell water had long been sacred.

To the goddess? The goddess who was Isis and Artemis and Hecate and Ceridwen and Brigid in all her forms.

It was at teacher-training college in the Midlands that Betty had been introduced to the goddess. One of her tutors there was a witch; this had emerged when Betty had confessed she found it hard to go into a particular changing room where, it turned out, a student had hanged herself. Alexandra had been entirely understanding about her reaction and had invited Betty home . . . into a whole new world of incense and veils, earth and water and fire and air . . . where dreams were analysed, the trees breathed, past and present and future coexisted . . . and the moon was the guiding lamp of the goddess.

The recent Walton Basin archaeological project had discovered evidence of a prehistoric ritual landscape here, including the remains of a palisade of posts, the biggest of its kind in Britain. Being here, at the centre of all this, ought to be as exciting to Betty as it was to Robin, who was now – thanks to George – totally convinced that their church occupied a site which too had once been very much part of this sacred complex.

So why had her most intense experience there been the image of a tortured figure frenziedly at prayer, radiating agony and despair, in the ruined nave of St Michael's? She'd tried to drive it away, but it kept coming back to her; she could even smell the sweat and urine. How sacred, how euphoric, was *that*?

Three lanes met in Old Hindwell, converging at an undistinguished pub. Across the road, the former school had been converted into a health centre – by the famous Dr Coll, presumably. The stone and timbered cottages had once been widely spaced, but now there were graceless bungalows slotted between them. In many cases it would be indigenous local people – often retired farmers – living in these bungalows, freed at last from agricultural headaches, while city-reared incomers spent thousands turning the nearby cottages into the period jewels they were never intended to be.

She didn't particularly remember this place from her Radnorshire childhood, and she didn't yet know anyone here. It was actually pretty stupid to move into an area where you knew absolutely nobody, where the social structure and pattern of life were a complete mystery to you. Yet people did it all the time, lured by vistas of green, the magic of comparative isolation. But Betty realized that if there was to be any hope of their long-term survival here, she and Robin would have to start forming links locally. Connecting with the landscape was not enough.

Robin still had this fantasy of holding a mini fire festival at Candlemas, bringing in the celebrants from outside but throwing open the party afterwards to local people. Like a barbecue: the locals getting drunk and realizing that these witches were OK when you got to know them.

Candlemas – Robin preferred the Celtic 'Imbolc' – was barely a week away, so that was madness. Lights in the old church, chanting on the night air? Somebody would see, somebody would hear.

Too soon. Much too soon.

Or was that an excuse because Wicca no longer inspired her the way it did Robin? Why had she found George so annoying last weekend? Why had his ideas – truths and certainties to him – seemed so futile to her?

When she got home, Robin was waiting for her in the cold dusk, down by the brook. He wore his fez-thing with the mirrors, no protection at all against the rain. He looked damp and he looked agitated.

'We have a slight difficulty,' he said.

Robin was like those US astronauts; he saved the understatements for when things were particularly bad.

SEVEN

Possession

Even in embittered January, the interior of Ledwardine Church kept its autumnal glow. Because of the apples.

This was an orchard village and, when the orchards were bare, Merrily would buy red and yellow apples in Hereford and scatter them around: on the pulpit, down by the font, along the deep window ledges.

The biggest and oldest apple there was clasped in the hand of Eve in the most dramatic of Ledwardine's stained-glass windows, west-facing to pull in the sunset. Although there'd been no sun this afternoon, that old, fatal fruit was still a beacon, and its warmth was picked up by the lone Bramley cooking apple sitting plump and rosy on Minnie's coffin.

'Um . . . want to tell you about this morning,' Merrily said. 'How the day began for Gomer and me.'

She wasn't in the pulpit; she was standing to one side of it, in front of the rood screen of foliate faces and carved wooden apples, viewing the congregation along the coffin's shiny mahogany top.

'Somehow, I never sleep well the night before a funeral. Especially if it's someone I know as well as I'd got to know Minnie. So this morning, I was up before six, and I made a cup of tea, and then I walked out, intending to stroll around the square for a bit. To think about what I was going to say here.'

There must have been seventy or eighty people in the church, and she recognized fewer than half of them. As well as Minnie's relatives from the Midlands, there were several farmer-looking blokes who must have known Gomer when he was digging drainage ditches along the Welsh border. *'You wanner know why most of them buggers've come yere,'* he'd hissed in Merrily's ear, *'you watch how high they piles up their bloody plates with pie and cake in the village hall afterwards.'*

Now, she looked across at Gomer, sitting forlorn in the front pew, his glasses opaque, his wild white hair Brylcreemed probably as close to flat as it had ever been. Sitting next to him was Jane, looking amazingly neat and prim and solemn in her dark blue two-piece. Jane had taken the day off school, and had helped prepare the tea now laid out at the village hall.

'It was very cold,' Merrily said. 'Nobody else in the village seemed to be up yet. No lights, no smoke from chimneys. I was thinking it was true what they say about it always being darkest just before the dawn. But then . . . as I walked past the lychgate . . . I became aware of a small light in the churchyard.'

She'd approached carefully, listening hard – remembering, inevitably, the words of Huw Owen, her tutor on the Deliverance course. *'They'll follow you home, they'll breathe into your phone at night, break into your vestry and tamper with your gear. Crouch in the back pews and masturbate through your sermons . . . Little rat-eyes in the dark.'*

The light glowed soft in the mist. It was down at the bottom of the churchyard, where it met the orchard, close to the spot where Merrily had planned a small memorial for Wil Williams, seventeeth-century vicar of this parish and the vicarage's one-time resident ghost.

The light yellowed the air immediately above the open space awaiting Minnie Parry. Merrily had stopped about five yards from the grave and, as she watched, the light grew brighter.

And then there was another light, a small red firefly gleam, and she almost laughed in relief as Gomer Parry, glowing ciggy clamped between his teeth, reached up from below and dumped his hurricane lamp, with a clank, on the edge of the grave.

'Oh, hell.' Gomer heaved himself out. 'Din't disturb you, nor nothing, did I, vicar? Din't think you could see this ole lamp from the vicarage. Din't think you'd be up, see.'

'I didn't see it from the vicarage. I was . . . I was up anyway. Got a lot of things to do before . . . Got to see the bishop – stuff like that.' She was burbling, half embarrassed.

'Ar,' said Gomer.

Merrily was determined not to ask what he'd been up to down there in the grave; if he was doing it under cover of darkness, it was no business of anyone else's. Besides, he'd made himself solely responsible for Minnie's resting place, turning up with his mini-JCB to attack the ice-hard ground, personally laying down the lining.

'Fancy a cup of tea, Gomer?'

Gomer came over, carrying his lamp.

'Bugger me, vicar,' he said. 'Catch a feller pokin' round your churchyard at dead of night and you offers him a cup o' tea?'

'Listen, pal,' Merrily said, echoing the asphalt tones of the verger of the Liverpool church where she'd served as a curate, 'I'm a bloody Christian, me.'

Gomer grinned, a tired, white gash in the lamplight.

'So . . . we went back to the vicarage.' Merrily's gaze was fixed on the shiny Bramley on Minnie's coffin. 'And there we were, Gomer and me, at six o'clock in the morning, sitting either side of the kitchen table, drinking tea. And for once I was at a bit of a loss . . .'

She heard light footsteps and saw a stocky figure tiptoeing up the central aisle; recognized young Eirion Lewis, in school uniform. He was looking hesitantly from side to side . . . looking for Jane. He must be *extremely* keen on the kid to drive straight from school to join her at the funeral of someone he hadn't even known.

It was, you had to admit, a smart and subtle gesture. But Eirion had been raised to it; his old man ran Welsh Water or something. Eirion, though you wouldn't know it from his English accent, had been raised among the Welsh-speaking Cardiff aristocracy: the *crachach*.

When he saw that Jane was in the front pew, a leading mourner, he quietly backed off and went to sit on his own in the northern aisle which was where, in the old days, the women had been obliged to sit – the ghetto aisle. Eirion was, in fact, a nice kid, so Jane would probably dump him in a couple of weeks.

Merrily looked up. 'Then, after his second mug of tea, Gomer began to talk.'

'All it was . . . just buryin' a little box o' stuff, 'fore my Min goes down there, like. So's it'll be underneath the big box, kind of thing. En't no church rules against that, is there?'

'If there are,' Merrily had said, lighting a cigarette, 'I can have them changed by this afternoon.'

'Just bits o' stuff, see. Couple o' little wedding photos. Them white plastic earrings 'er insisted on wearing, 'cept for church. Nothing valuable – not even the watches.'

She had stared at him. He looked down at his tea, added more sugar. She noticed his wrist was bare.

'Mine and Min's, they both got new batteries. So's they'd go on ticking for a year or so. Two year, mabbe.'

Don't smile, Merrily told herself. Don't cry. She remembered Gomer's watch. It was years old, probably one of the first watches ever to work off a battery. And so it really did tick, loudly.

'Dunno why I done it, really, vicar. Don't make no sense, do it?'

'I think, somehow . . .' Merrily looked into the cigarette smoke, 'it makes the kind of sense neither of us is clever enough to explain.'

'And I'm not going to try too hard to explain it now,' she said to the congregation. 'I think people in this job can sometimes spend too long trying to explain too much.'

In the pew next to Gomer, Jane nodded firmly.

'I mean, I *could* go on about those watches ticking day and night under the ground, symbolizing the life beyond death . . . but that's not a great analogy when you start to think about it. In the end, it was Gomer making the point that he and Minnie had something together that can't just be switched off by death.'

'Way I sees it, vicar, by the time them ole watches d'stop ticking, we'll both be over this – out the other side.' Gomer had pushed both hands through his aggressive hair. 'Gotter go on, see, isn't it? Gotter bloody go on.'

'Yeah.'

'What was it like when your husband . . . when he died?'

'A lot different,' Merrily said. 'If he hadn't crashed his car we'd have got divorced. It was all a mistake. We were both too young – all that stuff.'

'And we was too bloody old,' Gomer said, 'me and Min. Problem is, nothin' in life's ever quite . . . what's that word? Synchronized. 'Cept for them ole watches. And you can bet one o' them buggers is gonner run down 'fore the other.'

Gomer smoked in silence for a few moments. He'd been Minnie Seagrove's second husband, she'd been Gomer's second wife. She'd moved to rural Wales some years ago with Frank Seagrove, who'd retired and wanted to come out here for the fishing, but then had died, leaving her alone in a strange town. Merrily still wasn't sure quite how Minnie and Gomer had first met.

Gomer's mouth opened and shut a couple of times, as if there was something important he wanted to ask her but he wasn't sure how.

'Not seen your friend, Lol, round yere for a while,' he said at last – which wasn't it.

'He's over in Birmingham, on a course.'

'Ar?'

'Psychotherapy. Had to give up his flat, and then he got some money, unexpectedly, from his old record company and he's spent it on this course. Half of him thinks he should become a full-time psychotherapist – like, what mental health needs is more ex-loonies. The other half thinks it's all crap. But he's doing the course, then he's going to make a decision.'

'Good boy,' Gomer said.

'Jane still insists she has hopes for Lol and me.'

Gomer nodded. Then he said quickly, 'Dunno quite how to put this, see. I mean, it's your job, ennit, to keep us all in hopes of the hereafter: 'E died so we could live on, kinder thing – which never made full sense to me, but I en't too bright, see?'

61

Merrily put out her cigarette. Ethel, the cat, jumped onto her knees. She plunged both hands into Ethel's black winter coat.

The big one?

'Only, there's gotter be times, see, vicar, when you wakes up cold in the middle of the night and you're thinkin' to youself, is it bloody *true*? Is anythin' *at all* gonner happen when we gets to the end?'

From the graveside there came no audible ticking as Minnie's coffin went in. Gomer had accepted that his nephew, Nev, should be the one to fill in the hole, on the grounds that Minnie would have been mad as hell watching Gomer getting red Herefordshire earth all over his best suit.

Walking away from the grave, he smiled wryly. He may also have wept earlier, briefly and silently; Merrily had noticed him tilt his head to the sky, his hands clasped behind his back. He was, in unexpected ways, a private person.

Down at the village hall, he nudged her, indicating several tea plates piled higher with food than you'd have thought possible without scaffolding.

'Give 'em a funeral in the afternoon, some of them tight buggers goes without no bloody breakfast and lunch. 'Scuse me a minute, vicar, I oughter 'ave a word with Jack Preece.' And he moved off towards a ravaged-looking old man, whose suit seemed several sizes too big for him.

Merrily nibbled at a slice of chocolate cake and eavesdropped a group of farmer-types who'd separated themselves from their wives and didn't, for once, seem to be discussing dismal sheep prices.

'Bloody what-d'you-call-its – pep pills, Ecstersee, wannit? Boy gets picked up by the police, see, with a pocketful o' these bloody Ecstersee. Up in court at Llandod. Dennis says, "That's it boy, you stay under my roof you can change your bloody ways. We're gonner go an' see the bloody rector . . .'"

'OK, Mum?'

Merrily turned to find Jane holding a plate with just one small egg sandwich. Was this anorexia, or love?

'What happened to Eirion, flower?'

'He had to get home.'

'Where's he live exactly?'

'Some gloomy, rotting mansion out near Abergavenny. It was quite nice of him to come, wasn't it?'

'It was incredibly nice of him. But then . . . he *is* a nice guy.'

'Yeah.'

Merrily tilted her head. 'Meaning he'd be more attractive if he was a bit of a rogue? Kind of dangerous?'

'You think I'm that superficial?'

'No, flower. Anyway, I expect he'll be going to university next year.'

'He wants to work in TV, as a reporter. Not – you know – *Livenight*.'

'Good heavens, no.'

'So you're going to do that after all then?' Jane said in that suspiciously bland voice that screamed *hidden agenda*.

'I was blackmailed.'

'Can I come?'

Merrily raised her eyes. 'Do I *look* stupid?'

'See, I thought we could take Irene. He's into anything to do with TV, obviously. Like, he knows his dad could get him a job with BBC Wales on the old Taff network, but he wants to make his own way. Which is kind of commendable, I'd have thought.'

'Very honourable, flower.'

'Still, never mind.'

'Sorry.'

'Sure. You told that – what was her name? Tania?'

'Not yet.'

'She'll be ever so pleased.'

And Jane slid away with her plate, and Merrily saw Uncle Ted, the senior churchwarden, elbowing through the farmers. He was currently trying to persuade her to levy a charge for the tea and coffee provided in the church after Sunday services. She wondered how to avoid him. She also wondered how to avoid appearing on trash television to argue with militant pagans.

'Mrs . . . Watkins?'

She turned and saw a woman looking down at her – a pale, tall, stylishly dressed woman, fifty-fiveish, with expertly bleached hair. She was not carrying any food.

'I was impressed,' she said, 'with your sermon.' Her accent was educated, but had an edge. 'It was compelling.'

'Well, it was just . . .'

' . . . from the heart. Meant something to people. Meant something to me, and I didn't even know . . . er . . .'

'Minnie Parry.'

'Yes.' The woman blinked twice, rapidly – a suggestion of nerves. She seemed to shake herself out of it, straightened her back with a puppet-like jerk. 'Sister Cullen was right. You seem genuine.'

'Oh, you're from the hospital . . .'

'Not exactly.' The woman looked round, especially at the farmers, her eyes flicking from face to florid face, evidently making sure there was nobody she knew within listening distance. 'Barbara Buckingham. I was at the hospital, to visit my sister. I think you saw her the other night – before I arrived. Menna Thomas . . . Menna . . .' Her voice hardened. 'Menna Weal.'

'Oh, right. I did see her, but . . .'

'But she was already dead.'

'Yes, she was, I'm afraid.'

'Mrs Watkins,' the woman took Merrily's arm, 'may I talk to you?' Not a request. 'I rang your office, in Hereford. Sister Cullen gave me the number. She said you were probably the person to help me. The person who deals with *possession*.'

'Oh.'

'I rang your office and they said you were conducting a funeral here, so I just . . . came. It seemed appropriate.' She broke off. She was attracting glances.

'It's a bit crowded, isn't it?' Merrily said. 'Would you like –?'

'I'll come to the point. Would it be possible for you to conduct a funeral service for me?'

Merrily raised an eyebrow.

'For my sister, that is. I suppose I mean a memorial service. Though actually I don't. She should have . . . she should have a real funeral in church. A proper funeral.'

'I'm sorry, I'm not getting this.'

'Because I can't go, you see. I can't go to the . . . interment.'

'Why not?'

'Because . . . it's going to take place in that bastard's garden.' Her voice rose. 'He won't let her go. It's all about *possession*, Mrs Watkins.'

'I don't . . .' Several people were staring at them now, over their piled-up plates.

'Possession of the dead by the living,' explained Barbara Buckingham.

'I think we'd better go back to the vicarage,' Merrily said.

EIGHT

The E-Word

'Oh my God,' Betty said. 'The only time I go out on my own, in walks number one on the list of situations I wouldn't trust you to handle.'

Robin couldn't keep still. He was pacing the kitchen, touching walls and doors, the sink, the fridge – as if the permanence of this place in his life was no longer certain.

'So he's in this old green Cherokee, right? And he has on this well-worn army jacket with, like, camouflage patches. And it's unzipped, and all the time I'm hoping what's underneath is just gonna turn out to be some kind of black turtleneck. With, like, a thick white stripe around the neck.'

Betty took off her coat, hung it behind the door and came to sit down. It wasn't the vicar that worried her – every newcomer sooner or later had a visit from the vicar. It was how Robin had dealt with him.

'Pretty damn clear from the start he wasn't just coming to ask the way to someplace.' Robin went over to the kitchen table; there were two half-pint glasses on it and four small beer bottles, all empty. 'Guy wanted to talk. He was waiting for me to ask him in.'

'I don't suppose he had to wait long.'

'Soon's we get inside, it's the firm handshake. "Hi, I'm Nick Ellis." And I'm wondering do these guys drink beer? So I offer him a Michelob from the refrigerator.'

'Normal practice is to offer them tea, Robin.'

'No . . . wait . . . Transpires he spent some years in the States –

which became detectable in his accent. And then – what can I say? – we . . .'

'You exchanged history. You drank beer together.'

'I confess, I'm standing there pouring out the stuff and I'm like . . .' Robin held up a glass with a trembling hand. 'Like, all the time, I'm half-expecting him to leap up in horror, pull out his cross . . . slam it in my face, like the guy in the Dracula movies. But he was fine.'

She looked sceptical. 'What did you tell him about us?'

'Well . . . this was hard for me. I'm a straight person, I've no time for deception, you know that.'

'What did you *tell* him?' Clenching her hands. 'What did you say about us?'

'Fucksake, whaddaya think I said? "Hey, priest, guess how *we* spent Halloween"?' Robin went over and pulled out a chair and slumped down. 'I told him I was an illustrator and that you were into alternative therapy. I told him you were British and we met when we were both attending a conference in New England. I somehow refrained from identifying the conference as the 1993 Wiccan International Moot in Salem, Mass. And although I did not say we were married I didn't mention handfasting either. I said we had gotten *hitched*.'

'Hitched?'

'Uh-huh. And when he brought up the subject of religion, as priests are inclined to do when they get through with football and stuff, I was quite awesomely discreet. I simply said we were not churchgoers.'

Betty breathed out properly for the first time since sitting down. 'All right. I'm sorry. I do trust you. I've just been feeling a little uptight.'

'Because you're not being true to yourself and your beliefs,' Robin said severely.

'So what was he like?'

'Unexceptional at first. Friendly, but also watchful. Open, but . . . holding back. He's of medium height but the way he holds himself makes him look taller. Rangy, you know? Looks like a backwoods boy. Looks fit. He drank just one beer while I appear to have drunk three. His hair is fairish and he wears it brushed straight back, and in a ponytail, which is cool. I mean, I have no basic problem with these guys – as a spiritual grouping. As a profession.'

'But?'

Robin got up and fed the Rayburn some pine. The Rayburn spat in disgust. Robin looked up at Betty; his eyes were unsteady.

'But, if you want the truth, babe, I guess this is probably a very sick and dangerous example of the species.'

Robin had been anxious the priest remained in the kitchen. He would have had problems explaining the brass pentacle over the living-room fireplace. Would not be happy to have had the Reverend Nicholas Ellis browsing through those books on the shelves. He was glad his guest consumed only one beer and therefore would be less likely to need the bathroom.

And when Ellis asked if he might take a look at the ancient church of St Michael, Robin had the back door open faster than was entirely polite.

Still raining out there. The priest wore hiking boots and pulled out a camouflage beret. They strolled back across the farmyard, around the barn into the field, where the ground was uneven and boggy. And there it was, on its promontory above the water, its stones glistening, its tower proud but its roofless body like a split, gutted fish.

'Cool, huh, Nick?' Robin had told the priest about St Michael's probably becoming disused on account of the Hindwell Brook, the problem of getting cars close enough to the church in the wintertime.

The priest smiled sceptically. 'That's *your* theory, is it, Robin?'

'Well, that and the general decline in, uh, faith. I guess some people'd started looking for something a little more progressive, dynamic.'

The Reverend Ellis stopped. He had a wide, loose mouth. And though his face was a touch weathered, it had no lines, no wrinkles. He was maybe forty.

'What do you mean by that, Robin?'

'Well . . . uh . . .' Robin had felt himself blushing. He talked on about how maybe the Church had become kind of hidebound: same old hymns, same old . . . you know?

The minister had said nothing, just stood there looking even taller, watching Robin sinking into the mud.

'Uh . . . what I meant . . . maybe they began to feel the Church wasn't offering too much in the direction of personal development, you know?'

And then Ellis went, 'Yeah, I do know. And you're dead right.'

'Oh. For a minute, I was worried I was offending you.'

'The Church over here *has* lost much of its dynamism. Don't suppose I need tell you that in most areas of the United States a far higher proportion of the population attends regular services than in this country.'

'So how come you were over there?' Robin had grabbed his chance to edge the talk away from religion.

'Went over with my mother as a teenager. After her marriage ended. We moved around quite a bit, mainly in the South.'

'Really? That's interesting. My mom was English and she met my dad when he was serving with the Air Force in the North of England, and she went home with him, to New Jersey. So, like—'

'And it was there,' Nicholas Ellis continued steadily, 'that I first became exposed to what you might consider a more "dynamic" manifestation of Christianity.'

'In the, uh, Bible Belt?' *Snakes and hot coals?*

'Where I became fully aware of the power of God.' The priest looked up at the veiled church. 'Where, if you like, the power of the Holy Spirit reached out and touched me.'

No, Robin did *not* like. 'You notice how the mist winds itself around the tower? As a painter, that fascinates me.'

'The sheer fervour, the electric *momentum*, you encountered in little . . .' Ellis's hands forming fists for emphasis, 'little clapboard chapels. The living church – I knew what that meant for the first time. Over here, we have all these exquisite ancient buildings, steeped in centuries of worship . . . and we're losing it, *losing it*, Robin.'

'Right,' Robin had said neutrally.

Ellis nodded toward the ruins. 'Poets eulogizing the beauty of country churches . . . and they meant the *buildings*, the surroundings. Man, is that not beauty at its most superficial?'

'Uh . . . I guess.' Robin considered how Betty would want him to play this and so didn't rise to it. But he knew in his soul that what those poets were evoking, whether they were aware of it or not, was an *energy of place* which long pre-dated Christianity. The energy Robin was experiencing right there, right this minute, with the tower uniting with the mist and the water surging below. Sure, the Christians picked up on that, mainly in medieval times, with all those soaring Gothic cathedrals, but basically it was out of their league.

Because, Robin thought, meeting the priest's pale eyes, this is a pagan thing, man.

And this was when he had first become aware of an agenda. Sensing that whatever the future held for him and this casual-looking priest in his army cast-offs, it was not going to involve friendly rivalry and good-natured badinage.

'Buildings are jewellery,' Ellis had said, 'baubles. When I came home, I felt like a missionary in my own land. I was working as a teacher at the time. But when I was subsequently ordained, ended up here, I knew this was where I was destined to be. These people have their priorities right.'

'How's that?'

Ellis let the question go by. He was now talking about how the States also had its *bad* side. How he had spent time in California, where people threw away their souls like candy wrappers, where the Devil squatted in shop windows like Santa Claus, handing out packs of tarot cards and runes and I Ching sets.

'Can you *believe* those people?' Robin turned away to control a grin. For, albeit he was East Coast raised, he *was* those people.

'Over here, it's less obvious.' Ellis shuddered suddenly. 'Far more deeply embedded. Like bindweed, the worst of it's underground.'

Robin hadn't reacted, though he was unsure of whether this was the best response or not. Maybe some normal person bombarded with this bullshit would, by now, be telling this guy he had things to do, someplace else to go, calls to make – nice talking with you, Reverend, maybe see you around.

Looking over at the rain-screened hills, Ellis was saying how, the very week he had arrived here, it was announced that archaeologists had stumbled on something in the Radnor Valley – evidence of one of the biggest prehistoric wooden temples ever discovered in Europe.

Robin's response had been, 'Yeah, wasn't that terrific?'

When Ellis had turned to him, there was a light in his eyes which Robin perceived as like a gas jet.

'He said it was a sign of something coming to the surface.'

'Them finding the prehistoric site?' Betty sat up, pushing her golden hair behind her ears.

'It was coming out like a rash, was how he put it,' Robin said. 'Like the disease under the surface – the disease which you only identify when the rash starts coming out?'

'What's he talking about?'

'Man with an agenda, Bets.' Robin detected a half-inch of beer in one of the Michelob bottles and drained it, laid down the bottle with a thump. 'If there's anything I can recognize straight off, it's another guy with an agenda.'

'Robin, *you* don't have an agenda, you just have woolly dreams.'

'You wanna hear this, or not?'

'Sorry,' Betty said, frayed. 'Go on.'

Robin told her that when Ellis had first come here, before the Church let him go his own way, he looked after four small parishes, on both sides of the border. New Radnor was the biggest. All the parishes possessed churches, except one of these was in ruins.

'But don't take this the wrong way. Remember this is a guy doesn't *go* for churches. He's into clapboard shacks. Now, Old Hindwell is a village with no church any more, not even a Baptist chapel. But one thing it does have is a clapboard fucking *shack*. Well, not exactly clapboard – more like concrete and steel. The parish hall in fact.'

'Is there one?'

'Up some steps, top of the village. Built, not too well, in the early sixties. Close to derelict, when Ellis arrived. He hacks through the brambles one day and a big light comes down on him, like that guy on the road to Damascus, and he's like, *"This is it. This is my church!"*

You recall that film *Witness*, where the Amish community build this huge barn in, like, one day?'

'Everybody mucking in. Brilliant.'

'Yeah, well, what happens here is Christians converge from miles around to help Nick Ellis realize his vision. Money comes pouring in. Carpenters, plumbers, sundry artisans giving their work for free. No time at all, the parish hall's good as new . . . better than new. And there's a nice big cross sticking out the roof, with a light inside the porch. And every Sunday the place is packed with more people than all the other local churches put together.'

Robin paused.

Betty opened out her hands. 'What do you want me to say? Triumph of the spirit? You think I should knock that?'

'Wait,' Robin told her. 'How come all this goes down in a place with so little religious feeling they abandoned the original goddamn church?'

'Evangelism, Robin. It spreads like a grass fire when it gets going. He's a new kind of priest with all that American . . . whatever. If it can happen there, it can happen here – and obviously has. Which shows how right we were to keep a low profile, because those born-again people, to put it mildly, are *not* tolerant towards paganism.'

Robin shook his head. 'Ellis denies responsibility for the upsurge. Figures it was waiting to happen – to deal with something that went wrong. Something of which Old Hindwell church is symptomatic.'

Betty waited.

'So we're both moving in closer to the church, and I'm finding him a little irritating by now, so I start to point out these wonderful ancient yew trees – how the building itself might be medieval but I'm *told* that the yews in a circle and the general positioning of the church indicate that it occupies a pre-Christian site. I'm talking in a "this doesn't mean much to me but it's interesting, isn't it?" kind of voice.'

'Robin,' Betty said, 'you don't *possess* that voice.'

Ellis was staring at him. 'Who told you that, Robin?'

Robin floundered. 'Oh . . . the real estate agent, I guess.'

Furious with himself that, instead of speaking up for the oldest religion of these islands, he was scuttling away like some shamed vampire at dawn, allowing this humourless bastard to go on assuming without question that his own 2,000-year-old cult had established a right to the moral high ground. *So how did they achieve that, Nick? By waging countless so-called holy wars against other faiths? By fighting amongst themselves with bombs and midnight kneecappings, blowing guys away in front of their kids?*

'All right,' Ellis had then said, 'let me tell you the truth about this church, Robin. This church was dedicated to St Michael. How much do you know about him?'

Robin could only think of Marks and freaking Spencer, but was wise enough to say nothing.

'The Revelation of St John the Divine, Chapter Twelve. "And there was war in heaven. Michael and his angels fought against the dragon, and the dragon fought Michael and his angels."'

Robin had looked down at his boots.

'"And the great dragon was cast out . . . that old serpent called the Devil, and Satan, which deceiveth the whole world. He was cast out . . . into the earth."'

'Uh, right,' Robin said, 'I'd forgotten about that.'

'Interestingly, around the perimeter of Radnor Forest are several other churches dedicated to St Michael.'

'Not too much imagination in those days, I guess.'

Ellis had now taken off his beret. His face was shining with rain.

'The Archangel Michael is the most formidable warrior in God's army. Therefore a number of churches dedicated to him would represent a very powerful barrier against evil.'

'What evil would this *be* precisely, Nick?' Robin was becoming majorly exasperated by Ellis's habit of not answering questions – like your questions are sure to be stupid and inexact, so he was answering the ones you ought to have asked. It also bugged Robin when people talked so loosely about 'evil' – a coverall for fanatics.

Ellis said, 'I visit the local schools. Children still talk of a dragon in Radnor Forest. It's part of the folklore of the area. There's even a line of hills a few miles from here they call the Dragon's Back.'

Robin shrugged. 'Local place names. That so uncommon, Nick?'

'Not awfully. Satanic evil is ubiquitous.'

'Yeah, but is a dragon necessarily evil?' Robin was thinking of the fantasy novels of Kirk Blackmore, where dragons were fearsome forces for positive change.

Ellis gave him a cold look. 'It would seem to me, Robin, that a dragon legend and a circle of churches dedicated to St Michael is incontrovertible evidence of something requiring perpetual restraint.'

'I'm not getting this.'

'A circle of churches.' Ellis spread his hands. 'A holy wall to contain the dragon. But the dragon will always want to escape. Periodically, the dragon rears . . . and snaps . . . and is forced back again and again and keeps coming back . . .' Ellis clawing the air, a harsh light in his eyes, 'until something yields.'

Now he was looking over at the ruins again, like an army officer sizing up the field of battle. This was one serious fucking fruitcake.

'And the evil is now *inside* . . . The legend says – and you'll find references to this in most of the books written about this area – that if just one of those churches should fall, the dragon will escape.'

Then he looked directly at Robin.

Robin said, 'But . . . this is a legend, Nick.'

'The circle of St Michael churches is not a legend.'

'You think this place is *evil*?'

'It's decommissioned. It no longer has the protection of St Michael. In this particular situation, I would suggest that's a sign that it requires . . . attention.'

'Attention?'

Robin put on a crazy laugh, but his heart wasn't in it. And Betty didn't laugh at all.

'What does he want?'

'He . . .' Robin shook his head. 'Oh, boy. He was warning me. That fruitcake was giving me notice.'

'Of what? What does he want?'

'He wants to hold a service here. He believes this church was abandoned because the dragon got in. Because the frigging dragon lies coiled here. And that God has chosen him, Ellis, given him the muscle, in the shape of the biggest congregations ever known in this area, given him the power to drive the dragon out.'

Betty went very still.

'All he wants, Bets . . . *all* he wants . . . is to come along with a few friends and hold some kind of a service.'

'What kind of a service?'

'You imagine that? All these farmers in their best suits and the matrons in their Sunday hats and Nick in his white surplice and stuff all standing around in a church with no roof singing goddamn "Bread of Heaven"? In a site that they stole from the Old Religion about 800 years ago and then fucking sold off? Jeez, I was so mad! This is *our* church now. On our farm. And we *like* dragons!'

Betty was silent. The whole room was silent. The rain had stopped, the breeze had died. Even the Rayburn had temporarily conquered its snoring.

Robin howled like a dog. 'What's happening here? Why do we have to wind up in a parish with a priest who's been exposed to the insane Bible-freaks who stalk the more primitive parts of my beloved homeland? And is therefore no longer content with vicarage tea parties and the organ fund.'

'So what did you say to him?'

'Bastard had me over a barrel. I say a flat "no", the cat's clean out the bag. So, what I said . . . to my shame, I said, Nick, I could not *think* of letting you hold a service in there. Look at all that mud! Look at those pools of water! Just give us some time – like we've only been here days – give us some time to get it cleaned up. How sad was *that*?'

Just like Ellis, she didn't seem to have been listening. 'Robin, what kind of service?'

'He said it would be no big deal – not realizing that any kind of damn service here *now*, was gonna be a big deal far as we're concerned. And if it's no big deal, why do it? Guy doesn't even *like* churches.'

'What kind of service?' Betty was at the edge of her chair and her eyes were hard.

'I don't know.' Robin was a little scared, and that made him angry. 'A short Eucharist? Did he say that? What is that precisely? I'm not too familiar with this Christian sh—'

'It's a Mass.'

'Huh?'

'An Anglican Mass. And do you know why a Mass is generally performed in a building other than a functioning church?'

He didn't fully. He could only guess.

'To cleanse it,' Betty said. 'The Eucharist is Christian disinfectant. To cleanse, to purify – to get rid of bacteria.'

'OK, let me get this . . .' Robin pulled his hands down his face, in praying mode. 'This is the E-word, right?'

Betty nodded.

An exorcism.

NINE

Visitor

The answering machine sounded quite irritable.

'Mrs Watkins. Tania Beauman, Livenight. *I've left messages for you all over the place. The programme goes out Friday night, so I really have to know whether it's yes or no. I'll be here until seven. Please call me . . . Thank you.'*

'Sorry.' Merrily came back into the kitchen, hung up her funeral cloak. 'I can't think with that thing bleeping.'

Barbara Buckingham was sitting at the refectory table, unwinding her heavy silk scarf while her eyes compiled a photo-inventory of the room.

'You're in demand, Mrs Watkins.' The slight roll on the 'r' and the barely perceptible lengthening of the 'a' showed her roots were sunk into mid-border clay. But this would be way back, many southern English summers since.

Walking through black and white timber-framed Ledwardine, across the cobbled square to the sixteenth-century vicarage, the dull day dying around them, the lights in the windows blunting the bite of evening, she'd said, 'How quaint and cosy it is here. I'd forgotten. And so close.'

Close to what? Merrily had made a point of not asking.

'Tea?' She still felt slightly ashamed of the kitchen – must get round to emulsioning it in the spring. 'Or coffee?'

Barbara would have tea. She took off her gloves.

Like her late sister, she was good-looking, but in a sleek and sharp way, with a turned-up nose which once would have been cute but

PHIL RICKMAN

now seemed haughty. '*The sister's a retired teacher and there's no arguing with her*,' Eileen Cullen had said.

'I didn't expect you to be so young, Mrs Watkins.'

'Going on thirty-seven?'

'Young for what you're doing. Young to be the diocesan exorcist.'

'Diocesan deliverance consultant.'

'You must have a progressive bishop.'

'Not any more.' Merrily filled the kettle.

Mrs Buckingham dropped a short laugh. 'Of course. That man who couldn't take the pressure and walked out. Hunt? Hunter? I try to keep up with Church affairs. I was headmistress of a Church school for many years.'

'In this area? The border?'

'God no. Got out of there before I was twenty. Couldn't stand the cold.'

Merrily put the kettle on the stove. 'We can get bad winters here,' she agreed.

'Ah . . . not simply the climate. My father was a farmer in Radnor Forest. I remember my whole childhood as a kind of perpetual February.'

'Frugal?' Merrily tossed tea bags into the pot.

Mrs Buckingham exhaled bitter laughter. 'In our house, those two tea bags would have to be used at least six times. The fat in the chip pan was only renewed for Christmas.' Her face grew pinched at the memories.

'You were poor?'

'Not particularly. We had in excess of 130 acres. Marginal land, mind – always appallingly overgrazed. Waste nothing. Make every square yard earn its keep. Have you heard of hydatid disease?'

'Vaguely.'

'Causes cysts to grow on internal organs, sometimes the size of pomegranates. Originates from a tapeworm absorbed by dogs allowed to feed on infected dead sheep. Or, on our farm, *required* to eat dead sheep. Human beings can pick it up – the tapeworm eggs – simply through stroking the sheepdog. When I was sixteen I had to go into hospital to have a hydatid cyst removed from my liver.'

'How awful.'

78

'That was when I decided to get out. I doubt my father even noticed I was gone. Had another mouth to feed by then. A girl again, unfortunately.'

'Menna?'

'She would be . . . ten months old when I left. It was a long time before I began to feel guilty about abandoning her – fifteen years or more. And by then it was too late. They'd probably forgotten I'd ever existed. I expect he was even grateful I'd gone – another opportunity to try for a son, at no extra cost. A farmer with no son is felt to be lacking in something.'

'Any luck?'

'My mother miscarried, apparently,' Mrs Buckingham said brusquely. 'There was a hysterectomy.' She shrugged. 'I never saw them again.'

'Where did you go?'

'Found a job in Hereford, in a furniture shop. The people there were very good to me. They gave me a room above the shop, next to the storeroom. Rather frightening at night. All those empty chairs: I would imagine people sitting there, silently, waiting for me when I came back from night classes. Character-building, though, I suppose. I got two A levels and a grant for teacher-training college.'

It all sounded faintly Dickensian to Merrily, though it could have been no earlier than the 1960s.

'So you never went back?' The phone was ringing.

'After college, I went to work in Hampshire, near Portsmouth. Then a husband, kids – grown up now. No, I never went back, until quite recently. A neighbour's daughter – Judith – kept me informed, through occasional letters. She was another farmer's daughter, from a rather less primitive farm. Please get that phone call, if you want.'

Merrily nodded, went through to the office.

'As it happens' – closing the scullery door – 'she's here now.'

'Listen, I'm sorry,' Eileen Cullen said. 'I couldn't think what else to tell her. Showed up last night, still unhappy about the sister's death and getting no cooperation from the doctor. I didn't have much time to bother with her either. I just thought somebody ought to persuade her to forget about Mr Weal, and go home, get on with her life. And I thought she'd take it better coming from a person of the cloth such as your wee self.'

'Forgive me, but that doesn't sound like you.'

'No. Well . . .'

'So she didn't say anything about holding a special service in church then?'

'Merrily, the problem is I'm on the ward in one minute.'

'Bloody hell, Eileen—'

'Aw, Jesus, all the woman wants is her sister laid to rest in a decent, holy fashion. She's one of your fellow Christians. Tell her you'll say a few prayers for the poor soul, and leave it at that.'

There was an unexpected undercurrent here.

'What happened with Mr Weal after I left the other night?'

'Well, he came out. Eventually.'

'Eventually?'

'He came out when *she* did. And he chose to accompany her down to the mortuary.'

'Is that normal?'

'Well, of course it isn't fockin' normal. We're not talking about a normal feller here! It was a special concession. Merrily, I really have to go. If the sister's tardy, how can you expect the nurses—'

'Eileen!'

'That's all I can tell you. Just persuade her to go home. She'll do no good for herself.'

'What's *that* supposed to—'

Cullen hung up.

It was dark outside now, and the thorns were ticking against the scullery window.

When Merrily returned to the kitchen, Barbara Buckingham was standing under a wall lamp, her silk scarf dangling from one hand as if she was wondering whether or not to leave.

'Mrs Watkins, I don't want to be a pain . . .'

'Merrily. Don't be silly. Sit down. There's no—'

'I try to be direct, you see. In my childhood, no one was direct.

They'd never meet your eyes. Keep your head down, avoid direct conflict, run neither with the English nor the Welsh. Keep your head down and move quietly, in darkness.'

The woman had been too long out of it, Merrily thought, as the kettle boiled. She'd turned her spartan childhood into something Gothic. 'Tell me about the . . . possession.'

'In essence, I believe, your job is to liberate them. The possessed, I mean.'

Merrily carefully took down two mugs from the crockery shelf. 'Milk?' Through the open door, she could still hear that damned rosebush scratching at the scullery window.

'A little. No sugar.'

Merrily brought milk from the fridge. She left her own tea black, and carried both mugs to the table.

'It's a big word, Barbara.'

'Yes.'

'And often abused – I have to say that.'

'We should both be direct.'

'And I should tell you I've yet to encounter a valid case of possession. But then I've not been doing this very long.'

'It may be the wrong word. Perhaps I only used it to get your attention.' Looking frustrated, Barbara tossed her scarf onto the table. I've attended church most of my life. Much of the time out of habit, I admit; occasionally out of need. I have no time for . . . mysticism, that's what I'm trying to say. I'm not fey.'

Merrily smiled. 'No.'

'But Menna has been possessed for years. Do you know what I mean? Weal suffocated her in life; now he won't let her go after death.'

Cullen: *'He asks for a bowl and a cloth and he washes her. Very tenderly, reverently you might say. And then he'll wash himself: his face, his hands, in the same water.'*

And followed her down to the mortuary. Did Barbara know about that?

Merrily heard a key in the side door, beyond the scullery, and then footsteps on the back stairs: Jane coming in, going up to her apartment.

'They were our family solicitors,' Barbara said. 'Everybody's solicitors, in those days, it seemed. Weal and Son . . . the first Weal was Jeffery's grandfather, the "and son" was Jeffery's father R.T. Weal. Weal and Son, of Kington, and their gloomy old offices with the roll-top desks and a Victorian chair like a great dark throne. I first remember Jeffery when he was fifteen going on fifty. A lumbering, sullen boy, slow-moving, slow-thinking, single-minded, his future written in stone – Weal and Son and Son, even unto the ends of the earth. I hated them, the complete *unchangingness* of them – same chair, same desks, same dark tweed suits, same dark car creeping up the track.'

'Eileen Cullen told me she thought he probably became a father figure,' Merrily said. 'After Menna had spent some years looking after her own father. Your dad was widowed, presumably.'

'Sixteen or seventeen years ago. I had a letter from Judith – my friend in Old Hindwell. My father wouldn't have told me; I no longer existed for him. And he was ailing, too. Later I learned that Menna never had a boyfriend or any social life, so she lost the best years of her life to her bloody father, and the rest of it to Weal. Who, of course, became the proverbial tower of strength when the old man died.'

'He looked after her then?'

'Seized his chance with a weak, unworldly girl. I . . . came to find her about two years ago. I'd recently taken early retirement. My daughter had just got married, my husband was away – I was at a *very* loose end. One morning, I simply got in my car and drove up here, and knocked on their door . . .' She stared into space. 'Menna seemed . . . unsurprised, unmoved, entirely incurious. I'd forgotten what these people can be like. She just stood there in the doorway – didn't even ask me in. Talked in an offhand way, as though I was a neighbour whom she saw occasionally but didn't particularly care for.'

'And you actually hadn't seen each other since she was a baby?'

The woman shook her head. There was distance now in her voice. 'She . . . wore no make-up. She was pale, in an unnatural, etiolated kind of way, like grass that's been covered up. And quite beautiful. But she didn't seem to either know or care who I was. She might as well already have been dead.'

*

82

Jane nicked the cordless from Mum's bedroom and took it upstairs to the trio of attic rooms that now made up her apartment: bedroom, sitting room–study and a half-finished bathroom. She put on the lights, took off her jacket, sat on the bed. Thinking about poor Gomer going home on his own to a house full of Minnie's things. It made her cry.

Fucking death!

Jane dried her eyes on a corner of the pillowcase. Gomer wouldn't cry. Gomer would get on with it. But how much in life was really worth getting on with? Where was it leading? Was Minnie any closer now to knowing the answer? *Oh God.*

Jane picked up the phone and looked at it and shrugged. If this didn't work, it didn't work. She rolled up her sleeve. The *Livenight* number was written in fibre-tip on the inside of her left arm. Jane pushed in the numbers, asked for Tania Beauman. The switchboard put her on hold and made her listen to Dire Straits – which could have been worse, though Jane would never admit it.

She leaned back against the headboard and contemplated the Mondrian walls, wondering if anyone else had ever had the idea of painting the squares and rectangles between sixteenth-century beams in different colours. She wondered what Eirion would think of it.

If she was ever to bring him up here.

If? Time was running out if she was going to fit in two *serious* lovers before she hit twenty. Serious could mean six months. Longer.

'Tania Beauman.'

'Oh, hi.' Jane sat up. 'You know who this is?'

'Oh,' said Tania.

'Hey, don't be like that. I may have cracked it for you.'

'Cracked . . . what?'

Jane swung her feet to the floor. 'I'm telling you, Tania, it wasn't easy. She really didn't want to know. *Livenight?* Pff! But I'm, like, "Look, Merrily, being elitist is what put the Church of England in the hole it's in today. You can't just turn a blind eye to paganism and pretend it isn't happening all over again. Or before you know it there'll be more of *them* around than you . . ."'

'That's a very cogent argument,' Tania said, 'but why aren't I talking to your mother?'

83

'Because I've, like, *nearly* got her convinced – but I'm not quite there yet.'

'Well, I have to tell you, you don't have much time.'

'But do I have the incentive, Tania? That's the point.'

'I wondered if there'd be a point.'

'To be blunt,' Jane said, 'I need a very, very small favour.'

Home burial. It was becoming, if not exactly commonplace, then less of an upper-class phenomenon than it used to be. Merrily tried to explain this to Barbara Buckingham: that it was a secular thing, or sometimes a green issue; that you often didn't even need official permission.

'The main drawback for most people is the risk of taking value off their house if and when it's sold. No one wants a grave in the garden.'

'He's not . . .' Barbara had picked up her scarf again; she began to wind it around her hands. 'He is not going to bury Menna; that's the worst of it. She's going into a . . . tomb.' She pulled the scarf tight. 'A mausoleum.'

'Oh.' *To be loved like that.*

'He has a Victorian house at Old Hindwell,' Barbara said. 'The former rectory. Do you know Old Hindwell?'

'Not really. Is it in this diocese, I can't remember?'

'Possibly. It's very close to the border, about three miles from Kington, on the edge of the Forest. Radnor Forest. Weal's house isn't remote, but it has no immediate neighbours. In the garden there's a . . . structure – wine store, ice house, air-raid shelter, I don't know precisely what it is, but that's where she's going to be.'

'Like a family vault?'

'It's sick. I went to see a solicitor in Hereford this morning. He told me there was nothing I could do. A man has a perfect legal right to keep his dead wife in a private museum.'

'And as a solicitor himself, your brother-in-law is going to be fully aware of his rights.'

'Don't call him that!' Barbara turned away. 'Whole thing's obscene.'

'He loved her,' Merrily said uncertainly. 'He doesn't want to be parted from her. He wants to feel that she's near him. That's the usual reason.'

'No! It's a statement of ownership. Possession is – what is it? – nine points of the law?'

'That word again. Do you mind if I smoke?'

'Go ahead.'

Merrily lit a Silk Cut, pulled over an ashtray.

'What about the funeral itself? Is it strictly private? I mean, are you kind of barred?'

'My dear!' Barbara dropped the scarf. 'It's going to be a highly public affair. A service in the village hall.'

'Not the church?'

'They don't have a church any more. The minister holds his services in the village hall.'

'Ah. And the minister is . . .?'

'Father Ellis.'

'Nick Ellis.' Merrily nodded. This explained a lot.

'I don't know *why* so many Anglicans are choosing to call themselves "Father" now, as if they're courting Catholicism. You know this man?'

'I know *of* him. He's a *charismatic* minister, which means—'

'Not happy-clappy?' Barbara's eyes narrowed in distaste. 'Everybody hugging one another?'

'That's one aspect of it. Nick Ellis is also a member of a group known as the Sea of Light. It's a movement inside the Anglican Church, which maintains that the Church has become too obsessed with property. Keepers of buildings rather than souls. They claim the Holy Spirit flows through people, not stones. So a Sea of Light minister is more than happy to hold services in village halls, community centres – and private homes, of course.'

'And the same goes for burial.'

'I would guess so.'

'So Jeffery has an accomplice in the clergy.' Barbara Buckingham stood up. 'He would have, wouldn't he? It's such a tight little world.'

'Look,' Merrily said, 'I know how you feel, but I really don't think there's anything you can do about it. And if Nick Ellis is conducting a funeral service at the village hall and a ceremony in J.W. Weal's back garden, I'm not sure I can hold another one in a church. However—'

'Mrs Watkins . . . Merrily . . .' She'd failed with the solicitor, now she was trying the Church.

Merrily said awkwardly, 'I'm really not sure this is a spiritual problem.'

'Oh, but it *is*.' Barbara splayed her fingers on the table, leaned towards Merrily. 'She comes to me, you see . . .'

The bereavement ghost: the visitor. Maybe sitting in a familiar chair or walking in the garden, or commonly – like Menna – in dreams. Barbara Buckingham, staying at a hotel near Kington, had dreamt of her sister every night since her death.

Menna was wearing a white shift or shroud, with darkness around her.

'You'd prefer, no doubt, to think the whole thing is a projection of my guilt,' Barbara said.

'Perhaps of your loss, even though you didn't know her. Perhaps an even greater loss, because of all those years you *might* have known her, and now you realize you never will. Is your husband . . .?'

'In France on a buying trip. He has an antiques business.'

'How do you feel when you wake up?'

'Anxious.' Barbara drank some tea very quickly. 'And drained. Exhausted and debilitated.'

'Have you seen a doctor?'

'Yes. As it happens' – a mild snort – 'I've seen Menna's doctor, Collard Banks-Morgan. We were at the same primary school. "Dr Coll", they all call him now. But if you were suggesting that a little Valium might help to relax me, I didn't go to consult him about myself.'

'You wanted to know why she'd suffered a stroke.'

'I gatecrashed his surgery at the school in Old Hindwell. Made a nuisance of myself, not that it made any difference. Bloody man told me I was asking him to be unethical, pre-empting the post-mortem. He was like that as a child, terribly proper. If they'd had a head boy at the primary school, it would've been Collard Banks-Morgan.'

'*Did* you find out if there was a long-term blood pressure problem?'

'No.' Barbara Buckingham put on her scarf at last. 'But I will.'

'Look,' Merrily said, 'why don't we say a prayer for Menna before you go? For her spirit. Why don't we pop over to the church?'

'I've taken too much of your time.'

'I think it might help.' Fifth rule of Deliverance: whether you believe the story or not, never leave things without at least a prayer. 'I *would* like to help, if I can.'

And there was more to this. Merrily was curious now. Everything suggested there was more. Why should this woman feel robbed of a sister she'd never really known?

'Then come to the funeral,' Barbara said.

'Me?'

'Is that too much of an imposition?'

'Well, no but—'

'You were at the hospital with her.'

Merrily agonized then about whether she should tell Barbara Buckingham what she'd witnessed in the side ward. It was clear Cullen hadn't or Barbara would have mentioned that. She remembered the feeling she'd had then of something ritualistic about the way Weal was putting dabs of water on Menna's corpse and then himself. Refusing to let the nurses try to feed her. Refusing to let Merrily pray for her. Wanting to do everything himself. It was, she suppposed, a kind of possession.

But she decided to say nothing. It might only inflame an already fraught situation.

'OK. I'll try to come. What day?'

'Saturday. Three thirty. Old Hindwell village hall.'

'That should be OK. If something comes up, where can I get a message to you?'

'Doesn't matter. If you aren't there, you aren't there.'

'I'll do my best. Have you . . . spoken to Mr Weal?'

'I'm not ready for that yet,' Barbara said. 'But I shall do. Thank you, Merrily.'

TEN

Nightlife of Old Hindwell

Robin had the map spread out under a wine-bottle lamp on the kitchen table, after they'd finished supper.

'Come take a look, Bets.' Holding his thick, black drawing pencil the way he held his *athame* in a rite. 'Whole bunch of churches around the Forest.'

The lamplight sheened his dense, Dark Ages hair. Betty leaned over him. He smelled sweet and warm, like a puppy. She felt an unexpected stirring; he was so lovably uncomplicated.

And so simplistic, sometimes, in his thinking. Why, since they'd arrived here, had any physical desire always been so swiftly soured by irritation? She gazed around the still-gloomy farmhouse kitchen. Why, with the stove on for over a week, was there still an aura of damp – always worse after sunset? She felt clammy and uncomfortable, as though she had the curse. If Robin had said, 'Let's give this place up, and leave now, tonight,' she wouldn't have hesitated.

But since that mention of the E-word, his attitude had unsubtly altered. A couple of seconds of trepidation then the male thing was kicking in. Robin wanted to find out precisely where Ellis was coming from, then get in his face. It hadn't been helped, Betty guessed, by Ellis wearing army gear. Combat gear? She was appalled to think that she might even once have shared Robin's zeal, if only this had been someone else's house, the home of a fellow pagan in need of moral support.

If only she wasn't already growing to hate their church too much to want to defend it.

She'd tried to remember her reaction on first seeing it, and couldn't. Probably because she was being practical at the time and paying more attention to the farmhouse, leaving Robin to moon over the ruins, take dozens of photographs.

He'd now finished ringing churches on the Landranger map. Although it didn't identify individual ones except by symbols, nearby place names sometimes would give a clue to the dedication. Betty could help him out there a little, from childhood knowledge of Welsh. She put a thumbnail to the southernmost symbol.

'That one: the village is Llanfihangel nant Melan. Llanfihangel's Welsh for "The Church of St Michael".'

'Cool.' Robin drew an extra ring around the church and then tracked around the others with the tip of his pencil until he came to the northern part of the forest perimeter. 'What's this? Same word, right?'

'Llanfihangel Rhydithon. That's another, yeah. And then ours, of course. Three St Michael churches around the Forest. He was right, I suppose.'

'Gotta be more. Three doesn't make a circle.'

With swift, firm pencil strokes, he redrew the plan on his sketch-pad. Graphics were important to Robin. Making a picture made things real.

'Of course,' Betty said, 'there's nothing to suggest all these churches were built at the same time. I vaguely remember going to Llanfihangel Rhydithon as a kid, and I don't think it's even medieval.'

'It's the site that counts. Come on, Bets, what are you, agnostic now? Look through Ellis's eyes. Guy thinks he's fighting an active Devil.'

'Or, more specifically, in the absence of people actually sacrificing cockerels and abusing children on his doorstep – against us,' Betty said bitterly.

'I'm still not sure he knows. Ellis was fishing. Like, who could've told him? Who *else* knows, or could've seen anything? We didn't even use removal men.'

Betty said, 'It scares me. I don't want this.'

'Aw, come on,' he said. 'You're a witch. Hey, you know, damn near all these churches have just gotta be on older sites, when you see how close they are to standing stones and burial mounds.' He leaned back in satisfaction. 'This valley's a damned prehistoric ritual freaking wonderland. Which explains everything.'

'It does?'

'You got all these sacred sites, right? It's a good bet most of them were still being used by surviving pagan groups well into medieval times, and probably long after that. This was a remote area with a small and scattered population. Closed in, secretive. I think it's fair to assume that even when they'd been brutally eradicated from most of the rest of the country, the Old Ways were still preserved here.'

'Possibly.'

'The Archangel Michael's the hard guy of the Church. It's them saying to the pagans, you bastards better come around, *or else*. Ellis, as a fundamentalist, relates to all of that. Plus, he's been influenced by insane Bible Belt evangelists who persecute snakes. Plus, his ego's already been blown up sky high by the size of congregations he's pulling when all the neighbouring churches are going down the tubes. I've decided the guy sucks. The only remaining question is how long we keep stalling before we tell him that he and his exorcism squad can go screw themselves.'

'I was going to say that if we don't make an issue of it, if we let it go quiet, then he'll probably forget about us,' Betty said lamely.

'Not gonna happen. Believe me, this guy's on some kind of crusade under the banner of St Michael. Hey! Would that explain the army surplus stuff? *Shit*.'

Robin smiled at his own flawed logic. Betty saw, with a plummeting heart, that he *wanted* to be a target of Christian fanaticism.

'When *we* look at those ruins,' he said, 'we see a resurgence of the true, indigenous spirituality. Whereas *he* sees a naked tower giving him and his religion the finger. He *so* wants to be the guy who killed the dragon and claimed it all back. It's an ego thing.'

'You and him both.'

The smile crashed. 'Meaning *what*?'

'You have a few beers together, you size each other up, and now you're both flexing your muscles for the big fight. You can't wait, can you? You love it that he's got this huge mass of followers and there's just the two of us here, newcomers, isolated . . .'

'Now listen, lady.' Robin was on his feet, furious. 'My instinct was to kick his ass, right from the off, but no . . . I play it the way I figure *you* would want me to! Mr Nice Guy, Mr Don't Frighten The Horses . . . Mr Take A Faceful Of Shit And Keep Smiling kind of guy!'

'No, you didn't. You thought you could play with him, lead him around the houses, take the piss out of him a little . . . when in fact he was playing with *you*.'

'You weren't even there!'

'And you've never given a thought to where this could leave us. We have to live here . . . Whatever happens, we have to live here afterwards. And we *will* have to live here, because – in case you haven't thought about this – who is going to buy a run-down house along with a ruined church which the local minister insists is infested with demonic evil?' She spun away from him. 'You shithead.'

Robin snatched in a breath that was halfway to a sob then threw his pencil down on the table. 'I need some air.'

'You certainly do!'

He turned his back on her, strode across the kitchen like Lord bloody Madoc and tore open the back door. Before he slammed it behind him, she heard the rushing of the rain-swollen Hindwell Brook in the night, like a hiss of glee.

Betty let her head fall into her hands on the tabletop.

What have we done? What have we walked into?

Robin stomped across the yard, hit the track toward the gate and the road. It was cold and the going wasn't so easy in the dark, but he was damned if he was going back for a coat and flashlight.

Why, *why* was whatever he said, whatever he did, whatever he tried to do, always the wrong fucking thing?

Four years he and Betty had been together and, sure, they were different people, raised in different cultures. But they'd previously come through on shared beliefs, a strong respect for natural forces and each other's destiny.

And he'd thought the road to Old Hindwell was lit for them both.

All the portents had been there, just as soon as they decided they would look for a place in the countryside where they might explore the roots of the old spirituality. They'd let it be known on the pagan network that they were looking for something rural and it didn't have to be luxurious. The Shrewsbury coven had worked a spell on their behalf and, before that week was out, they'd received – anonymously, but with a wellwisher's symbol and the message 'Thought you might be interested in this . . . Blessed Be!' – the estate agent's particulars of St Michael's Farm. And – in the very same post – a letter from Al Delaney at Talisman to say that Kirk Blackmore was impressed with Robin's work and would like him to design the new cover . . . with the possibility of a contract for the soon-to-be-rejacketed backlist of SEVEN VOLUMES!

Even Betty had to agree, it was like writing in the sky.

Robin joined the lane that led first past the Prosser farm and then on to the village. The farm was spread across the council roadway, like it owned it, sheds and barns on either side, mud from tractor wheels softening the surface of the road. A Land Rover was parked under an awning. It had a big yellow sticker in the back window, and even at night you could read 'Christ is the Light!' in luminous yellow. Robin gave a moan, stifled it. He hadn't known about this. If Ellis denounced them, they'd have no support from their neighbours.

When he got clear of the farm he surveyed the night. Ahead of him, the moon lay on its back over a long hill bristling with ranks of conifers – a hedgehog's back, a dragon's back. Robin held out his arms as if to embrace the hill, then let them fall uselessly to his sides and walked on down the middle of the narrow lane, with ditches to either side and banks topped by hedges so savagely pleached they were almost like hurdles. Gareth Prosser was clearly a farmer who liked to keep nature under his thumb. *His farm, his land.* Robin wondered how Prosser had reacted to the team of archaeologists who'd moved in and sheared the surface from one of his fields to uncover postholes revealing that, 4,000 years ago, the farm had been a key site of ritual pagan worship. Maybe Prosser had gotten Ellis in to sanctify the site.

Whatever, there was virtually nothing to see there now. Robin had sent off to the Council for British Archaeology for the report on the Radnor Valley dig. A couple of weeks ago, when he and Betty had driven down with a vanload of books, he'd checked out the site but found just a few humps and patches where the soil had been put back and reseeded. The team had taken away their finds – the flint arrowheads and axes – and hundreds of photos, and given the temple back to the sheep.

And to the pagans.

Well, why not? The night before they moved in, they'd agreed there should be a sabbat here at Imbolc – which Betty preferred to call by its old Christian name, Candlemas, because it was prettier. They'd agreed there should be the traditional Crown of Lights, which Betty would wear if there was no more suitable candidate. At the old church above the water, it was all going to be totally beautiful; Robin had had this fantasy of the village people coming along to watch or even join in and bringing their kids – this atmosphere of joy and harmony at Imbolc, Candlemas, the first day of Celtic Spring, the glimmering in the darkness.

But that had not been mentioned since, and he was damned if he was gonna bring it up again.

Robin walked on, uphill now. Presently, the hedge on the right gave way to a stone wall, and he entered the village of Old Hindwell. As if to mock the word 'Old', the first dwelling in the village was a modern brick bungalow. A few yards further on was the first street-light, a bluish bulb under a tin hat on a bracket projecting from a telephone pole. Older cottages on either side now. At the top of the hill, the road widened into a fork.

On the corner was the pub, the Black Lion, the utility bulkhead bulb over its porch clouded with the massed corpses of flies. It was an alehouse, not much more; the licensee, Greg Starkey, had come from London with big ideas but not pulled enough customers to realize them.

Tonight, Robin could have used a drink. Jacketless, therefore walletless, he dug into his pockets for change, came up with a single 50p piece. Could you get any kind of drink for 50p? He figured not.

'Robin. Hi.'

'Jeez!' He jumped. She'd come out of an entrance to the Black Lion's back yard. 'Uh . . . Marianne.'

Greg's wife. She moved out under the bulb, so he could see she was wearing a turquoise fleece jacket over a low-cut black top. Standard landladywear in her part of London, maybe, but not so often seen out here. But Marianne made no secret of how much she'd give to get back to the city.

'Haven't seen you for days and days, Robin.'

'Oh . . . Well, lot of work. The house move, you know?'

The last time he'd seen her was when he'd driven down on his own with a vanload of stuff, grabbing some lunch at the Lion. She'd seemed hugely pleased that he was moving in, with or without a wife. *'Anything you wanna know about the place, you come and ask me; Wednesdays are best, that's when Greg goes over to Hereford market.'*

Yeah, well.

'Bored already, Robin? I did warn you.'

She was late thirties, disillusion setting up permanent home in the lines either side of her mouth.

Robin said, 'I, uh . . . I guess I just like the night.'

'Robin, love,' she said, 'this ain't *night*. This is just bleedin' darkness.'

She did this cackly laugh. He smiled. 'So, uh . . . you still don't feel too good about here.'

'Give the boy a prize off the top shelf.'

Her voice was too loud for this village at night. It bounced off walls. She moved toward him. He could smell that she'd been drinking. She stopped less than a foot away. There was no one else in sight. Robin kind of wished he'd turned around at the bottom of the street.

'This is the nearest I get to a night out, you know that? We got to *work*. We got to open the boozer every lunchtime and every bleedin' night of the week, and we don't get the same day off 'cause we can't afford to pay nobody, and we wouldn't trust 'em to keep their fingers out of the bleedin' till, anyway.'

'Aw, come on, Marianne . . .'

'They all hate us. We'll always be outsiders.'

'Come on . . . Nobody hates you.'

'So we take our *pleasures* separately. Greg whoops it up at Hereford market on a Wednesday. Me, I just stand in the street and wait for a beautiful man to come along who don't stink of sheep dip.'

'Marianne, I think—'

'Oh, sorry! I forgot – except for this Saturday when I'm going to a funeral. Because it is potilic . . . what'd I say? *Politic* – that's what Greg says: politic. I'm pissed, Robin . . .' Putting out her hands as if to steady herself, gripping his chest. 'And you're very appealing to me. I been thinking about you a lot. You're a different kind of person, aincha?'

'I'm an American kind of person is all. Otherwise just a regular—'

'Now don't go modest on me for Gawd's sake. I tell you what . . .' She started to rub her hands over his chest and stomach. 'You can kiss me, Mr American-kind-of-person. Think of it as charity to the Third World. 'Cause if this ain't the Third bleedin' World . . .'

'Uh, call me old-fashioned' – Robin gently detached her hands – 'but I really don't think that would be too wise.'

'Well, if anybody's watching . . .' Marianne's voice rose. 'If anybody's spying from behind their lace bleedin' curtains, they can *go fuck themselves*!'

Robin panicked; no way he wanted to be associated with this particular attitude. He backed off so fast that Marianne toppled towards him, clawed vaguely at the air and fell with her hands flat on the cindered surface of the pub's parking lot.

Where she stayed, on all fours, looking down at the road.

Oh shit.

Robin moved to help her. She looked up at him and bared her teeth like a cornered cat. 'You pushed me.'

'No, no, I really didn't. You know I didn't.'

Marianne staggered to her feet, hands waving in the air for balance.

'How about we get you inside,' Robin said.

'You pushed me!' Backing towards the yard entrance, holding up her scratched hands like she was displaying crucifixion scars. If the people of Old Hindwell hadn't been watching from behind their curtains before, they sure were now.

'Fuck you!' Marianne said. '*Fuck you!*' she screamed and flew at him like a crazy chicken.

Robin backed off and spun around and found himself running any which way, until he was out of breath.

He stopped. Apart from his own panting, the place was silent again. He looked around, saw only night. The buildings had gone. He didn't know where he was.

And then he looked up and there, set into the partially afforested hillside, was the tip of a golden light, a shining ingot in the dense, damp, conifered darkness. It was, by far, the brightest light in Old Hindwell village and, as he stepped back, it lengthened and branched out. Became a cross, in golden neon.

Nick Ellis's clapboard church.

The cross hung there as if unsupported, like a big, improbable star.

The truth was, Robin found it kind of chilling. It was like he'd been driven into a trap. Away in the darkness, he heard footsteps. He froze. Was she coming after him?

Too heavy, too slow. And the steps were receding. Robin walked quietly back the way he'd come and presently the light above the pub door reappeared. He moved cautiously into the roadway in case Marianne was still around, claws out.

A few yards ahead of him, passing the entrance to the school-turned-surgery, was a man on his own. A man so big he was like an outsize shadow thrown on a wall. *Must be a head taller than most of the farmers hereabouts.* But he hadn't come out of the pub. He was not drunk. He had a steady, stately walk and, as he passed the pub, Robin saw by the bulkhead light that the man was dressed in a dark suit and a white shirt and tie. The kind of attire farmers wore only for funerals.

The guy walked slowly back down the street, the same way Robin was headed. After a dozen or so paces, he stopped and looked over his shoulder for two, three seconds. Robin saw his face clearly: stiff, grey hair and kind of a hooked nose, like the beak of an eagle.

The guy turned and continued on his way down the street. Robin, having had to take the same route, hung around a while to put some distance between them; he didn't feel too sociable right now, but he did feel cold. He stood across from the pub, shivering and hugging himself.

The big guy was a shambling shadow against curtained windows lit from behind. Halfway down the street, he stopped again, looked back over his shoulder. *Looked*, not glanced. Robin only saw his face in silhouette this time. He was surely looking for someone, but there was no one there.

Robin shook his head, uncomprehending – a little more spooked.

The nightlife of Old Hindwell.

ELEVEN

No Ghosts, No God

Huddled in Jane's duffel coat, she walked past the village square, where the cobbles were glassy with frost. The moon was in the west, still hard and brighter than the security lamp beside the front door of the Swan.

It was 5.30 a.m. She clutched the church keys in a gloved hand. She planned to pray before the altar for Barbara Buckingham and for the soul of her sister, Menna.

Merrily walked in through the lychgate. Somewhere, beyond the orchard, a fox yelped. Down in the churchyard she saw a soft and now familiar glow.

'Last time, vicar. Honest to God.'

'Gomer, I don't mind, really.'

'Unnatural, sure t'be. Be thinkin' I'm some ole pervert, ennit?'

Merrily smiled. He was crouching by Minnie's grave, an area of raised earth, an elongated mole-tump, with the hurricane lamp on it. No memorial yet. No sound of underground ticking.

'I was just thinking, like,' Gomer said. 'I don't want no bloody stone. I got to have a stone?'

'Don't see why.'

'Wood. I likes wood. En't no good with stone, but I could carve out a nice piece of oak, see.' He looked up at Merrily, lamplight moons in his glasses. 'En't nothing to do with the money, like. Be a proper piece. We never talked about it, but her liked a nice bit of oak, my Min. I'll put on it about Frank as well, see.'

'Whatever you like, Gomer. Whatever you think she'd have wanted.'

'Summat to do, ennit? Long ole days, see, vicar. Long ole days.'

Merrily sat on a raised stone tomb, tucking her coat underneath her. 'What else will you do, Gomer?'

'Oh.' Gomer sniffed meditatively. 'Bit o' this, bit o' that.'

'Will you stay here?'

'Never thought about moving.'

'Jane thought you might go back to Radnorshire.'

'What for?'

'Roots?'

Gomer sniffed again abruptly. 'People talks a lot of ole wallop 'bout roots. Roots is generally gnarled and twisted. Best kept buried, my experience.'

'Yeah, you could be right.' She had a thought. 'You ever know a family called Thomas down on the border?'

'Knowed 'bout half a dozen families called Thomas, over the years. Danny Thomas, up by Kinnerton, he's a good ole boy. Keeps a 'lectric guitar and amplifiers in his tractor shed, on account his wife, Greta, she hates rock and roll. They was at Min's funeral.'

'Around Old Hindwell, I was thinking.'

'Ole Hindwell.' Gomer accepted a Silk Cut from Merrily's packet. 'Gareth Prosser, he's the big man in Ole Hindwell. Laid some field drainage for him, years back. Then he inherits another 200 acres and a pile o' cash, and the bugger buys hisself a second-hand digger at a farm sale. Always thought theirselves a cut above, the Prossers. County councillor, magistrate, all this ole wallop.'

'These particular Thomases had two daughters. Barbara was one?'

'Got you now. Her runned away?'

'That's right.'

'An' the other one wed Big Weal, the lawyer.'

'Menna.'

'Their ole man was Merv Thomas, Maesmawr, up by Walton. Never worked for 'em, mind – too tight, digged their own cesspits, never drained a field. Merv's dead now, ennit? Ar, course he is. Her'd never be wed otherwise.'

'You know Weal?'

99

'Always avoided lawyers,' Gomer said. 'Thieving bastards, pardon me, vicar. Weal's ole-fashioned, mind, but that don't make him any less of a thieving bastard. Looks after his wife, though, 'cordin' to what they says.'

'Menna's dead, Gomer.'

'Never!' Gomer was shocked enough to whip the ciggy out of his mouth.

'Died in the County, same night as Minnie.'

'But her was no more'n a kiddie!'

'Thirty-nine. A stroke.'

'Bugger me.' Gomer stared down at the soil. 'Big Weal must be gutted.'

'Could say that.'

Gomer put his ciggy back, shook his head. 'Ole Hindwell, eh? You know what they says about that place, don't you, vicar?'

'Tell me.' Merrily managed to get her cigarette going before the breeze doused the Zippo.

'"Place as God give up on",' explained Gomer.

'Lot of places like that.'

'With the church, see. Lets their church fall into ruin and never had another.'

'Until now.'

'Ar?'

'There's a kind of missionary minister who's holding services in the parish hall. Father Ellis?'

'Oh hell, aye.' Gomer puffed on his ciggy. 'Nutter.'

'That's what they say about him, is it? Nutter?'

'Had two or three proper, solid ole churches under his wing, and they says he favoured Ole Hindwell village hall above the lot of 'em. An' all this clappin' and huggin' and chantin' and stuff. Mind, in Ole Hindwell they wouldn't notice another bloody nutter if he was stark naked in the snow.'

'How do you mean?'

'Inbreedin'.' Gomer chuckled. 'We always says that. Some places gets that kind o' reputation for no reason at all other'n being a bit off the beaten track. And havin' its church falled into ruins.'

'Why *did* it fall into ruins? Apart from God giving up.'

'Now, there's a can of ole worms, ennit?'

'Is it?'

'Last but one vicar, they reckoned he went mad.'

'Like Ellis?'

'No, *mad* mad. All kinds o' rumours, there. Never come out, proper. You got a problem out there, vicar?'

'Well, erm . . . Mr Weal seems to be set on putting Mrs Weal into some kind of tomb in his garden.'

'Well, well,' Gomer said non-committally.

'And Barbara doesn't think that's a good idea. She doesn't think Weal's quite grasped the need to let go of the dead. And she wants me to go to the funeral with her, to hold her hand . . . or maybe to restrain her. And I think there's something odd about that whole situation. Would, er, would you happen to know anybody who might know the score there?'

Gomer nodded slowly. 'I reckon.'

'And maybe a bit about Barbara and why she hates that area so much.'

'Likely. Anythin' else?'

'Father Ellis? Seems to me that for everybody who thinks he's a nutter, there must be another five can't get enough, if you see what I mean.'

'No accountin' for the way folks is gonner go, them parts. Seen it before, oh hell, aye. Gimme a day or two.'

This time, Gomer declined the offer of tea and breakfast, said he'd got himself a nice, crusty cob needed using up. She could tell he was pleased to have something to occupy his time.

And *digging* was what Gomer did best.

Merrily went into church and prayed for Barbara and Menna and asked the Boss about another matter – kind of hoping she'd get a strong negative response.

Back at the vicarage just before seven, she punched out Tania Beauman's *Livenight* number. Waited for the answering machine to kick in.

'Oh . . . this is Merrily Watkins at the Hereford Diocese. Sorry for not getting back to you last night. I'll be in the office from about half nine, if you want to talk about . . . what I might be able to contribute to your programme. Thanks.'

No backing out now.

Be something different, anyway: bright lights, hi-tech hardware, the fast chat, the tat, the trivia, the complete, glossy inconsequentiality of it.

Jane came down for breakfast, all fresh and school-uniformed.

'Been up long, Mum?'

'Couple of hours. Couldn't sleep.'

'So, you rang *Livenight*, then?'

'Not much gets past you, does it, flower?'

'It'll be fun.'

'Be fun for *you*, watching at home.'

'Er . . . yeah,' Jane said airily.

That night, after a wedding rehearsal at the church for a couple whose chief bridesmaid would be their own granddaughter, Merrily phoned Eileen Cullen from the scullery.

'I just got the feeling you might have heard from Barbara Buckingham again.'

'And why would you be thinking that, Reverend?' Cullen sounded more than usually impatient, as if she was carrying an overflowing bedpan in her other hand.

'She's keen to find out why Menna died.'

'High blood pressure.'

'Well, yes, sure. But why did she have high blood pressure at *her* age?'

'I told you why, and I haven't changed my mind. I reckon she'd been on the Pill for longer than she ought to've been. Years longer, that's my guess. Prolonged ingestion of synthetic oestrogen. Bad news – but then you'd know all that.'

'Eileen, I live the life of a nun. I've *forgotten* all that.'

'Well, it's not your problem, and it's not mine either and it's not poor Menna's any longer.' A pause, then she came back a little softer.

'Listen, if you've got the Buckingham woman on your back in a big way, I'm sorry. I'm sorry I sent her over, so I am.'

'You must have felt at the time that she had a valid problem.'

'Just wanted her out of me hair. You know what I'm like.'

'Mmm, that's why I don't think you're being entirely upfront.'

'Jesus Christ, I'm always upfront. Nobody in this fockin' job's got time to go round the side any more.'

'Did you by any chance tell her about Weal and that business with the water?'

'You mean so they could have a big row and disturb all my patients? Are you kidding? Did *you* tell her?'

'No.'

'Well, good.'

'Confidentially—'

'Merrily, when the hell do we ever talk any other way?'

'Barbara's getting troubled dreams.'

'Troubled, how?'

'Says she sees Menna.'

A pause. 'Does she?'

'Night after night.'

'Stress,' Cullen said. 'Look, I've got to—'

'Well, you would say that. No ghosts, no God. You think my whole life's a sorry sham.'

'Aye, but you're a well-meaning wee creature. Listen, I really do have to go.'

'So you haven't seen her then?'

'Of course I haven't fockin' seen her!' Cullen snapped. 'What the hell d'you think I am?'

Merrily's head spun. She stared at the circle of light thrown on the Holy Bible. The rosebush chattered at the dark window.

'I meant Barbara,' Merrily said.

'I have to go.' Cullen hung up.

Part Two

Witchcraft may be underestimated by Christians on the grounds that it is phoney and synthetic and that its covens are completely eclectic and belong to no national organization. There are, however, dangers . . .

Deliverance (ed. Michael Perry)
The Christian Deliverance Study Group

TWELVE

Bear Pit

She first became aware of him in the green room.

Her initial thought was that he must be a priest, because he was wearing a suit, though not a dog collar – well, how many *did* these days, outside working hours? And then, because he was so smooth and assured, and – perhaps, she thought afterwards, because his shirt was wine-coloured – she even wondered if he might be a bishop.

He brought her a coffee. 'This stuff could be worse,' he said. 'BBC coffee is *much* worse.'

'You do this kind of thing fairly often then?' she said. God, that wasn't quite, 'Do you come here often?' but it was dangerously close.

'When I must,' he said. 'Edward Bain, by the way.'

'Merrily Watkins.'

'I know,' he said.

He was, of course, attractive: lean, pale features and dark curly hair with a twist of grey over the ears. He'd made straight for Merrily across the green room – it sounded like some notoriously haunted, country house bedchamber, but was simply the area where all the participants gathered before the show. It was long and narrow and starting to look like a pantomime dressing room because of some of the costumes: Dark Age *chic* meeting retro-punk in a tangle of braids and bracelets.

The producer and his team mingled with the main guests and the support acts, observing and listening, picking out the potential stars-for-an-hour. Meanwhile the guests drank tea and coffee and spring water – no alcohol – and nibbled things on sticks, talking a lot, losing

107

inhibitions, unblocking their adrenal glands, developing that party mentality. As if most of them hadn't brought it with them.

'Lord,' Edward Bain murmured, 'do they really *want* to be taken seriously?' He looked at Merrily with a faint, pained smile.

The smile chilled her. It was Sean's smile – her dead husband's. Boyish, disarming. Sean's smile when accused. She turned sharply away, as though distracted by an argument in progress between a tight-faced security officer and a ginger-bearded man wearing a short, white cloak over a red tunic with a belt. Into the belt was stuck a knife with a black handle

'It's my fucking *athame*, man. It's a *religious* tool. You wouldn't ask a fucking bishop to hand over his fucking crozier!'

Edward Bain's smile became a wince, wiping away the similarity to Sean. If it had ever really been there. Merrily swallowed.

The security man turned to Tania Beauman for support. Tania wrinkled her nose. 'Oh, leave it, Grant. I suspect it looks more dangerous than it actually is.'

'Tania, it's a knife. If we start allowing weapons in the studio, we may as well—'

'It's a f—' The ginger guy blew out his cheeks in frustration, turned to Tania. 'This doorman is really hacking me off, you know? This is religious persecution.'

'Sure.' Tania was a short, capable bottle-blonde of about forty. 'If we just agree that it's purely ornamental – yeah, sorry, *religious* – and that you won't be taking it out of—'

'Of course I won't be fucking taking it out!'

'And if you use that word on camera before midnight, you realize you'll be excluded from the debate, yeah?'

The ginger man subsided in a surly kind of way, a semi-chastened schoolboy.

'That's *his* card marked,' Edward Bain told Merrily. 'He'll be used purely for decoration, now. Won't get asked a single question unless it starts to slow up and they're really desperate for confrontation.'

'I don't see that happening, somehow,' Merrily said, 'do you?'

'The boy's an idiot, anyway. If the *athame* is to have any potency at all it should hardly be displayed like some sort of cycling club badge.'

He smiled down at Merrily – instant Sean once more – and glided away, leaving her feeling clammy. And she thought, Oh my God. He's one of them.

'Ooooooooh.' Tania went into a sinuous shudder. 'Magnetic – and more.'

Over by the door, Edward Bain was into an intense conversation with a woman in a long, loose, classical kind of dress, like someone from rent-a-Muse. Merrily saw now that one of Bain's middle fingers wore a silver ring with a moonstone. She saw him and the woman clasp hands lightly and smile, and she imagined tiny blue electric stars crackling between their fingers. She wondered if they'd even met before tonight.

'Who is he?' Merrily muttered. 'I mean, *what* is he?'

'Don't you vicars ever read the *News of the World?*'

'Only if we're really desperate for a sermon.'

'He's the Man,' Tania said. 'If you call him something like King of the Witches, he'll look pained. He doesn't like the word "witch". He's a champagne pagan, if you like. Works as a publishing executive and would rather be profiled in the *Observer* than the *News of the World* . . . and, yeah, he's getting there.'

'By way of *Livenight?*'

Tania frowned. 'Don't take this programme too lightly, Merrily. You can get deeply shafted out there. And we are watched by all kinds of people you wouldn't expect.'

Especially this week! By the acting Bishop of Hereford this week, and probably half of Lambeth Palace. Take it *lightly?* She'd had to put down her glass of spring water because she couldn't hold it still. Ridiculous; she conducted services every Sunday, she talked to hostile teenagers, she talked to God, she . . .

Sean was there, smiling in her mind. In getting here, she'd had to drive past where he died, on the M5, in flames. *Go away!*

She said, too loudly, 'Tania, can you . . . give me a rundown? Who else is here?'

'OK.' Tania nodded briskly. 'Well, we get the programme peg out of the way first, right? The couple who want their kid to be allowed to do his pagan prayers and whatnot at school.' She nodded towards a solemn, bearded man in a home-made-looking sweater. His partner had a waist-length plait. They might have been Muslims. They might even have been Christians.

Merrily said, 'Am I right in thinking you're not going to be spending very long on them?'

'Dead right. Boring, boring, boring. Actually, the headmaster of the school's going to be better value. Born-again Christian. Actually talks like Sir Cliff, like he's got a boiled sweet in his cheek. OK, over there . . . Patrick Ryan – long hair, velvet jacket – Cambridge professor who's done a study of pagan practices. And shagged half the priest-esses in the Home Counties by all accounts, but I doubt he'll be discussing *that*. If Ryan's too heavy, the little guy with the shaven head's Tim Fagan, ex-hack from the *Sun*, was sent out to do an exposé on some sexy coven and wound up joining them. Now edits a popular witchy magazine called – ha ha – *The Moon*.'

Edward Bain excepted, they all looked fairly innocuous.

'What about the other side?'

'Right. Well, we've got a really angry mother who claims paganism turned her daughter into a basket case. She is *very* strong. The kid got drawn into white witchcraft and ended up peeing in churches. Which leads neatly into you, I think.'

'Thanks.'

'You know what I mean.'

'Mmm.' Tania had revealed on the phone that she had seen news cuttings on last year's Herefordshire desecration case, involving the sacrifice of a crow in a country church. Not entirely appropriate, in Merrily's view.

'I mean, I can't say that was your orthodox paganism – if there is such a thing, which I doubt. It was a peculiar kind of black magic. It was a one-off.'

Tania Beauman shrugged.

'By "the other side",' Merrily said, 'I actually meant *us*, the Church. You said I wouldn't be on my own here.' How pathetic did *that* sound?

Tania looked mildly concerned. 'I didn't say that, did I? I'm sure I didn't say that.'

'You did, Tania.'

'Oh, well, what happened, the other bloke let us down. I think his wife had a miscarriage or something.' She was blatantly improvising. 'But if you're looking for back-up, the headmaster's brought along a few members of his church. See the guy in the white—'

'Which church would that be?'

'Well, Christian, obviously, but I suppose you'd probably call it more of a cult.'

'Wonderful.'

'They'll be doing some heavy apocalyptic stuff about the Antichrist walking the earth disguised as . . . Hang on – looks like Steve wants to do his pep talk.'

A bald man of about thirty, in white jeans and a crumpled paisley shirt, strode into the centre of the green room, lifted up his arms for silence, and went – Merrily guessed – into autopilot.

'OK, listen up, everybody, my name's Steve Ewing. I'm the editor of *Livenight*. I'd like to welcome you all to the programme and point out that we'll be on the air in about fifty minutes. You've all seen the show – if not, then that's your problem for sticking with boring old Paxman or the dirty movie on Channel 5. OK, now what I mainly want to stress to you is that *Livenight* is like life – you don't get a second chance.'

A woman cackled. 'All *you* know, mate.'

'Yeah, very good.' Steve Ewing smiled thinly. 'What I'm trying to get over here is that we don't hang around and neither should you. If you have something to say, don't hold back, because it'll be too late and we'll have moved on to another aspect of the debate, and you'll be kicking yourself all the way home because you missed your chance of getting your argument across on the programme.'

Merrily looked around for any exit sign. Wasn't too late to get the hell out of here.

'What I'm looking for,' said Steve, 'is straight talking and – above all – quick, snappy responses. There's a lot of choice material to get across, and we want to help you do that. So it's straight to the point, no pussyfooting, and if it's going to take longer than about thirty seconds, save it for your PhD thesis. John Fallon's the ringmaster.

You won't meet him until you go in, but you've all seen John, he's a smart guy, a pro, and his bullshit threshold is zero. Any questions?'

There was some shuffling but no direct response.

'Why don't we get to meet Fallon before the programme?' Merrily whispered.

Tania Beauman hardly moved her lips. 'You'd know more about this than me, but I don't imagine they'd normally introduce the Christians to the lion.'

They called this the gallery. It was a narrow room with a bank of TV monitors, through which the director and the sound and vision mixers could view the studio floor from different angles. Once the show was on the air, the director would be in audio contact with the producer and the presenter, John Fallon, down in the bear pit. They actually called it that. In fact, Jane had found it a little disappointing at first. It was much smaller than it looked on the box – like a little theatre-in-the-round, with about six rows of banked-up seating.

'Does the whole audience have some angle on the debate?' she asked a white-haired bloke called Gerry, an ex-*Daily Star* reporter who was the senior member of Tania Beauman's research team.

'Nah,' he said. 'We've got a decent enough budget now, but it's not *that* big. The audience are just ordinary punters bussed in – tonight's bunch is from a paint factory in Walsall: packers, cleaners, management – a cross section of society.'

Gerry glanced at Eirion, who looked awfully young and innocent – and not happy. He had no stomach for subterfuge, Jane was realizing. He'd been appalled to discover that her mum, down there, did not know they were up here. Or, indeed, within sixty miles of *Livenight*.

Even in Eirion's car, with the patched-up silencer, it hadn't taken long to get here. The Warehouse studio complex had been quite easy to find, on the edge of a new business park, under a mile from the M5 and ten miles out of the central Birmingham traffic hell.

It was not until they'd actually left the motorway that Jane had revealed to Eirion the faintly illicit nature of this operation. 'Irene,

I'm doing this for *you*. This could be your future. This is like cutting-edge telly. It's an *in*, OK. You might even get a holiday job.'

Eirion had looked appalled, like a taxi driver who'd just discovered he was providing the wheels in a wages snatch. He'd thought they were only driving up separately because Jane's mum might have to stay the night. He did not know how Jane came to have Tania Beauman in her pocket, and would probably not be finding out. Neither would Mum; the plan was, they'd clear off about two minutes before the programme ended, go bombing back down the motorway, and Jane would be up in her apartment with the lights out by the time Mum got home.

Tania Beauman had turned out to be actually OK. She'd told both Gerry and the grizzled director, Maurice, that Jane was her cousin, doing a media studies college course. Which could well be true, one day.

'How old is she?' Maurice had enquired suspiciously.

'Nineteen next month,' Jane said crisply. Eirion looked queasy.

'Stone me,' Gerry muttered. 'When the nineteen-year-olds start looking fourteen, you know you're getting too old for it.'

Maurice took off his cans. 'See, the problem with this particular programme is that we're not *Songs of Praise* and this is not the God Slot. What we do *not* want is a religious debate. We don't want the history of Druidism, we want to know what they get up to in their stone circles when the film crew's gone home. We don't want to hear about the people the witches've healed, we want to know about the ones they've cursed and the virgins they've deflowered on their altars. This is late-night TV. Our job – to put it crudely – is to send you off to bed with a hard-on.'

'I'll be interested to see how the little priest handles it,' Gerry said thoughtfully. 'She's got enough of her own demons.'

Jane stared at him.

'Marital problems,' Gerry said. 'Husband playing away . . . though what the hell possessed him, with that at home.'

'You never know what goes on behind bedroom doors.' Maurice shook his head, smiling sadly. 'You turned all that up, did you, Gerald?'

'And then, when it's all looking a bit messy . . . *Bang!* The husband goes and gets killed in the car, with his girlfriend. Merrily wakes up a widow . . . and soon after that she's become a priest. Interesting, do I detect guilt in there somewhere, or do I just have a suspicious—'

'Christ!' Jane snarled. 'She didn't become a bloody nun! She—' She felt Eirion's hand on her arm and shook it off and bit her lip.

Gerry grinned. 'My, my. Women do stick together, don't they?'

'Lay off, Gerald.' Maurice slipped on his headphones, flipped a switch on his console. 'You there, Martin? Speak to me, son.'

'So.' Gerry leaned against the edge of the mixing desk. 'There you are, Jane. Now you know how easy it is to get people going. You just watch the monitors. Within about seven minutes, everybody's forgotten there are cameras.' He pencilled a note on a copy of the programme's running order; Jane made out the word *Merrily.* 'Be a lot of heat, tonight, I think. When it gets going, it's very possible one of those weirdos is gonna try some spooky stuff.'

Eirion stiffened. 'Spooky stuff?'

'I dunno, son. A spell or something, I suppose. Something to prove they can make things happen. I dunno, basically – it's all cobblers, anyway.'

Jane looked at Eirion. She was still shaking. They had a little file on Mum; if the show lost momentum, shafting her became an option.

THIRTEEN

A Surreal Memory

Betty's day clearly hadn't been too great either. You could tell not so much from her face as from her manner: no bustle.

'You don't tell me yours, and I won't tell you mine.' Robin didn't even lift his head from the kitchen table where he'd fallen into a sleep of dismay and frustration. 'We'll call it a shit amnesty.'

Ten fifteen on this cold, misty, moonless night. Betty had been out since mid-afternoon. She'd been to see the widow Wilshire in New Radnor again, taking with her an arthritis potion involving 'burdock and honeysuckle, garlic and nettle and a little healing magic'. Betty was good with healing plants; after pissing off her parents by walking out of teacher training, she'd worked at a herb garden and studied with a herbalist at nights for two and a half years. She'd gone to a whole lot of trouble with this potion, driving over to a place the other side of Hereford yesterday to pick up the ingredients.

'How is she now?'

'Oh . . . more comfortable. And happier, I think.'

Around six she'd phoned him to say she was hanging on there a while. Seemed Mrs Wilshire's home help had not made it this week and she was distressed about the state of her house and her inability to clean it up. So Betty would clean up, sure she would. Wherever she went, Betty added to her collection of aunts.

'OK,' Robin said, 'if she's so much better, I give up. Where's the bad stuff come in?'

'It isn't necessarily bad – just odd.' Betty took off her coat, hung it behind the back door, went to get warm by the stuttering Rayburn. 'So you first. It's Ellis, isn't it?'

'No, haven't heard a word from Ellis. This is Blackmore. He faxed. He doesn't like the artwork.'

'Oh.' Betty pushed her hands through her hair, letting it tumble. 'I did say it was a mistake, dealing with him directly. You should have carried on communicating through the publishers. If he can get hold of you any time he wants, he'll just keep on quibbling.'

'It was what he wanted. And *he* is Kirk Blackmore. And, frankly, quibbling doesn't quite reach it.'

'Not something you can alter easily?'

Robin laughed bleakly. 'What the asshole doesn't like is . . . everything. He doesn't like my concept of Lord Madoc – his face is wrong, his hair is wrong, his clothes are wrong, his freaking *boots* are wrong. Oh, and he walks in the wrong colour of mist.'

'I'm sorry.' Betty came round the back of his chair, put her hands on his shoulders, began to knead. 'All that work. What does it mean? What happens now?'

'Means I grovel. Or I take the one-off money and someone else's artwork goes on the book.'

'There's no way—'

'Betty . . . OK. I am a well-regarded illustrator. Any ordinary, midlist fantasy writer, they'd have to go with it. Blackmore, however, is now into a one-and-a-half-million-pound three-book deal. He walks with the gods. Different rules apply.'

Betty scowled. 'Doesn't change the fact that he writes moronic crap. Tell him to sod off. It's just one book.'

He sat up. 'It's not moronic. The guy knows his stuff. And it's not just one book. His whole backlist's gonna be rejacketed in the *Sword of Twilight* format, whoever's artwork that should be. Which is *seven* books – a lot of work. Face it, I *need* Blackmore. I need to have my images under his big name. Also, we need the money if we're gonna make a start on getting this place into any kind of good condition. We were counting on that money, were we not?'

'I suppose.'

'Right, end of story. Back to the airbrush.'

She bent and kissed his hair. 'You've gone pale.'

'Yeah, well, I didn't expect it. It was a kick in the mouth. Do me good – getting too sure of myself. All right, go ahead. Regale me with the unglad tidings you bring back from the big metropolis.'

They'd taken to calling New Radnor the big metropolis, on account of it had three shops.

'Well . . .' Betty sat down next to him. 'Mrs Wilshire was all worked up because she remembered she'd promised to get the home help to hunt out some of the Major's papers relating to . . . this place. He kept them in a wooden summerhouse in the garden. And of course, the home help didn't show up. Anyway, she gave me the key. That's why I'm so late. I was in there for over an hour. Quite a little field HQ the Major had there: lighting, electric heater, kettle, steel filing cabinet.'

'And she let you loose in there? Almost a stranger?'

'She needs somebody to trust.'

'Yeah.' People trusted Betty on sight; it was a rare quality.

'And she wanted it sorting out, but quite clearly couldn't face going down there, because of the extra responsibility it might heap on her, which she's never been good at. And also because there's a lot of him still there. You can feel him – a clean, precise sort of mind; and frustration because he couldn't find enough to do with it. So when he was buying a house, he was determined to know everything, get the very best deal.'

'Not like me, huh?'

Betty smiled. 'You're the worst kind of impulse buyer. You even hide things from yourself. You and the Major wouldn't have got on at all.'

'So what did you find?'

'Mrs Wilshire said I could bring anything home that might be useful. I've got a cardboard box full of stuff in the car.'

'But you didn't bring it in?'

'Tomorrow.' Betty leaned her head back. 'I've read enough for one night. No wonder he kept it in the shed.'

'What are you saying?'

'I mean, in one respect, Major Wilshire *was* like you – once he'd seen this place, he had to have it. But it also had to be at the right price. And of course he wasn't remotely superstitious. An old soldier, he wasn't afraid of anything that couldn't shoot him. But I suppose that if he happened to come up with certain information that might upset any *other* potential buyers . . .' Betty stopped and rolled her head around to ease tension. 'It's funny . . . the first time I ever went in those ruins, I thought, this is really not a happy place.'

'This is something the agent should've told us? We get to sue the agent?'

'How very American of you. No, I rather doubt it. All too long ago. Anyway, they told us about Major Wilshire's death, which was the main drawback, presumably, as far as they were concerned.'

'So what is this? The ruins are haunted?'

'We jumped to conclusions. We assumed the church was abandoned because of flooding or no access for cars. Or at least *you* did.'

'I assumed. Yeah, assuming is what I do. All the time. OK.' Robin stood up. 'I can't stand it. Gimme the car keys, I'll go fetch your box of goodies.'

When he arrived back with the stuff, she had cocoa coming up. He slammed and barred the door. He was tingling with cold and damp.

'Whooo, it's turned into fog! Was it like that when you were driving home?'

'Some of the way.'

Just as well he'd fallen asleep earlier and hadn't known about the fog; he'd have been worried sick about her, with the ice on the roads and all.

He dumped the cardboard wine box on the table. 'Best not to go out at night this time of year, living in a place like this. Suppose it was so thick you drove into the creek?'

'Brook,' Betty said.

'Whatever.' Robin unpacked the box. Mostly, it seemed to be photocopies, the top one evidently from some official list of historic buildings.

CHURCH OF ST MICHAEL, OLD HINDWELL.
Ruins of former parish church. Mainly C13 and C14, with later south porch and chancel. Embattled three-stage tower

of late C14, rubble-construction with diagonal buttresses to north-west and south-west . . .

And so on. There were a couple more pages of this stuff, which Robin put aside for further study.

'Like you said, looks like the Major built up a fairly comprehensive background file.'

He turned up some sale particulars similar to the one he and Betty had received. Same agent – and same wording, give or take.

'A characterful, historic farmhouse with outbuildings and the picturesque ruins of a parish church, in a most unusual location . . .'

All true enough, as far as it went. Next, Robin found several pages ripped out of a spiral-bound notebook and bunched together with a bulldog clip. There was handwriting on them, not too intelligible, and a string of phone numbers.

'What's this?'

'Don't know. Couldn't make it out. There's all kinds of junk in there. Mrs Wilshire told me to take it anyway. I think she just wanted to get rid of as much as she could. Right, there you are . . . that's the start of it.'

He lifted out a news cutting pasted to a piece of A4. The item was small and faded. 'Rector Resigns due to Ill Health.'

It said little more than that the Reverend Terence Penney had given up the living of Old Hindwell and had left the area. A replacement was being sought.

'When was this?' A date had been scrawled across the newsprint but he couldn't make it out.

'1967.'

'*That* late? You mean the Old Hindwell church was still operational until '67?'

''68, actually.'

'Why did I have it in mind it must have been abandoned back in the '30s or '40s?'

'Because you were sold on the idea that it was due to motor vehicles and the brook. Read the letter underneath. It's from the same woman who wrote the piece in the newspaper.'

It had been typewritten, on an old machine with an old ribbon.

119

Lower Lodge
Monkshall
Leominster
Herefordshire
18 May

Dear Major Wilshire,

Thank you for your letter. Yes, you are quite right, I did have the dubious honour of being appointed Radnor Valley correspondent of the Brecon and Radnor Express for a few years in the 1960s, receiving, if I recall correctly, something like one halfpenny a line for my jottings about local events of note!

My reports on the departure of the Reverend Penney were not, I must say, the ones of which I am most proud, amounting, as they did, to what I suppose would be termed these days a 'cover up'. But my late husband and I were comparatively recent incomers to the area and I was 'walking on eggshells' and determined not to cause offence to anyone!

However, I suppose after all this time there is no reason to conceal anything any more, especially as there was considerable local gossip about it at the time.

Yes, the Reverend Penney was indeed rather a strange young man, although I am still inclined to discount the rumours that he 'took drugs'. There were some hippy types living in the area at the time with whom he was quite friendly, so I suppose this is how the rumour originated.

In retrospect, I think Mr Penney was not the most appropriate person to be put in charge of St Michael's. He was a young man and very enthusiastic, full of ideas, but the local people were somewhat set in their ways and resistant to any kind of change. The church itself was not in very good condition (even before Mr Penney's arrival!), and the parish was having difficulty raising money for repairs – there were not the grants available in those days – and it was a big responsibility for such a young and inexperienced minister.

Yes, I am afraid that what you have been told is broadly correct, though I must say that I never found any signs of mental imbalance in Mr Penney, in his first year at least. He was always friendly, if a little remote.

My memories of THAT day remain confused. Perhaps we should have suspected something after the small fire, the slippage of tiles from the roof and the repeated acts of apparent vandalism (I realize no charges ever resulted from these continued occurrences, so I hope I can trust you, as a soldier, to treat this correspondence as strictly confidential), but no one could really have predicted the events of that particular October morning. It would not have seemed so bad had it not been raining so hard and the brook in such spate. Naturally, quite a crowd – for Hindwell – gathered and there was much weeping and wailing, although this was quickly suppressed and after that day I do not remember anyone speaking of it – quite extraordinary. It was as if the whole village somehow shared the shame.

No, as you note, the big newspapers never 'got on' to the story. Small communities have always been very good at smothering sensational events almost at birth. And what was I, the village correspondent, supposed to write? I was not a journalist, merely a recorder of names at funerals and prize-winners at the local show. Furthermore, later that day, I received a visit from Mr Gareth Prosser Snr, together with Mr Weal, his and our solicitor, who stressed to me that it would 'not be in the best interests of the local people' for this to be publicized in any way. Mr Prosser was the county councillor for the area and served on the police committee and was a personage of considerable gravitas. It was not for me, a newcomer, to cross him over an issue of such sensitivity!

The Church of England (the village is in Wales, but the parish is in the Diocese of Hereford) chose not to take any proceedings against Mr Penney. After his departure, another minister was appointed but did not stay long and thereafter the parish became part of a 'cluster' which is not so uncommon these days! I suppose one could say Old Hindwell 'lost heart' after the extraordinary behaviour of Mr Penney.

I do hope I have been able to help you, but I am rather 'out of touch' with events in Old Hindwell. Although I live no more than half an hour's drive away.

I seem never once to have revisited the village since we moved house in 1983. Old Hindwell is one of those places which it is easy to forget exists, except as a rather surreal memory!

With very best regards,
Juliet Pottinger (Mrs)

'The Local People,' Robin said. 'Whoooeee! Those local people sure like to wield power.'

'No more than in any small community.' Betty brought over cocoa for them both. She knew he'd go for the cover-up aspect first, rather than the significance of the event that had been covered up. She almost wished she could have censored the papers before letting him see them.

The idea of this panicked her. It was like the Wilshires in reverse. Until they came here, she'd never even *thought* of keeping secrets from Robin.

'And who is this Weal?' he said. 'Was the plan that they might have to lean on this old broad legally?'

'She wouldn't have been an old broad then. She was probably quite a young broad.'

'Whatever, this smells of real redneck intrigue. Prosser Senior – that would be Gareth Prosser's old man?'

'Sounds like it,' Betty said. And then came to the point. 'But the main issue is, what happened to the Reverend Penney? What did he do that day that scandalized the community so much that he had to resign on so-called health grounds?'

'Didn't the widow Wilshire know any of this?'

'She'd never even seen the letter. Bryan would not have wanted to worry the little woman.'

'Well,' Robin said, 'it's clear that the Reverend Penney was under a lot of pressure and it drove him a little crazy. She talks about him feeling isolated. Maybe he came from some English city, couldn't cut it in the sticks. And the Local People resented him, gave him a hard time.'

'To the extent of vandalizing his church? Starting a fire? You don't think that sounds a little inner-city for a place like this?'

'Sounds like he was getting some hassle. Sounds like there could be something the Local People are a tad ashamed about, wouldn't you say?'

He looked pleased about this. He would make a point now of finding out precisely what had happened and what, if anything, the community had to hide. Betty, on the other hand, could sympathize with Juliet Pottinger's low-profile approach. Yes, it would be necessary to find out what had happened on what was now their property – but not to go about this in a conspicuous way. They were incomers and foreigners. And had a different religion, which may somehow have become known to certain people. Unspoken opinion might already be stacked against them; they must not be seen to be too nosy or too clever. They must move quietly.

'After Penney left,' she said, 'the church appeared to "lose heart". It was in full use until 1968 and now it's a ruin. In just over thirty years. Not exactly a slow decay.'

'Aw, buildings go to pieces in no time at all when they're left derelict. She implies in the letter that it was already falling apart. And maybe in those days the authorities weren't so hot on preserving old buildings. I'm more curious about what the Local People did to this Penney. Where's he now?'

'I don't know. And we're the last people to know anyone in the clergy who might be able to find out. We—'

'Look, I'll go find out the truth tomorrow. I'll go see Prosser. We're gonna need more logs – real logs. I'll go find out if Prosser knows a reputable log dealer and at the same time I'll ask him about Reverend Penney. See if he tries to lean on me, do the rural menace stuff.'

'I'll go, if you like,' Betty said, without thinking.

Robin put down his cocoa mug. 'Because I will rub him up the wrong way? Because I will be gauche and loud and unsubtle? Because I will say, you can't touch me, pal, I got the Old Gods on my side?'

'Of course not. I'm sorry. You're right. You should go. Men around here prefer to deal with other men.'

'What I thought.' He looked at her and grinned. 'This is nothing to worry about.'

'No,' Betty said.

Far from representing her and Robin's destiny and the beautiful future of the pagan movement in this country, she was now convinced that the old church of Michael was a tainted and revolting place that should indeed be left to rot. But how could she lay all this on him now, after his crushing disappointment over the Blackmore illustrations?

'Let's go to bed,' she said.

FOURTEEN

Armageddon

No way could she ever have imagined it was going to be like this.

She'd thought that it could never be worse than the pulpit that first time, up in Liverpool, when those three creaking wooden steps were like the steps to the gallows.

And may God have mercy on your soul.

She'd drunk very little of the spring water on offer in the green room, never once thinking of the fierce heat from the studio lights and what it might do to the irrigation of the inside of her mouth.

With ten minutes to go, she'd popped outside for a cigarette, sharing a fire-escape platform with two sly-smiling New Age warriors and their seven-inch spliff, shaking her head with a friendly, liberal smile when they'd offered it to her.

Never *really* imagining that the nerves wouldn't just float away once they were on the air. Because . . . well, because this was trivial, trash, tabloid television, forgotten before the first editions of tomorrow's papers got onto the streets.

This really mustn't be taken too seriously.

Merrily froze, 2,000 years of Christianity setting like concrete around her shoulders. The light was merciless and hotter than the sun. She was in terror; she couldn't even pray.

'Merrily Watkins,' he'd said, 'you're a vicar, a woman of God. Let's hear how you defend your creator against that kind of logic. Isn't there really a fair bit of sense in what Ned's saying?'

He was slight, not very tall. His natural expression was halfway to a smile, the lips in a little V. He was light and nimble and chatty. He earned probably six times as much as a bishop – the shiny-suited, eel-like, non-stick, omnipotent John Fallon.

'Well, Merrily,' he said. '*Isn't* there?'

And yet, there were no tricks, no surprises. It had started, exactly as Tania Beauman had said it would, with the parents Jean and Roger Gillespie, goddess-worshippers from Taunton, Somerset, who wanted their daughter's religion to be formally accepted at her primary school. They'd have a second child starting school next year; later a third one; they wanted new data programmed into the education machine, respectful references to new names: Isis, Artemis, Aradia. Roger was an architect with the county council; he maintained that his beliefs were fully accepted on the executive estate where the Gillespies had lived for three years.

They were both so humourless, Merrily thought, as Jean demanded parity with Islam and boring old Christianity, and special provision for her family's celebration of the solstices and the equinoxes, the inclusion of pagan songs, at least once a week, at the school assembly.

Fallon had finally interrupted this tedious monotone. 'And what do you do exactly, Jean? Do you hold nude ceremonies in your garden? What happens if the neighbours've got a barbecue going?'

'Well, that's just the kind of attitude we *don't* get, for a start.' Jean's single plait hung like a fat hawser down her bosom. 'Our rituals are private and discreet and are respected by our neighbours, who—'

'Fine. Sure. OK.' John Fallon had already been on the move, away from Jean, who carried on talking, although the boom-mic operator had moved on. Fallon had spun away through ninety degrees to his next interviewee: the elegant Mr Edward Bain, nothing so vulgar as King of the Witches.

'We're here to talk about religious belief,' Fallon had read from the autocue at the beginning of the show, 'and the right of people in a free society to worship their own gods. Some of you might think it's a bit loony, even scary, but the thousands of pagan worshippers in Britain maintain that theirs is the only true religion of these islands, and they want their ceremonies – which sometimes include nudity, simulated and indeed actual sex – to be given full charitable status and full recognition from the state and the education system . . .'

When he had his back to Merrily, she saw the wire to his earpiece coming out of his collar, like a ruched scar on the back of his neck. Relaying instructions or suggestions, from the programme's director in some hidden bunker.

'Ned Bain,' Fallon said, 'you're the high priest of a London coven – can we use the word "coven"? – and also a publisher and an expert on ancient religions of all kinds. I want you to tell me, simply and concisely, why *you* think paganism is, today, more relevant and more important to these islands than Christianity.'

And Edward Bain had sat, one leg hooked casually over the other like . . . like Sean had sat sometimes . . . a TV natural, expounding without pause, his eyes apparently on Fallon, but actually gazing beyond him across the studio. His eyes, in fact, were lazily fixed on Merrily's . . . and they – she clutched her chair seat tightly – they were *not* Sean's.

'Well, for a start, they've had their two millennia,' he said reasonably. '2,000 years of war and divison, repression and persecution, torture, genocide . . . in the name of a cruel, despotic deity dreamed up in the Middle East.'

From the seats tiered behind Merrily came the swelling sound of indrawn breath, like a whistling in the eaves. Part awe, part shock, part admiration at such cool, convincing blasphemy.

'2,000 years of the cynical exploitation, by wealthy men, of humanity's unquenchable yearning for spirituality . . . the milking of the peasants to build and maintain those great soaring cathedrals . . . created to harness energies they no longer even understand. 2,000 years of Christianity . . . a tiny, but ruinous period of Earth's history. A single dark night of unrelenting savagery and rape.'

There was a trickle of applause. He continued to look at Merrily, his mouth downturned in sorrow but a winner's light in his eyes. The space between them seemed to shrink, until she could almost feel the warm dusting of his breath on her face. On a huge screen above him was projected the image of a serene, bare-breasted woman wearing a tiara like a coiled snake.

'Now it's our turn,' he said softly. 'We who worship in woods and circles of rough stone. We who are not afraid to part the curtains, to peer into the mysteries from which Christianity still cowers, screaming shrilly at us to *come away, come away.* To us – and to the rest of you, if you care to give it any thought – Christianity is, at best, a dull screen, a block. It is *anti*-spiritual. It was force-fed to the conquered and brutalized natives of the old lands, who practised – as we once did, when we still had sensitivity – a natural religion, in harmony with the tides and the seasons, entirely beneficent, gentle, pacific, not rigid nor patriarchal. The Old Religion has always recognized the equality of the sexes and exalted the nurturing spirit, the spirit which can soothe and heal the Earth before it is too late.'

The trickle of applause becoming a river. John Fallon standing with folded arms and his habitual half-smile. Someone had dimmed the studio lights so that Ned Bain was haloed like a Christ figure, and when he spoke again it might have been Sean there, being reasonable, logical. Merrily began to sweat.

'The clock of the Earth is running down. We've become alienated from her. We must put the last 2,000 years behind us and speak to her again.'

And the river of applause fanned out into a delta among not only the myriad ranks of the pagans, but also the shop-floor workers and the wages staff and the middle and upper management of the paint factory in Walsall. The claps and cheers turned to an agony of white noise in Merrily's head and she closed her eyes, and when she opened them, there was the fuzzy boom-mic on a pole hanging over her head, and the camera had glided silently across like an enormous floor-polisher and John Fallon, legs apart, hands behind his back, was telling her and the millions at home, ' . . . really a fair bit of sense in what Ned's saying? Well, Merrily . . . isn't there?'

She's frozen, Jane thought in horror, as two seconds passed.

Two entire seconds. . . . on *Livenight*! A hush in the bear pit.

'Come on, love.' Gerry's hands were chivvying at the monitors. 'You're not in the bloody pulpit now.'

Maurice, the director, said into his microphone, 'John, why don't you just ask her, very gently, if she's feeling all right?'

Jane wanted to haul him from his swivel chair and wrestle him to the ground among the snaking wires. But then, thank Christ, Mum started talking.

It just wasn't her voice, that was the problem. She sounded like she'd just been awakened from a drugged sleep. Well, all right, it was going to be a tough one. Ned Bain was a class act, a cool, cool person, undeniably sexy. And Jane admittedly felt some serious empathy with what he was saying. Like, hadn't she herself had this same argument with Mum time and again, pointing out that paganism – witchcraft – was a European thing, born in dark woodland glades, married to mountain streams. It was practical, and Jane didn't even see it as entirely incompatible with Christianity.

The camera was tight on Mum – so tight that, *oh no*, you could see the sweat. And she was gabbling in that strange, cracked voice about Christianity being pure, selfless love, while paganism seemed to be about sex at its most mechanical and . . . feelingless.

Feelingless? Jesus, Jane thought, is that a real word? *Oh God.*

'This is bloody trite crap, especially after the pagan guy,' Maurice told John Fallon. 'Let's come back to her when, and if, she gets her shit together.'

'All right.' John Fallon spun away, a flying smirk. 'That's the, ah, Church of England angle.'

Someone jeered.

Oh God! When she was sure the camera was away from her, Merrily dabbed a crumpled tissue to her forehead, knowing immediately what she *should* have said, how she *could* have dealt with Bain's simplistic generalizations. Now wanting to jump up and tug Fallon back. But it was, of course, too late.

From halfway up an aisle between rows of seats, she caught a glance from Steve Ewing, the producer, his mouth hidden under a lip-microphone as used by ringside boxing commentators. It was as if he was ironically rerunning his pre-programme pep talk '... *you'll be kicking yourself all the way home because you missed your chance of getting your argument across on the programme.*'

From the adjacent seat to her left, a hand gently squeezed her arm: Patrick Ryan, the sociologist who was supposed to have shagged half the priestesses in the southern counties while compiling his thesis on pagan ritual practice. 'You'll get used to it,' he whispered.

She nodded. She sought out the eyes of Ned Bain, but they were in shadow now; he seemed to be looking downwards. He appeared very still and limp, as though his body was recharging. She thought, He was staring at me the whole time. And afterwards I couldn't do a thing.

'... gonna talk to Maureen now,' John Fallon was saying, back on the other side of the studio floor, just across the aisle from Ned Bain. 'Maureen, your teenage daughter was into all this peaceful, New Age nature worship. But that was only the start, because Gemma ended up, I believe, in a psychiatric unit.'

Oh, sure ... blame Bain for your own deficiencies. Merrily shook herself, furious. *Blame poor dead Sean.*

'She's still attending the unit, John.' Maureen was a bulky woman, early fifties, south London accent. 'Apart from that, she won't hardly leave the house any more, poor kid.'

'She became a witch, right?'

'She became a witch when she was about seventeen, when she first went to the tech college. There was a lecturer there like ... him.' Maureen jerked a thumb at Ned Bain, who tilted his head quizzically. 'Smooth, good-looking guy, on the make.'

Ned chuckled. *Really nothing like Sean. How could she have—*

'But let's just make it clear,' Fallon said, 'that this was *not* Ned Bain here. So this other man recruited Gemma into a witch coven.'

Maureen described how her daughter had been initiated in a shop cellar converted into a temple, and within about six months her personality had completely changed. She'd broken off her engagement to a very nice boy who was a garage mechanic, and then they found out she was into hard drugs.

'But I never knew the worst of it till her mate come to see me one day. This was the mate she'd joined the coven with, and she told me Gemma had got involved with this other group what was doing black magic. She said Gemma went with the rest of them to St Anthony's Church – and I know this happened, 'cause it was in the papers – and they desecrated it.'

'Desecrated, how?'

'Well . . . you know . . . did . . . did their dirt.' The big face crumpled. 'Things like—'

'John, let me say . . .' Ned Bain was leaning forward. The camera pulled back, the boom-mic operator shifted position. 'This is satanism, and satanism is a specifically anti-Christian movement. It is entirely irrelevant to Wicca or any of the other strands of paganism. We do not oppose Christianity. We—'

'The hell you don't!' Merrily was half out of her seat, but well off-mic.

'We are an *alternative* to Christianity,' Bain stressed. 'And also, I should perhaps point out at this stage, a precursor, of the tired, politicized cult of Jesus. And I say precursor, because there's evidence that Christianity itself is no more than a fabrication, a modification of the cult of Dionysus, in which the story of the man-god who dies and is resurrected . . .'

'Yeah, yeah,' Fallon stopped him. 'Fascinating stuff, Ned, but I want to stay with satanism for a moment.'

'As you would,' Merrily muttered.

'Now, Ned, *you* would say that satanism is as much anathema to pagans as it is to the Christian Church. And yet young Gemma graduated – or descended – to some kind of devil worship after being initiated as a witch. I want to come back . . .' Fallon wheeled ' . . . to Merrily Watkins . . .'

Merrily's hands tightened on the arms of her chair. *Please God . . .*

'Now, what we didn't say before about Merrily is that, as well as being one of the new breed of female parish priests, she's also the official exorcist – I believe Deliverance Minister is the correct term these days – for the Diocese of Hereford. That's right?'

'Yes.' *Ignore the camera, the lights. Don't look at Bain's eyes.*

'So what I want to ask you, do people like Maureen often come to you with this same kind of story?'

'I . . .' She swallowed. How could she say she hadn't been in the job long enough to have accumulated any kind of client base. 'I have to say ... John ... that what you might call *real* satanism is uncommon. What you have are kids who're playing old Black Sabbath albums and get a perverse buzz out of dressing up and doing something horribly antisocial. Quite often, you'll find that these kids will join a witch coven in the belief that it's far more ... extreme, if you like, than it actually is. That they're entering a world of sex rites and blood sacrifice.'

'Which is *your* fault!' one of the pagans shouted. 'Because that's how the Church has portrayed us for centuries.'

'She's saying,' Maureen shrilled, extending a finger at Merrily, 'that my daughter only joined the witches because she thought they were evil?'

'No, what I'm—'

'She's sitting on the fence!' A heavy man bounded down one of the aisles. 'That's what she's doing.'

Two security heavies moved in from different directions. Fallon blocked the man's path. 'You are?'

'The Reverend Peter Gemmell.' He was grey-bearded and big enough to take on either of the two security men. 'You won't find me on your list. I'm an industrial chaplain, and I came with the factory group from Walsall. But that's beside the point. What I want is to tell you all the truth that my colleague here is too diplomatic, too delicate, too wishy-washy to introduce. And that is to say that Satan himself is present in this studio tonight.'

'Oh hell,' Jane said glumly, 'a fruitcake. Just when I thought she might be really cooking.'

'Lovely.' Gerry leaned back in his canvas chair with his hands behind his head.

Voice-crackle from Maurice's cans. He nodded, scanning the monitors to make sure Gemmell was alone. 'OK, Steve, thanks, will do. John, let's see where this one goes, OK?'

Eirion looked shell-shocked. 'Anything could happen down there, couldn't it? Suppose that guy had a gun?'

'Probably wouldn't be that much use against Satan, anyway,' Jane reasoned.

'Why don't you tell them?' The Rev. Peter Gemmell hissed at Merrily. 'Why don't *you* tell them that Satan is in our midst? That he's here now. Why don't you stand up and denounce him?'

Fallon saved her.

'Well, *you* tell us, Peter, since you're here. You point him out. Where exactly is Satan sitting?'

'I *shall* tell you.' Gemmell didn't hesitate. 'He's sitting directly behind you.'

Fallon stepped aside to reveal Ned Bain smiling and shaking his head, pityingly.

'That man . . .' Gemmell glared contemptuously at Bain. 'That man speaks from the Devil's script. From his lips spews the slick rhetoric of Satan the seducer.'

Sea of Light? Merrily wondered.

'"The satyr shall cry to his fellow!"' Gemmell roared. ' "Yea, there shall the night hag alight, and find for herself a resting place!" Isaiah.'

Merrily thought of the number of interpretations you could put on that. In fact, she was sure there was a rather more innocent translation in the Revised English Bible. She just couldn't remember what it was. Couldn't remember anything tonight.

'The satyr,' Gemmell explained, 'is the so-called horned god of the witches – the god Pan. The night hag is the demon Lilith. And so the Bible tells us quite plainly that paganism invites the demonic to share its bed. And that is as true today as it was when it was written.'

'The Old Testament,' Bain said wearily. 'This guy comes down here and quotes at me from a hotchpotch of myth and legend and old wives' tales . . .'

'The voice of Satan!' Gemmell snarled, and Merrily was aware of Steve Ewing to her right, putting the bouncers on alert.

'Thank you, Peter.' John Fallon placed an arm on the big priest's shoulder. 'We're grateful for that, but I don't think we're quite ready for the battle of Armageddon tonight.'

'I have made my point,' Gemmell said with dignity and, with a baleful glance at Merrily, walked back up the aisle and then stopped and turned and, before the security men could reach him, roared out, 'We must – and *will* – put out the false lights in the night of filth!'

'Good man,' Fallon said. 'Well . . . Ned Bain's either the saviour of our planet or he's the Antichrist. But before that interruption, Merrily, you were saying so-called satanists are just a bunch of delinquent kids . . .'

'No, what I said was that real satanism is uncommon. I do know it exists. I *have* encountered the use of occult practices for evil purposes and I think Ned's being a bit optimistic if he thinks all pagans are in it to heal the earth.' Her mouth was dry again. She swallowed.

'Go on,' Fallon said.

'Well, I know for a fact that pagan groups are infiltrated by people with less . . . altruistic aims – whether it's money, or drugs or iffy sex.'

'Black propaganda!' a woman screeched. Fallon held up a hand for quiet.

'I do know a young girl,' Merrily said carefully, thinking of Jane watching at home. 'She's a girl who was very nearly ensnared by the people who were secretly running what appeared to be a fairly innocent mystical group for women. It's a minefield. In the glamorous world of goddesses and prophecy and . . . and nude dancing at midnight, it's very hard to distinguish between the people who truly and sincerely believe all this will heal the earth and free our souls . . . and the ones who are into personal power and gratification of their—'

'What group?' the woman shouted. 'She's making it up! John, you make her tell us where it was!'

'Ssssh,' Fallon said. 'OK, where was this, Merrily?'

'It was . . . around Hereford. Around the Welsh border. Obviously, I'm not going to name anybody who—'

'All right.' Fallon turned to the young woman who'd shouted out. 'It's Vivienne, right? And you're the priestess of a coven in Manchester. How do you know what kind of people you're initiating? How do you vet them?'

'You just . . . know.' Vivienne had cropped hair and earrings that

seemed to be made from the bejewelled bodies of seahorses. 'The
initiation process itself weeds out the scumbags and the weirdos. It's
a psychic thing. You learn to pick up on it, and the goddess herself—'

'That is rubbish,' Merrily interrupted.

Vivienne paused. John Fallon smiled.

Merrily said, 'People *don't* get vetted before they're allowed to
mess with other people's minds. You *don't* have any real organization
or any fixed creed. Your rituals *don't* go back to pre-Christian times,
they were all made up in the last half century. You're a complete
ragbag of half-truths and good intentions and bad intentions and—'

'And that's any different from your Church?' Vivienne reared out
of her seat. 'Half of you don't believe in a Virgin Birth! Half of you
don't believe in the Resurrection! And you call *us* a ragbag. I'm
telling you, lady, you'll have come to bits long before we do. It's
happening right now. And you . . . you're part of the decay. We look
at you and the blokes see a pretty face and nice legs, and that's just
the Church's latest scheme to deflect attention from the rot in its
guts.'

A build-up of cheers among the pagan ranks. John Fallon stepped
back to let the camera catch it all.

'Your Church is dying on its feet!' Vivienne grinned triumphantly.
'It's not gonna see the new century out. You took our sacred sites
from us, and we're gonna take them back. Your fancy churches will
fall, and honest grass will grow up through their ruins, and towers
will stand alone, like megaliths—'

'Whoah!' Fallon stepped back into the action 'What *are* you
banging on about?'

'All right,' Vivienne said. 'She's from the Welsh border, yeah? I
can show you a church on her actual doorstep where that's already
happened. I can show you a church with a tower and graves and
everything . . . which is now a *pagan* church. *You* don't know what's
happening on your own doorstep. You don't know *nothing*!'

FIFTEEN

Fairground

'Move it!' Jane raced along the bright corridor, trailing her fleece coat over a shoulder. The building appeared to be still only half finished; there were lumps of plaster everywhere, and the panes of many windows still had strips of brown tape across them. 'Irene, move!'

'I was just trying to thank Maurice and Gerry.'

'We'll write them a letter! Come on. Believe me, she is not going to hang on here. She's going to be out of that bear pit before any of them can pin her in a corner. She'll be driving like a bat out of hell down the motorway, swearing that she'll never, never, never again . . .'

'I thought she did OK,' Eirion said, blundering behind her, 'in the end. She got that woman very annoyed.'

'*You* thought she did OK. *I* think she just about managed to rescue the situation. *She'll* think she was absolutely crap and like disgraced the Church and the bishop and . . . Jesus Christ!' Jane hit a pair of swing doors, still running. 'Can't you move any faster? I thought you were in the rugby team.'

'The chess team.' Eirion caught the doors on the rebound. 'You know it was the chess team.'

In the old Nova, with Jane leaning back, panting, against a peeling headrest, Eirion said, 'I wonder what Gerry meant, when that woman was going on about the pagan church.'

'Huh?'

'He said, "*That'll* flog, if I'm quick," and made a note on his script.'

'That church, you mean?'

'No, the story, I suppose.' Eirion drove out of the parking area, past a red and white striped barrier which was already raised. 'He means sell the story.'

'Who to?'

'Who would you normally sell a story to? To the papers. He was a tabloid journalist, wasn't he? And John Fallon didn't even follow it up on the programme, so . . .'

'He doesn't follow up anything that'll take longer than thirty seconds or won't lead to a fight. Irene, was that crass, meaningless and totally inconclusive, or what?'

'Bit like the Welsh Assembly without a vote.'

'You still want to do TV one day?'

'What? Oh . . . well, not quite that, obviously. Not exactly *that*. I want to be a TV news reporter.'

'So did those guys at one time, I expect. I mean, nobody starts out wanting to shovel shit for a living, do they?'

'That was you, wasn't it?' Eirion slowed for a roundabout. 'We're looking for M5 South, aren't we?'

'Huh?'

'Yeah, this one.' Eirion hit the slip road. 'That girl your mother was talking about. The girl who nearly got ensnared by those people running that women's mystical group in Hereford.'

'You already know it was me. You saw how it ended.'

'I wasn't sure.'

'Well, it was.'

'And yet you're still interested in paganism and all that. Because that's why we're here, isn't it? I mean, I know you did think *I* might get something out of it, career-wise . . . but you *are* kind of drawn to all that, aren't you? I mean, *still*.'

Jane snorted a laugh. A big motorway sign loomed up, wreathed in tendrils of mist: 'Worcester. The South West'. So many options. The motorway was romantic at night, despite those dark, blurred, nightmare memories that were more nightmare than memory, but fading.

'Like, despite everything,' Eirion persisted, 'you're still turned on by weird mystical stuff.'

'Irene, it's not "weird mystical stuff", it's about what we are and where we're going. Do you never lie in bed and wonder what we're part of and where it all ends?'

'I could lie awake all night and agonize about it, but it wouldn't make any difference, would it? I don't like the look of this fog, Jane.'

'But suppose it would? Suppose you could? I mean, suppose you could go places, deep into yourself and into the heart of the universe at the same time?'

'But I know I couldn't. I wouldn't have the – what is it? – the application. Neither would most of those people there tonight. They think they can discover enormous, eternal, mind-blowing truths by summoning gods and spirits and things, but they're just fooling themselves. I mean they were just . . . kind of sad tossers.'

'Ned Bain wasn't sad.'

'Course he was. He was just the tosser in the suit.'

Eirion drifted onto the motorway. It wasn't *too* foggy, but you couldn't see the sky. Jane hoped Mum wasn't feeling too choked about her performance to drive carefully.

She said, 'He was making the point that paganism is no longer a crank thing; that it has to be taken seriously as a major, continuing tradition in this country and a genuine, valid force for change. He was like . . . very controlled and eloquent. I'd guess he's quite a way along the Path.'

'You mean the garden path?'

'You know exactly what I mean.'

'He's manipulative. You couldn't trust him.'

'Because he's kind of good-looking?'

'Well,' Eirion said, 'that's obviously a small plus-factor with you.'

'Sod off. If I was that superficial, would I be going out with you?'

'Are you?'

'Superficial?'

'Going out with me?'

'Possibly. I don't know. I might be too weird for you.'

'Yeah, that's my principal worry, too,' Eirion said, deadpan.

'Bastard.' Jane leaned her shoulder into his. 'I wish there'd been time to wait and grab that Vivienne when she came out.'

'She wouldn't have told you where that church is. You notice how quick she clammed up, as though she knew she'd said too much? Because if some witchcraft sect are secretly practising at a Christian church . . . well, I don't know. If they haven't actually broken in, is that some kind of crime? Probably not.'

'Well, there you go.'

'Your mother's going to have to find out about it, though, isn't she?'

'Probably.'

'And what will she do when she does find out?'

'Go in there with a big cross? How should I know?'

'You could be more sympathetic to her.'

'I *am* sympathetic.'

'You're also sympathetic to paganism.'

'I'm interested. I've had . . . experiences, odd psychic things I can't explain.'

'Like what?'

'I don't want to talk about it really.'

'Oh.' Eirion drove in silence. Yellow fog-warning lights signalled a 40 m.p.h. speed limit.

'I'm not being funny,' Jane said. 'This just isn't the time.'

'No.'

'Haven't you? Had things happen to you you can't explain? Feelings about places? Things you thought you saw? Times when your emotions and your, like, sensations are so intense that you feel you're about to burst through into . . . something else. Some other level? I mean, the Welsh are supposed to be like . . .'

'My gran's a bit spooky.'

'Tell me in what way.'

'No, you tell me about your mum. Tell me about your dad.'

'That bloody Gerry,' Jane said.

Eirion was hesitant. 'Was what he said . . .?' The rest of it was lost under the rattling of a lorry passing them in the centre lane, a low-loader without a load, fast and free in the night.

'Yeah,' Jane said. 'He had it more or less right. My dad met my mum at university, where they were both studying law, and she . . . got pregnant with me and left the university, and he carried on and became a bent solicitor.'

'There was a special course for bent solicitors?'

'Ha ha. They were both going to do legal aid stuff and defend people who couldn't afford solicitors and all kinds of liberal, crusading stuff like that, according to Mum. But Dad wanted money – because of me, maybe he'd have said. Because of the responsibility. Though Mum says she was already learning things about him she didn't like. And, anyway, he got into iffy deals with some clients and Mum found out about it and there was this big morality scene, not helped by him screwing his clerk.' Jane paused for breath. 'Around this time, Mum had been helping the local vicar with community work and also she had this quite heavy experience of her own.'

'What sort of experience?'

'This was when things were really, really bad, and she was desperately trying to sort things out in her own head. She drove off into the sticks and came across this tiny little church in a wood or something and there was, like, a lamplit path . . .'

'It was night?'

'No, it was daytime, dickhead. The lamplit path was, like, metaphorical or in her head or a visionary thing. And listen, if she ever asks, I didn't tell you this, because she hates . . . Can't you go any faster?'

'There's a speed limit.'

'I can't even see any fog now. Because if she catches us up . . .'

'There's still a speed limit. And so your dad was killed?'

'He hit a motorway bridge. They were both killed. I mean, Karen, too. I read some newspaper cuttings I wasn't supposed to find. It was horrible – a ball of fire.'

'I'm sorry.'

'It was years ago,' Jane said without emotion.

'Which motorway?'

'The M5. I suppose this is the M5, isn't it?'

'It's a long motorway.'

'Well, it wasn't on this stretch, I don't think. I don't quite know where it was. I didn't read that bit. You don't want to keep looking out for a certain bridge all your life, do you?'

'No, you don't.'

'What Gerry said about a guilt trip, that's bullshit. I mean, why should *she* feel guilty? She was never mixed up in any of those crooked deals. Well, all right, it's easier for a widow to get into the Church than a newly divorced woman. Maybe she did feel guilty at the way that decision was so neatly taken out of her hands.'

'How do you feel about your dad?'

'He was kind of fun,' Jane said, 'but I was very little. Your dad's always fun when you're little. What was your home like? Did you all speak Welsh? I mean, *do* you?'

'Only when we have certain visitors. As everybody can speak English and English is a much bigger language and more versatile, you don't *have* to speak Welsh to anybody. But there are some people it's more *correct* to speak Welsh to. If you see what I mean.'

'Wow, minefield.'

'It's a cultural minefield, yeah. But I like Welsh. It's not my first language, but it's not that far behind.'

'Do you swear in Welsh? I mean you could swear in Welsh at school, in front of the teachers, and nobody would know.'

'That's an interesting point,' Eirion said. 'Actually, most Welsh people, when they swear, revert automatically to English. They're walking along the street conversing happily in Welsh, then one trips over the kerb and it's, like, "Oh, shit!"'

'Oh shit.' Jane whispered.

It was sudden – like a grey woollen blanket flung over your head.

'Oh, dear God,' Jane said.

It was like they'd entered some weird fairground. Red lights in the air. Also white lights, at skewed angles, intersecting across all three carriageways.

She heard Eirion breathe in sharply as he hit the brakes and spun the wheel. Spun into a carnival of lights. Lights all over the place. *False lights in the night of filth.* Grabbed by her seatbelt, Jane heard screams, dipping and rising like the screams of women on a roller coaster.

The engine stalled. The car slid and juddered.

And stopped? Had they stopped?

Under the fuzzed and shivering lights, there was a moment of massive stillness in which Jane registered that Eirion had managed to bring the car to a halt without hitting anything. She breathed out in shattered relief. 'Oh, Jesus.'

'It's a pile-up,' Eirion said. 'I don't know what to do. Should we get out?'

'We might be able to help someone.'

'Yeah.'

There was fog and there was also steam or something. And the silhouettes of figures moving. Even inside the car, there was a smell of petrol. Jane scrubbed at the windscreen, saw metal scrunched, twisted, stretched and pulled like intestine. The fog swirled like poison gas, alive with shouting and wailing and the waxy, solidified beams of headlights.

Jane screamed suddenly and thudded back into the passenger seat. Eirion frenziedly unbuckled his seatbelt, leaned across her. 'Jane?'

'I saw an arm. In the road. An arm sticking out. With a hand and fingers all splayed out and white. Just an arm, it was just—'

Brakes shrieked behind them.

Behind.

You never thought about behind. Jane actually turned in time to see it, the monster with many eyes, before it reared and snarled and crushed them.

SIXTEEN

Lurid Bit

Gareth Prosser was loading hay or silage or whatever the hell they called it in these parts onto a trailer for his sheep out on the hills. He was panting out small balloons of white breath. He didn't even look up when Robin strolled over, just muttered once into the trailer.

''Ow're you?'

Robin deduced that his neighbour was enquiring after his health.

'I'm fine,' he said, although he still felt like shit after the Blackmore put-down. 'Nice morning. Specially after all that fog last night.'

'Not bad.'

Gareth Prosser straightened up. He wore a dark green nylon coverall and an old discoloured cap. Behind him, you could hardly distinguish the grey farmhouse from the barns and tin-roofed shacks. There was a cold mist snaking amongst a clump of conifers on the hillside, but the sun had risen out of it. The sun looked somehow forlorn and out of place, like an orange beachball in the roadway. It was around 8.15 a.m.

'Wonder if you can give me some advice,' Robin said.

Gareth Prosser looked at him. Well, not in fact *at* him, but at a point just a couple degrees to his left, which was disconcerting – made you think there was someone behind you with an axe.

'Firewood,' Robin said. 'We need some dry wood for the stove, and I figured you would know a reputable dealer.'

Gareth Prosser thought this over. He was a shortish, thickset guy in his fifties and now well overweight. His face was jowly, the colour and texture of cement.

Eventually, he said, 'Mansel Smith's your man.'

'Ah.' Robin was unsure how to proceed, on account of, if his recollection was accurate, the dealer who had sold them the notorious trailerload of damp and resinous pine also answered to the name of Mansel Smith.

'You get your own wood from, uh, Mansel?'

Prosser slammed up the tailgate on the trailer.

'We burns anthracite,' he said.

'Right.' If Mansel Smith was the only wood dealer around, Robin could believe that. And yet somehow he thought that if Gareth Prosser did ever require a cord of firewood from Mansel it would not be pine and it would not be wet.

'Well, thanks for your advice.'

'No problem,' Prosser said.

Right now, if this situation was the other way about, Robin figured he himself would be asking his neighbour in for a coffee, but Prosser just stood there, up against his trailer, like one of those monuments where the figure kind of dissolves into uncarved rock. No particular hostility; chances were this guy didn't know or didn't care that Robin was pagan.

Well, this was all fine by Robin, who stayed put, stayed cool. If there was one thing he'd learned from the Craft it was the ability to become still, part of the landscape like an oak tree. Prosser stayed put because maybe he *was* part of the landscape, and Robin figured they could both have stood there alongside that trailerload of winter fodder until one of them felt hunger pains or he – unlikely to be Prosser – burst out laughing.

But after about five seconds, the farmer looked up when a woman's voice called out, 'Gareth! Who was that?'

Prosser didn't reply, and she came round the side of one of the sheds onto the half-frozen rutted track.

'Oh,' she said.

'Hi there,' Robin said.

The woman was a little younger than Gareth, maybe fifty, and a good deal better preserved. She wore tight jeans and boots and a canvas bomber jacket. She had a strong, lean face and clear blue eyes and short hair with, possibly, highlights.

'Good morning,' the woman said distinctly. 'I'm Councillor Prosser's wife.'

'Hi. Robin Thorogood. From, uh, next door.'

'Judith Prosser.'

They shook hands. She had a firm grip. She even looked directly into his eyes.

'I've got some coffee on,' she said.

'That would be wonderful.'

'I'll be in now,' Gareth said.

Robin had learned, from Betty, that when they said 'now' they meant 'in a short while'. So he smiled and nodded at Gareth Prosser and gratefully followed Judith up the track toward the farmhouse complex. In the middle distance, their two teenage sons were wheeling their dirt bikes out to the hill. There was a sound like a chainsaw starting up and one of the boys splattered off.

'Be an international next year, our Richard,' Judith Prosser said proudly. 'Had his first bike when he was four. All Wales Schoolboy Scrambling champion at eleven. Perfect country for it, see.'

'Doesn't it mess up the fields?'

'Messes up the footpaths a bit.' Mrs Prosser smiled ruefully. 'We gets complaints from some of the rambling groups from Off. But not from the local people.'

Robin nodded.

'Councillor Prosser's boys, see,' Mrs Prosser said, like it was perfectly reasonable that being a councillor should automatically exclude you from certain stifling social impositions. Robin didn't detect any irony, but maybe it was there.

'I see,' he said.

'This is Juliet Pottinger.' An efficient and authoritative Scottish voice. *'I'm afraid I am away this weekend, but you may wish to leave a message after the tone. If you are a burglar uninterested in thousands of books which are essentially old rather than antiquarian, then I can tell you that you are almost certainly wasting your time.'*

Betty thought she sounded like a woman who would at least give you a straight answer – if not until Monday.

Bugger. She cleared away the breakfast things, ran some water for washing up. Whatever Robin learned about the Reverend Penney from the Prossers, she didn't trust him not to put some pagan-friendly spin on it, and it was important to her now to find out the truth. What had Penney done to cause 'weeping and wailing' in the village? Why had the local people hushed it up? Did the priest, Ellis, know the full story and did this explain why he was so determined to subject the site to some kind of exorcism? She'd never settle here until she knew.

The phone rang, had her reaching for a towel before the answering machine could grab the call.

'Oh, my dear, I'm sure it's working already!'

'Mrs Wilshire?'

'I have had what, without doubt, was the best night's sleep I've had in months!'

'That's, er, wonderful,' Betty said hesitantly, because the likelihood of her arthritis remedy kicking in overnight was remote, to say the least.

'I can bend my fingers further than . . . Oh, I must show you. Will you be in this area today?'

'Well, I suppose . . .'

'Marvellous. I shall be at home all day.'

'Er . . . you didn't stop taking your cortisone tablets, did you? Because steroids do need to be wound down slowly.'

'Oh, I wouldn't take any chances.'

'No.'

It was psychological, of course, and Betty felt a little wary. Mrs Wilshire was a woman who could very easily become dependent on people. If Betty wasn't careful, she'd wind up having to call in to see her every other day. Still, if it hadn't been for Mrs Wilshire they would never have got onto the Penney affair.

'OK, I'll drop in later this morning if that's all right. Er, Mrs Wilshire, the papers you kindly let me take – about the church? There was one from a Mrs Pottinger, relating to the Reverend Penney. Do you know anything about that?'

'Oh, there was a lot of trouble about him, my dear. Everyone was very glad when he left, so I'm told.'

'Even though the church was decommissioned and sold soon afterwards?'

'That was a pity, although I believe it was always rather a draughty old place.'

'Er, do you remember, when you bought the house – and the church – did the Reverend Ellis come to visit you there?'

'Oh, I don't know. I was hardly ever there. It was Bryan's project. Bryan's house, until it was finished. Which I confess I really rather hoped it never would be.'

'So you don't know if the Reverend Ellis went to see Bryan there?'

'I'm afraid I don't. Though I'm sure he would have mentioned it. He never mentioned Mr Ellis in connection with that house. I don't *remember* him ever mentioning Mr Ellis.'

'No suggestion of Mr Ellis wanting to conduct a service in the church?'

'A church service?'

'Er . . . yes.'

'Oh no, my dear. I'm sure I would have remembered that.'

Just us, then.

The first thing Mrs Judith Prosser asked him was if they would be keeping stock on their land. Robin replied that farmers seemed to be having a hard enough time right now without amateurs creeping in under the fence. Which led her to ask what he did for a living and him to tell her he was an artist.

'That's interesting,' Mrs Prosser said, though Robin couldn't basically see how she could find it so; there wasn't a painting on any wall of the parlour – just photographs, mainly of men. Some of the photos were so old that the men had wing collars and watch chains.

As well as chairman's chains. Robin wondered if 'Councillor' was some kind of inherited title in the Prosser family – like, even if you had all the personality of a bag of fertilizer, they still elected you, on account of the Prossers knew the way to County Hall in Llandrindod.

Mrs Prosser went through to the kitchen, leaving the door open. There was a black suit on a hanger behind the door.

'We have a funeral this afternoon,' she explained.

'I guess councillors have a lot of funerals to attend.'

She looked at him. 'In this case, it's for a friend.'

'I'm sorry.'

'We all are. Sit down, Mr Thorogood.'

The furniture was dark and heavy and highly polished. The leather chair he sat in had arms that came almost up to his shoulders. When you put your hands on them, you felt like a dog begging.

Funerals. Was this an opening?

'So it's, uh, *local*, this funeral?' Boy, how soon you could grow to hate one simple little word.

'In the village, yes.'

'So you still have a graveyard – despite no church?'

Mrs Prosser didn't reply. He heard her pouring coffee. It occurred to him she hadn't commented on him being American. Maybe 'from Off' was all-inclusive; how far 'Off' was of no major consequence.

He raised his voice a little. 'I guess there must've been problems with funerals when the old St Michael's Church was in use. What with the creek and all.' OK, it might not be in the best of taste to keep on about funerals, but it was his only way into the Reverend Penney, and he wasn't about to let go.

'Because of the brook, no one's been buried there in centuries.' She came back with two brown cups and saucers on a tray.

'Thank you, uh, Judith. Hey, I met the vicar. He came round.'

'Mr Ellis is a good rector.'

'But not local,' Robin said.

'You don't get local ministers anywhere any more, do you? But he brings people in. Very popular, he is. Quite an attraction.'

'You like to see new people coming in?'

She laughed: a good-looking woman, in her weathered way. 'Depends what people they are, isn't it? Nobody objects to church-goers. And the collections support the village hall. They're always very generous.'

'Just Nick doesn't seem your regular kind of minister,' Robin said.

'He suits our needs,' said Mrs Prosser. 'Father Ellis's style of worship might not be what we've been used to in this area, but a breath of something new is no bad thing, we're always told. Jog us out of our routine, isn't it?'

'I guess.' He tasted the coffee. It was strong and surprisingly good. Judith Prosser put the tray on a small table and came to sit on the sofa opposite. She was turning out to be unexpectedly intelligent, not so insular as he'd figured. He felt ashamed of his smug preconceptions about rural people, *local* people. So he went for it.

'From what I hear, this area seems to attract kind of off-the-wall clergy. This guy, uh . . . Penney?'

'My,' she said, 'you *have* picked up a lot of gossip in a short time.'

'Not everybody finds themselves buying a church. You feel you oughta find out the history.'

'Or the lurid bits, at least.'

'Uh . . . I guess.' He gave her his charming, sheepish smile.

'Terry Penney.' Judith sipped her coffee. 'What's to say? Quiet sort of man. Scholarly, you know? Had his study floor to ceiling with books. Not an unfriendly person, mind, not reclusive particularly. Not at first.'

'He didn't live at the farmhouse – our house?'

'Oh, no, that was always a farm. No, the rectory was just out of the village, on the Walton road. Mr Weal has it now – the solicitor.'

Robin recalled the name from someplace. Juliet Pottinger's letter?

'So . . .' He put down his coffee on a coaster resting on the high chair arm. 'The, uh, lurid bit?'

'Restrain yourself, Mr Thorogood, I'm getting there.'

Robin grinned; she was OK. He guessed the Christ is the Light sticker was just the politically correct thing to do in Old Hindwell.

'Well, it was my husband, see, who had the first inkling of something amiss – through the county council. Every year Old Hindwell Church would apply for a grant from the Welsh Church Acts Committee, or whatever they called it then, which allotted money to old buildings, for preservation. Although the church was in the Hereford diocese it's actually in Wales, as you know. However, this particular year, there was no request for money.'

She turned on a wry smile. She was – he hadn't expected this – enjoying telling this story.

'The Reverend Penney had been yere . . . oh, must have been

nearly eighteen months by then. Thought he must have forgotten, we did, so Councillor Prosser goes to see him. And Mr Penney, bold as you please, says, oh no, he hasn't forgotten at all. He doesn't want a grant. He doesn't think the church should be preserved!'

Robin widened his eyes.

'The church is *wrong*, says Mr Penney. It's in the wrong place. It should never have been built where it is. The water's not healthy. The fabric's rotten. Parking's difficult. Oh, a whole host of excuses. He says he's written to the diocese and whoever else, suggesting that they dispense with St Michael's at the earliest possible opportunity.'

Robin was fazed. 'He called for them to get rid of his own church? Just like that?'

'*Just* like that. No one could believe it.'

'Wow.' Robin was thinking furiously. Had Penney realized this was a powerful pagan site? Was it that simple? Had he made some kind of discovery? He tried to hide his excitement. 'Was he mad?'

'Perhaps he'd always been a little mad,' said Mrs Prosser. 'But we just never saw it until it was too late.'

'So, like . . . what did he do?'

Judith Prosser put down her coffee. 'No one likes to talk about it. But, as the owner now, I suppose you have a right to be told.'

One of the few good things about living here was that the post usually arrived before nine; in some rural areas you couldn't count on getting it before lunchtime.

Today's was a catalogue from a mail order supplier of garden ornaments – how quickly these people caught up with you – and a letter addressed to '*Mrs*' Thoroughgood with a Hereford postmark.

That 'Mrs' told her what this was going to be.

She sat down at the table with the letter in front of her. Usual cheap white envelope. They'd received two when they were living in Shrewsbury. They said things like: *We Know About Your Dirty Nude Ceremonies Worshipping Heathen Gods. The Lord Will Punish You.*

How had they found out? Who'd told them? Had Robin been indiscreet?

Betty felt gutted. The sick irony of this was that she hadn't practised as a witch since they moved here and, the way she was feeling now, never would again – at least, not in any organized way.

She contemplated tossing the letter in the stove unopened. But if she did that it would dwell in her, would be twice as destructive.

With contempt, Betty slit the envelope.

She read the note three times. Usual capitals, usual poor spelling. But otherwise not quite what she'd expected.

YOU HAD BETTER TELL THAT LONG HAIRED
LOUT THAT IF HE WANTS TO GO HELPING
HIMSELF TO THE FAVOURS OF THE
BIGGEST HORE IN THE VILLAGE HE OUGHT
TO BE MORE DISCREAT ABOUT IT.

SEVENTEEN

Revelations

It was incredible! So wonderfully bizarre that, walking back to St Michael's Farm, Robin forgot all about agonizing over that asshole Blackmore who thought bestsellerdom had conferred upon him an art critic's instincts.

On the footbridge over the Hindwell Brook, he stopped a moment, evoking the incredible scene on that October morning back in the sixties when the brook was in flood. Had anyone photographed it? Could there be pictures still around?

Naw, anyone who'd pulled out a camera would probably have been compelled by some local by-law to hand over the film to Councillor Prosser – whichever Prosser happened to be the councillor at the time.

Judith Prosser had let him out the front way, through a dark-beamed hallway with some nice oak panelling. Up against the panelling there had been an outsize chair with a leather seat and a brass plate on the back. The chairman's chair, Judith had explained when he asked about it, from the Old Hindwell Community Council, disbanded some years ago under local government reorganization. And, yes, Gareth had been its chairman – twice.

Robin wondered if Judith Prosser called her husband by his title. Maybe got a little bedtime buzz out of it: *Oh, oh . . . give it to me harder, Councillor . . .*

He grinned at the winter sun. He felt a whole lot lighter. Holy shit, he'd actually spoken, in a meaningful way, to a Local Person! It was a seminal thing.

Indeed, when he looked across at the church on its promontory he even had the feeling that the Imbolc sabbat could go back on the schedule. He could see it now – using his visualization skills to cancel the brightness, and paint the sky dark, he could see lights awakening in the church, its ruins coming alive. He conjured the sound of Celtic drums and a tin whistle. *Son et lumière.* He saw, in the foreground, Betty's graceful silhouette – Betty in her pale cloak and a headdress woven from twigs. And, in the headdress, a ring of tiny flames, a sacred circle of candle-spears, a crown of lights.

He came in through the back door of St Michael's farmhouse so much happier than when he'd gone out of it. Returning with the breeze behind him.

'Siddown, babe,' he told her. 'You should hear this.'

'Should I?' She was already sitting down.

Robin halted on the stone flags. His mood fell, like a cooling meteor, to earth.

Her voice was flat as nan bread. At gone ten in the morning she was still in her robe. She looked pale and swollen-eyed, sitting at the kitchen table with a glass of the hot water she sometimes drank early in the day.

'You OK?'

Her hair also looked flat, like tired barn-straw. She'd been sleeping when he'd slipped out of bed around seven. He'd first made some coffee and toast for himself, not keeping especially quiet, and left a note for her on the table before he went over to the Prosser farm. He was half suspecting then that it was going to be one of *those* days, the kind he'd hoped there wouldn't be any more of after they moved to the country. In fact, since they'd moved here those days had accumulated one after the other, sure as sunrise. It was now reaching the point where it seemed they could never, simultaneously, be in a good mood. Like the sun would only shine on one of them at any one time.

Is this a psychic malaise? Could this be solved?

'Bets?' He was burning to bring her comfort, but he didn't know how. There were always going to be areas of her he could not reach;

153

he accepted this. He also accepted that in some ways he was no more than her attendant. This was not *necessarily* sad, was it?

'I'm sorry. Time of the moon.' She gave him the palest smile he could recall. 'Tell me what you learned at the farm.'

She was evidently not going to talk about whatever it was. He sat down opposite her and, in a voice from which the oil of narrative enthusiasm had now been well drained, told her what he'd learned about the Reverend Penney.

It was obviously his change of mood, but now he saw beyond the bizarre; he saw the sadness of it all.

'It's like early in the morning, still only half light and a mist down by the water, so not everyone sees it. Just the Prossers, that's the two brothers who lived here, and their older brother – Gareth's father – and his wife. And Gareth himself, who'd have been in his twenties back then. And this Mrs Pottinger, she was there soon enough, in her role as the eyes and ears of Old Hindwell for the *Brecon and Radnor Express*. Because she'd seen a . . . what do you call that thing they kneel on to pray?'

'Hassock,' Betty said. 'I think.'

'Yeah. Pottinger was out for an early walk with the dog and she'd seen a hassock floating down the brook. Maybe her first thought was that this was the vandals she talked about in her letter to Major Wilshire. Seems she wanted to call the cops, but she ran into the Prossers, and the Prossers stopped her. They knew it was an inside job.'

'Yes,' Betty said, like she knew it would have to be.

'Well, the brook was already high, with all the rain, and close to bursting its banks, and that's what they think's happened at first. It's overflowed into the field by the barn and it's halfway up the promontory where the church is. It's like there's a dam – like a tree or something fell into the brook – but as the day gets lighter they can see the full extent of what's going down here.'

While he told her, he was seeing it so clearly, hearing the voices over the rushing and roaring of the water. Shrieks of shock from the women, Pottinger's dog barking in excitement. Judith Prosser hadn't been there, of course; it would be another fifteen years before she and Gareth were married, but she must have heard the story many times since.

'Everything!' Robin said. 'Everything that wasn't part of the fabric or nailed down. All the pews, the lectern, a big tapestry from the wall, the choir stalls . . . all floating down the Hindwell Brook. Until the first stuff reaches the bend and gets snagged on some branches and it all starts to pile up.'

He could see the great dam, one of the pews on end, wood groaning and splintering like the wreck of a sailing ship on the rocks, the water rising all around. He wanted so much to paint it, like Turner would have painted it, all mist and spray.

Betty said, 'The altar?'

'Oh yeah, that too. He'd stripped off the cloth and dragged it out through the doors and out to the end of the promontory, like he'd done with all the pews, and just . . . just tipped it into the water.'

Visualizing the great spout of water as the altar crashed into the brook.

'He was apparently a big guy. Played rugby. Very strong. His most impressive feat was to rip out the stone font. He must've rolled it out the double doors. They found it sticking out of the water, like a big rock.'

Betty glanced bleakly across at him, then picked up her glass and drank the rest of the warm water like it was a double Scotch.

'And where was he? Where was Penney?'

'Gone. They never saw him again. The Prossers and some other guys they could trust salvaged what they could. Took about four of them to get the font out – they waited nearly a week till the water level dropped down, and draped tarpaulin and stuff over it meantime. Couple of weeks later, the diocese gets a cheque for several thousand. Whole damn thing was hushed up.'

'They never found out why he did it?'

'Just he'd grown to hate the church, was all. There was no further explanation. He'd cleaned it out. Musta taken him hours, working at it through the night, by the oil lamps – no electricity in there. Trashing his own church like a maniac. When they went inside, it was all bare. Just the Bible from off of the lectern. The Bible lying there in the middle of the nave. Lying open.'

Betty waited a long time before she asked him.

'Open at?'

Robin smiled, shaking his head.

'The Book of Revelations, wouldn't you guess? About Michael and his angels taking on the Devil and *his* angels? The great dragon getting cast out into the earth? All of this underlined in ink.'

'I see.' Betty stood up.

'Shows us where Ellis is coming from, doesn't it? He's clearly heard about Penney and the dragon fixation that gets him so screwed up he trashes his own church. Well, OK, maybe the poor guy experiences some pre-Christian energy on that site which is so awesome it shakes his Christian faith, scares the shit outa him. To Penney it's devilish. It blows his mind . . . he wrecks the joint.'

'Thereby becoming a *vehicle* for this energy, I suppose,' Betty said wearily.

'Holy shit!' A big light came on in Robin's head. 'Hey, that's so cool! The priest is unwittingly helping the church to cast off Christianity – to revert.'

Betty took her glass to the sink, not looking at him, like she didn't want to hear what was coming next. But, hell, he had to say it. It was staring them right in the face.

'Bets . . . it's down to us, now, isn't it? To, like, finish the job. It puts us hard against Ellis, but . . . like, is this fate, or what?'

He was tingling with excitement. This was their clear future.

At the sink, Betty put down the glass, turned both taps on full. She was staring into the water running out of the taps. 'I doubt this is as simple as you imagine.'

'Or maybe it just *is*. Maybe it's also fate that the local people weren't so attached to the church the way it was that they wanted to fight to save it.'

'It was in a poor state, anyway. It was going to cost a fortune in repairs. That's what the Pottinger woman said.'

'And maybe Ellis was right about something coming to the surface. Bad news for him . . . but not for us, babes.'

'Oh, don't be so bloody simplistic! Just for a moment stop trying to make *everything* fit into your dream scenario.'

'Well, sure . . . OK.' He felt hurt. 'I mean let's talk this thing through.'

'I have to go out. I have to go and see Mrs Wilshire.'

'Again? What the fuck *is* this?'

'It's not your problem.'

'Oh really?' Hell, this needed saying, this was long overdue. 'Well what *is* my problem is why you always have to find excuses to get out of here. Like going in the *car*. Why don't you ever even go into the village? The place we live next to? Why don't you get to know the people *here*? People like Judith Prosser next door. OK, Gareth might be a dumb bastard, but she's OK, not what I imagined. Maybe we were wrong to start condemning the local people as total redneck bigots, purely on your flawed fucking childhood memories.'

Betty didn't flare up. She just stared hard at him for a couple of seconds, and he stared back.

And then she said, 'I never said that. I'm sure there are some decent, liberal, perceptive, outward-looking people down there.' She went to the table, picked up a piece of white notepaper, pushed it at him. 'Like, for instance, the person who sent that.'

EIGHTEEN

Cold, Earthly, Rational . . .

The Gothic letter D was still on the office door, but hanging loose now, at an angle. D for Deliverance – Bishop Hunter's idea.

As had been the Reverend Watkins becoming Deliverance Consultant.

She stood on the stone stairs, in front of the closed door, and decided, after all, to go back home. Her head ached. What the hell was she doing here? As she turned to creep back down the stairs, the office door opened.

'I *thought* it was!'

Merrily stopped, and slowly and sheepishly turned around again.

'I *thought* it was your car.' Sophie was expensively casual in a blue and white Alpine sweater. 'What on earth are you doing here? Nobody would have expected you to come in today.'

She'd spoken briefly to Sophie on the phone, asking her to put the bishop in the picture.

'Merrily, you look—'

'Yeah, I know.'

'Starved.' Sophie stood aside for her.

Merrily slung Jane's duffel coat on the back of her chair, and slumped into it. 'If I hadn't come in *today*, I might never have come in again.'

Sophie frowned and began making tea. Through the gatehouse window, above Broad Street, the late morning sun flickered unstably in and out between hard clouds. The air outside had felt as though it was full of razor blades. The weather forecast had said there might be snow showers tonight – which was better than fog.

'The bishop tried to ring you.' Sophie laid out two cups and saucers. 'He said if I spoke to you to tell you there was no need to phone back.'

'Ever.'

'Don't be silly, Merrily. On reflection, I'm glad you did come in. Are you listening to me?'

'I'm listening.'

'You *cannot* drive to Worcester.'

'I'll be perfectly—'

'You will not. *I* shall drive you. Leave your car here. I don't want an argument about this, do you understand?'

'Well, I can take a bit of a rest this afternoon. They're not releasing her until after five.'

'She should stay there another night,' Sophie said stiffly. 'Concussion's unpredictable.'

'I think, on the whole, I can probably do without her discharging herself and stalking the streets of Worcester at midnight.'

'I should have thought that she'd be sufficiently penitent not to dare to—'

'Sophie' – Merrily cradled her face in cupped hands, looked up sorrowfully – 'this is Jane we're talking about.'

'If she were *my* daughter . . .'

'Don't give yourself nightmares.' Merrily dropped her hands, trying not to cry from exhaustion, anxiety, confusion and a terror which seemed to be lodged deep inside her, which every so often would pulse, hot-wiring her entire nervous system.

'Delayed shock, Merrily.'

'If you tell me I need trauma counselling, I'll put this computer through the window.'

Sophie brought over a chair, sat down opposite Merrily.

'Tell *me* then.'

The sun had put itself away again. Sophie added two sugars into Merrily's tea and switched on the answering machine.

*

Sophie? Sophie in her incredibly expensive Alpine sweater. Sophie who served the cathedral and all it represented. Yeah, why not?

'When you really contemplate the nature of this job,' Merrily said, 'you can start to think you're more than half mad. When the line between reality and whatever else there is . . . is no longer distinct. When it's no longer even a *line*.'

And when you swerve around a crashed lorry in the fog, and there's a figure staggering in the road that you just know you're going to hit, and in the last second, while you're throwing yourself around the wheel, you see her face.

'I'm starting actually to understand the Church's conservatism on the supernatural. Shut the door and bar it. Block the gap at the bottom with a thick mat. Let no chink of unnatural light seep in, because a chink's as good as a . . . whatever you call a big blast of light that renders you blind.'

'As in Paul on the road to Damascus?' Sophie said.

'Not exactly. Paul was . . . sure.'

'You *are* tired.'

'I mean, *I'm* sure . . . I'm just not quite sure what I'm sure *of*. It's only by being dull and conservative that the Church remains relatively intact. Bricks and mortar and *Songs of Praise*. Leave the weird stuff to Deliverance. It's a dirty job, and they've never been totally convinced someone has to do it.'

'I did watch the *Livenight* programme,' Sophie said. 'I didn't really see how else you could have handled it. Without coming over as a . . . crank.'

'Or a bigot. Both of which are probably better than a drowning wimp.' Merrily drank her tea, both hands around the cup, like someone pulled out of the sea and wrapped in a blanket. 'You spend an interminable hour making a fool of yourself on TV, you walk out thinking all religion's a joke. You're unhappy and ashamed and cynical all at the same time. You get in your car, you drive maybe not quite as carefully as you ought to, given the ubiquitous fog warnings and the fact that your husband just happened to have died horrifically on this same stretch of motorway. You drive into a fog bank. You become aware of two dull specks of red that you think must be a hundred yards away and which turn out to be this bloody great crashed lorry dead in your path. You spin the wheel in panic. You become aware of a figure dragging another figure across the road in front of you. The second figure stares full into your headlights, and you see . . . you see the face of your daughter who you know for a fact is at home in bed fifty-odd miles away. Your daughter's face . . . blank, white, expressionless. Like the face of a corpse.'

Sophie shuddered. 'It must have been . . . I can't imagine what that must have been like.'

'Like . . . Nemesis,' Merrily said. 'You know what I was thinking about in the few minutes before? I was thinking about this woman who believes she's seeing her sister's ghost. I was just deciding she really didn't have a psychiatric problem— Oh *no!*'

'What's the matter?'

'I told her I'd go with her to her sister's funeral. It's this after-noon. It's in about two hours. Or less.'

'Oh, Merrily, nobody could possibly expect—'

'I've got to.'

'You've had no *sleep.*'

'Oh, I've had . . . had an hour on the sofa. Fed the cat, grabbed a slice of toast, rung Worcester Infirmary twice to make sure Jane's not . . . worse. No, look, I've got to go, because . . .' *Because if I don't and something awful happens* . . . 'Beause it's something I can't just leave in the air.'

'Then you must lie down for a while first. I'll find somewhere in the palace. Look at you – you're trembling. Are you saying this pile-up actually happened in the same area where your husband was killed?'

'Well, that was on the other side, the northbound lanes. He was . . . I suppose he was on my mind, when . . .'

When she'd walked into that studio? Was Sean stalking her then? Was he already deep-harboured in her head when she'd entered the TV building? Having driven along the same stretch of the M5, under the very same bridge against which his car had balled on impact and bounced in its final firedance, while he and Karen were torn and roasted.

Couldn't tell Sophie any of that. Couldn't tell her about the eloquent pagan, Ned Bain, sitting there with his lazy, knowing Sean-like eyes, and even his legs crossed à la Sean.

Just stay with the main event.

'And, you think . . . what you think is that this can't be happening. And if it can't be happening then it's a hallucination. And you *know* you're not hallucinating. Therefore – click, click – it has to be a paranormal experience, just like all the paranormal experiences other people have told you about and you've nodded sagely and given your balanced opinion.'

'But only you would think that. Only someone in your—'

'Only someone in my weird, cranky job.'

'But you didn't hit her,' Sophie said intensely. 'Did you? You did not hit Jane.'

'No. There was no impact. I didn't hit anyone. But still a complete nightmare – I mean dreamlike. You haven't physically driven into your daughter, therefore it must be a premonition: a vision of *killing your own child.*'

'But it wasn't, was it?'

'I could see Sean in her face . . . that little bump in the nose, the twist of the lips. I could see Sean in her, like I'd never seen him there before.'

'Juxtaposition of ideas,' Sophie said, 'or something.'

'I swerved, violently. Stopped the car and got out, terrified out of my mind. Only to discover . . .' Sophie reached across the desk, squeezed Merrily's cold right hand. ' . . . that this really was Jane. The actual Jane, being pulled away by a terrified Eirion after being very nearly killed when this speeding low-loader smashed into the back of his car. She was pale and expressionless not because she was dead, but because she was semi-concussed. This is the mind-blowing perversity of it, that there is *an absolutely cold, earthly, rational explanation* . . . for everything. For every aspect of it. Why do I find that even more frightening? The most horrifying moment in my life, and there is, in the end, a simple, rational explanation.'

'You're afraid that you've stopped looking for simple rational explanations? Is that what you mean?'

'Maybe.'

'How many people were killed?' Sophie asked. 'In the end.'

'Three. And one critical in hospital. I think about four slightly hurt, including Jane. There were about six cars involved, and a couple of lorries. Seemed like the parameds and the fire brigade were on the scene before I was out of my car. There was one poor woman . . .'

Merrily shook her head, blinked away the unbelievably horrific image of a torn-off arm on the central reservation.

'You were very lucky, both of you. And the boy?'

'Eirion. His car was a write-off.'

'He's not injured, that's all that matters.'

'Some whiplash. They kept him in for the night, too, but I think his father picked him up this morning. Or his father's chauffeur. I talked to his stepmother on the phone. Eirion seems to be blaming himself for what happened. *Nice* kid.'

'So, altogether . . .'

'What I keep coming back to is, suppose I'd arrived one second earlier? Suppose I'd killed her? In one of those one-in-a-billion freak family tragedies? What would I have done with the rest of my life? What would any of it be worth?'

'But you didn't. Someone didn't want to lose you – and didn't want you forever damaged either.'

Merrily leaned back, shook out a cigarette. 'You ever thought of getting ordained, Sophie?'

'God forbid.' Sophie stood up. 'Put that thing away and get your coat.'

'It's Jane's coat. What for?'

'Jane's coat, then. I'm going to drive you to this funeral. You can perhaps sleep on the way. If we leave now, we might even stop for a sandwich.'

'Sophie, it's Saturday. You can't . . . You have things to do.'

'Oh,' Sophie said, 'I think Hereford United can manage without me for one week.'

Merrily blinked. Sophie unhooked a long, sheepskin coat and a woollen scarf from the door. It did rather look like the sort of outfit you would wear to a football match in January. Bizarre?

'This is above and beyond, Soph.' Merrily got unsteadily to her feet.

'I should be grateful if you didn't smoke in my car,' Sophie said.

NINETEEN

Abracadabra

The main road from Old Hindwell to New Radnor passed through the hamlet of Llanfihangel nant Melan. The church of St Michael was right next to the road and, although it didn't actually look very old, there were indications of a circle of ancient yew trees, which suggested it had been rebuilt.

Although there were a number of other cars nearby, Betty stopped the Subaru. She was in no mood to talk to Mrs Wilshire or anybody else right now. She would check out the atmosphere of the church. It might even calm her down.

She was still furious with Robin. If he'd been accosted the other night by the drunken wife of Greg Starkey, feeling him up in the street, why hadn't he told Betty when he arrived home? Old Hindwell wasn't exactly known for its red-light quarter. So why had he kept quiet?

Why? Because they'd just had a goddamn row over his handling of Nick Ellis. Because he'd slammed out of the house and didn't think she'd be speaking to him anyway. Because he was cold and tired. *Because.*

So why hadn't he mentioned it the next day, even?

Because . . . Jeez, was it important? Did she think he *enjoyed* it? Did she think he'd snatched this chance to feel Marianne's tits?

Actually, she didn't think that. What she thought was that Robin hated to tell her anything that might make her think less of Old Hindwell. *Why don't you get to know the people here? Like Judith Prosser – she's OK, not what I imagined.*

Dickhead.

Betty walked over to the church. The stonework suggested exten-sive Victorian renovation. Did anything remain of the church built as part of some alleged St Michael circle? How would this one feel inside?

Sooner or later, when Robin was not around, she would have to go back into the Old Hindwell ruins to face the question now looming large: the stained and sweating, fear-ridden man at prayer – was that him? Was that the Reverend Terry Penney? Was he dead now?

But this wasn't an exercise in psychic skills. Before she went back there, she wanted to know all there was to be known about *all* the churches in the St Michael circle.

However, in Llanfihangel Church, she was immediately accosted by a man in a light suit who asked her if she was on the bride or the groom's side. So much for standing there in the silence and feeling for the essence of the place. Betty apologized and escaped with a handful of leaflets, which she inspected back in the Subaru.

And just couldn't believe it. One, apparently produced as a result of a community tourism initiative, was blatantly entitled, 'Where sleeps the Dragon on the trail of St Michael's churches'.

Betty slumped back in her seat, broke into a peal of wild, stupid laughter. A tourist leaflet. Was that how all this had started?

The text explained that there were four St Michael churches around Radnor Forest – at Llanfihangel nant Melan, Llanfihangel Rhydithon, Cefnllys and Cascob. It presumably didn't mention Old Hindwell because it was a ruin, now on private land.

An inside page was headed: 'St Michael and the Dragon of Radnor Forest'.

It referred to the introduction by Jewish Christians of 'angel-ology'. Angels guarded nature and local communities. St Michael guarded Israel and was named in the Book of Revelations, etc., etc. Most Welsh churches dedicated to him had appeared in the tenth and eleventh centuries.

The specific Radnor reference had been pulled from a book called *A Welsh Country Parson* by D. Parry-Jones, who recounted a legend that the last Welsh dragon slept in Radnor Forest and, to contain it, local people had built four St Michael churches in a circle around the Forest. It was said that if any of these churches was destroyed, the dragon would awaken and ravage the countryside once more.

This was it? This was the source of Nicholas Ellis's paranoia? Crazy!

Still, it did look as though Robin and Ellis were right. Assuming there was no fire-breathing elemental beast locked into the landscape, this appeared to be a simple metaphor for paganism, the Old Religion.

'. . . *if any one of these churches is destroyed* . . .'

Old Hindwell *had* been virtually destroyed . . . and initially by its rector, which didn't make any obvious sense. Why would a clergyman make a gesture which was bound to be adversely interpreted by anyone superstitious enough to give any credence to the dragon legend?

Unless Penney had been a closet pagan. Was that likely?

Not really. Something was missing. For a moment, Betty smelled again the rich, sickening stench from the praying man in the skeletal nave.

She drove off too quickly, the Subaru shuddering.

Lizzie Wilshire greeted her with a spindly embrace.

'I don't know whether it's your herbal mixture or just *you*, my dear, but I feel *so* much better.' Holding out her right hand and making it into a claw, the fingertips slowly but effectively closing on the palm.

'Gosh,' Betty said.

'I haven't been able to do that for months!' Those ET eyes shining like polished marbles. 'You're a wonder, my dear!'

'I wouldn't quite say that.'

Psychological? The potion couldn't possibly have had such a spontaneous and dramatic effect unless her problem was essentially, or to an extent, psychosomatic.

And yet . . . Betty caught an unexpected sidelong glimpse of Lizzie's aura. It was, without a doubt, less fragmented. And she was talking constantly, garrulous rather than querulous now.

'Were you originally called Elizabeth? Like me?'

'A long time ago,' Betty admitted, as they sat down.

'A *long* time ago, my dear, you weren't even born.' Lizzie Wilshire laughed hoarsely. 'Now, were those papers useful? If not, just throw them away. I'm in a clearing-out mood. Clutter frightens me. I'm even thinking of selling the summerhouse. Every time I look out at it, I expect to see Bryan walking across the garden. Do people buy summerhouses second-hand like that? Can they take them away?'

'I should think so. You could advertise it in the paper. I could do that for you, if you want.'

'Oh, would you? That's terribly kind. Yes. I told Dr Coll – I hope you don't mind . . .'

'About the summerhouse?'

'About you, of course! About your wonderful herbal preparation. He called in this morning, even though it's Saturday – such a caring, caring man – and said how much better I was looking, and naturally I told him about you.'

'Oh.' In Betty's experience the very last thing a doctor liked to be told was that some cranky plant remedy had had an instantaneous effect on a condition against which powerful drugs had thus far failed to make a conspicuous impact.

'He was delighted,' Lizzie said.

'He was?'

'Far be it from him, he said, to dismiss the old remedies. Indeed, he's often suggested I might benefit from attending one of the Reverend Ellis's services – but that's all too brash and noisy for me.'

'He must be a very unusual doctor.'

'Simply a very caring man. I didn't realize how *pastoral* country doctors could be until Bryan died. Bryan had a thing about the medical profession, refused to call a doctor unless in dire emergency. He'd have liked *you*. Oh, yes. His army training involved finding treatments in the hedgerows. A great believer in natural medicine, was Bryan. Although, one does need to have a fully qualified medical man in the background, don't you think?'

'Yes,' Betty said. 'I suppose so. Shall I make some tea?'

She knew now where everything was kept. She knew on which plate to arrange which biscuits. On which tray to spread which cloth.

All of which greatly pleased Mrs Wilshire. When it was done, Betty sat down with her and they smiled at one another.

'You've brightened my life in such a short time, Betty.'

'You've been very helpful to me, too.'

'I won't forget it, you know. I never forget a kindness.'

'Oh, look . . .'

'We never had children, I've no close relatives left. At my age, with my ailments, one doesn't know how long one has left . . .'

'Come on . . . that's daft.'

'I'm quite serious, my dear. I said to Dr Coll some time ago, is there anything I can do to help you after my death? Is there anything you need? New equipment? An extension to the surgery? Of course, he brushed that aside, but I think when you've been treated so well by people, by a community, it's your *duty* to put something back.'

'Well . . .'

'In the end, the most he would do was give me the name of a local charity he supports, but . . . Oh dear, I've embarrassed you, I'm so sorry. We'll change the subject. Tell me how you're getting on with that terrible old place. Have you been able to do anything with the damp?'

'These things take time,' Betty said, careful not to mention the need for money.

Getting into the car, she felt deeply uncomfortable. It might be better if she didn't return to Mrs Wilshire's for a while. The old girl probably wasn't aware of trying to buy attention, even if it was only with compliments about a very ordinary herbal preparation, but . . . Oh, why was *everything* so bloody complicated, suddenly?

She leaned back in the seat, rotating her head to dispel tension. She noticed the dragon leaflet on the passenger seat. Where, out of interest, was the next church on the list?

Cascob.

Nestles in the hills near the head of the Cas Valley . . . village appears in the Domesday Book as Casope – the mound overlooking the River Cas.

Promising, she supposed. And was about to throw the leaflet back on the seat, when another word caught her eye.

It was 'exorcize'.

A couple of miles into Radnor Forest, Betty became aware of an ominous thickening of cloud . . . and, under it, a solitary signpost.

She must have passed this little sign twenty times previously and never registered it, perhaps because it pointed up that narrow lonely lane, a lane which didn't seem to lead anywhere other than: Cascob.

Strange name. Perhaps some chopped-off, mangled Anglicization of a Welsh phrase which meant 'obscure-church-at-the-end-of-the-narrow-road-that-goes-on-for-ever'. Or so it seemed, perhaps because this was the kind of road along which no stranger would dare travel at more than 20 m.p.h. It was deserted, sullen and moody. Robin would be enchanted.

There wasn't much to Cascob. A bend in a sunken, shaded lane, a lone farmhouse and, opposite it, a few steep yards above the road, the wooden gate to the church itself, tied up with orange binder twine. Betty left the Subaru in gear, parked on the incline, untied the twine around the gate.

Sheep grazed the sloping, circular churchyard among ancient, haphazard gravestones and tombs that were crumbly round the edges, like broken biscuits. There was a wide view of a particularly lonely part of the Forest, and the atmosphere was so dense and heavy that Betty couldn't, for a while, go any further.

Some places, it was instantaneous.

The old man in the cellar at Grandma's place in Sheffield . . . that had probably been the first. None of them had frightened her for quite a while, not until she'd learned from other kids that you were *supposed* to be afraid of ghosts. Until then, she'd been affected only by the particular emotions specific to each place where something similar happened: fear, hatred, greed and – the one emotion she hadn't at first understood – lust.

She steadied her breathing. Cascob Church squatted under low, grey cloud. It looked both cosy and creepy. To what extent had the present sensations been preconditioned by what she'd read in the leaflet?

' . . . to exorcize a young woman . . .'

She walked on, towards the church.

The stone and timbered building, like many this old, seemed to have grown out of the site organically. There were oak beams in its porch and under the pyramid-cap of the tower. It snuggled against an earthmound which was clearly not natural, possibly a Bronze Age tumulus. From the base of the mound grew an apple tree, spidery winter branches tangled against the cold light. There was a gate across the porch – more twine to untie.

Betty stepped inside. There were recent posters on the wall and a framed card invited all who entered to say a prayer before they left. She would not be so crass as to offer a prayer to the goddess. When she put out a hand to the oak door, Cascob Church seemed to settle around her, not unfriendly, certainly ancient and comfortably mysterious.

And locked.

She wondered for a moment if this was a sign that she was not supposed to enter this place. But then, all churches were kept locked these days, even – perhaps especially – in locations this remote.

She walked back across the churchyard and the narrow road to the farmhouse to enquire where she might borrow a key. The bloke there was accommodating and presented her with a highly suitable one, about six inches long. It made her right hand tingle with impressions, and she twice passed it quickly to her left hand and back again before reaching the porch.

The lock turned easily. She went in and stood tensely, with the door open behind her.

The church inside was dark and basic. Betty stood poised to banish anything invasive. But there was nothing. It was quiet. So far removed from the foetid turmoil swirling in the Old Hindwell ruins that she banished *that* from her thoughts, lest she somehow infest Cascob.

The place was tiny and probably little changed since the fourteenth or fifteenth century. A farmers' church, with a font for christenings but no room for gentry weddings.

There was a wooden table with literature on it, including the sleeping dragon leaflet and a similar one about Cascob Church itself. A collection box had Betty fumbling for a fiver, an offering to appease the God of the Christians. She stood for a moment behind one of the back pews, not touching its dark wood, her head hanging down so as not to face the simple altar. It was not *her* altar, it faced the wrong direction, and she'd turned away from all this eight years ago.

Betty closed her eyes. It had been her decision. She'd turned from the east to face the north: a witch's altar was always to the north. There was no turning back . . . was there?

When she reopened her eyes, she was facing the whitewashed north wall, where a document hung in a thin, black frame.

Betty looked at it, breathed in sharply. The breathing came hard. The air around her seemed to have clotted. She stared at the symbols near the bottom of the frame.

And saw, with an awful sense of déjà vu:

$$\mathcal{X} \mathfrak{I} \mathfrak{4} \mathcal{X} \odot \mathfrak{4} \mathcal{X} \mathfrak{q} \mathfrak{4} \Delta \odot \mathfrak{I} \Delta \mathfrak{4} \mathfrak{q}$$

She felt almost sick now, with trepidation. There was nothing coincidental about this.

At the top of the document, under the funeral black of the frame, was something even more explicit.

ABRACADABRA

ABRACADABR

ABRACADAB

ABRACADA

ABRACAD

ABRACA

ABRAC

ABRA

ABR

AB

A

Betty spun away from the wall, snatched up one of the leaflets about the church and ran outside.

Under the Zeppelin cloud, she opened the leaflet to a pen and ink drawing of the church and a smaller sketch of the Archangel Michael with wings outstretched and a sword held above his head.

Under the drawing of the church, she read:

' . . . the Abracadabra charm, dated from the seventeenth century, purported to have been used to exorcize a young woman. Heaven knows what she went through, but it sheds an interesting light on the state of faith in Radnorshire at the time.'

Betty stilled herself with a few minutes of chakra breathing, then went back into the church and up to the document itself, again leaving the door open for light.

What she'd read was a transcript of the original charm produced, it said in a tiny footnote, by an expert from the British Museum. The original was at the bottom: a scrap of paper with the ink faded to a light brown and now virtually indecipherable. There were no details about exactly how or when it had been found in the church.

But there was no inglenook fireplace where a box might be placed.

Hands clenched in the pockets of her ski jacket, Betty read the transcript. The two charms might be a century or more apart, but the similarities were obvious.

In the name of the Father, Son and of the Holy Ghost Amen
X X X and in the name of the lord Jesus Christ I will delive
Elizabeth Loyd from all witchcraft and from all Evil Spirites
and from all evil men or women or wizardes or hardness of
heart Amen X X X

It went on with a mixture of Roman Catholic Latin – *pater noster, ave Maria* – and cabbalistic words of power like 'Tetragrammaton', the name of God. At the bottom were two rows of planetary symbols. The sun, the moon and Venus were obvious. The one that looked like a '4' was Jupiter.

Wizards . . . spirits . . . hardness of heart. All too similar. Another solid link, apart from St Michael, between the two churches.

There was more obsessive repetition:

I will trust in the Lord Jesus Christ my Redeemer and Saviour
from all evil spirites and from all other assaltes of the Devil and
that he will delive Elizabeth Loyd from all witchcraft and from all
evil spirites by the same apower as he did cause the blind to see,
the lame to walke and that thou findest with unclean spirites to
be in thire one mindes amen X X X as weeth Jehovah Amen.
The witches compassed her abought but in the name of the lord
i will destroy them Amen X X X X X X X

It was signed by Jah Jah Jah.

Poor Elizabeth Loyd. A 'young woman'. How old. Twenty?
Seventeen? Was she really possessed by evil? Or was she schizophrenic?
Or, more likely, simply epileptic?

*Heaven knows what she went through, but it sheds an interesting
light on the state of faith in Radnorshire at the time.*

Had it been carried out here, in the church? If so, Betty wasn't
picking up anything. What kind of minister had mixed this bizarre
and volatile cocktail of Anglicanism, Roman Catholicism, paganism,
cabbalism and astrology?

Or was it the local wise man, the conjuror?

Or were they one and the same?

Betty was glad the charm lay behind glass, that she wouldn't have
to force herself to touch it, where it had been held by the exorcist,
didn't even like to look too hard at the original manuscript, was glad
that the ink had faded to the colour of soft sand.

She walked back outside into the churchyard and was drawn back
– felt she had no choice – to that spot amongst the graves where
she'd previously felt the weight of something. She wondered what
had happened if, after the exorcism, the epilepsy or whatever persisted? There was something deeply distasteful about the whole
business – and there had probably been villagers at the turn of the
eighteenth century who also found it disturbing. But they'd have to
keep quiet. Especially if the exorcism was performed by the minister.

She was gazing out towards the Forest – yellowed fields, a wedge
of conifers – when the pain came.

It was so sudden and so violent that she sank to her knees in the
long, wet grass, both hands at her groin. There was an instant of

shocking cold inside her, and then it was over and she was crawling away, sobbing, to the shelter of a nearby gravestone.

She stayed there for several minutes, her breathing rapid and her heart rate up. She pushed her hair back out of her eyes and found that it was soaked with sweat.

When she was able to stand again, she was terrified there might be physical damage.

She stumbled back to the church wall and, trembling, wrote a huge banishing pentagram, clockwise on the air.

And then followed it with the sign of the cross.

TWENTY

Blessed Beneath the Wings of Angels

Been a while since he was here last, but it might as well have been yesterday. Nothing changed, see. A new bungalow here, a fancy conservatory there. A few new faces that started out bright and shiny and open . . . and gradually closed in, grew cloudy-eyed and worried.

Like this boy in the pub. Londoner, sounded like. Gomer had seen it before. They came with their catering certificates and visions of taking over the village inn and turning it into a swish restaurant with fiddly little meals and vintage wine, fifty quid a time. Year or so later, it was back to the ole steak pie and oven chips and a pint of lager – three diners a night if they was lucky, at a fiver apiece.

Gomer sucked the top off his pint of Guinness. Ole Hindwell, he thought, where city dreams comes to die.

'Not seen you around before,' the London boy said.

'That's on account you en't been around yourself more'n a week or two,' Gomer told him.

'Two years, actually. Two years in March.' The boy had dandruffy hair, receding a bit, greying a bit. You could tell those two years had felt to him like half a lifetime. He'd be about forty years old; time to start getting anxious.

'Bought the place off Ronnie Pugh, is it?'

'That's right.'

'Ar.' Gomer nodded, spying the creeping damp, already blackening walls they must have rewhitewashed when they moved in. 'Tryin' to get rid for six year or more, ole Ronnie.'

'So it appears,' the boy said, regrets showing through like blisters.

As well they might. Never fashionable, the Forest. No real old money, see. Radnorshire always was a poor county: six times as many sheep as people, and you could count off the mansions on one hand. Not much new money, neither: the real rich folk – film stars, pop stars, stockbrokers, retired drug dealers and the like – went to the Cotswolds, and the medium-rich bought theirselves some rambling black-and-white over in Herefordshire.

While Radnorshire – no swish shops, no public schools, no general hospital, no towns with much over 3,000 people – collected the pioneer-types. Trading in the semi in Croydon or Solihull for two scrubby acres, a dozen sheep and a crumbly old farmhouse with rotting timbers, loose slates and stone-lice.

And the pensioners. Radnorshire got them too, by the thousand. Couples like Minnie and Frank, buying up the old farm cottages and the cheap bungalows. And then one of them dies and the other's stuck, all alone in the middle of nowhere, on account of Radnorshire property prices don't rise much year to year, and the poor buggers can't afford to move away.

'Not going up the funeral?' the boy said. Though the car park was full, there was only himself and Gomer in the Black Lion. Mourners for Menna Weal had parked up outside, stopped in for one drink, and trailed off to the village hall. Funny old set-up, doing church services at the village hall. But that was Radnorshire – lose your church and you makes do.

Gomer shook his head. 'Well, I never knowed her that well, see.' Truth was, with Min only days in the ground, he couldn't face it, could he? Good to help the little vicar, but he realized the vicar was only giving him something to do to take his mind off his own loss; she wouldn't want him attending no funeral.

'Nor me,' the boy said. 'Mrs Weal never came in here. Her husband comes in occasionally.'

'Picks up his business in the pub, what I yeard. Folks from Off. Friendly local lawyer, sort o' thing.' Gomer had heard this from a few people. He didn't say much, Big Weal, played his cards close, but he put himself about in all the right places.

The boy came over bashful. 'He picked *us* up, actually. He was in here when we were looking over the place. Knew the agent, wound up doing the conveyancing.' He laughed, a bit uncomfortably. 'Bloke's so big you don't feel you dare refuse, know what I mean?'

'Likely it was the same with poor Mrs Weal,' Gomer said.

He'd gathered a fair bit of background about Menna from Danny Thomas, the rock-and-roll farmer at Kinnerton who, it turned out, was a distant cousin. Danny had fancied her himself at one time, but Merv Thomas kept her out of the way of men. Selfish bastard, old Merv, especially after his wife passed on; he had to have another woman around doing the things women had been put on God's earth to do.

Frail, pale little person, Menna, it seemed. All right for washing and cleaning, but too frail for farming, definitely too frail for Merv Thomas's farm. Sons was what Merv had needed, but never got. So now the Thomas farm had gone to folk from Off, the deal sorted by J.W. Weal who then married the profits. '*What a bloody waste,*' Danny Thomas had said, guitar on his knee in the barn, crunching Gomer's eardrums with something called 'Smoke on the Water'.

'Like I said, he never brought her in here.' The boy leaned over his bar, confidentially. 'You never saw her round the village neither. We used to wonder if she had agoraphobia or somefing, but I never liked to ask.'

'Ar.' Wise attitude. Nobody liked a new landlord nosing into the affairs of local people. 'Her never had no friends yere, then?'

'Mrs Prosser, Councillor Prosser's wife, she used to go there once or twice a week, apparently.'

Judy Prosser. This figured. Judy Prosser was born and raised the other side of the quarry, no more than half a mile from Merv Thomas's farm. She'd have known the Thomas girls, likely Barbara better than Menna, being nearer her age. Judy Prosser would know the score. Smart girl that one; not much got past her, whereas most everything got past that dull bugger Gareth.

Well, Gomer had always got on well enough with Judy, in the days before Gareth bought his own digger. Likely he'd hang around here, see if she came in the pub after the funeral.

'My missus went across there once,' the boy continued.

'To visit Menna?'

'They'd be about the same age, near enough, and she reckoned

177

maybe they could be friends. But she got short shrift. Never got further'n the doorstep.'

'This is the ole rectory?'

'Blooming great big place for just the two of them. Never seemed to have guests to stay or anyfing, even in the summer. Never went on holidays either.'

'Solicitor, see,' Gomer said. 'Gotter have hisself a big house. Status in the community. Plus, his ole man likely got a good deal on it when they ditched the church. You drinking . . .?'

'Greg. Fanks very much,' the boy said. 'I'll have a half. So you were from round here, originally, Mr—'

'Gomer Parry Plant Hire,' Gomer said. 'Radnor Valley born an' bred. Used to run a bunch o' diggers and bulldozers. We done drainage, soakaways, put roads in, all over the valley. My nephew, Nev, he does it now, see.'

'Oh, yeah, *I* know. He was filling in after the archaeological digs, yeah? Used to come in for a sandwich and a pint at lunchtime?'

'Sure t'be.'

'They were digging all over the place. We all got excited when it came out they'd found an old temple. We fought it was gonna be like Stonehenge and we'd get thousands of tourists. But all it was – it was just a few holes in the ground where there'd been like wooden posts what rotted away centuries ago. Noffing to see, apart from all the stone axeheads and stuff they dug up. Terrible disappointment.'

'Ar. Typical Radnorshire tourist attraction, that is.' Gomer took out his tin to roll a ciggie. 'Sounds good till you sees it.'

Crossing the Welsh border, you came, unexpectedly, out of darkness into light, Merrily thought, raising herself up in the passenger seat of Sophie's Saab. The last English town, Kington, with its narrow streets and dark surrounding hills, had been more like a Welsh country town. The hills beyond were densely conifered until the trees thinned to reveal a rotting cathedral of fissured rocks.

And then, suddenly, the Radnor Valley opened up and the whole landscape was washed clean under a sandy sky, and Merrily sank back again, just wanting to go on being driven through the winter countryside, not having to make any decisions . . . not having to answer difficult questions with a boom-mic hanging over her like a club.

Sophie took a left, and the car began to burrow under high banks and high, naked hedges. As the lanes narrowed, Old Hindwell began to be signposted, but by now they might just as well have followed any vehicle on that road; every car and Land Rover seemed to contain people dressed in black.

'One forgets,' Sophie mused, 'that rural funerals are such social events.'

The lanes seemed to have brought them in a loop, back into conifer country. The official Old Hindwell sign was small and muddied. Just beyond it, set back into a clearing, sat a well-built, stone Victorian house with a small, conical turret at one end. In most of its windows, curtains were drawn; the others probably didn't have curtains.

'The old rectory, do you think?' Sophie said.

'Weal's house? You could be right. There's obviously nobody about. If it is the rectory, we ought to be able to see the old church nearby.'

She peered among the trees, an uneasy mixture of leafless, twisted oaks and dark, thrusting firs.

'I suppose it must have occurred to you,' Sophie said, 'that the old church here might have been the one referred to by that woman on your TV programme.'

'The pagan church, mmm?' The road took them through a farm layout – windowless buildings on either side. 'But let's not worry about that until someone asks us to.'

The first grey-brown cottages appeared up ahead.

And the cars. The village was clogged with cars.

The pub car park was full, as was the yard in front of what had once been a school. Cars and Land Rovers also lined the two principal lanes, blocking driveways and entrances, until the roads became so narrow that another parked vehicle would have made them impassable. Could it possibly be like this every Sunday?

Sophie slowed for a drab posse of mourners. They crossed the road and filed into a tarmac track between two big leylandii.

'The village hall,' Merrily said, unnecessarily.

It stood on what she judged to be the western edge of the village, partly concealed a little way up a conifered hillside, and was accessed by a footpath and steps. Sophie wondered aloud how they got any wheelchairs up there, for all the disabled people who thought Nicholas Ellis's prayers might cure them.

'So it's true then?' Merrily said. 'He does healing, too?'

'I copied cuttings from the local papers onto your computer file.' Sophie reversed into a field entrance to turn round again in the hope of finding a space. 'I don't suppose you had time to read them yet. I don't know how many people he's actually supposed to have healed.'

'You don't usually get statistics on it.'

Sophie frowned. 'That sort of thing is just not Anglican, somehow.'

'No? What about the shrine of St Thomas, in the cathedral?'

'*Not* the same thing.'

'What – because Ellis spent some time in the States?'

'My information is that he learned his trade with the more extreme kind of Bible Belt evangelist.' Sophie shuddered. 'Would you like to borrow my coat? It may not be exactly funereal, but it's at least . . .'

'Respectable?'

'I'm sorry,' Sophie said. 'I didn't mean—'

'Of course you didn't.' When Merrily smiled her face felt so stiff with fatigue that it hurt. 'If anyone does notice me, I could pretend to be a poor single-parent whom Mr Weal defended on a shoplifting charge.'

When the strangers came in, Gomer was getting the local take on the planting of Menna Weal in the rectory garden.

'Most people couldn't equate it wiv him being a lawyer and into property, Greg said. "Who's gonna wanna buy a house wiv a bleedin' great tomb? They say he'll leave it to his nephew who's started in the firm, but would you wanna live in a house wiv your dead auntie in the garden?'

Gomer wondered how he'd feel if his Min was buried in the back garden, and decided it wouldn't be right for either of them. In the churchyard she wasn't alone, see. Not meaning the dead; it was the coming and going of the living.

'But what I reckon . . .' Greg said. 'That building's right down the bottom of the garden, OK? You could lop it off, make it separate. A little park, with a footpath to it. The Weal memorial garden. I reckon that's what he's got in mind.'

'Nobody ask him?'

'Blimey, you don't ask *him* nothing. Not even the time – you'd get a bleedin' bill. It's like there's a wall around him, wiv an admission charge. And no first names. It's Mr Weal. Or J.W., if you're a friend.'

'He got many friends?'

'He knows a lot of people. That's the main fing in his profession.' Greg turned to his two new customers. 'Yes, gents . . .'

They wore suits – but not funeral suits. Both youngish fellows, in their thirties. One was a bit paunchy, with a half-grown beard; he ordered two pints.

'Not here for the funeral?' Greg said.

'Ah, that's what it is.' The plump, bearded one paid for their drinks. 'Must be somebody important, all those cars.'

'Oh, that's not unusual. There's a mass of cars every Sunday. Popular man, our minister. You get people coming from fifty miles away.'

Gomer looked up, gobsmacked. Most of these folks were not here for Menna at all, but part of some travelling fan club for the rector? Bloody hell.

'Hang on,' the plump feller with the beard said. 'Are there *two* churches, then?'

'Kind of,' Greg said. 'Our minister uses the village hall for his services.'

'But the old one, the old church – that's disused, right?'

'Long time ago. It's a ruin.'

'Can you still get to it?'

'You probably can,' Greg said, 'but it's on private land. It's privately owned now.'

'Only my mate wanted to take some pictures. With permission, of course. We don't want to go sneaking about. Who would we ask? Who owns it?'

'Well, it's new people, actually – only been moved in a week or so. There's a farmhouse, St Michael's. If you go back along the lane, past the post office, and on out of the village, you'll see a big farm, both sides of the road, then there's a track off to your left. If you go over a little bridge and you get to the old rectory, on your right, you've gone too far.'

'They all right, the people?'

'Sure,' Greg said. 'Young couple. He's American, an artist – book illustrator. Yeah, they're fine.'

'What's the name?'

Gomer was suspicious by now. Gomer was always suspicious of fellers in suits asking questions. Not Greg, though; suspicious land-lords didn't sell many drinks.

'Oh blimey, let me think. Goodfellow. Goodbody? Somefing like that.'

The paunchy bloke nodded. 'Thanks, mate, we'll go and knock on their door.'

'You can take a picture of my pub, if you like,' Greg said. 'What is it, magazine, holiday guide?'

The two men looked at each other, swapping grins.

'Something like that,' said the one who did the talking.

The village hall was like one of those roadside garages built in the 1950s, with a grey-white facade and a stepped roof. From its summit projected a perspex cross which would obviously light up at night. Conifers crowded in on the building, so you had the feeling of a missionary chapel in the jungle.

It was coming up to 3.45 p.m., the sky turning brown, the air raw. As Sophie drove away, Merrily felt unexpectedly apprehensive. From inside, as she walked up the steps, came the sound of a hymn she didn't recognize.

Below her, Old Hindwell was laid out in a V-shape. Beyond one arm arose the partly afforested hump which, Sophie had told her, was topped by the Iron Age hill fort, Burfa Camp. The northern horizon was broken by the shaven hills of Radnor Forest. The small, falling sun picked up the arc of a thin river around the boundary, like an eroded copper bangle.

Across the village, divided from it by a fuzz of bare trees, she could see the tower of the old church. She wondered if Nicholas Ellis would have made Old Hindwell his main base if that church had still been in use. Arguably not, since using the community hall was a good demonstration of his personal creed: the Church was people, ancient churches were museums.

The hymn she didn't know, sung unaccompanied by organ or piano, came to an end, and then there was the sound of a communal subsidence into rickety chairs. Merrily pushed open the double doors and went in.

Into darkness. Into a theatre with the house lights down. But the stage – she stifled a gasp – was lit, as though for a Nativity play. *Just not Anglican, somehow.* Gently, she pulled the doors together behind her and stood under a cracked green exit sign.

There was a row of shadowed heads and shoulders no more than four feet in front of her. The chairs were arranged like theatre-in-the-round under the girdered ceiling. The industrial window blinds were all lowered.

It was alarmingly like the *Livenight* studio, and the audience must have been at least as big: maybe 200 people, some on wooden benches pushed back to the walls. Spotlights in the ceiling lit the stage where stood a man in a white, monkish robe, head bowed, eyes cast down to hands loosely clasped on his stomach.

Merrily's first, disappointing glimpse of the Reverend Nicholas Ellis was a definite *so-what* moment.

' . . . is a particularly poignant occasion for me,' she heard. 'It's only weeks since Menna came to me, with her loving husband, to be baptized again, to pledge herself to the Lord Jesus in the presence of the Holy Spirit. I wonder . . . if somehow . . . she knew.'

His face was bland and shining, his mouth wide, like a letter box. His light brown hair was brushed straight back, a modest pony-tail disappearing into the folds of his monk's cowl. Monastic gear was less unorthodox than it used to be for Church of England ministers, but in dazzling white this was hardly a sign of humility. Too messianic for Merrily. His words rang coldly in the factory acoustic.

'I conducted the solemn but joyful service of rebaptism at their home. And on that day the very air was alive with hope and rejoicing, and these two souls were blessed beneath the wings of angels.'

From the shadows, someone, a man, cried out – involuntarily, it seemed, like a hiccup – 'Praise God!' As though the heavenly host had suddenly burst through the ceiling.

Nicholas Ellis was silent for a moment. Merrily couldn't make out his expression because the spotlights in the ceiling were aimed not at him but at the uncovered coffin.

Lidless! In the American style, Menna Weal lay in an open casket. Wrapped in her shroud. Her face looked like marble under the lights. A curtain of shadows surrounded her.

Merrily didn't like this, found it eerie. She looked for Barbara Buckingham in the congregation, but in this light it was hopeless. How could Barbara, wherever she was, stand this performance? How could any of them?

Eerie – what a funeral should *never* be.

Nicholas Ellis said, 'And it is to that same loving home that, in a short time, Menna's body will return. The final laying to rest of these earthly remains will be a small private ceremony which, in the context of that loving relationship, is as it should be.'

Merrily saw the seated figure of J.W. Weal, hunched like a big rock, gazing steadily at the body of his wife. Her thoughts were carried back to the county hospital, that first sight of him with his bowl of water and his cloth. An act of worship?

'Let us thank God for love,' Ellis said, 'when the black dragon wings of evil beat above our heads and the night air carries the stench of Satan.'

Merrily wrinkled her nose.

' . . . let us remember that only the strong light of love can bring us through the long hours of darkness. Now let us all rise and, with Menna and Jeffery together in our hearts, sing number two on our hymn sheet, 'Take Me, Lord, To Your Golden Palace'.

The lights blinked on, so that they could all read the words. Everyone rose, with a mass scraping of metal chair legs that was almost a shriek, and Merrily saw, at the front, one broad head thrust above all the others. J.W. looking down on the remains of his wife.

'A statement of ownership,' Barbara had said. *'Possession is nine points of the law.'*

Merrily found herself outside in the cold again, feeling slightly shocked.

She stopped about halfway down the steps, with her back to a Scots pine tree. The sand colour in the sky had all but disappeared, washed under the rapid, grey estuary of dusk. Below her, Old Hindwell settled into its umbered shadows. Merrily stood watching for the lights of Sophie's Saab, listening for its engine.

Just not Anglican, somehow.

You could say that again. She sank her hands far into her coat pockets.

It had been a singalong, gospelly, country-and-western hymn. It was cloying, trite – no worse but certainly no better than the stilted Victorian hymns which Merrily had been trying for months to squeeze out of her services. She'd had no hymn sheet, but the dipping of the house lights told her when the last verse had finished. Then words that were not on the hymn sheet took over – when, in the darkness, the tune and the rhythm disappeared but the singing itself did not stop.

Merrily stood silent, not having been exposed for quite some years to this phenomenon: the language of the angels according to some evangelists. Nonsense words, bubbling and flowing and ululating between slackened jaws.

Tongues. The gift of. The sign that the Holy Spirit was here in Old Hindwell village hall.

Right now, she was in no position to dispute this. It wasn't the hymn or its ghostly coda which had brought her out here, nor the sight of the silent, sombre Jeffery Weal, his gaze still fixed on his wife while the congregation summoned angels to waft her spirit into paradise.

It was just that, during the hymn, while the lights were on, she'd had an opportunity to investigate the congregation, row by row, and Barbara Buckingham was definitely not there. And while that meant she hadn't had to listen to Ellis's Gothic nonsense and stand in fuming silence while all around her sang themselves into a religious stupor, it did raise a possible problem.

Barbara was a determined woman. She had a serious grudge against this area, arising from a deprived childhood, which had become narrowed and focused into a hatred of the lumbering, sullen, slow-moving, single-minded Jeffery Weal.

Suppose she was already at Weal's house? Outside somewhere, waiting for the mourners at the small private ceremony that would follow.

Merrily hurried down the rest of the steps. After what she'd seen in there, she too wanted very much to know how this was going to end.

TWENTY-ONE

Lord Madoc

'Robin, it's Al.'

But this was *not* Al. Al was so cheerful that if he called you too early in the morning it hurt.

And this was not early morning, it was late afternoon and Betty had gone to see the goddamn widow Wilshire again and the voice on the phone was like the voice of a relative calling to say someone close to you was dead.

As art director handling Talisman, the fantasy imprint of the multinational publisher, Harvey-Calder, Al Delaney did not know any of Robin's relatives; he kept his dealings strictly to artists and writers and editors. So Robin was already feeling sick to his gut.

'Hi,' he said. 'How's it going?'

With the light failing fast, he stood by the window in his studio. Or, at least, the north-facing room that was to go on serving as his studio until they'd gotten enough money together to convert one of their outbuildings. The room had two trestle tables, one carrying his paints and his four airbrush motors, only two of which now worked. Airbrushes seemed to react badly to Robin. Must be all that awesome psychic energy.

Haw!

'I'm calling you from home,' Al said.

'That would be because it's Saturday and the offices are closed, right?'

'And because I've just heard from, er . . . Kirk Blackmore.'

'Uh-huh.' Robin moistened his lips.

'And I'd rather say what I want to say from home. Like that Blackmore's an insufferable egomaniac who'd stand there and tell Botticelli he couldn't draw arses, and that there are a few of us who'd like to use the Sword of Twilight to publicly disembowel him. But, tragically—'

'Tragically, he is also the hottest fantasy writer in Britain, so it would be unwise to say that to his face. Yeah, yeah. OK, Al, just listen for one minute. Since I got Blackmore's fax, I've been giving it a whole lot of thought and I've come up with something which I think he's gonna like a whole lot more. I accept that the purple mist was too lurid, the lettering too loud, so what I propose, for starters—'

'Robin, he now doesn't want you to do it at all.'

On the second table, the work table, lay Robin's preliminary watercolour drawings for the proposed new Kirk Blackmore format, the one which would run down the backlist like gold thread. The one, in fact, which would launch the fund which would finance the restoration of the outbuildings – providing Betty with her own herbal haven and Robin, in a year or two, with the most wonderful, inspiring, *sacred* studio.

'He just . . . he just said he didn't like the painting,' Robin said. His whole body seemed very light. 'He said he . . . he said there were *elements* of the painting he didn't like, was all.'

Al said, 'He wants someone else to do it, Robin.'

'Who?' Robin couldn't feel his hands.

'It doesn't matter who. Nobody in particular – but not you. Mate, I'm sorry. I was so convinced you were the man for this, I would've . . . I had to tell you today. I didn't want you spending all weekend working out something that wasn't even going to get—'

'And the backlist?'

'The backlist?'

'What I'm saying, this isn't just the one cover he doesn't like . . .?'

'It *is* the one cover he doesn't like, obviously, and you'll get paid in full for that, no problem at all. But it's also . . . How many ways can I put this? He wants . . . he wants another artist. He doesn't want you.'

*

Robin held up the core design which Blackmore should have loved, took a last look into the eyes of Lord Madoc who, in times of need, would stand in his megalithic circle and summon the Celtic Ray.

Robin's Madoc – who would not now be Blackmore's Madoc. A lean, noble, beardless face, its hairstyle – or glorious *neglect* of style – shamelessly modelled on Betty's own delicious profusion. Sympathetic magic: Madoc's hair was full of electricity and pulsed in the mist around him; Madoc, the hack fantasy hero, had been permitted to reflect the bright essence of Betty's holy power. How could frigging Blackmore have failed to respond to that?

And what were they gonna live on now?

Maybe not love. He recalled Betty's face before she had gone out, the light gone from her eyes, the shine from her skin. And her hair all brushed. She'd brushed her hair flat!

She also wore a skirt he didn't even remember her owning, a dark, mid-length skirt – a very ordinary skirt. This was the true horror of it. When she left the house she was looking like *an ordinary person.*

And it was his fault. Ever since they got here, everything he did was wrong. And everything he didn't do – or say.

Jeez, he'd never even thought much about what had happened with Marianne outside the pub. That whole sequence was like a dream – the glowing cross in the sky, the big, weird guy looking over his shoulder at no one right behind him. Robin had gone home and he'd slept, and tomorrow had been another lousy day.

He felt cold to his gut. Lately, Betty had lain with her back to him in bed, feigning sleep, a psychic wall between them.

Very tired, she would say, with the move and all.

'Fuck!' Robin tore the Madoc drawings end to end and let the strips fall to the floorboards. 'Fuck, oh fuck, oh *fuck.*'

Trying to picture Blackmore as he was ripping them, but he'd never seen the guy. The face that came to him was the smug, unlined, holy face of the Reverend Nicholas Ellis. Ellis had done this. Ellis who had made Robin his devil, focused his smug, holy Christian hatred on the ruins of St Michael's, the lair of the dragon. Ellis had brought down bad luck on them.

And they were innocent.

He broke down and wept in frustration and despair, his head

among the scattered paint tubes. Robin Thorogood, illustrator, seducer of souls, guardian of the softly lit doorways? What a fucking joke.

By seed, by root, by bud and stem, by leaf and flower and fruit, by life and love, in the name of the goddess, I Robin, take thee, Betty, to my hand, my heart and my spirit at the setting of the sun and rising of the stars.

A handfasting. None of this till-death-do-us-part shit.

In the fullness of time we shall be born again, at the same time and in the same place as each other, and we shall meet and know and remember and love again.

It made you cry. Every time you thought of that it made you cry. How much of the prosaic Christian marriage ceremony could do that to you?

Robin cried some more. He saw her in her wedding dress. He saw her slipping out of the dress, when they were left alone, for the consummation, the Great Rite.

How could it be that their souls were sailing away from each other? How could this happen in the sacred place which, it had been prophesied – it had been fucking *prophesied* – was their destiny?

Robin rose from the table. He figured what he would do now was take a walk down to the barn.

And from the barn he would retrieve the box containing the charm which promised to protect this house and all the chickens and pigs and local people therein from the menace of the Old Religion.

And he, Robin Thorogood, guardian of the softly lit doorways, would take this box and carry it to the edge of the promontory on which the Christians had built their church and, with due ceremony and acknowledgement to the Reverend Penney, hurl the mother-fucker into the hungry torrent of the Hindwell Brook.

Robin wiped his eyes with a paint cloth. He thought he heard a knocking at the front door.

Local people. It was probably only *Local People*. Like the deeply local person who wrote the anonymous letter to his wife, shafting him good.

Well, these local people could just remove themselves from off of his – and the building society's – property. Robin's fists bunched.

A CROWN OF LIGHTS

They could very kindly evacuate their asses from said property right now.

The guy said, 'Mr Thorogood?'

Not a local person. Even Robin was getting so he could separate out British accents, and this was kind of London middle class.

Two of them, and one carried a biggish metal-edged case. When Robin saw the case, he thought sourly, Whaddaya know, it's another local person bringing us another box with another charm to guard us against ourselves and thus turn our idyllic lives into liquid shit.

'Mr Thorogood, my name's Richard Prentice. This is Stuart Joyce.'

Robin flicked on the porch light. Overweight guy with a beard, and a thinner, younger guy in a leather jacket. Double-glazing, Robin figured; or travelling reps from some company that would maximize your prospects by investing the contents of your bank account in a chain of international vivisection laboratories.

'We both work for the *Daily Mail* newspaper,' Prentice said. 'If it's convenient, I'd like a chat with you – about your religion.'

'About my . . .?' Robin glanced at the case. Of course, a camera case.

'I understand you and your wife are practising witches.'

Robin went still. 'How would you have come to understand that?'

Relax. No camera around the thin guy's neck.

Prentice smiled. 'You didn't happen to watch a TV programme called *Livenight*, by any chance?'

'We don't have a TV.'

'Oh.' The man smiled. 'That would certainly explain it. Well, Mr Thorogood, you and your wife were referred to on that programme.'

'What?'

'Not by name – but your situation was mentioned. Now, it sounds as though we're the first media people to approach you. And that's a good thing for both of us, because—'

'Hold on a moment,' Robin said. 'If, as you say, we *are* witches – which, in these enlightened times, I'm hardly gonna deny . . . Why are you interested? There are thousands of us. It's, like, the fastest growing religion in the country right now. What I'm saying is, what kind of big deal is that for a paper like yours?'

'Well, I'll be straight with you, Robin, it's primarily the church. How many witches have actually taken over a Christian church for their rituals?'

'Well, Richard,' Robin said, 'if I can reverse that question, how many Christian churches have taken over pagan sites for *their* rituals?'

Richard Prentice grinned through his beard. '*That*, my friend, is an excellent point, and we'd like to give you the opportunity to amplify it.'

'I don't think so, Richard.'

'Could we come in and talk about it? It's perishing out here.'

'I really don't think so. For starters, my wife—'

'Look,' Prentice said. 'You were more or less outed – if I can use that term – on a TV programme watched by millions of viewers. I'd guess you're going to be hearing from a lot of other journalists over the next few days. And I mean tabloid journalists.'

'Isn't that what you are?'

'We like to call ours a *compact* paper. There's a difference.'

'Don't make me laugh, Richard.'

'Robin . . . look . . . what we have in mind – and this would be for Monday's paper, so we'd have a whole day to get it absolutely right – is a serious feature explaining exactly what your plans are for this church, and why you believe you're no threat to the community.'

'Somebody say we're a threat to the community here?'

'You know what local people are like, Robin.'

'Out,' Robin said.

'I'm sorry?'

'Go, Richard.'

'Robin, I think you'll find that we can protect you from the unwanted intrusion of less responsible—'

'Leave now. Or I'll, like, turn you into a fucking toad.'

'That's not a very sensible attitude. Look, this was probably a bad time. I can tell something's happened to upset you. We're going to be staying in the area tonight. I suggest we come back in the morning. All right?'

Robin stepped out of the porch. Through the trees, he could hear the racing of the Hindwell Brook.

'OK,' Prentice said, 'that's your decision.'

And if they'd gone at that moment, things might all have been so much less fraught.

Unfortunately, at this point the porch and Robin were lit up brightly, and Robin realized the younger guy suddenly had a camera out.

The rushing of the brook filled his head. *Cold white noise.* Robin thought of silent Betty with her back to him in the sack. He thought he heard, somewhere on the ether, the rich sound of Kirk Blackmore laughing at his artwork.

Robin made like Lord freaking Madoc.

TWENTY-TWO

Wisp

Merrily could see the battlemented outline of Old Hindwell church tower over the bristle of trees, and the spiteful voice cawed in her head.

'I can show you a church with a tower and graves and everything . . . which is now a pagan church. You don't know what's happening on your own doorstep.'

If these pagans had been around for a while, it would explain why Ellis had adopted Old Hindwell – extremes attract extremes. The only other abandoned Anglican church she could think of in the diocese was at Llanwarne, down towards Ross-on-Wye, and that was close to the centre of a village and open to the road, a tourist attraction.

But whether this was or wasn't the alleged neo-pagan temple was not the issue right now. What she needed to make for was the former rectory, which was not ruined, far from abandoned . . . but about to accommodate its first grave.

She would probably encounter Sophie's car along the way.

And Barbara Buckingham?

That grumbling foreboding in her stomach – that was subjective, right? Merrily walked faster, aware that the only sound on the street was the soft padding of her own flat shoes. She walked into the centre of the village, where there was a small shop and post office – closed already – and the pub had frosted windows and looked inviting only compared with everywhere else.

In one of the cottages, a dog howled suddenly, a spiralling sound;

maybe it had picked up a distant discordant wailing emanating from the village hall. Something which was not, perhaps, quite human.

The pub car park was still full. With the cars – of course – of outsiders. The singing in tongues should have given it away: many people in today's congregation were not, in fact, family mourners or friends or long-time clients of J.W. Weal, but core members of Nicholas Ellis's church.

And the tongues was not a spontaneous phenomenon; for them it had become routine, a habit, almost an addiction, a Christian trip. She'd learned that while at theological college when a bunch of students, well into the born-again thing, had persuaded her to join them at a weekend event known as the Big Bible Fest, held in a huge marquee near Warwick. Two long days of everybody smiling at everybody else and doing the '*Praise Him!*' routine like kids with a new schoolyard catchphrase, and by the end of the first day Merrily had been ready to swing for the next person who addressed her as 'sister'.

It had been Jeremy, one of the faithful, who'd told her that the cynical bitch persona was simply concealing her fear of complete surrender to the Holy Spirit. He was challenging her to go along that night with an open mind, without prejudice, without resistance. Praise Him! So, OK, she'd attended a service where all the hymns had been simple, rhythmic pop anthems, sung by happy people in Hawaiian shirts and sweatpants – and all ending in tongues.

Tongues was the gift of Christ, originally granted to a select few. The Bible did not spell out what tongues actually sounded like, its linguistic roots, its grammatical structure, but modern evangelical Christians insisted it was a way of talking directly to God, who Himself did not necessarily speak English.

Not entirely convincing, but for the first two hymns she'd held out. After all, hadn't her own formative mystical moment occurred in total silence, lit by the blue and the gold, alone in a little hermit's cave of a church?

And then – *Praise Him, praise God!* – her mouth had been open like everyone else's, and out it all came like those flimsy coloured scarves produced by conjurers. Words which were flowing and lyrical and meant nothing, but sounded as if they ought to. Lush, liquid worship. Dynamic, wordless prayer. A disconnecting of the senses. A transcendent experience, up there around the marquee's striped roof.

She could, in fact, still bring it on when she wanted to, could summon that wild Christian high, simple as popping a pill, as though just doing it that once had been a lifetime's initiation. It was easy.

Maybe too easy.

She wondered to what extent the locals had joined in. Were slow-speaking farmers now singing in tongues? Did they say 'Praise God' when they met by the sheep pens on market day, instead of the time-honoured ''Ow're you?'

You couldn't rule that out. After all, it was in Wales that traditional church worship had been massively abandoned in the rush to build stark, spartan Noncomformist chapels. So how far down the charis-matic road did Old Hindwell go? Was it like the Toronto Blessing, with people collapsing everywhere? Were they discovering Galilean sand in the palms of their hands and gold fillings in their teeth?

But how appropriate was this at a funeral?

Merrily scanned the cars by the pub. Was one of them Barbara's? What make had Barbara been driving? Merrily didn't know.

She turned and walked on down the darkening street, a headache coming on, although it was dulled by the cold. Beyond the village shop and a lone bungalow with a 1970s-style rainbow-stone porch, the grass verge came to an end, so Merrily walked in the road, down into a conifered valley which would eventually open out to the hill country of Radnor Forest.

Soon afterwards, she heard the low mutter of approaching vehicles, and then dipped headlights began to cast a pale light on the road, and she pressed close to the hedge as the cortège came past.

As the mourners had started coming for their cars, Gomer had moved to the pub window to look out for Gareth and Judy Prosser. Chances were the Prossers would be on foot, but they'd still have to come this way. Most of the people picking up their vehicles Gomer didn't recognize.

'There a funeral tea up the hall?' he asked Greg.

'If there is, we weren't asked to provide it. Nah, they say Father Ellis don't go for eating and drinking in church.'

'It's a bloody village hall!'

'Not when he's there it ain't.'

Gomer looked over his shoulder at Greg polishing glasses for the customers that didn't come in. 'You're not a churchgoer, then, boy?'

'Never was. But the bloody pressure's on now.' The anxious look flitted across Greg's face again. 'Lot of people've started going. He don't look much, Ellis, but they reckon you come out feeling on cloud nine. I mean, whatever it is, I'm not sure I wanna catch it. The wife's gone to this funeral. And I let 'em use the car park – all his fans from miles around. Not that many of 'em drop in for a pint or anyfing afterwards. Don't need drink when you're high on God.'

'You got a few yere now, boy,' Gomer observed. 'Stand by your pumps.'

Two men and three women came in, all in black. One of the men was Tony Probert, farmer from Evenjobb – Gomer knew him to speak to, just about – and one of the women was . . .

'Gomer Parry!'

'Greta,' Gomer said, '"ow're you?'

Greta Thomas, wife of Danny, the rock-and-roll farmer from Kinnerton. She was little and busty, with a voice Nash Rocks could've used for blasting. Used to be receptionist for Dr Coll.

'I hope you're lookin' after yourself, Gomer,' Greta yelled. 'Not goin' back to the wild?' Never one to make a meal of the ole condolences; once the funeral was over Greta believed it was time to start cheering you up.

'I'm doing fine, Gret.'

'"Cause if Min thought you was on the bevvy . . .'

'Moderation in all things, you know me, girl. I dunno, I seen bloody Danny earlier, he never said you was goin' to see Menna off.'

'Never remembers nothing, 'cept his bloody chords. Tony and Julie was coming, so I had a lift.' Greta pulled Gomer towards a table. 'Reckoned *somebody* ought to represent Danny's side of the family.'

'Nothin' to do with wantin' to see the famous Reverend Ellis in action without goin' to a reg'lar service, like?'

Greta looked sheepish. 'No harm in that, is there?'

'Worth it, was it?'

'Well . . . strange, it is, actually, Gomer.'

'Ar?'

'Specially the funny singing. Like a trance – beautiful really, when it gets going. The voices are like harmonizing natural, the men and the women. Really gets you. It's quite . . . I don't know . . . sexy. That's a stupid thing to say, ennit?'

'Better get you a drink, Gret.'

He went to Greg at the bar, bought Greta a brandy. He might learn something here, and it beat going home to an empty bungalow with no fire, no tea, nothing but crap Saturday night telly and then a cold bed.

Greta looked up at him from under a fringe of hair dyed the colour of Hereford clay.

'I didn't mean that how it sounded, Gomer. I mean, I've never been that religious, but it makes you think. A lot of people's saying that. Dr Coll – even Dr Coll – reckons Mr Ellis is the best thing ever happened to this area.'

'Why do he reckon that?' Clergy, in Gomer's experience, came and went and never got noticed much, unless they started messing with people's wives – or they were little and pretty.

'The way it's bringing the community together,' Greta said. 'You'd never get that with an ordinary parson and an ordinary church. When did you ever see local people and folk from Off hugging each other?'

'En't natural,' Gomer conceded.

'And they also reckons you can get a private consultation.'

'What for?'

'Anything, really. Sickness, emotional problems . . .'

'What's he do for that?'

'Fetches them out of you, Gomer. Lays his hands on you, fetches it all out.'

'Bloody hell, Gret.'

'There's folk swears by it.'

'Bloody hell.'

He leaned back and thought for a bit. Doctor's receptionist for what – ten years? Her'd have been no more than a young girl when her first went to work for Dr Coll's old feller. Still . . .

'How well did you actually know Menna Thomas, Gret?'

Doctor's receptionists, it was easier for them to talk about the dead than the living, and Greta Thomas was still talking when Tony Probert and his wife and the other couple had finished up their drinks and looked a bit restive, so Gomer told them it was OK, he'd take Greta home himself.

On the way, he said, 'And how well did you know her sister Barbara?'

Which was how he found out the truth about the hydatid cyst.

Behind the hearse came an old-fashioned taxi, like a London black cab. Merrily saw brake lights come on about a hundred yards down the lane and she moved quietly towards them. Stone posts stood stark against the last of the light and she heard the grating of metal gates.

Silhouettes now. Someone in a long overcoat pushing a bier. Merrily watched the coffin sliding onto it under the raised tailgate of the hearse, saw the bier pushed through the gates. It was followed by several people fused into one moving shadow.

Against the band of light below the grey roller blind of evening, she could see the roof of the old rectory. No lights on there. The taxi started up, rolled away down the lane. No sign of another car.

No sign of Barbara Buckingham.

Suppose Barbara had accosted Weal, made a nuisance of herself, and Weal – as a solicitor, able to expedite these things – had responded with some kind of injunction to restrain her. In which case, why hadn't Barbara told Merrily? Why hadn't she left a message?

At the gates, peering down an alley of laurels, Merrily was pulled sharply back by the realization that this whole situation was entirely ridiculous. Only Jane would do something like this. But then more headlights were glaring around the bend behind her, and she slipped inside the gates to avoid them.

The vehicle went past on full beams: not Sophie's Saab but a fat four-wheel drive with two men in it. Leaving Merrily standing on the property of J.W. Weal as, somewhere beyond the laurels, a single warm light was anointing the bruised dusk with an amber balm.

She followed the laurel alley towards the house, now only half expecting the dramatic eleventh-hour appearance of Barbara Buckingham like the dissenting wedding guest with just cause for stopping the service.

By the house, the drive split into a fork, one prong ending at a concrete double garage, the other dropping down a step and narrowing into a path, its tarmac surface fragmenting into crazy paving to cross the lawn – which was wedge-shaped and bordered by spruce and Scots pine. At the narrow end of this wedge stood a conical building, the source of the light.

The wine store . . . the ice house . . . Menna's waiting tomb.

Merrily stood by the last of the laurels, on the edge of the lawn, and looked up at the Victorian house – substantial, grey and gabled, three storeys high. The light from the open door of the tomb, maybe forty yards away, was bright enough to outline the regular stone blocks in the back wall of the house. She could see the shadows of heavy, lumpen furniture in the room immediately behind a bay window on the ground floor. This house was very J.W. Weal.

At its end of the lawn, the mausoleum was a squat Palladian temple. Victorian kitsch, its interior was creamed with electric light from two wrought-iron hanging lanterns. Then the light was suddenly blocked and diffused . . . two men looming. Merrily backed up against the house wall, laurel leaves wet on her face.

'Mind the step, George.'

'He could use a light.'

'Knows his way down yere in his sleep, I reckon.'

The undertakers maybe? Must be the departure of the last outsiders.

Feeling very much on her own now, Merrily moved down the lawn, stopping about fifteen yards from the door of the mausoleum. From an oblique angle, she could see inside, to where mourners were grouped around a stone trough set into the middle of the floor. She saw Ellis, in his white robe. She saw a wiry bearded man, a squat bulky man, and a woman. They were still as a painted tableau, faces lit with a Rembrandt glow. And she thought, aghast, This is intrusion, this is voyeurism, this is none of my business!

This was about a man – not an affable man, not an immediately likeable man, but a man who had loved his wife, who had treated her with great tenderness till the last seconds of her life. Who had – whatever you thought of rebaptism, rebirth in the faith – come with her to Christ. Who could not bear to be entirely parted from her. Who had chosen to gaze out every morning from their bedroom window, probably for the rest of his life, across to where she lay.

That's it. I'm going. She turned abruptly away.

And walked into the man himself.

Her face was suddenly buried in the cold, crisp shirt-front in the V of his waistcoat.

It smelled of camphor.

For a moment, she was frozen with shock, let out a small 'Oh' before his big arms came around her, lifting her off her feet. For a flowing second, she was spun in space through the path of light from the tomb, and then put down in shadow and held.

'Men-na,' he breathed.

The great body rigid, compressing her. Camphor. Carbolic. She was gripped for a too-long moment, like a captured bird, and then the arms sprang apart.

'I'm sorry . . .' she whispered.

He was silent. Neither of them moved.

A small night breeze had arisen, was rippling the laurels and sighing in the conifers. The firs and pines were like sentries with spears. J.W. Weal was just another shadow now; she didn't feel that he was looking at her. The line of light shivered, and Merrily saw figures standing in the doorway of the mausoleum. Nobody spoke, nobody called to her. It was dreamlike, slow-motion.

She turned and walked away – trying not to run – across the lawn, in and out of the path of light, her arms pressed into her sides, as though his arms were still around her. The strong light from the mausoleum haloed the old rectory, illuminating the inside of the bay-windowed room on the ground floor.

And then, as she was looking up at that same window, it became dark all round. The door of the mausoleum had been closed. They'd been waiting for Jeffery Weal to return from the house, and now they'd shut themselves away for the finale, leaving darkness outside. The lawn was black, the track of light from the tomb having vanished. Merrily felt small and bewildered and ashamed, like a child who should be in bed but had peered through the bannisters into an unknown, unknowable, grown-up world.

'*Men-na*.'

What was he *thinking* then?

She searched for the entrance to the drive. Without light, she would need to go carefully.

Yet there *was* light: a dull, diffused haze behind the bay window, where the backs of chairs threw rearing shadows up the interior walls. She now hated that room. She knew it was very cold in there, colder than it was out here. She didn't want to be looking in. She didn't want to see . . .

. . . the pale figure flitting across the wide windows, from pane to pane.

The slight, moth-like thing, the wisp of despair.

She didn't want to see it. She *couldn't* see it.

But as the room came out to her, enclosing her in its pocket of cold, she could almost hear the flimsy, flightless, jittering thing beating itself against the glass in its frenzy, with a noise like tiny crackling bones.

Merrily flailed and stumbled into the laurels, slipped on numbed legs and grabbed handfuls of leaves to keep from falling. Only these weren't the laurels; they had thorns, winter-vicious. Still she clutched them in both hands, almost relishing the entirely physical pain, then she scrambled up and onto the drive, hobbling away towards the gateposts.

Part Three

The vast majority of charismatic churches are aware of the dangers of confusing demonic attack with psychological problems . . . There are, however, some charismatic groups which are inclined to carry out a ministry of deliverance which concerns most other charismatic churches and which leads to 'casualties'.

Deliverance (ed. Michael Perry)
The Christian Deliverance Study Group

TWENTY-THREE

Tango with Satan

Since coming home to her apartment at the vicarage, Jane had . . . well, just slept, actually. Longer, probably, than she'd ever slept before. She woke up briefly, thought of something crucially important, went back to sleep, forgot about it. Just like that for most of a day.

It was the hospital's fault. Hospitals were, like, totally knackering. Unless you were drugged to the eyeballs, you *never* slept in a hospital – be more relaxing bedding down on a factory floor during the night shift. Naturally, Jane had tried telling them this, but no, they'd insisted on keeping her in, in case her skull was fractured or something worse. Which she knew it wasn't, and *they* knew really, but it was, like – yawn, yawn – procedure, to forestall people suing the Health Service for half a million on account of her having gone into a coma on the bus.

Sleep was all you really needed. Real sleep, home sleep. Sleep was crucial, because it gave the body and the brain time to repair themselves, and because it was a natural thing.

And, also, in this particular case, because it postponed that inevitable Long Talk With Mum.

The Long Talk had not taken place, as expected, in the car coming home from Worcester Royal Infirmary last night, because it was Sophie's car and Sophie was driving it, and Sophie – to Jane's slight resentment – seemed more concerned about Mum, who had herself at one point fallen asleep in the passenger seat and awoken with a start – like a really *seismic* start – which made Sophie judderingly slam on the brakes going down Fromes Hill. Mum had shaken herself fully awake and said – in that flustered, half-embarrassed way of hers when lying – that something must have walked over her grave.

And, like, trod on her hands? Why were both her hands clumsily criss-crossed with broad strips of Elastoplast, like *she* was the motorway pile-up casualty?

Fell among thorns, was all Mum would say when they finally got home, must have been around ten. Bewilderingly, she'd hugged Jane for a long time before they'd staggered off to their respective bedrooms, without mention of the impending Long Talk.

Odd.

Jane slept through most of Sunday morning, venturing dowstairs just once for a bite to eat from the fridge – lump of cheese, handful of digestive biscuits – while Mum was out, doing the weekly pulpit gig. Then leaving her plates conspicuously on the draining board so that Mum would know she'd eaten and wouldn't come up to ask about lunch and initiate the Long Talk.

She vaguely remembered awakening to see Mum standing by the bed in her clerical gear, like a ghost, but she must have fallen asleep again before either of them could speak. She kept half waking to hear the ting of the phone: a lot of calls. *A lot of calls.* Was this about the accident? Or *Livenight* – Mum apologizing to half the clergy for screwing up on TV?

For Sunday lunch, alone with Ethel the cat, Merrily had just a boiled egg and a slice of toast. Which was just as well because, before 2 p.m., the bishop was on the phone, enquiring after Jane and revealing himself to be a worried man.

The *Daily Mail* had phoned him at home. Did he know that a former church in his diocese had become a temple for the worship of pagan gods?

Well, of course he did. He'd seen the damned TV programme like everyone else, but he was hoping that either nothing more would be heard of it or it would turn out to be safely over the border in the Diocese of Swansea and Brecon.

Not that he'd told the *Mail* that. He'd told the *Mail* he was 'concerned' and would be 'making enquiries'.

And this was one of them.

'As it happens,' Merrily said, 'I was in Old Hindwell yesterday.'

Bernie Dunmore went quiet for a couple of seconds.

'That's an extraordinary coincidence,' he said.

'It is. But nothing more than that.'

'Did you see the church?'

'Only the tower above the trees. I didn't see any naked figures dancing around a fire, didn't hear any chanting. Is it really true? Who are they?'

'Witches, apparently. People called Thorogood, ironically enough. Young couple, came from Shrewsbury, I think. But he's American.'

'In parts of America, witchcraft is awfully respectable these days.'

'Merrily, this is Radnorshire.'

'Er . . . quite.'

'As for the church – well, strictly speaking it isn't a church at all any more. Did all the right things when they let it go. Took away the churchyard bones to a place of suitable sanctity. Virtually *gave* it to the farming family whose land had surrounded it for generations. Stipulating, naturally, that relatives of people whose names were on the graves should be able to visit and lay flowers, by arrangement.'

'Why *did* they let it go? It's not as though the village has an alternative church.'

'Usual reasons: economics coupled with a very convenient period of public apathy.'

'You could dump half the parish churches in Britain on that basis.'

'Also, this isn't a building of any great architectural merit,' Bernie said. 'Old, certainly, but the only *history* it seems to have is one of more or less continuous major repairs and renewals, dating back to the fifteenth century or earlier. The dear old place never seems to have wanted to stay up, if you get my meaning. Close to a river or something, so perhaps built on ground prone to subsidence. Things apparently came to a head when the rector at the time actually suggested it should be decommissioned.'

'Really?'

'Anyway, all that's irrelevant. The unfortunate fact is, if it's got a

207

tower or a steeple and a handful of gravestones, the general public will still see it as holy ground, and there'll be protests.'

'But there's nothing you can do about that, is there? You can't actually vet new owners.'

'The Church *can* vet them, obviously, when the Church is the vendor. And the Church does – we're not going to sell one to someone who wants to turn it into St Cuthbert's Casino or St Mary's Massage Parlour. But when it's being sold on for the second or, in this case, third time, you're right, it's more or less out of our hands.'

'So is there any reason for this to escalate into anything –?'

'Merrily, this is Nicholas Ellis's patch. This is where he holds his gatherings . . . in the village hall.'

'I know. I was there for a funeral. The congregation was singing in tongues over the coffin.'

The bishop made a noise conveying extreme distaste.

'But the point I was about to make, Bernie, is that Ellis is Sea of Light. He doesn't *care* about churches.'

'Oh, Merrily, you don't really believe the bugger isn't going to start caring very deeply – as of now?'

'You've spoken to him?'

'Never spoken to the man in my life, but the press have. They didn't tell us what he said, but I expect we'll all be reading about it at length in the morning.'

'Oh. Anything I can do?'

Bernie Dunmore chuckled aridly. 'You're the Deliverance Consultant, Merrily, so what do *you* think you could do?'

'That's not fair. Look, I'm sorry I messed up so badly on TV, if that's what—'

'Not at all. No, indeed, you were . . . fine. As well as being probably the only woman on that programme who looked as if she shaved her armpits. Was that sexist? What I'm trying to say . . . you're the only one of us who officially knows about this kind of thing and is able to discuss it in a balanced kind of way. Not like Ellis, that's what I mean. Obviously, I can't forbid the man to speak to the media, but I'd far rather it were you . . .'

'The only problem, Bishop—'

' . . . and if all future requests for information could be passed directly to our Deliverance Consultant. As the official spokesperson for the diocese on . . . matters of this kind.'

Merrily felt a tremor of trepidation. And recalled the whizz and flicker, the crackle and tap-tap on the window of a room full of shadows.

'But, Bernie, this job . . . deliverance—'

'I know, I know. It's supposed to be low-profile.' He paused, to weight the punchline. 'But you have, after all, been on television now, haven't you?'

Ah.

'I won't dress it up,' Bernie said. 'You'll probably have problems as a result. Extremists on both sides. The pagans'll have you down as a jackboot fascist, while Ellis is calling you a pinko hippy doing the tango with Satan. Still, it'll be an experience for you.'

She stripped off the plasters Sophie had bought from the pharmacy at Tesco on the way to Worcester last night – a fraught journey, from the moment she'd stumbled into the Saab's headlight beams somewhere on the outskirts of the village.

She then changed out of her clerical clothes and went up to the attic to check that Jane was OK.

The kid was asleep in her double bed under the famous Mondrian walls of vermilion, Prussian blue and chrome yellow. Merrily found herself bending over her, like she hadn't done for years, making sure she was breathing. Jane's eyes fluttered open briefly and she murmured something unintelligible.

Merrily quietly left the room. They'd assured her at the hospital that her daughter was absolutely fine but might sleep a lot.

Downstairs, the phone was ringing. She grabbed the cordless.

It was Gomer. He'd just been to the shop for tobacco for his roll-ups and learned about the motorway accident.

'Her's all right?'

'Fine. Sleeping a lot, but that's good.'

'Bloody hell, vicar.'

'One of those things.'

'Bloody hell. Anythin' I can do, see?'

'I know. Thanks, Gomer.'

'So you wouldn't've gone to Menna's funeral then? I never went to look for you. One funeral's enough . . . enough for a long time.'

'You were in Old Hindwell yesterday?'

'Reckoned it might be a good time. Found out a few things you might wanner know, see. No rush, mind. You look after the kiddie.'

'In the morning?'

'Sure t'be,' Gomer said.

Good old Gomer.

'Mum.'

'Flower!'

Jane was standing in the kitchen doorway in her towelling dressing gown. She looked surprisingly OK. You wouldn't notice the bruise over her left eye unless you were looking for it.

'You hungry?'

'Not really. I just went to the loo and looked out the window, and I think you've got the filth.'

'What?'

'He's outside in his car, talking on his radio or his mobile. Over-weight guy in a dark suit. I've seen him before. I think it's that miserable-looking copper used to tag around after Annie Howe, the Belsen dentist. I'll go for another lie-down now, but just thought I'd warn you.'

Merrily let him in. 'DC Mumford.'

'DS Mumford, vicar. Amazingly enough.'

'Congratulations.'

'They have accelerated promotion for young graduates like DI Howe,' Mumford said heavily. 'For plods like me, it can still take twenty-odd years. How's your little girl?'

'You're just a late starter,' Merrily assured him. 'You'll whizz through the ranks now. Jane's doing OK, thanks. But that's not why you're here?'

Andy Mumford's smile was strained as he stepped into the kitchen. Another two or three years and he'd be up for retirement. Merrily had coffee freshly made and poured him one. She'd left the door open for Jane, for once hoping she was listening – a strong indication of recovery.

'You've been in contact with Mrs Barbara Buckingham,' Mumford said. 'We traced her movement back through the hospital. Sister Cullen says she referred her to you.'

Merrily stiffened. 'What's happened?'

'She's been reported missing, Mrs Watkins.'

'Barbara? By whom?'

'Arranged to phone her daughter in Hampshire every night while she was here. But hasn't rung for two nights. Does not appear to have attended her sister's funeral.'

'Oh my God.'

'Checked with Hampshire before I came in. No word there. It's an odd one, Mrs Watkins. Teenagers, nine times out of ten they'll surface after a while. A woman Mrs Buckingham's age, middle class, we start to worry.' Mumford sipped his coffee. 'You saw her last when?'

'Tuesday evening, here. It was the only time. How much did Eileen Cullen tell you?'

'She said Mrs Buckingham was very upset, not only over her sister's premature death but the fact that she wouldn't be getting buried in the churchyard like normal people. She said she thought you'd be the minister most likely to give the woman a sympathetic hearing.'

'I'm just the only one Eileen knows.'

Mumford smiled almost shyly. 'To be honest, Mrs Watkins, I got the feeling there might have been another reason she put the lady on to you, apart from this objection to the burial. But that might just be promotion making me feel I ought to behave like a detective. Of course, if you don't think that would throw any light on our inquiry . . .'

'Well . . . there was another reason, relating to my other job. You can put this down to stress if you like but don't go thinking she was nuts because I don't think she was – *is*.'

'Not my place, Reverend.'

'She was having troublesome dreams – anxiety dreams probably – about her sister. Barbara left home in Radnorshire when Menna was just a baby, and they'd hardly seen each other since. Anybody would feel . . . regrets in that situation. She's a Christian, she was headmistress at a Church school. Eileen thought she might appreciate some spiritual, er, counselling.'

'She explain *why* she was alone? Why her husband wasn't with her?'

'She said he was away – in France, I think. He deals in antiques.'

'Didn't say anything about him leaving her, then?'

'Oh God, really?'

'For France, read Winchester.' Mumford pulled out his pocket-book. 'Richard Buckingham moved out two months ago.'

'Another woman?'

'That's the information we have from the daughter. So, were you able to ease Mrs Buckingham's mind? I mean, if I was to ask you if you thought there was any possibility of her taking her own life . . .?'

'Oh no. She was too angry.'

'Angry.'

'Yeah, I'd say so.'

'At anybody in particular?'

'At J.W. Weal, I suppose. Know him?'

'Paths have crossed in court once or twice. He used to do quite a bit of legal aid work, maybe still does. I don't get out that way much these days.'

'Really?' She'd made a joke out of it to Sophie, but she couldn't imagine Weal defending small-time shoplifters and car thieves and dope smokers; that would mean he'd have to *talk* to them. 'I had him down as a wills and conveyancing man.'

'Place like that, a lawyer has to grab what he can get,' said Mumford. 'Mrs Buckingham didn't care for her brother-in-law, I take it.'

'Not a lot. You have a situation where Menna spends her young life looking after her widowed father and then gets married to a much older bloke, in the same area. No life at all, in Barbara's view. And then can't even get away when she dies.'

'You don't like him either then, Mrs Watkins?'

'I don't know him.'

Mumford considered. 'You'd wonder, does anybody? So, when

you spoke to her, did Mrs Buckingham give you any idea what she was going to do next?'

'She wanted me to go to the funeral with her. I went along, but she apparently didn't.'

'*You* were there?'

'We were supposed to meet.'

'Seems an unusual arrangement, if you don't mind me saying.'

'I thought she needed somebody.'

'You didn't know Mrs Weal, then?'

'Well, I was actually at the county hospital, with a friend, just after she died. But, no, I didn't actually know her. I don't really know why I said I'd go along. It's not like I don't have enough to do. Maybe . . .' Why did coppers always make you feel unaccountably guilty? 'Maybe I thought Barbara might do something stupid if I wasn't there, which I might have been able to prevent. It's hard to explain.'

'Stupid how?'

'Maybe cause some kind of scene. Start hurling accusations at J.W. Weal, or something, at the funeral.'

'But you didn't find her there?'

'To be honest, it was a difficult day. I had Jane to pick up from hospital in Worcester. If I'd known Barbara had been reported missing, I'd have . . . tried harder.'

She returned from seeing Mumford out to find Jane at the kitchen table. The kid was dressed in jeans and her white fluffy sweater. She looked about ten. Until, of course, she spoke.

'He thinks she's dead.'

'Police always think that, flower.'

'I think you think she's dead, too.'

'I don't think that, but I do feel guilty.'

'You always feel guilty,' Jane said.

TWENTY-FOUR

Against the World

Old Hindwell post office was a brick-built nineteenth-century building a little way down from the pub, on the opposite side of the street. Betty was there by eight fifteen on this dry but bitter Monday morning. The newsagent side of the business opened at eight. There were no other customers inside.

'*Daily Mail*, please.'

The postmistress, Mrs Eleri Cobbold, glanced quickly at Betty and went stiff.

'None left, I'm sorry.'

'You've only been open fifteen minutes.' Betty eyed her steadily. It was the first time she'd been in here. She saw a thin-faced woman of about sixty. She saw a woman who had already read today's *Daily Mail*.

'Only got ordered copies, isn't it?' Mrs Cobbold swallowed. 'Besides two extras. Which we've sold.'

Betty was not giving up. She glanced at the public photocopier at the other end of the shop. 'In that case, could I perhaps borrow one of the ordered papers and make a copy of one particular page?'

Mrs Cobbold blinked nervously. 'Well, I don't . . .'

Betty sought her eyes, but Mrs Cobbold kept looking away as though her narrow, God-fearing soul was in danger. She glanced towards the door and seemed very relieved when it was opened by a slim, tweed-suited man with a neat beard.

'Oh, good morning, Doctor.'

'A sharp day, Eleri.'

'Yes. Yes, indeed.' Mrs Cobbold bent quickly below the counter and produced a *Daily Mail*. She didn't look at Betty. 'You had better take mine. Thirty-five pence, please.'

'Are you sure?'

'Yes,' Mrs Cobbold whispered.

This was ridiculous.

'Thank you.' Betty also bought a bottle of milk and a pot of local honey. She took her purse from her shoulder bag. She didn't smile. 'And if I could have a carton of bat's blood as well, please.'

This, and the presence in the shop of the doctor, seemed to release something.

'Take your paper and don't come in here again, please,' Mrs Cobbold said shrilly.

The doctor raised a ginger eyebrow.

Betty started to shake her head. 'I really can't believe this.'

'And' – Mrs Cobbold looked at her at last – 'you can tell that husband of yours that if he wants to conduct affairs with married women, we don't want to have to watch it on the street at night. You tell him that.'

Betty's mouth fell open as Mrs Cobbold stared defiantly at her. The doctor smiled and held open the door for her.

Robin paced the freaking kitchen.

She wouldn't let him fetch the paper. She didn't trust him not to overreact if there were any comments . . . to behave, in fact, like a man who'd been cold-shouldered by his wife, told his artwork was a piece of shit and then stitched up by the media.

She'd been awesomely and unapproachably silent most of yesterday, like she was half out of the world, sealing herself off from the awful implications of the whole nation – worse still, the whole *village* – knowing where they were coming from. Implications? Like *what* implications? A lynch mob? The stake? Their house torched? Was this the twenty-first century or, like, 1650?

Later in the day he'd actually found her sunk into a book on the seventeenth-century witch-hunts. The chapter was headed 'Suckling Demons'; it was about women accused of having sex with the Devil. But she wouldn't talk about it. He just wanted to snatch away the book and feed it to the stove.

She'd hardly moved from the kitchen for the rest of the morning, drinking strong herbal tea and smoking – Robin counted – eleven cigarettes. And still he hadn't told her the *truly* awful news, about Blackmore, because things were bad enough. He'd just spent the entire day trying to persuade her just to talk to him, which was like trying to lure a wounded vixen from her lair.

Was she blaming *him* for the truth leaking out – like he'd been down the pub handing out invitations to their next sabbat. And the journalists . . . well, how *was* he supposed to have handled them? Invite the bastards in to watch them perform the Great Rite on the hearthrug?

Some chance.

If he'd had the brains he was born with, she'd told him, her voice now inflected with hard Yorkshire – this was while they were still speaking – he'd've kept very quiet, not answered the door. There was no car there, so they could quite easily have been away from home.

What? This had made him actually start pulling at his hair. Like, how the fuck was he supposed to know it was the goddamned media at the door? Might have been insurance salesmen, the Jehovah's freaking Witnesses. How *could* he have known?

No reply. No reply either when he'd twice called George Webster and Vivvie, up in Manchester, to see if they knew anything about this damn TV show. He'd left two messages on their answering machine.

And then yesterday, after a lunch of tomato soup and stale rolls, Betty had said she needed time to think and went outside to walk alone, leaving Robin eking out the very last of the sodden pine wood. Maybe she went to the church to try and communicate with the Reverend freaking Penney. Robin wasn't interested any more. When she came back, she started moving furniture around and drinking yet more herbal tea.

Maybe there was something on her mind he didn't know about. Dare he ask? What was the damn use?

It was like she was waiting for something even worse to happen.

This was all down to Ellis. No question there. It was Ellis sicked the press on them.

Goddamn Christian bastard.

*

She came in from the post office and laid a newspaper on the kitchen table. She didn't even look at Robin. 'I'm going to change,' she said and went out. He heard her going upstairs.

The room felt cold. The colours had faded.

This was bad, wasn't it? It was going to be worse than he could have imagined, although he accepted that he maybe hadn't endeared himself to the *Mail* hacks by going for their camera like that.

He looked at the paper. At least it wasn't on the front. Nervously, he turned over the first page.

Holy shit . . .

Just the whole of page three, was all.

Down the right-hand side was a long picture of St Michael's Church, in silhouette against a sunset sky, the tower starkly framed by winter trees. It was a good picture, black and white. The headline above it, however, was just crazy: 'Witches possess parish church. "Nightmare evil in our midst," warns rector'.

'Evil?' Robin shouted. 'They really *listened* to that crazy mother-fucker?'

But it was the big picture, in colour, that made him cringe the most.

It was a grainy close-up of a snarling man, eyes burning under long, shaggy black hair. On his sweat-shiny cheeks were streaks of paint, diluted – if you wanted the truth – by bitter tears, but who was ever gonna think that? This was blue paint. It had obviously come off the cloth he'd used to wipe his eyes. In the picture, it looked like freaking woad. The guy looked like he would cut out your heart before raping your wife and slaughtering your children. Aligned with the picture, the story read:

> This is the face of the new 'priest' at an ancient village church.
>
> Robin Thorogood is a professional artist. He and his wife, Betty, are also practising witches. Now the couple have become the owners of a medieval parish church – while the local rector has to hold his services in the village hall.

'This is my worst nightmare come true,' says the Rev. Nicholas Ellis. 'It is the manifestation of a truly insidious evil in our midst.'

Now the acting Bishop of Hereford, the Rt Rev. Bernard Dunmore, is to look into the bizarre situation. 'It concerns me very deeply,' he said last night.

It is more than thirty years since the church, at Old Hindwell, Powys, was decommissioned by the Church of England. For most of that time, it stood undisturbed on the land of farming brothers John and Ifan Prosser. When the last brother, John, died two years ago it passed out of the family and was bought by the Thorogoods just before Christmas.

Robin Thorogood, who is American-born, says he and his wife represent 'the fastest-growing religion in the country.'

He claims that many of Britain's old churches were built on former pagan ritual sites – one of which, he says, he and his wife have now repossessed.

However, when invited to explain their plans for the church, Mr Thorogood became abusive and attacked *Daily Mail* photographer Stuart Joyce, screaming, 'I'll turn you into a f—ing toad.'

Now villagers say they are terrified that the couple will desecrate the ruined church by conducting pagan rites there. They say they have already seen strange lights in the ruins late at night.

The Thorogoods' nearest neighbour, local councillor Gareth Prosser, a farmer and nephew of the former owners, said, 'This has always been a God-fearing community and we will not tolerate this kind of sacrilege.

'These people sneaked in, pretending to be just an ordinary young couple.

> 'Although this is a community of old-established families, newcomers have always been welcome here as long as they respect our way of life.
>   'But we feel these people have betrayed our trust and that is utterly despicable.'

'Trust?' Robin exploded. 'What did that fat asshole ever trust us with?' Jeez, he'd hardly even spoken to the guy till a couple days ago, and then it was like Robin was some kind of vagrant.

He sat down, beating his fist on the table. It was a while before he realized the phone was ringing. By that time, Betty had come down and answered it.

When she came off the phone she was white with anger.

'Who?' Robin said.

She didn't answer.

'Please?'

She said in low voice, 'Vivvie.'

'Good of them to call back after only a day. *Did* they know anything about that programme? For all it matters.'

'She was on the programme.'

He sat up. '*What?*'

'They were both there in the studio, but only Vivienne got to talk.' Betty's voice was clipped and precise. 'It was a late-night forum about the growth of Dark Age paganism in twenty-first-century Britain. They had Wiccans and Druids, Odinists – also some Christians to generate friction. It's a friction programme.'

Robin snorted. TV was a psychic drain.

'Vivienne was one of a group of experienced, civilized Wiccans put together by Ned Bain for that programme.'

'Jesus,' Robin said, 'if she was one of the civilized ones, I sure wouldn't like to be alone with the wild children of Odin.'

And Ned Bain? Who, as well as being some kind of rich, society witch, just happened to be an editorial director at Harvey-Calder, proprietors of Talisman Books. Robin had already felt an irrational anger that Bain should have allowed Blackmore to dump a fellow pagan – although, realistically, in a big outfit like that, it was unlikely Bain had anything at all to do with the bastard.

Betty said, 'She claims she lost her cool when some woman priest became abusive.'

'She doesn't *have* any freaking cool.'

'This priest was from Hereford. Ned Bain had argued that, after 2,000 years of strife and corruption, the Christian Church was finally on the way out and Vivienne informed the Hereford priest that the erosion had already started in her own backyard, with pagans claiming back the old pagan sites, taking them back from the Church that had stolen them.'

Robin froze. 'You have *got* to be fucking kidding.'

She didn't reply.

'She . . . Jeez, that dumb bitch! She *named* us? Right there on network TV?'

'No. Some local journalist must have picked it up and tracked us down.'

'And sold us to the *Mail*.'

'The paper that supports suburban values,' Betty said.

The phone rang. Robin went for it.

'Mr Thorogood?'

'He's away,' Robin said calmly. 'He went back to the States.' He hung up. 'That the way to handle the media?'

Betty walked over and switched on the machine. 'That's a better way.'

'They'll only show up at the door.'

'Well, *I* won't be here.'

He saw that she was wearing her *ordinary person* outfit, the one with the ordinary skirt. And this time with a silk scarf around her neck. It panicked him.

'Look,' he cried, 'listen to me. I'm sorry. I'm truly sorry about that picture. I'm sorry for looking like an asshole. I just . . . I just lost it you know? I'd just had . . . I'd just taken this really bad call.'

'From your friend?' Betty said.

'Huh?'

'From your friend in the village?'

The phone rang again.

'From Al,' he said. 'Al at Talisman.'

The machine picked up.

'This is Juliet Pottinger,' the voice told the machine. *'You appear to have telephoned me over the weekend. I am now back home, if you would like to call again. Thank you.'*

'Look' – Robin waved a contemptuous hand at the paper – 'this is just . . . complete shit. Like, are we supposed to feel threatened because the freaking Bishop of Hereford finds it a matter warranting *deep concern?* Because loopy Nick Ellis sees us as symptoms of some new epidemic of an old disease? What is he, the Witchfinder freaking General, now?'

He leapt up, moved toward her.

Betty's hair was loose and tumbled. Her face was flushed. She looked more beautiful than he'd ever seen her. She always did look beautiful. And he was losing her. He'd been losing her from the moment they arrived here. He felt like his heart was swollen to the size of the room.

'We're not gonna let them take us down, are we? Betty, this is . . . this is you and me against the world, right?'

Betty detached her car keys from the hook by the door.

'Please,' Robin said. 'Please don't go.'

Betty said quietly, 'I'm not *leaving* you, Robin.'

He put his head in his hands and wept. When he took them down again, she was no longer there.

TWENTY-FIVE

Cyst

Ledwardine sat solid, firmly defined in black and white under one of those sullen, shifty skies that looked as if it might spit anything at you. Just before nine Merrily crossed the square to the Eight-till-Late to buy a *Mail*.

A spiky white head rose from the shop's freezer, its glasses misted.

'Seems funny diggin' out the ole frozen pasties again, vicar.'

They ended up, as usual, in the churchyard, where Gomer gathered all the flowers from Minnie's grave into a bin liner.

'Bloody waste. Never liked flowers at funerals. Never liked cut flowers at all. Let 'em grow, they don't 'ave long.'

'True.' She knotted the neck of the bin liner, spread the *Daily Mail* on the neighbouring tombstone and they sat on it.

'Barbara Buckingham's missing, Gomer. Didn't show up for Menna's funeral. Never got back to me, and hasn't been in touch with her daughter in Hampshire either.'

'Well,' Gomer said, 'en't like it's the first time, is it?'

'She just go off without a word when she was sixteen?'

'Been talkin' to Greta Thomas, vicar. No relation – well, her man, Danny's second cousin twice removed, whatever.'

'Small gene pool.'

'Ar. Also, Greta used to be secertry at the surgery. Dr Coll's. En't much they don't find out there. Barbara Thomas told you why her was under the doctor back then?'

'Hydatid cyst.'

Barbara had talked as though the cyst epitomized all the bad things about her upbringing in the Forest – all the meanness and the narrowness and the squalidness. So that when she had it removed, she felt she was being given the chance to make a clean new start – a Radnorectomy.

Gomer did his big grin, getting out his roll-up tin.

Merrily said, 'You're going to tell me it wasn't a hydatid cyst at all, right?'

Gomer shoved a ready-rolled ciggy between his teeth in affirmation.

'I never thought of that,' Merrily said. 'I suppose I should have. What happened to the baby?'

'Din't go all the way, vicar. Her miscarried. Whether her had any help, mind, I wouldn't know. Even Greta don't know that. But there was always one or two farmers' wives in them parts willin' to do the business. And nobody liked Merv much.'

'Hang on . . . remind me. Merv . . .?'

'Merv Thomas. Barbara's ole feller.'

'Oh God.'

Gomer nodded. 'See, Merv's wife, Glenny, her was never a well woman. Bit like Menna – delicate. Havin' babbies took it out of her. Hard birth, Menna. Hear the screams clear to Glascwm, Greta reckons. After that, Glenny, *her* says, that's it, that's me finished. Slams the ole bedroom door on Merv.'

Merrily stared up at the sandstone church tower, breathed in Gomer's smoke. She'd come out without her cigarettes.

'Well, Merv coulder gone into a particlar pub in Kington,' Gomer said. 'Even over to Hereford. Her'd have worn that, no problem, long as he din't go braggin' about it.'

'But Merv thought a man was entitled to have his needs met in his own home.'

It explained so much: why Barbara left home in a hurry, also why she had such a profound hatred of Radnor Forest. And why Menna had invaded her conscience so corrosively – to the extent, perhaps, that after she was dead, her presence was even stronger. When Menna no longer existed on the outside, in a fixed place in Radnorshire, she became a permanent nightly lodger in Barbara's subconscious.

'But the bedroom door musn't have stayed closed, Gomer.

Barbara said her father was determined to breed a son, but her mother miscarried, and then there was a hysterectomy.'

Gomer shrugged.

'But then his wife died. Hang on, this friend of yours . . .' Merrily was appalled. 'If she knew about Barbara, then she must've known what might have been happening to Menna.'

'Difference being, vicar, that Menna had protection. There was a good neighbour kept an eye on Menna, specially after her ma died. Judy Rowland. Judy Prosser now.'

Judy . . . Judith. 'Barbara said she had letters from a friend called Judith, who was looking out for Menna. That eased her conscience a little.'

'Smart woman, Judy. I reckons if Judy was lookin' out for Menna, Menna'd be all right. Her'd take on Merv, would Judy, sure to.'

'She still around?'

'Oh hell, aye. Her's wed to Gareth Prosser – councillor, magistrate, on this committee, that committee. Big man – dull bugger, mind. Lucky he's got Judy to do his thinkin' for him. Point I was gonner make, though, vicar, I reckon Judy was still lookin' out for Menna, seein' as both of 'em was living in Ole Hindwell.'

'You mean after her marriage?'

'No more'n five minutes apart, boy at the pub told me.'

'So if she also still kept in touch with Barbara, maybe Barbara went to see her, too, while she was here.'

'Dunno 'bout that, but her went to see Greta, askin' questions 'bout Dr Coll.'

Gatecrashed his surgery. Made a nuisance of myself. Not that it made any difference. Bloody man told me I was asking him to be unethical, pre-empting the post-mortem.

'What did Barbara want to know about Dr Coll?'

'Whether he was treatin' Menna 'fore she died, that kind o' stuff.'

'What's he look like, Dr Coll?'

'Oh . . . skinny little bloke. 'Bout my build, s'pose you'd say. Scrappy bit of a beard, like that political feller, Robin Cook.'

'He was at Menna's funeral. The private bit.'

'Ar, would be.'

'So where's Barbara then, Gomer? Where is Barbara Thomas?'

'I could go see Judy Prosser, mabbe. Anybody knows the score, it's her. I'll sniff around a bit more. What else I gotter do till the ole grass starts growin' up between the graves again?'

It was colder now. The mist had dropped down over the tip of the steeple. Gomer's roll-up was close to burning his lips. He took it out and squeezed the end. He looked sadly at the grave, his bag of frozen pasties on his knees and his head on one side like a dog, as if he was listening for the ticking of those two watches under the soil.

'I've got to go back there today.' She told him about Old Hindwell seemingly metamorphosed into Salem, Mass. 'You, er, don't fancy coming along?'

Gomer was on his feet. 'Just gimme three minutes to put these buggers in the fridge, vicar.'

Jane was not happy. Jane was deeply frustrated. She telephoned Eirion from the scullery.

'They've found out where that church is! The pagan church? I had *completely* forgotten about it! The one that woman was going on about on *Livenight*? I'd *forgotten* about it. Like, you apparently lose all these brain cells when you have a bump, and I just didn't *remember* that stuff, and then bits started coming back, and I knew there was something vital, but I couldn't put my fing— Anyway, it's all over one of the papers. It's somewhere just your side of the border. And she's just raced off over there . . . on account of there's this *major* scene going down.'

'Major scene?' Eirion said.

'And I'm, like, I have *got* to check this out! But would she let me go with her? Like, she's even taken Gomer with her. But not me – the person who is profoundly interested in this stuff? And, like, because of the other night there is, of course, not a thing I can do about it. She just puts on this calm, sorrowful expression and she looks me in the eyes, and she's like, "You're going to stay here, this time, aren't you, flower?" I am completely, totally, utterly *stuffed.*'

Eirion said calmly, 'So how are you now, Eirion? How's the whiplash? Is there any chance your car isn't a complete write-off?'

'Ah.' Jane sat down at the desk. 'Right. Sorry, Irene. You have to understand that self-pity is, like, my most instinctive and dominant emotion.'

'You OK?'

'Yeah, slept a lot. Still feel a bit heavy when I first get up, but no headaches or anything. No scars at all. Like I said, some things I can't remember too clearly. About that programme and stuff. But . . . yeah. Yeah, I'm OK.'

'My stepmother spoke to your mother. I've been feeling I ought to ring her, too. Do you think she'd be OK about that?'

'With you she'd be fatally charming. So *is* it a write-off?'

'Interesting you should ask about the car before asking about me.'

'I know *you're* OK. Your stepmother told Mum you were OK.'

'I might have subsequently suffered a brain haemorrhage in the night.'

'Did you?'

Eirion paused. 'Yes, it *is* a write-off. A car that old, if you break a headlamp, it's a write-off.'

'I'm sorry.'

'I loved that car. I worked all summer at a lousy supermarket for that little Nova. I should get just about enough on the insurance to replace it with a mountain bike.'

'Irene, I'm really, really sorry.' Jane felt tears coming. 'It's all my fault. Everything I touch these days I screw up. I don't suppose you want to see me ever again, but one day – I swear this on my mother's . . . altar – I'll get you another car.'

'What, you mean in fifteen years' time I'll come home one day in my Porsche and find a thirty-year-old Vauxhall Nova outside my penthouse?'

'In my scenario,' Jane said, 'you're actually trudging home to your squat.'

'Let's forget the car,' Eirion said. 'You can sleep with me or something instead.'

'OK.'

Silence.

Eirion said, 'Listen, I'm sorry. That just came out. That was a joke.'

'I said it was OK.'

'You don't understand,' Eirion said. 'I don't want it to be like that.'

'You don't want to sleep with me?'

'I mean, I don't want it to be like . . . like you shag first and then you decide if you want to know the person better. I don't want it to be like that. It never lasts. Most of the time that's where it all ends.'

'You've done a lot of this?'

'Well . . . erm, I was in a band. You get around, meet lots of people, hear lots of stories. It's just not how I want it to be with us, OK?'

'Wow. You don't mess around on the phone, do you?'

'Yeah, I'm good on the phone,' Eirion said. 'Listen . . . It's been weird. I can't stop thinking about that stuff. I've just been walking round the grounds and turning it all over and over—'

'Oh, the *grounds* . . .'

'I can't help my deprived upbringing. No, I was thinking how close we came to being like—'

'Dead?'

'Well . . . yeah, it really bloody shakes you up when you start thinking about it.'

'Brings your life into hard focus. Unless you've had concussion, when it seems to do the opposite most of the time.'

'I started thinking about your mum, what that would've done to her, with both her husband and her daughter – and it doesn't matter what kind of shit he was, he was still her husband and your dad – like, both her husband and her daughter wiped out on the same bit of road. And maybe her, too, if she hadn't stopped in time – these pile-ups can just go on and on in a fog. And . . . I don't know what I'm trying to say, Jane . . .'

'I do. It was like when I said to you in the car – I remember this because it was just before it happened. I said, do you never lie in bed and think about where we are and how we relate to the big picture?'

'I just don't lie in bed and think about it, I tramp around the grounds and the hills and think about it.'

'That's cool,' Jane said.

'And I was thinking how, when we were talking to Gerry earlier . . . you remember Gerry, the researcher?'

'Gerry and . . . Maurice?'

'That's right. You remember Gerry saying, before the show started, that he wouldn't be surprised if one of them – one of the pagans in the studio – tried some spooky stuff, just to show they could make things happen?'

'He said that?'

'He said *spooky* stuff. And I said, "What? What would they do?" And Gerry said a spell or something, just to prove they could make things happen. It was just after he was going on about your mum, and how your dad was killed and maybe she felt guilty—'

'Oh *yeah* – the bastard.'

'And you jumped down his—'

'Sure. I mean, where *did* he get that stuff?'

'He got it from that guy Ned Bain.'

'Ned . . .? Oh, the really cool—'

'The smooth-talking git,' Eirion said. 'But that whole thing was getting to me. Because they *didn't* do anything, did they? There was no spell, no mumbo-jumbo, no pyrotechnics; they were all actually quite well behaved. But somehow Gerry had got it into his head that they were going to pull some stunt. So, anyway, I rang him this morning. You know . . . how I'm that bloke who wants to be a TV journalist? So I'm writing a piece on my adventures in the *Livenight* gallery for the school magazine . . .'

'You're not!'

'Of course I'm not. It's just what I told Gerry to get him talking. I told him I was explaining in my piece how the programme researchers get their information, and there were things I didn't have a chance to ask him there on the night.'

'And where *do* they get it?'

'Cuttings files, obviously. But they also talk to the guests beforehand. Like this Tania talked to your mum . . . and Gerry talked to Ned Bain and a few others. But Gerry reckoned it was Bain had provided all this detailed background on the Church of England's first woman diocesan exorcist.'

'Gerry just told you that?'

'It took a bit of digging, actually, Jane. After which Gerry said how he thought I had a future in his profession; said to give him a call when I get through college.'

'Wow, big time.'

'Sod off.'

'So he was genned up on Mum? Like *know thine enemy*?

'But is that sort of stuff about your dad going to be readily available from the *Hereford Times* or something.'

'She won't do interviews about herself.'

'So where did he get it?'

'It's no big secret, Irene. Maybe it's all floating around on the Internet.'

'Exactly. I'm going to check it out, I think.'

'Who told Gerry they were going to pull a stunt? That from Ned Bain too?'

'Gerry claimed he'd never said that. He said I must've misunderstood. But he bloody *did* say it, Jane. He just didn't want it going in a school magazine that they were happy for stuff like that to happen on a live programme.'

'Stuff like what?'

'I don't know, it just—'

'I mean, OK, let's spell it out, bottom line. Are you suggesting the evil Ned Bain and his satanic cronies did some kind of black magic resulting in a fog pile-up which caused the deaths of several people? Is that what you're saying?'

'Not exactly that . . .'

'What are you, some kind of fundamentalist Welsh Chapel bigot?'

'Unfair, Jane.'

'So what *are* you suggesting?'

'I don't know, I just . . . I mean no, it would be ridiculous to suggest that those tossers in fancy dress could do anything like that, even if they *were* evil, and I don't think they are. Not evil, just totally irresponsible. They're like, "Oh, can we work hand in hand with nature to make *good* things happen and save the Earth?" How the fuck can *they* know that what they're going to make happen is going to be *good* necessarily?'

'You sound like Mum.'

'Well, maybe she's right.'

'Don't meddle with anything metaphysical? Throw yourself on God's mercy?'

'Unless you know what you're doing, maybe yes. And they don't, they *can't* know what they're doing. How can they, Jane?'

'It never occurred to you that by working on yourself for, like, years and years and studying and meditating, you can achieve wisdom and enlightenment?'

'But most of those people haven't, have they? It's just, "Oh, let's light a fire and take all our clothes off . . ."'

'That is a totally simplistic *News of the World* viewpoint.' Jane's head was suddenly full of a dark and fuzzy resentment. 'You haven't the faintest idea . . .'

'At least I'm not naive about it.'

'So I'm *naive*?'

'I didn't say that.'

There was a moment of true, sickening enlightenment. 'You've been talking to her, haven't you?'

'Who?'

'My esteemed parent, the Reverend Watkins. She didn't just speak to your stepmother on the phone, she spoke to you as well, didn't she?'

'No. Well only at the hospital. I mean you were *there* some of time.'

'*That's* why there's been no big row. Why she hasn't asked me what the hell I was doing on the M5 at midnight. Why she's so laid-back about it.'

'Look, Jane, I'm not saying Gwennan didn't also fill her in on some of the details, but I've never even—'

'I've been really, really stupid, haven't I? It really *must* have destroyed some of my brain cells. While I'm sleeping it off, you're all having a good chat. *You* told her how I'd rigged the whole trip, making you think she knew all about us going. Then she's like, "Oh, you have to understand Jane found it hard coming to terms with me being a priest, has to go her own way." This cosy vicar-to-cathedral-school-choirboy tête-à-tête. Gosh, what are we going to *do* about that girl?'

'Jane, that is totally . . .'

'And you're like, "Oh, I'm trying to understand her too, Mrs Watkins. If you think I'm just one of those reprehensible youths who only want to get inside her pants, let me assure you—"'

'For Christ's sake, Jane . . .'

'That is just *so* demeaning.'

'It would be if it—'

'You are fucking well dead in the water, Lewis.'

'J—'

Demonstration of Faith

Merrily pulled the old Volvo up against the hedge.

'I'm sure *that* wasn't there on Saturday.'

A cross standing in a garden.

'Mabbe not,' Gomer said.

It wasn't any big deal, no more than the kind of rustic pole available from garden centres everywhere, with a section of another pole nailed on as a horizontal. It had been sunk into a flowerbed behind a picket fence in the garden of a neat, roadside bungalow about half a mile out of Walton, on the road leading to Old Hindwell. There were three other bungalows but this was the only one with a cross. Although it was no more than five feet high, there was a white light behind it, leaking through a rip in the clouds, and the fact that it was out of context made you suddenly and breathlessly aware of what a powerful symbol this was.

The bungalow looked empty, no smoke from the chimney. Merrily drove on. 'You know who lives there?'

'Retired folk from Off, I reckon.'

'Mmm.' Retired incomers were always useful for topping up your congregation. If the affable local minister turned up to welcome them, just when they were wondering if they were going to be happy here among strangers, they would feel obliged to return the favour, even if it was only for the next few Sundays. But if the friendly minister was the Reverend Nicholas Ellis, drifting away after a month or so could be more complicated.

This was what Bernie Dunmore had been afraid of. She'd received a briefing on the phone from Sophie before they left.

'Apparently there was something of a record turn-out at the village hall yesterday. The bishop understands that a number of people were out delivering printed circulars last night, and bulletins were posted on Christian websites, warning of pagan infestation. Today there's to be what's been described as "a Demonstration of Faith", which the bishop finds more than a little ominous.'

'I wonder what he said to them in his sermon. You know any regular churchgoers in the village, Gomer?'

'We'll find somebody for you, vicar, no problem.'

'The bishop's in conference all day . . .'

Unsurprisingly.

' . . . but what he wants you to do initially, Merrily, is to offer advice and support to the Reverend Mr Ellis. By which I understand him to mean restraint.'

What was she supposed to do exactly? Put him under clerical arrest?

But if Merrily felt a seeping trepidation about this exercise, it clearly wasn't shared by Gomer, who was hunched eagerly forward in the passenger seat, chewing on an unlit ciggy, his white hair on end like a mat of antennae. Describing him to someone once, Jane had said: 'You need to start by imagining Bart Simpson as an old man.'

The lane dipped, darkening, into a channel between lines of forestry. The old rectory appeared on the left, in its clearing. Merrily kept her eyes on the narrowing road. How would she have reacted if she'd turned then and seen a pale movement in a window? She gripped the wheel, forestalling a shudder.

'Not a soul, vicar,' Gomer observed ambivalently.

'Right.' Her voice was huskier than she would have liked. The towering conifers were oppressive. 'This must be the only part of Britain where you plunge into the trees when you *leave* the Forest.'

'Ar, we all growed up never thinkin' a forest had much to do with trees.'

Merrily slowed at the mud-flecked Old Hindwell sign. A grey poster with white lettering had been attached to its stem.

'Christ is the Light!'

That hadn't been there on Saturday either. She accelerated for the hill up to the village. Halfway up, to the right, the tower of the old church suddenly filled a gap in the horizon of pines. It was like a grey figure standing there.

The manifestation of a truly insidious evil in our midst.

A seriously inflammatory thing to say – Ellis playing it for all it was worth.

She'd read the *Daily Mail* story twice. Robin Thorogood sounded typical of the type of pagan recruited for *Livenight*. Primarily political, and an anarchist – what they used to call in Liverpool a tear-arse – but not necessarily insidiously evil. She wondered what his wife was like; no picture of her in the paper.

Sophie had said, *'The bishop would like you to point out to whoever it might concern that, while this might have previously been a church, it is also now this couple's private property, and they do not appear to be breaking any laws – which the Reverend Ellis and his followers might well be doing if any of them sets foot inside it.'*

Merrily slowed to a crawl at the side road to the church and farm. This was where you might have expected to find a lychgate. There was a small parking area, and then an ordinary, barred farm gate. She saw that, while St Michael's Church had never been exactly in a central position, trees and bushes had been allowed to grow around what was presumably the churchyard, hedging it off from the village. Somewhere in there, also, was the brook providing another natural barrier.

They moved on up the hill. 'I wouldn't mind taking a look at that place without drawing attention. Would that be possible, Gomer?'

'Sure t'be. There's a bit of an ole footpath following the brook from the other side. They opened him up a bit for the harchaeologists last summer, so we oughter be able to park a good way in.'

'You know everything, don't you?'

'Ah, well, reason I knows this, vicar, is my nephew, Nev, he got brought in to shovel a few tons o' soil and clay back when the harchaeologists was finished. I give Nev a bell last night. Good money, he reckoned, but a lot o' waitin' around. Bugger me, vicar, look at *that . . .'*

Merrily braked. There was a cottage on the right, almost on the road. It had small windows, lace-curtained, but in one of the downstairs ones the curtains had been pushed back and a candle was alight. Although the forestry was thinning, it was dark enough here for the flame to be visible from quite a distance. Power cut?

Not exactly. The candle was fixed on a pewter tray, which itself sat on a thick, black book, almost certainly a Bible. *Christ is the Light.*

'Annie Smith lives there,' Gomer said. 'She's a widow. Percy Smith, he had a little timber business, died ten year ago. Their boy, Mansel, he took it over but he en't doin' too well. Deals mostly in firewood now, for wood-burners and such.'

Merrily stopped the car just past the cottage. 'She overtly religious, this Annie Smith?'

'Never made a thing of it, if she is. But local people sticks together on things, see. Gareth Prosser goes along with the rector, say, then the rest of 'em en't gonner go the other way. It's a border thing: when the Welsh was fightin' the English, the border folk'd be on the fence till they figured out which side was gonner be first to knock the ole fence down, see. And that was the side they'd jump down on. But they'd all jump together, see.'

'Border logic.'

'Don't matter they hates each other's guts the rest o' the time, they jumps together. All about survival, vicar.'

'And *does* Gareth Prosser go along with the rector?'

'They d'say he's got one o' them Christ stickers in the back of his Land Rover.'

'What does that mean, then?'

'Means he's got a sticker,' said Gomer.

Before they reached the village centre, they'd passed five homes with candles burning in their windows, and two of them with Bibles stood on end, gilt crosses facing outwards. A fat church candle gleamed greasily in the window of the post office. Merrily, usually at home with Bibles and candles, found this uncanny. *'We don't do this kind of thing any more.'*

'It's medieval, Gomer. One couple. One pagan couple – OK,

young, confrontational, but still just one couple. Then it's like there's a contagious disease about, and you put a candle in the window if it's safe to go inside. Is this village . . . I mean, is it normally . . . normal?'

'Just a village like any other yereabouts.' He pondered a moment. 'No, that en't right. Ole Hindwell was always a bit set apart. Not part o' the Valley, not quite in the Forest. Seen better times – used to 'ave a little school an' a blacksmith. Same as there used t'be a church, ennit? But villages around yere, they grows and wanes. I never seen it as not normal.'

A big, white-haired man was walking up the hill, carrying something on his shoulder.

'They d'say he does a bit o' healin',' Gomer said.

'Ellis? Laying on of hands at the end of the services?'

At the Big Bible Fest in Warwickshire, the spiritual energy generated by power prayer and singing in tongues would often be channelled into healing, members of the congregations stepping up with various ailments and chronic conditions and often claiming remarkable relief afterwards. It was this aspect Merrily had most wanted to believe in, but she suspected that, when the euphoria faded, the pain would usually return and she hated to hear people who failed to make it out of their wheelchairs being told that their faith was not strong enough.

'They reckons he does a bit o' house-to-house. And it en't just normal sickness either.'

'Know any specific cases?' A snatch of conversation came back to her from Minnie's funeral tea at Ledwardine village hall. *Boy gets picked up by the police, with a pocketful o' these bloody ecstersee. Up in court . . . Dennis says, "That's it, boy, you stay under my roof you can change your bloody ways. We're gonner go an' see the bloody rector . . ."'*

When the big man stepped into the middle of the road and swung round, the item on his shoulder was revealed to be a large grey video camera. He took a step back, to take in the empty, sloping street, where the only movement was the flickering of the candles. He stood with his legs apart, recording the silent scene – looking like the sheriff in a western in the seconds before doors flew open and figures appeared, shooting.

No doors opened. Clouds hung low and heavy; there was little
light left in the sky; the weather was cooperating with the candles.
The cameraman shot the scene at leisure.

'TV news,' Merrily said. 'There'll be a reporter around somewhere, too. I'm supposed to make myself known to them.'

Gomer nodded towards the cameraman. 'Least that tells you why
there's no bugger about. Nobody yere's gonner wanner explain on
telly about them candles.'

Even if they could, Merrily thought.

'What you wanner do, vicar?'

'It's not what I *want* to do,' Merrily said, 'but I do have to talk
to the Reverend Nick Ellis. He lives on the estate. Would that be . . .?'

Past the pub, about a hundred yards out of the village centre,
were eight semi-detached houses on the same side of the road.

'That's the estate.' Gomer pointed, as they approached.

Merrily parked in front of the first house. Though these were
once council houses, fancy gates, double glazing and new front doors
showed that most of them had been purchased.

They all had candles in the windows.

Only one house, fairly central, kept its maroon, standard-issue
front door and flaking metal gates. It was the only one still looking
like a council house. Except for the cross on the door: wood, painted
gold, and nailed on.

There was a large jeep crowding the brief drive. A sticker over a
nameplate on the gate announced that Christ was the Light. In the
single downstairs window, two beeswax candles burned, in trays, on
Bibles.

Merrily had heard that Ellis was living in a council house because,
when he'd given up his churches, he'd also given up his rectory. The
Church paid the rent on this modest new manse. A small price to
pay per head of congregation, and it wouldn't do Ellis's image any
harm at all, and he would know that.

She felt a pulse of fury. From singing in tongues to erecting a
wall of silence, this man had turned a whole community, dozens
maybe hundreds of people, against a couple who hadn't yet been
here long enough for anyone really to know them. The Thorogoods
would need to be very hard-faced to survive it.

TWENTY-SEVEN

Spirit of Salem

'This is no coincidence,' George said on the phone. 'This is fate. We all know what tomorrow is.'

'Probably the last day of my freaking marriage.'

'You have to go with it, Robin. We can turn this round. We can make it a triumph.'

Robin wanted to scream that he couldn't give a shit about Imbolc; he just wanted things to come right again with his wife, some work to bring in some money, his religious beliefs no longer to be national news. He just wanted to become a boring, obscure person.

In the background, the old fax machine huffed and whizzed. He watched the paper emerge.

Thou shalt not suffer a witch to live

Poison faxes? Creepy Bible quotes? Someone had unleashed the Christian propaganda machine. The spirit of Salem living on.

'It's all our fault, man,' George said.

'Not your fault. Vivvie's fault.'

'I share the blame. I was there too. I also now share the responsibility for getting you and Betty through this.'

'We could maybe get through this, George, if people would just leave us the fuck alone.'

He wasn't so sure about that, though, the way Betty was behaving.

By 9 a.m. the answering machine had taken calls from BBC Wales,

238

Radio Hereford and Worcester, HTV, Central News, BBC Midlands and 5 Live. And from some flat-voiced kid who said he was a pagan too and would like to pledge his support and his magic.

Already they were starting to come to the front door. By 11 a.m., there'd been four people knocking. He hadn't answered. Instead he'd closed the curtains and sat in the dimness, hugging the Rayburn. He'd listened to the answering machine, intercepting just this one call from George.

The whole damn story was truly out; it had been on all the radio stations and breakfast TV. Was also out on the World Wide Web, with emails of support – according to George – coming from Native Americans in Canada and pagans as far away as India. George claimed that already this confrontation was being seen as a rallying flashpoint for ethnic worshippers of all persuasions. Strength and courage were being transmitted to them from all over the world.

'We don't want it,' Robin told George. 'We came here for a *quiet* life. Pretty soon I'm gonna take the phone off the hook and unplug the fax.'

'In that case,' George said, 'surely it's better that the people you know—'

'You mean people *you* know. Listen, George, just hold off, can you do that? I would need to talk to Betty.'

'When's she going to be back?'

'I don't *know* when she's gonna be back. She's mad at me. She thinks I screwed up with the *Mail* guys. *I* think I screwed up with the *Mail* guys. *I'm* mad at me.'

'You need support, man. And there's a lot of Craft brothers and Craft sisters who want to give you some. I tell you, there's an unbelievable amount of strong feeling about this. It'll be very much a question of *stopping* people coming out there.'

'Well you fucking *better* stop them.'

'Plus, the opposition, of course,' George said. 'We don't know how many they are or where they're coming from.'

Robin peered round the edge of the curtain at the puddles in the farmyard and along the side of the barn. It looked bleak, it looked desolate. In spite of all the courage and strength being beamed at them, it looked lonely as hell. Sure he felt vulnerable; how could he not?

When he sighed, it came out rough, with a tremor underneath it. 'How many were you thinking?'

'Well, we need a coven,' George had said. 'I'll find eleven good people which, with you and Betty makes . . . the right number. We could be there by nightfall. Don't worry about accommodation, we'll have at least two camper vans. We'll bring food and wine and every-thing we need to deck out the church for Imbolc. Be the greatest Imbolc ever, Robin. We'll set the place alight.'

'I dunno. I dunno what to do.' For George this was cool, this was exciting. If you'd put it to Robin, even just a few days ago, he'd have said yeah, wow, great. It was what he'd envisaged from the start: the repaganized church becoming a centre of the old religion at the heart of a prehistoric ritual landscape. *The idyll.*

But this was not Betty's vision any more – if it ever had been.

'Leave it with me, yeah?' George said. 'Blessed be, man.'

'I'm quite psychic, you know.' Juliet Pottinger had what Betty regarded as a posh Lowland Scottish accent. 'I was about to go into town, and then I thought, no, if I go out now I shall miss something interesting.'

Which was a better opening than Betty could have hoped for.

Lower Lodge was an extended Georgian cottage on the edge of a minor road about two miles out of Leominster and a good twenty-five miles east of Old Hindwell. Once away from Old Hindwell, Betty's head had seemed to clear. The day was dull but dry, the temperature no worse than you could expect in late January. Out here, she felt lighter, less scared, less oppressed.

Mrs Pottinger's house was full of books. Six bookcases in the hall, with two piles of books beside one of them, propped up by an umbrella stand. In the long kitchen, where she made Betty tea, the demands of reading and research seemed to have long since overtaken the need for food preparation. Books and box-files were wedged between pans on the shelves and under cups and plates on the dresser. The only visible cooker was a microwave, and an old Amstrad word processor with a daisywheel printer took up half the kitchen table. There was – small blessing – no sign of a *Daily Mail*.

Juliet Pottinger was about sixty-five, with a heavy body, layered in cardigans, and what you could only call wide hair. Her seat was a typist's chair, which creaked when she moved. She was working, she said, on a definitive history of the mid-border.

'I'm sorry I didn't phone first,' Betty said. 'I just happened to be . . . passing.'

'But you live at Old Hindwell, you say?'

'At St Michael's.'

'Oh,' said Mrs Pottinger. 'Oh . . .'

It meant Betty didn't have to spend too long explaining her interest in the church, and no need to make reference either to her religion or the ruined building's palpable residue of pain.

'The widow sold it, then?' said Mrs Pottinger. 'Thought she would. It was in the *Hereford Times* about Major Wilshire . . . old regiment man. The SAS. He wrote to me – as you know, of course.'

'Mrs Wilshire passed over to me some documents relating to the house and the church, and your letter was one of them. That's how we learned about Mr Penney.'

'Oh, I feel such a terrible wimp about that, Mrs Thorogood. I wanted to write up the whole story, but I doubt the *Brecon and Radnor* would have printed it, for legal reasons. Also, I ramble so, become over-absorbed in detail – always been more of a historian than a journalist. And, of course, the local people were against *anything* coming out.'

'Why do you think that was?'

'In case it reflected poorly on them, I suppose. In case it drew attention to *their* affairs. Gareth Prosser the elder was the councillor then, upholding the family's local government tradition of conserving the community in whatever ways are most expedient and saying as little as possible about it in open council. My brief, as local correspondent for the paper, was to report nothing that everyone didn't already know. Except, of course, in the case of poor Terry, when I was instructed *not* to report what everyone already knew. Oh dear, it really has not been a happy place, I'm afraid.'

'You felt that?'

'I always knew that. However, I don't want to depress you. You do, after all have to . . .'

'Live with it? That's why I need to know about its true history. It oppresses me otherwise.'

'Does it?' Mrs Pottinger's eyes became, in an instant, shrewdly bird-like.

'Yes, it . . . I . . .' Betty's banging heart was confirming that it was too late for subterfuge. 'I'm, I suppose you'd say, sensitive to atmosphere – acutely sensitive.'

'*Are* you indeed?'

'The first time I saw that ruined church, I had a very negative reaction, which I kept to myself because my husband loved it . . . was enraptured. For some time I kept trying to tell myself we could, you know, do something about it.'

'You mean feng shui or something?'

'Or something,' Betty said carefully. 'The place upsets me. It unbalances me in ways I can't handle. After we moved in, that became stronger, until I could feel it almost through the walls of the farmhouse. I hope I don't sound like an idiot to you, Mrs Pottinger.'

She was amazed at what she'd just said – all the things she hadn't been able to say to Robin. Mrs Pottinger did not smile. She pulled off her half-glasses and thought for a few moments, tapping one of the arms on a corner of the Amstrad.

'While we were living in Old Hindwell,' she said at last, 'we acquired for ourselves a dog. It was a cocker spaniel we called Hopkins. My husband would take him for walks morning and evening. By using the footpath which follows the brook past the church, it was possible almost to circumnavigate the village. Have you walked that particular path yet?'

'I haven't, but I think my husband has.'

'It's a round trip of about a mile and a half, a perfect evening walk. But would Hopkins follow it? He would *not*. Within about twenty yards of the church – approaching from either direction – that dog would be off! Disappeared for a whole night once. Well, after this had happened two or three times, Pottinger tried putting him on a lead. But when they reached some invisible barrier – as I say, about twenty yards from the church, where the yew trees began –

242

Hopkins would start tugging in the opposite direction with such force that he almost strangled himself. Pottinger used to say he was afraid the poor creature would choke himself to death rather than continue along that path.'

Mrs Pottinger replaced her glasses.

'As you can imagine, that's another story I didn't write for the *Brecon and Radnor Express*.'

Betty found the story chilling, but not surprising. The only time she'd ever seen anyone on that path was the night the witch box was delivered.

'Did you try to find out what might have scared your dog?'

'Naturally, I did. I was fascinated, so I went to visit Terry.'

Betty registered that Penney was the only male – not even her own husband – whom Mrs Pottinger had referred to by his first name.

'It was the first time I'd actually been up to the rectory, as he never seemed to invite people there. Normally I'd collect his notes and notices for the *B and R* at the church, on Sundays after morning service. The rectory was far too large for a bachelor, of course – or even for a married clergyman with fewer than four children. One can understand why the Church is now shedding so many of its properties, but in those days it was still expected that the minister should have a substantial dwelling. Terry, however, was . . . well, it was quite bizarre . . .'

Betty remembered how Mrs Pottinger's letter to Major Wilshire had ended, with the suggestion that Old Hindwell existed for her now as little more than a 'surreal memory'.

'His appearance, I suppose, was becoming quite hippyish – although this was the mid-60s, when that term was not yet in circulation. He'd seemed quite normal when he first arrived in the village. But after a time it began to be noticed that he was allowing his hair to grow and perhaps not shaving as often as he might. And when I arrived at the rectory that day – it was about this time of year, perhaps a little later – Terry showed me into a reception room so cold and sparsely furnished that it was clear to me that it could not possibly be in general use. I remember I put my hand on the seat of an old armchair and it was actually damp! "Good God, Terry," I said, "we can't possibly talk in *here*." I don't know about you, Mrs Thorogood, but I can't even *think* in the cold.'

Betty smiled. The book-stuffed kitchen was stiflingly warm.

'And so, with great reluctance, Terry took me into his living room. And when I say *living* room . . . it contained not only his chair and his writing desk, but also his bed, which was just a sleeping bag! He told me he was repainting his bedroom, but I wasn't fooled. This single room was Terry's home. He was camping in this one room, like in a bedsitter, and, apart from the kitchen, the rest of the rectory was closed off. I doubt he even used a bathroom. Washed himself at the sink instead, I'd guess – when he even remembered to. Not terribly . . . Is there something the matter, Mrs Thorogood?'

Betty shook her head. 'Please go on.'

'Well, he'd chosen this room, I guessed, because of the built-in bookshelves. He might not have had much furniture or many private possessions, but he had a good many books. I always examine people's bookshelves, and Terry's books included a great deal of theology, as one would expect, but also an element of what might be termed the *esoteric*. Do you know the kind of thing I mean?'

'The occult?'

'That word, of course, merely means hidden. There was certainly a *hidden* side to Terry. He was perfectly affable, kind to the old people, good with children. But his sermons . . . I suppose they must have been beyond most of the congregation, including me occasionally. They were sometimes close to meditations, I suppose – as though he was still working out for himself the significance of a particular biblical text. When I told him about our dog Hopkins, he didn't seem in the least surprised. He asked me how much I knew about the history of the area. At that time not a great deal, I admit. He asked me, particularly, if I knew of any legends about dragons.'

Betty cleared her throat. 'Dragons.'

'In the Radnor Forest.'

'And did you?'

'No. There's very little recorded folklore relating specifically to Radnor Forest. The only mention I could find was from . . . Hold on a moment.'

Mrs Pottinger jumped up, her hair rising like wings, an outstretched finger moving vaguely like a compass needle. 'Ah!' She crossed the room and plucked a green-covered book from the row supported by tall kitchen weights on a window ledge. 'You *are* enlivening my morning no end, Mrs Thorogood. So few people nowadays want to discuss such matters, especially with a garrulous old woman.'

She laid the book in front of Betty. It was called *A Welsh Country Parson*, by D. Parry-Jones. It fell open at a much-thumbed page.

'Parry-Jones records here, if you can see, that a dragon had dwelt "deep in the fastnesses" of the Forest. And he records – this would be back in the 1920s or '30s – a conversation with an old man who insisted he had heard the dragon *breathing*. All rather sketchy, I'm afraid, and somewhat fanciful. Anyway, it soon became clear to the people he was involved with on a day-to-day basis that Terry was becoming quite *obsessed*.'

Betty looked up from the book, shaken.

'As a symbol of evil,' Mrs Pottinger said, 'a satanic symbol, the dragon from the Book of Revelations represents *the old enemy*. My impression was that Terry thought he was in some way being tested by God – by being sent to Old Hindwell, where the dragon was at the door. That God had a mission for him here. Well, English people who come to Wales sometimes do pick up rather strange ideas.'

Mrs Pottinger put on a rather superior smile, as though Scots were immune to such overreaction. Ignoring this, Betty said, 'Did he believe there were so-called satanic influences at work in the Forest? I mean, is there a history of this . . . of witchcraft, say?'

'If there was, not much is recorded. No famous witchcraft trials on either side of the border in this area. But, of course' – a thin, sly smile – 'that doesn't mean it didn't go on. Quite the reverse, one would imagine. It may have been so much a part of everyday life, something buried so deep in the rural psyche, that rooting it out might have been deemed . . . impractical.'

'What about Cascob?'

'Cascob? Oh, the charm.' Mrs Pottinger beamed. 'That is rather a wonderful mixture, isn't it? Do you know some of those phrases are thought to have been taken from the writings of John Dee, the Elizabethan magus, who was born not far away, near Pilleth?'

'Do you know anything about the woman, Elizabeth Loyd?'

'Some poor child.'

'Could *she* have been a witch? I mean, the wording of the exorcism suggests she was thought to be possessed by satanic evil. Suspected witches around that time were often thought to have .. relations with the Devil.'

. . . some women are known to have boasted of it, Betty had read yesterday. 'The Devil's member was described as being long and narrow and cold as ice . . .'

'Nothing is known of her,' Mrs Pottinger said, 'or where her exorcism took place, or who conducted it. The historian Francis Payne suggests that the charm was probably *buried* to gain extra potency for the invocation.'

'Buried?'

'It was apparently dug up in the churchyard.'

Betty sat very still and nodded and tried to smile, and felt again the weight of a certain section of Cascob's circular churchyard, and the chill inside the building.

'Mrs Pottinger,' she said quickly, 'what finally happened to Terry Penney?'

'Well, he'd virtually destroyed his own church – an unpardonable sin. He had effectively resigned. He'd already left the village before the crime was even discovered, taking with him his roomful of possessions in that old van he drove.'

'You suggested in your letter to Major Wilshire that there'd been previous acts of vandalism.'

'Did I? Yes, minor things. A small fire in a shed outside, spotted and dealt with by a churchwarden. Other petty incidents, too, as though he was building up to the main event.'

'Where did he go after he left?'

'No one knows, or much cared at the time. Except, perhaps, for me, for a while. But the Church was very quickly compensated for the damage done, so perhaps Terry had more money than it appeared. Perhaps his frugal lifestyle was a form of asceticism, a monkish thing. Anyway, he just went away – after setting in train the process which ultimately led to the decommissioning of Old Hindwell Church. And the village then erased him from its collective – and wonderfully selective – memory.'

'You really didn't like the place much, did you?' Betty said bluntly.

'You may take it that I did not feel particularly grateful to some of the inhabitants. We left in '83. My husband had been unwell, so we thought we ought to live nearer to various amenities. That was what we told people, at least. And that's . . .' Mrs Pottinger's voice became faint. 'That's what I've been telling people ever since.'

She sat back in her typing chair, blinked at Betty, then stared widely, as if she was waking up to something.

Betty returned the stare.

'You're really rather an extraordinary young woman, aren't you?' Mrs Pottinger said in surprise, as though she'd ceased many years ago to find young people in any way interesting. 'I wonder why it is that I feel compelled to tell you the truth.'

'The truth?'

'Tell me,' Mrs Pottinger said, 'who's your doctor?'

TWENTY-EIGHT

A Humble Vessel

There was no doorbell, so she knocked twice, three times. She was about to give up when he answered the door.

'Ah,' he said, 'Reverend Watkins.' Registering her only briefly before bending over the threshold, apparently to inspect the candles in the neighbouring windows. 'Good.'

Meaning the candles, she guessed.

'I'm sorry to bother you, Mr Ellis . . .'

'They told me you'd be dropping in.' He shrugged. 'I accept that.'

'I feel a bit awkward . . .'

'Yes,' he said, 'you must do. Do you want to come in?'

She followed him through a shoebox hall which smelled of curry, into a small, square living room which had been turned into an office. There was a steel-framed desk, two matching chairs. A computer displayed red and green standby lights on a separate desk, and there was a portable TV set on a stand with a video recorder underneath.

'The war room,' Nicholas Ellis said with no smile.

His accent sounded far more transatlantic than it had during Menna's funeral service. He wore a light grey clerical shirt, with pectoral cross, and creased grey chinos. His long hair was loosely tied back with a black ribbon. His face was wind-reddened but without lines, like a mannequin in an old-fashioned tailor's shop.

He waved her vaguely to one of the metal chairs.

'Not much time, I'm afraid. I'll help you all I can, but I really don't have much time today, as you can imagine. Events kind of caught up on me.'

When he sat down behind his desk, Merrily became aware of the aluminium-framed picture on the wall behind him, over the boarded-up fireplace. It was William Blake's *The Great Red Dragon and the Woman Clothed with the Sun*. Sexually charged, awesomely repulsive. Ellis noticed her looking at it.

'Revoltingly explicit, isn't it – shining with evil? I live with it so that when they look in my window they will know I'm not afraid.'

They? The war room?

Merrily sat down, kept her coat on.

'So . . .' he said, as if he was trying hard to summon some interest. 'You are the, uh . . . I'm sorry, I did write it down.'

'Diocesan Deliverance Consultant.'

It had never sounded more ludicrous.

'And the suffragan Bishop of Ludlow has sent you to *support* me. Well, here I am' – he opened his arms – 'a humble vessel for the Holy Spirit. Have you ever truly experienced the Holy Spirit, Merrily?'

'In my way.'

'No, in other words,' he said. 'It doesn't happen in *your* way, it happens in *His* way.'

'Damn,' Merrily said, prickling. 'You're right.'

He looked at her with half a smile on his wide lips. 'Diocesan . . . Deliverance . . . Consultant. I guess you're like one of those young female MPs . . . what did they call them . . . Blair's Babes? I suppose it was only a matter of time before we had them in the Church.'

'Like woodworm.'

He didn't reply. He'd lost the half-smile.

'Meaning I look vaguely presentable,' Merrily said, 'even though I must know bugger all.'

'And you feel you *must* throw in the odd swear word to show that the clergy doesn't have to be stuffy and pious any more.'

'Gosh,' Merrily said, 'it doesn't take you long to get the measure of a person, does it?'

Ellis smiled at last. 'My, we really aren't getting along, are we? You aren't going to want to "support" me at all, are you? Well, other priests tend not to, as I'm a fundamentalist. That's what the Anglican

Church calls someone who truly believes in the living God.' He leaned back. 'I'm sorry. Let's start again. How do you propose to support me?'

'How would you like to be supported?'

'By being left alone, I guess.'

'That's what I guessed you'd say.'

'Aren't you clever?'

He was looking not at her, but through her, as though she was, for him, without substance – or at least insufficiently textured to engage his attention. It made her annoyed, but then it was designed to.

She pressed on, 'Um . . . you said "war room".'

'Yes.'

'And, obviously, quite a few people here seem to agree with you on that.'

'Yes.'

'And it all *looks* quite dramatic and everything.'

'You make it sound like a facade. It's an initial demonstration of faith in the Lord. It will spread. You'll see twice as many candles on your way out.'

'Isn't it a bit . . . premature to call this a war zone? One story in a newspaper? Two amateur witches in a redundant church? Unless . . .'

He gave her just a little more attention. 'Unless?'

'Unless this goes back rather further than this morning's *Daily Mail*.'

'It goes back well over 2,000 years, Merrily. "The satyr shall cry to his fellow. Yea, there shall the night hag alight, and find for herself a resting place."'

'Isaiah.' Merrily remembered the taunts of the industrial chaplain, the Rev. Gemmell, in the *Livenight* studio, inviting her to stand up and denounce Ned Bain as an agent of Satan in front of seven million viewers. 'Meaning that, whether they accept it or not, all followers of pagan gods are actually making a bed for the Devil.'

'In this case,' Ellis said, 'to reflect the imagery of the Radnor Forest, a nest for the dragon.'

'Because the former church here is dedicated to St Michael?' Merrily glanced up at the Blake print, in which the obscene and dominant dragon, viewed from behind, was curly-horned and not really red but the colour of an earthworm. It was hard not to believe that William Blake himself must have seen one.

'One of five churches positioned around Radnor Forest and charged with the energy of heaven's most potent weapon. Cefnllys, Cascob, Llanfihangel nant Melan, Llanfihangel Rhydithon, Old Hindwell.'

'The Forest is supposed to be a nest for the dragon? Is that a legend?'

'No legend is *simply* a legend,' Ellis said. 'We have the evidence of the five churches dedicated to the warrior angel. If one should fall, it creates a doorway for Satan. You see merely two misguided idiots, I see the beginnings of a disease which, unless eradicated at source, will spread until all Christendom is a mass of suppurating sores. This is what the Devil wants. Will you deny that?'

'Hold on . . . You say there's a legend that if one of the churches falls, etcetera . . . Yet you're not interested in preserving churches, are you? I mean, as I recall, when the Sea of Light group was inaugurated, someone said that the only way faith could be regenerated was to sell off all the churches as museums and use the money to pay more priests to go out among the people.'

'Correct. And in the village here, a resurgence of faith has already restored a community centre which had become derelict, a home for rats. Look at it now. Eventually, the church will move out, put up its illuminated cross somewhere else. But in the meantime, God has chosen Old Hindwell for a serious purpose. I can see you still don't understand.'

'Trying.'

'You see a ruined church, I see a battleground. Look . . .'

He stood up and strode to the computer, touched the mouse and brought up his menu, clicked on the mailbox icon. His in-box told him he had two unread emails. One was: *From: warlock. Subject: war in heaven*. He clicked. The message read, 'I am a brother to dragons and a companion to owls.'

'Book of Job,' Merrily said.

Ellis reduced and deleted it. 'There's one every day.'

'Since when?'

'They like to use that Internet provider, Demon. Today's is a comparatively mild offering.'

'You reported this to the police?'

'The police? This is beyond the police.'

'They can trace these people through the server.'

'It'll only turn out to be some fourteen-year-old who received his instructions anonymously in a spirit message from cyberspace, and the police are gonna laugh. I would hardly expect them to understand that there's a chain of delegation here, leading back, eventually, to hell. That, of course – he nodded at the computer – is Satan's latest toy. I keep one here, for the same reason I have that repulsive picture on the wall.'

Masochism, Merrily thought. A martyrdom trip.

'I'm a defiant man, Merrily. Don't go thinking this began with the arrival of the Thorogoods. I've been set up for this. I've been getting poison-pen letters for months. And phone calls – cackling voices in the night. Recently had a jagged scratch removed from my car bonnet: a series of vertical chevrons like a dragon's back.'

'Maybe you *do* need support.'

He hit the metal desk with an open palm. 'I *have* all the support I will ever need.'

'What do you plan to do?'

'God shall cast out the dragon – through Michael. I made a civilized approach to Thorogood. I told him I wanted to perform a cleansing Eucharist in the church. He put me off. He can't do that now. He faces the power of the Holy Spirit.'

'And the cold shoulder from the people of Old Hindwell.'

'You mean our Demonstration of Faith? You disagree with that?'

She shrugged. 'Candles are harmless. I just hope that's where it ends.'

'My dear Merrily' – Ellis walked to the door – 'this is where it *begins*. And, with respect, it's not your place to *hope* for anything in relation to my parishioners.'

'Aren't the Thorogoods also your parishioners?'

He expelled a mildly exasperated hiss.

'And if they're trying to make a point about reclaiming ancient sites, hasn't it occurred to you that you're just helping to publicize their cause?'

'And what's Bernard Dunmore's policy on the issue?' Ellis demanded. 'Say nothing and hope they won't be able to maintain their mortgage repayments? Try to forget they're there? Is that, perhaps, why the Church is no longer a force in this country, while evil thrives unchallenged? Perhaps *you* should find out for yourself what kind of people the Thorogoods really are. Maybe you could visit their property. Under cover of darkness again?'

Damn! She stood up. 'OK, I'm sorry. It was a private funeral, and I had no right. But I was looking for someone. Someone who, as it happens, has now been reported missing from home.'

'Oh?' For the first time, he was thrown off balance.

'Barbara Buckingham, née Thomas? Menna's sister?'

'I've never heard of her. I didn't even know Menna had a sister.'

Merrily blinked. 'Didn't you ever talk to Menna about her background?'

'Why should I have probed into her background?'

'Just that when I have kids for confirmation we have long chats about everything. Rebaptism, I mean. I'd have thought that was something much more serious.'

'Merrily, I don't have to talk about this to you.'

She followed him into the hall. 'It's just I can't believe you're one of those priests who simply goes through the motions, Nick.'

'I do have an appointment. I'm sorry.'

'Splish, splash, you're now baptized?'

When he swiftly lifted a hand, she thought, for an incredible moment, that he was going to hit her and she actually cringed. But all he did was twist the small knob on the Yale lock and pull open the front door, but when he noticed that momentary cower, he smiled broadly and his smooth face lit up like a jack-o'-lantern.

She didn't move. 'I still don't fully understand this, Nick.'

'I know,' he said. 'And you must ask yourself why.'

'I mean I don't understand why you're using the enviable influence you've developed in this community to put people in fear of their immortal souls. You didn't have to make that inflammatory statement to the *Mail*.'

He looked at her as if trying, for the first time, to bring her into focus and then, finding she was too flimsy to define, turned away. 'I can't believe,' he said, 'that *you* have somehow managed to become a priest of God.'

She walked past him through the doorway, glanced back and saw a man with nothing much to lose. A man who had stripped himself down to the basics: cheap clothes, a small council house, a village hall for a church, and even that impermanent. There was something distinctly medieval about him. He was like a friar, a mendicant.

'Of course,' she said from the step, '*they're* also helping to publicize *you*. And maybe the villagers aren't afraid for their immortal souls at all, they're just assisting their rector to build his personal reputation. If you were in a town, virtually nobody would think this was . . . worth the candle.'

'This is a waste of time,' Nick Ellis said. 'I have people to see.'

The door closed quietly in her face.

Merrily stood on the path. She found she was shaking.

She hadn't felt as ineffectual since the *Livenight* programme.

TWENTY-NINE

Dark Glamour

As Merrily got back into the car, Gomer pointed to the mobile on the dash.

'Bleeped twice. Third time, I figured out how to answer him. Andy Mumford, it was, that copper. Jane gived him your number. He asked could you call back.'

'He say what about?'

'Not to me.'

She picked up the phone, entered the Hereford number Gomer had written on a cigarette paper, having to hold the thin paper close to the window because it was beyond merely overcast now – and not yet 1 p.m. Three fat raindrops blopped on the windscreen. This was, she told herself, going to be positive news.

'DS Mumford.'

'It's Merrily Watkins.'

'Ah.'

'Has she turned up?'

'Afraid not, Mrs Watkins.'

'Oh.' She heard Ellis's front door slam, and saw him coming down the path. He was carrying a medium-sized white suitcase. He walked past her Volvo without a glance and carried on towards the village centre.

'But I'm afraid her car has,' Mumford said. 'You know the Elan Valley? Big area of lakes – reservoirs – about thirty miles west of Kington? They've pulled her car out of one of the reservoirs.'

'Oh God.'

'Some local farmer saw the top of it shining under the water. Been driven clean through a fence. Dyfed-Powys've got divers in there. When I checked, about ten minutes ago, they still hadn't found anything else. Don't know what the currents are like in those big reservoirs. I'm sorry to have to tell you this, Reverend, but I thought you'd want to know.'

'Yes. Thank you.'

'If I hear anything else, I'll get back to you. Or, of course, if *you* hear anything. It's been known for people to . . .'

'What, you think she might have faked her own death?'

'No, I'm a pessimist,' Mumford said. 'I tend to think they'll pull out a body before nightfall.'

It began as a forestry track, then dropped into an open field with an unexpected vista across the valley to the Radnor Forest hills of grey green and bracken brown, most of which Gomer knew by name.

And strange names they were: the Whimble, the Smatcher, the Black Mixen. Evocative English-sounding names, though all the hills were in Wales. Merrily and Gomer sat for a moment in the car and took in the view: not a farm, a cottage or even a barn in sight. There were a few sheep, but lambing would come late in an area as exposed as this: hill farming country, marginal land. She remembered Barbara Buckingham talking about her deprived childhood – the teabags used six times, the chip fat changed only for Christmas. As they left the car at the edge of the field, she paused to say a silent prayer for Barbara.

She caught up with Gomer alongside a new stile which, he said, had been erected by Nev for the archaeologists. This was where the track became a footpath following the line of the Hindwell Brook, which was flowing unexpectedly fast and wide after all the rain. It had stopped raining now, but the sky bulged with more to come. Gomer pointed across the brook, shouting over the rush of the water.

'Used to be another bridge by yere one time, but now the only way you can get to the ole church by car is through the farm, see.'

'Where was the excavation?'

'Back there. See them tumps? Nev's work.' He squinted critically at a line of earthmounds, where tons of soil had been replaced. 'Boy coulder made a better job o' that. Bit bloody uneven, ennit?'

She went to stand next to him. 'You'd like to get back on the diggers, wouldn't you?'

'Minnie never liked it,' Gomer said gruffly. 'Her still wouldn't like it. 'Sides which, I'm too old.'

'You don't think that for one minute.'

Gomer sniffed and turned away, and led her through an uncared-for copse, where some of the trees were dead and branches brought down by the gales had been left where they'd fallen.

'Prosser's ground, all of this – inherited from the ole fellers. But he don't do nothin' with it n'more. Muster been glad when the harchaeologists come – likely got compensation for lettin' 'em dig up ground the dull bugger'd forgotten he owned.'

'Why's he never done anything with it?'

'That's why,' Gomer said, as they came out of the copse.

And there, on a perfect promontory, a natural shelf above the brook, on the opposite bank, was the former parish church of St Michael, Old Hindwell.

'Gomer . . .' Merrily was transfixed. 'It's . . . beautiful.'

The nave had been torn open to the elements but the tower seemed intact. A bar of light in the sky made the stones shimmer brown and grey and pink between patches of moss and lichen.

'It's the kind of church townsfolk dream of going to on a Sunday. I mean, what must it be like on a summer evening, with its reflection in the water? How could they let it go?'

Gomer grunted, rolling a ciggy. 'Reverent Penney, ennit? I tole you. Went off 'is trolley.'

'Went off his trolley how, exactly?' She remembered that Bernie Dunmore had made a brief allusion last night to the rector at the time actually suggesting that Old Hindwell Church should be decommissioned.

Now, with a certain relish, Gomer told her what the Reverend Terence Penney, rector of this parish, had done with all that ancient and much-polished church furniture on an October day in the mid-1960s.

'Wow.' She stared into the water, imagining it foaming around the flotsam of the minister's madness. 'Why?'

'Drugs,' Gomer said. 'There was talk of drugs.'

'Where is he now?'

Gomer shrugged.

She gazed, appalled, at the ruin. 'I bet we can find out. When we get back to the car, I'll call Sophie. Sophie knows everybody in a dog collar who isn't a dog.'

They went back through the dismal, dying copse.

'Not many folks walks this path n'more,' Gomer said, ''cept a few tourists. Place gets a bad reputation. Then this feller fell off the tower, killed hisself.'

Merrily stopped. 'When?'

'Year or so back? Bloke called Wilshire, army man, lived New Radnor way. Falls off a ladder checkin' the stonework on the ole tower. That's how come these Thorogoods got it cheap, I reckon.'

'I see.'

At the car, despite the extensive view, the mobile phone signal was poor and she had to shout at Sophie, whose voice kept breaking up into hiss and crackle, shouting out the name Penney.

Gomer said, 'You wanner go talk to the witches, vicar?'

'Dare we?' She thought about it. 'Yeah, why not.'

But when they drove back to the farm gate, there was a TV crew videotaping a thirtyish couple with a 'Christ is the Light' placard. You could tell by their outward bound-type clothing that they were not local. Merrily found herself thinking that some people just didn't have enough to do with their lives.

She was confused. She didn't *know* this place at all. It was like one of those complicated watches that did all sorts of different things, and you had to get the back off before you could see how the cogs were connected. Problem was, she didn't even know where to apply the screwdriver to prise off the back.

'Black Lion?' Gomer suggested. 'I'll buy you a pint and a sandwich, vicar.'

*

At the Black Lion there were no visible candles – no lights at all, in fact.

Merrily saw Gomer glance at his wrist, before remembering he'd buried his watch. 'About a quarter to two,' she said.

Gomer frowned. 'What's the silly bugger playin' at, shuttin' of a lunchtime with all these TV fellers in town?'

Merrily followed him up a short alley into a yard full of dustbins and beer crates. There was a door with a small frosted-glass window and Gomer tapped on it. Kept on tapping until a face blurred up behind the frosted glass, looking like the scrubbed-over face of one of the suspects in a police documentary. 'We're closed!'

'Don't give me that ole wallop, Greg, boy. Open this bloody door!'

'Who's that?'

'Gomer Parry Plant Hire.' Sounding like he was planning to take a bulldozer to the side of the pub if he couldn't gain normal access.

Bolts were thrown.

The licensee was probably not much older than Merrily, but his eyes were bagged, his mouth pinched, his shirt collar frayed. He'd shaved, but not well. Gomer regarded him without sympathy.

'Bloody hell, Greg, we only wants a pot o' tea and a sandwich.'

The man hesitated. 'All right . . . Just don't make a big fing about it.'

They followed him through a storeroom and an expensive, fitted kitchen with a tomato-red double-oven Aga, and the sound of extractor fans.

'Busy night, boy?'

'Yeah.' But he didn't sound happy about it. 'Go frew there, to the lounge bar. I won't put no lights on.'

'Long's we can see what we're eatin'.'

The lounge bar, grey-lit through more frosted glass, looked to have been only half renovated, as if the money had run out: new brass light fittings on walls too thinly emulsioned. Also a vague smell of damp.

'I can make you coffee, but not tea,' Greg said without explanation.

'We'll take it.' Gomer pulled out bar stools for Merrily and himself.

Greg threw out the dregs of a smile. 'Hope this is your daughter, Gomer?'

'En't got no daughter,' Gomer said gruffly. 'This is the vicar of our church.' As Greg's smile vanished, Gomer sat down, leaned both elbows on the bar top. 'Who made you close the pub, then, boy?'

'The wife.'

'And who made *her* close it?'

'Look,' Greg said, 'I'm not saying you're a nosy git, but this is your second visit inside a few days, asking more questions than that geezer from the *Mail*. What are you, Radnorshire correspondent for *Saga* magazine?'

Merrily was quietly zipping up her coat. It was freezing in there. 'Well, Mr . . .'

'Starkey.'

'Mr Starkey, the nosy git's me. I'm with the Hereford Diocese.'

Greg's eyes slitted. 'Wassat mean?'

'It means . . . Well, it means I'm interested, among other things, in what the Reverend Ellis is getting up to – you know?' Greg snorted; Merrily uwound her scarf to let him see the dog collar. 'This seems to be one of the few places without a candle in the window.'

Greg pushed fingers through his receding hairline. He looked as if there wasn't much more he could take.

'You wanna know what he's getting up to? Like *apart* from destroying marriages?'

'No, let's include that.' Merrily sat down.

Greg said there'd been a full house last night.

'First time in ages. Folks I ain't never seen before. Not big drinkers, but we got frew a lot of Cokes and shandies and if you know anyfing about the licensing trade you'll know that's where the big profit margins lie, so I got no complaints there.'

'Thievin' bugger,' Gomer said. 'So what brought this increase in trade, boy?'

'Wife went to church, Gomer. That funeral. Mrs Weal. Never

come back for a good while after you'd left. I mean hours. Said she'd got talking to people. First time she'd really talked to anybody since we come here.' He scowled. 'Including me.'

'She'd never been before?' Merrily said. 'To church – to the hall?'

'Nah. Not to any kind of church. See, what you gotta realize about Marianne – and I've never told a soul round here, and I would bleedin' hate for anybody—'

'Not a word, boy,' Gomer said. 'Not a word from us.'

'She got problems.' Greg's voice went down to a mutter. 'Depression. *Acute* depression. Been in hospital for it. You know what I mean – psychiatric? This is back in London, when we was managing a pub in Fulham. She was getting . . . difficult to handle.'

Merrily said nothing.

'Wiv men and . . . and that.' Greg waved it away with an embarrassed shake of the head. 'Ain't a nympho or noffink like that. It was just the depression. We had a holiday once and she was fine. Said she was sure she'd be fine the whole time if we went to live somewhere nice, like in the country.' He snorted. 'Country ain't cheap no more. Not for a long time.'

''Cept yere, mabbe,' Gomer said.

'Yeah.'

'It's a trap, Greg, boy.'

'Tell me about it. I've had people in here – incomers, you can pick 'em out from the nervous laughter – still lookin' for strawberries and cream on the village green and the blacksmith tap-tappin' over his forge. Be funny if it wasn't so bleedin' tragic.'

'That was you, was it?' Merrily said softly. 'When you first came here?'

'Her – not me. I ain't a romantic. I tried to tell her . . . yeah, all right, maybe I did fink it was gonna be different. I mean, there's noffink *wrong* with the local people, most of 'em . . .'

'I coulder tole you, boy,' Gomer said. 'You come to the wrong part o' the valley. Folks back there . . .' he waved a hand over his shoulder, back towards New Radnor. 'They're different again, see. Bit of air back there. Makes a difference.'

'So your wife went to church again yesterday?' Merrily prompted.

'Yeah. Off again. Up the village hall. Couldn't get out this place

261

fast enough. I didn't want *this*. Sure I wanted her to make friends, but not this way. I said, come on, we ain't churchgoers and it'd be hypocritical to start now.'

'Without the hypocrites, all our congregations would be sadly depleted,' Merrily admitted. 'But she went anyway. And came back all aglow, right?'

Greg didn't smile.

'Made lots of new instant friends,' Merrily said. 'People she'd only nodded to in the village shop hugged her as she left. She realized she'd never felt quite so much at home in the community before.'

'Dead on,' Greg said sourly.

'And she wants you to close the pub and go to church with her next week.'

'Says it's the only way we're gonna have a future. And I don't fink she meant the extra business. It won't . . .' He looked scared. 'It won't *last*, will it, Miss . . .?'

'Merrily.'

'It can't last. Can it? She's not a *religious* person. I mean . . . yeah, I coulda foreseen this, soon as people starting whispering about the new rector, what a wonderful geezer he was, how their lives was changed, how he'd . . . I dunno, helped them stop smoking, straightened out their kids, this kind of stuff. All this talk of the Holy Spirit, and people fainting in church. And Marianne kind of saying, "Makes you fink, don't it? Never had no luck to speak of since we moved in. Wouldn't do no harm, would it?"' Greg looked at Merrily's collar. 'Not your style, then, all this Holy Spirit shite?'

'Not my style, exactly . . .'

Gomer said, 'Don't do any good to let your feet get too far off the ground, my experience.'

'Why did they want you to close the pub today?' Merrily asked.

'Aaah.' Shook his head contemptuously. 'You seen the paper. He told 'em all yesterday this was coming off. Got bloody Devil-worshippers in the village and they gotta be prepared. Bleedin' huge turnout. Standing room only up the hall, 'cording to Marianne, when I could get any sense out of her. People hanging out the doors, lining the bloody steps.'

'This is local people or . . . newcomers?'

'Mainly newcomers, I reckon. A few locals, though, no question. And apparently Ellis is going . . .' Greg threw up his arms. '"There's a great evil come amongst us! We got to fight it. We are the chosen ones in the battle against Satan!"' Satan is this Robin Thorogood? All right, a Yank, a bit loud – in your face. But *Satan?* You credit that?'

'You know him, then?'

He shrugged. 'Americans. Talk to 'em for half an hour, you know 'em. His wife's more down to earth. I didn't know they was witches, though. They never talked about that. But why should they?'

'You were going to tell us why you'd closed the pub.'

'He don't want any *distractions.* He wants *concentration of faith.*'

'I don't understand,' Merrily said. 'Why?'

'Mondays he holds his healing sessions,' Greg said. 'Up the village hall.'

'So?'

There was a lot of pain and bewilderment in his eyes.

'I can help,' Merrily said. 'Just tell me.'

Greg breathed heavily down his nose. 'Last night, she says to me, "I'm unclean." Just like that – like out the Bible. "I've been tempted by Satan," she says.'

'En't we all, boy?' Gomer said.

'By *Thorogood.* Suddenly, she's being frank all the time. She's telling me stuff I don't wanna know. Like she was . . . tempted sexually by Robin Thorogood, agent of Satan. She was possessed by his "dark glamour". She wanted to sh— sleep wiv him. She comes out wiv all this. To *me.*'

'*Wanted* to sleep with him?'

'Ah, noffink bleedin' happened. I'm sure of that. He ain't been here two minutes. Plus she's ten years older than what he is, gotta be, and if you seen his wife . . . Nah, I doubt he even noticed Marianne. It's just shite.' Greg shook his head, gutted. 'I'll go get your coffee.'

'Greg, hang on . . . "Possessed by his dark glamour?"' This wasn't his wife speaking, this was Ellis. 'Did she actually use the word "possessed"?'

'I reckon, yeah. To be honest, I couldn't take no more. I was knackered out. I went to bed. This is totally stupid. This don't happen in places like this. This is city madness, innit?'

'And she's up at the hall now?'

Merrily slid from her stool, picked up her scarf.

THIRTY

Handmaiden

Out in the pub car park, she was ambushed.

'Mrs Watkins – Martyn Kinsey, BBC Wales. I gather you're speaking for the diocese today.'

'Well, I am, but—'

'We'd like to knock off a quick interview, if that's OK.'

He'd probably recognized her from *Livenight*. She asked him if there was any chance of doing this stuff later. From where she stood she could see the top of the cross on the village hall, and it was lit up, and it hadn't been lit before.

'Actually' – Kinsey was a plump, shrewd-eyed guy in his thirties – 'if we don't do it now, I suspect we could be overtaken by events. Nick Ellis is over there in the hall, having a meeting with some people. We're expecting him to come out and announce plans for a march to St Michael's Church, probably tonight.'

'That's what he's doing in there, is it?' The cross was lit up for a policy meeting? *I don't think so.*

'Isn't that going to be too late for your programme?'

'Oh sure – much too late. We might get a piece in the half nine slot, though that'll be only about forty seconds. But I think it's going to be a damp squib anyway, with no one there to protest at. The Thorogoods have been smart enough to vacate the premises.'

'You've not been able to speak to them?'

Kinsey shook his head. 'That's why we're going to have to make do – if you don't mind me putting it like that – with people like you.

Just tell us where the Church stands on this issue. A straightforward response. Won't take more than a couple of minutes.'

Of course, it wasn't straightforward. And, with the positioning and the repositioning and the *cutaways* and the *noddies*, it took most of twenty minutes. Kinsey asked her if the diocese was fully behind Ellis; Merrily said the diocese was *concerned* about the situation. So would she be joining in tonight's protest? Not exactly; but she'd be going along as an observer.

'So the diocese is actually sitting on the fence?'

Merrily said, 'Personally, I don't care too much for witch-hunts.'

'So you think that's literally what this is?'

'I just wouldn't like it to turn into one. The Reverend Ellis has a perfect right – well, it's his job, in fact – to oppose whatever he considers evil, but—'

'Do *you* think it's evil?'

'I haven't met the Thorogoods. I wouldn't, on face value, condemn paganism any more that I'd condemn Buddhism or Islam. But I *would*, like everyone else, be interested to find out what they're proposing to do in Old Hindwell Church.'

'You'd see that potentially as sacrilege?'

'The significant point about Old Hindwell Church is that it's no longer a functioning church. It's been decommissioned.'

'What about the graveyard, though? Wouldn't relatives of dead people buried there—'

'There never were all that many graves because the proximity of the brook caused occasional flooding. What graves there were are quite old, and only the stones now remain. Obviously, we're concerned that those stones should not be tampered with.'

'What about the way the village itself has reacted? All the candles in the windows . . . how do you feel about that?'

Merrily smiled. 'I think they look very pretty.'

'What do you think they're saying?'

'Well . . . lots of different things, probably. Why don't you knock on a few doors and ask?'

Kinsey lowered his microphone, nodded to the cameraman. It was a wrap. 'Out of interest, Martyn,' Merrily said, 'what *did* people have to say when you knocked on their doors?'

'Sod all,' said Kinsey. 'Either they didn't answer or they backed off or they politely informed us that Mr Ellis was doing the talking. And in some cases not so politely. Off the record, why *is* Ellis doing this? Why's he going for these people – these so-called pagans?'

'You tell me.'

'I can't. He's not your usual evangelical, all praising God and bonhomie. He's quiet, he chooses his words carefully. Also he gets on with the locals . . . which is unusual. They're canny round here, not what you'd call impressionable. Anyway, not my problem. You going to be around, if we need anything else?'

'For the duration,' Merrily said.

'Well, good luck.'

'Thanks.'

She ran all the way to the village hall, meeting nobody on the way, bounding up the steps and praying she wasn't too late, because if it was all over . . . well, hearsay evidence just wasn't the same.

At the top, she stopped for breath – and to assess the man in the porch, obviously guarding the closed doors to the hall. Slumped on a folding chair like a sack of cement. He was an unsmiling, flat-capped bloke in his fifties. She didn't recognize him.

He didn't quite look at her. ''Ow're you?'

'I'm fine. OK if I just pop in?'

'No press, thank you. Father Ellis will be out in a while.'

'I'm not press.'

'I still can't let you in.'

Merrily unwound her scarf. He took in the collar, his watery eyes swivelling uncertainly.

'You're with Father Ellis?'

'Every step of the way,' Merrily said shamelessly.

He ushered her inside. 'Be very quiet,' he said sternly, and closed the doors silently behind her.

Suddenly she was in darkness.

She waited, close to the place where she'd stood at Menna's funeral service, until her eyes adjusted enough to reassure her there was little chance of being spotted. Here, at the this end of the hall, she stood alone.

All the window blinds had been pulled down tight, and it seemed to have a different layout, no longer a theatre-in-the-round. Whatever was happening was happening in a far corner, and all she could see of it was a white-gold aura, like over a Nativity scene, a distant holy grotto.

And all she could hear was a sobbing – hollow, slow and even.

Merrily slipped off her shoes, carried them to the shelter of a brick pillar about halfway down the hall. It was cold; no heating on.

She waited for about half a minute before peering carefully around the pillar.

The glow had resolved into two tiers of candles. The sobbing had softened into a whispery panting. Merrily could make out several people – seemed like women – some sitting or kneeling in a circle, the others standing behind them, all holding candles on small tin or pewter trays, like the ones in the windows of the village.

Women only? This was why the guy on the door had let her in without too much dispute.

The scene, with its unsteady glow and its umber shadows, had a dreamlike, period ambience: seventeenth or eighteenth century. You expected the women to be wearing starched Puritan collars.

'In the name of the Father . . . and of the Son . . . and of the Holy Ghost . . .'

Ellis's voice was low-level, with that transatlantic lubrication. User-friendly and surprisingly warm.

But only momentarily, for then he paused. Merrily saw him rise up, in his white monk's robe, in the centre of the circle, the only man here. Next to him stood a slender table with a candle on it and a chalice and something else in shadow, probably a Bible.

His voice rose, too, became more distinct, the American element now clipped out.

'O God, the Creator and Protector of the human race, Who hast formed man in Thine own image, look upon this Thy handmaiden who is grievously vexed with the wiles of an unclean spirit . . . whom the old adversary, the ancient enemy of the earth, encompasses with a horrible dread . . . and blinds the senses of her human understanding with stupor, confounds her with terror . . . and harasses her with trembling and fear.'

Merrily's feet were cold; she bent and slipped on her shoes. She wouldn't be getting any closer; from here she could see and hear all she needed. And she was fairly sure this was a modified version of the Roman Catholic ritual.

Ellis's voice gathered a rolling energy. 'Drive away, O Lord, the power of the Devil, take away his deceitful snares.'

At some signal, the women held their candles high, wafting out the rich and ancient aroma of melted wax.

With a glittering flourish, Ellis's arm was thrust up amid the lights.

'Behold the Cross of the Lord! Behold the Cross and flee, thou obscene spirits of the night!'

His voice dropped, became intense, sneering.

'Most cunning serpent, you shall never again dare to deceive the human race and persecute the Holy Church. Cursed dragon, we give thee warning in the names of Jesus Christ and Michael, in the names of Jehovah, Adonai, Tetragrammaton . . .'

Merrily stiffened. *What?*

She leaned further out to watch Nick Ellis standing amongst all the women, brandishing his cross like a sword in the light, brandishing words which surely belonged originally to the Roman Church, to Jewish mysticism, to . . .

The candles lowered again, to reveal a single woman crouching.

More like cringing?

Ellis laid the cross on the tall table and bent down to the woman. 'Do you embrace God?' His voice had softened.

The woman looked up at him, like a pet dog.

'You must embrace God,' he explained, gently at first. 'You must embrace God, embrace Him, embrace Him . . .' His right arm was extended, palm raised, the loose sleeve of his robe falling back. 'Embrace *Him*!'

Shadows leaping. A short expulsion of breath – '*Hoh!*' – and a sound of stumbling.

Merrily saw he'd pushed the woman away; she lay half on her back, panting.

'Say it!' Ellis roared.

'I . . . embrace Him.'

And do you renounce the evil elements of this world which corrupt those things God has created?'

'Yes.' She came awkwardly to her feet. She was wearing a white shift of some kind, possibly a nightdress. She must feel very cold.

'Do you renounce all sick and sinful desires which draw you away from the love of God?'

She began to cry again. Her London accent said this had to be Greg Starkey's wife, Marianne, the sometime sufferer from clinical depression, not a nympho in the normal sense, but tempted by the dark glamour of the witch Robin Thorogood. Was that it? Was that really the extent of her possession?

And, oh God, even if there was a whole lot more, this was not right, not by any stretch.

'Say it!'

Her head went back. She started to sniff.

'Say, "I so renounce them"!'

'I s . . . so . . . renounce them.'

'And do you, therefore, wish with all your heart to expel the lewd and maleficent spirit coiling like a foul serpent within you?'

Her head was thrown right back, as if she expected to be slapped, again and again.

'I ask you once more . . .' Softly. 'Do you wish, with all your heart . . .?'

'*Yes!*'

'Then lie down,' Father Ellis said.

What? Merrily moved away from the pillar. She could see now that Ellis was pointing at a hessian rug laid out on the boarded floor. Marianne drew an unsteady breath and went to stand on the rug. The watching women kept still. But she caught a movement from a darkened doorway, with a 'Toilets' sign over the top, and moved back behind her pillar.

There was a man in that doorway, she'd swear it.

Ellis said, 'Don't be afraid.'

He turned to the table and took up another cross from a white cloth. Merrily saw it clearly. About nine inches long, probably gold-plated. He held it up to the candlelight, then lowered it again. One of the women leaned forward, handed him something.

Involuntarily, Merrily moved closer. The woman held up her candle for Ellis. Merrily saw a yellow tube, then an inch of pale jelly was transferred to Ellis's forefinger. She saw him smearing the jelly along the stem of the crucifix.

What?

Ellis nodded once. Marianne Starkey crumpled to her knees then went into an ungainly squat, holding the nightdress up around her thighs.

'Be calm now,' Ellis said. 'Sit. Relax.'

The woman sat still. Ellis raised his eyes from her. 'O God of martyrs, God of confessors, we lay ourselves before Thee . . .' He glanced at Marianne, whispered, 'Lie back.'

Merrily watched Marianne's body subside onto the rough matting, her knees up, the nightdress slipping back. Ellis knelt in front of her.

'I ask you again,' he whispered. 'Is it your heart's wish that the unclean spirit might be expelled for ever?'

'Yes.'

'And do you understand that a foul spirit of this nature may effectively be purged only through the portal of its entry?'

'Yes . . .' Marianne hesitated then let her head fall back over the edge of the mat and onto the boarded floor with a dull thump. She closed her eyes. 'Yes.'

Ellis began to pray, a long, rolling mumble, slowly becoming intelligible.

'Let the impious tempter fly far hence! Let thy servant be defended by the sign . . .' Ellis rose and put the cross swiftly on Marianne's forehead. ' . . . of Thy Name.' He placed the cross against her breast. 'Do Thou guard her inmost soul . . .'

Merrily thought, 'He won't. He can't. It isn't possible, not with all these women here.'

Ellis reared over Marianne. 'Do Thou rule...' Then he bent suddenly. ' . . . her inmost parts.'

Marianne gave a low and throaty cry, then Ellis sprang up, kissing

271

the cross, tossing it to the table, and it was over. And women were hugging Marianne.

And Merrily was frozen in horror and could no longer see a man in the doorway.

THIRTY-ONE

Jewel

The converging lanes were filling up with vehicles – like last Saturday. When Ellis and the women – but not Marianne – came down the steps, they were joined by more people. By the time they all reached the road there were about thirty of them, with Ellis seeming to float in their midst, glowingly messianic in his white monk's habit.

The sick bastard.

Merrily turned away, found her hands were clenched together. Shame. Fury. When she could stand to look again, she saw that someone was bearing a white wooden crucifix aloft, in front of Ellis. At the apex of the village hall roof, the neon cross became a beacon in the rain. Like it was all a crusade.

She didn't recognize anyone in Ellis's group, but why should she? She guessed they were not locals anyway. A couple of the men wore suits but most others were casually but warmly dressed, like members of a serious hiking club. Nobody was speaking. Shouldn't they be singing some charismatic anthem, swaying, clapping?

Killing the shakes, Merrily walked erratically along the lane to the corner where a bunch of reporters stood under umbrellas and Gomer was waiting for her in the rain, an unlit ciggy drooping from his mouth.

'Vicar . . . you all right, girl?' Following her behind a Range Rover parked under some fir trees, he regarded her gravely. 'You looks a bit pale.'

'Don't fuss, Gomer.' Merrily dropped a cigarette in the process of trying to light it.

Gomer straightened his glasses.

'Sorry.' She touched his arm. 'It's *me*. I'm furious with me, that's all.'

'Happened in there, vicar?'

'Exorcism – of sorts. I ought to have stopped it. I just' – she thumped her thigh with a fist – 'stood there . . . let it happen.'

'Hexorcism?' Gomer said, bewildered. 'This'd be Greg's missus?'

'Must've been.'

'The bugger hexorcized Greg's missus for fancyin' a feller?'

'For embracing the dark,' Merrily said, with unsuppressible venom. 'For letting herself become possessed by most unholy and blasphemous lust.'

'Load of ole wallop. You gonner tell Greg?'

'Perhaps not.'

'Boy oughter know,' said Gomer, 'whatever it was.' He nodded towards a man getting into the Range Rover. 'Dr Coll,' he observed.

The cameramen were backing away down the street ahead of Ellis and his entourage. Dr Coll drove away in his Range Rover, leaving Merrily and Gomer exposed.

'I can't believe I let it happen,' she said. 'I couldn't believe it *was* happening. I can't tell Greg. You saw the state he was in. He'd go after Ellis with a baseball bat. That . . . *bastard*.'

Ellis walked without looking to either side. When a couple of the reporters tried to get a word with him, his anoraked minders pressed closer around him – the holy man. Merrily and Gomer walked well behind, Merrily turning things over and over.

Internal ministry, it had been called when the phenomenon had first been noted in the North of England. Mostly it was for supposed incidents of satanic child abuse – a number of allegations, but not much proven. It was a charismatic extreme, an evangelical madness: the warped and primitive conviction that demonic forces entered through bodily orifices and could only be expelled the same way.

It had all happened too quickly, clinically, like a doctor taking a cervical smear. The fact that it was also degrading, humiliating – and, as it happened, amounted to sexual assault – would not be an issue for someone who had convinced himself of it being a legitimate weapon in the war against Satan. Someone invoking the power of the Archangel Michael against a manufactured dragon.

When, in fact, *he* was the monster.

Got to stop him.

But if she spoke out there would be a dozen respectable women ready to say she was a liar with a chip on her shoulder; about a dozen women who had watched the ritual in silence. Then, afterwards, tears and hugs and 'Praise God!'

'Gomer . . . those women over there, who are they?'

Gomer identified Mrs Eleri Cobbold, the village sub-postmistress, Mrs Smith whose cottage they'd passed, Linda Llewellyn who managed a riding stables towards Presteigne. The others he didn't know. Mostly from Off, he reckoned.

Marianne wasn't among them.

'No back way out of the hall, is there?'

'Yes, but not without comin' down them steps, vicar, less you wants to squeeze through a fence and lose yourself in the forestry.'

So she was still up there. That made sense; they'd hardly want to bring her out looking like a road casualty, not with TV crews around.

Ellis had reached the car park of the Black Lion. He was evidently about to hold a press conference.

'Gomer, could you kind of hang around and listen to what he says? I need to go back in there.'

All eyes were fixed on Ellis as Merrily walked inconspicuously back through the rain towards the steps.

Nobody on the door this time. Inside the hall, all the blinds were now raised, the chairs were spread out and a plain wooden lectern stood in the centre of the room. This time, one corner looked very much like another and only a vague smell of wax indicated that anything more contentious than an ad hoc meeting of the community council had taken place.

No, there *was* something else: the atmosphere you often caught in a church after a packed service – tiny shivers in the air like dust motes waiting to settle.

A black coat slung over one of the chairs suggested someone was still around, if only a cleaner. Presently, Merrily became aware of voices from beyond the door with the 'Toilets' sign above it – where that solitary man had stood. She crossed the hall, not caring about the sound of her shoes on the polished floorboards.

The door opened into an ante-room leading to separate women's and men's lavatories. It contained a sink and one of the chairs from the main room – Marianne sitting in it. A woman was bending over her with a moistened paper towel, patting her brow. Marianne didn't react when the door swung shut behind Merrily, but the other woman looked up at once, clear blue eyes unblinking.

'We can manage, thank you.'

The voice echoed off the tiles: cold white tiles, floor to ceiling, reminding Merrily of the stark bathroom at Ledwardine vicarage.

'How is she?'

'She's much better, thank you. Had problems at home, haven't you, my love?'

The woman wore jeans and a black and orange rugby shirt. She had a lean, wind-roughened face, bleakly handsome. A face which had long since become insensitive to slaps from the weather and the world. A face last seen lit by the lanterns in Menna's mausoleum.

The woman dabbed at Marianne's cheek, screwed up the paper towel and looked again at Merrily, in annoyance. 'You want the lavatory, is it?'

'No. I'd just like a word with Marianne – when you've finished.' Merrily unwound her scarf. 'Merrily Watkins. Hereford Diocese.'

'Oh? Come to spy on Father Ellis, is it? We're not stupid. We know what the diocese thinks of him.'

Marianne looked glassy-eyed. *She* didn't care one way or the other.

'And anyway,' the woman said, 'Mrs Starkey hasn't been through anything she didn't personally request. Father Ellis doesn't do a soft ministry.'

'Obviously not.'

'Practical man who gets results. She'll be fine, if people will let her alone. If you want to talk to anybody, you can talk to me. Judith Prosser, my name. Councillor Prosser's wife. Come outside.'

She gave Marianne's shoulder a squeeze then went and held open the door for Merrily, ushering her out and down the central aisle of the hall, past Ellis's lectern. She picked up the black quilted coat from a chair back, and they went out through the main doors.

The rain had stopped. At the top of the steps, Judith Prosser didn't turn to look at Merrily; she leaned on the metal railings and gazed over to the village centre, where Ellis and his entourage were assembling for the media.

'And was it the diocese sent you to Menna's funeral, too, Reverend Watkins?'

Above Old Hindwell, a hopeless sun was trying vainly to burn a hole in the clouds. Mist still filigreed the firs on Burfa Hill but the tower of the old church was clear to the north.

'I didn't think you'd recognized me,' Merrily said.

'Well, of course I recognized you.'

This was the intelligent woman who Gomer seemed to admire. Who did her husband's thinking for him. Who could sit and watch another woman physically invaded in the name of God.

'For what it's worth, that was nothing at all to do with the diocese,' Merrily told her. 'I'd arranged to meet Barbara Buckingham at her sister's funeral. You remember Barbara?'

Judith Prosser's head turned slowly until her eyes locked on Merrily's.

'*Had* you now?'

'She was referred to me by a nurse at Hereford Hospital, after her sister died there. I do . . . counselling work, in certain areas.'

'Didn't come to the funeral, though, did she?'

'She's disappeared,' Merrily said. 'She spent some days here and now she's disappeared. The police are worried about her safety.'

'Oh, her *safety*? An eyebrow arched under Judith's stiff, short hair. 'And what are we to assume they mean by that?'

'We both know what they mean, Mrs Prosser.'

The sun had given up the struggle, was no more than a pale grey circle embossed on the cloud.

'Poor Barbara,' Judith said.

Merrily did some thinking. While she hadn't come up here to discuss Barbara and Menna, as soon as the conversation had been diverted away from Ellis himself, Judith Prosser had become instantly more forthcoming.

'Barbara told me you used to write to her.'

'For many years. We were best friends for a time, as girls.'

'So you know why she left home.'

'Do *you?*'

'I know it wasn't a hydatid cyst.'

'Ha. Good informants you must have. What else did they tell you?'

'That you were looking out for Menna, and keeping Barbara informed. Menna was a source of . . . disquiet . . . for Barbara. Especially after their mother died.'

'Ah.' Judith Prosser nodded. 'So that's it.' She leaned back with her elbows against the railings. 'Well, let me assure you right now, Mrs . . . *is* it Mrs? Let me assure you emphatically that Mervyn Thomas never touched Menna. I know that, because I warned him myself what would happen to him if he ever did.'

'But you'd have been just a kid . . . or not much more.'

'This was not when Menna was a child. Good heavens, Merv was never a child-molester. He'd wait till they filled out. Ha! No, there was never anything for Barbara to worry about there. *Nothing.* She could go on living her rich, soft, English life without a qualm.'

'Hasn't she been to see you in the past week or so?'

Judith sniffed. 'I heard she was around, pestering people – including you, it seems. Evidently she couldn't face me.'

'Wasn't it you who told her about Menna's stroke?'

'I sent her a short note. Somebody had to.'

'But not her husband.'

Mrs Prosser smiled and nodded. 'Let me also tell you, Mrs Watkins, that Jeffery Weal was the best thing that could have happened to Menna. If you knew her – which Barbara, lest we forget, never really *did* – Menna was a wispy, flimsy little thing. Insubstantial, see, like a ghost. She— Are you all right?'

'Yes.' Merrily swallowed. 'I'm fine. Why was Mr Weal so good for her?'

'If you knew her, you would know she would always need someone to direct her life. And while he was not the most demonstrative of men, he adored her. Kept her like a jewel.'

In a padded box, Merrily thought, in a private vault.

'Anyway,' Judith said, 'I do hope the Diocese of Hereford is not going to interfere with Father Ellis. He suits this area very well. He meets our needs.'

'Really? How many other people has he exorcized?'

Judith Prosser sighed in exasperation. 'As far as local people are concerned, he's giving back the church the authority it *used* to have. Time was when we had a village policeman and troublesome youngsters would get a clip around the ear. Now they have to go up before people like my husband, Councillor Prosser, and receive some paltry sentence – a conditional discharge, or a period of community service if they're *very* bad. Time *was* when sinners would be dealt with by the Church, isn't it? They weren't so ready to reoffend *then*.'

'The way Father Ellis deals with them?'

Judith smiled thinly. 'The way God deals with them, he would say, isn't it? Excuse me, I must go back and minister to Mrs Starkey.'

Halfway down the steps, Merrily encountered Gomer coming up. There were now a lot of things she needed to ask him. But, behind his glasses, Gomer's eyes were luridly alive.

'It's on, vicar.'

'The march?'

'Oh hell, aye. Tonight. No stoppin' the bugger now. Somebody been over to St Michael's, and they reckons Thorogood's back. En't on his own, neither.'

Merrily felt dejected. All she wanted was to get home, do some hard thinking, ring the bishop to discuss the issue of *internal ministry*. She didn't want to even have to look at Nicholas Ellis again tonight.

'Bunch o' cars and vans been arrivin' at St Michael's since 'bout half an hour ago. One of 'em had, like, a big badge on the back, 'cordin' to Eleri Cobbold. Like a star in a circle?'

'Pentagram,' Merrily said dully.

'Ar,' said Gomer, 'they figured it wasn't the bloody RAC.'

279

'How's Ellis reacted?'

'Oh, dead serious. Heavy, grim – for the cameras. Man called upon to do God's holy work, kind o' thing.'

'Yeah, I can imagine. But underneath . . .'

'Underneath – pardon me, vicar – like a dog with two dicks.'

'I don't need this,' Merrily said.

THIRTY-TWO

Potion

Betty left Mrs Pottinger's lodge in weak sunshine, wanting nothing more than to collapse in front of that cranky farmhouse stove and pour it all out to Robin.

Except that Robin would go insane.

She called for a quick salad at a supermarket cafe on the outskirts of Leominster. By the time she reached the Welsh border, it was approaching an early dusk and raining and, in her mind, she was back in the shop with Mrs Cobbold and the slender man with the pointed beard.

'Oh, good morning, Doctor.'

'A sharp day, Eleri.'

Dr Coll.

She needed to tell somebody about Dr Coll and the Hindwell Trust. She wished it could be Robin. Wished she could trust him not to go shooting his mouth off and have them facing legal action on top of everything else.

The Hindwell Trust, Juliet Pottinger had explained, was a local charity originally started to assist local youngsters from hard-pressed farming families to go on to higher education. To become – for instance – doctors and lawyers, so that they might return and serve the local community.

A *local people's* charity.

Juliet Pottinger had come to Old Hindwell because of her husband's job. Stanley had been much older, an archaeologist with the Clwyd-Powys Trust, who had continued to work part-time after his official retirement. He was, in fact, one of the first people to suspect that the Radnor Basin had a prehistory as significant as anywhere in Wales. His part-time job became a full-time obsession. He was overworking. He collapsed.

'Dr Collard Banks-Morgan was like a small, bearded, ministering angel,' Mrs Pottinger had said wryly. 'Whisked poor Stanley into the cottage hospital. Those were the days when anyone could occupy a bed for virtually as long as they wished. Stanley practically had to discharge himself in the end, to get back to his beloved excavation.'

And while Stanley was trowelling away at his favoured site, a round barrow at Harpton, Dr Coll paid Mrs P. a discreet visit. He informed her, in absolute confidence, that he was more than a little worried about Stanley's heart; that Stanley, not to dress up the situation, had just had a very lucky escape, and he could one day very easily push the enfeebled organ . . . just a little too far.

'Oh, don't *tell* him that. Good heavens, don't have him carrying it around like an unexploded bomb!' said Dr Coll jovially. 'I shall keep tabs on him, myself.' Chuckling, he added, 'I believe I'm developing a latent interest in prehistory!'

Dr Coll had been discretion itself, popping in for a regular chat – perhaps to ask Stanley the possible significance of some mound he could see from his surgery window or bring him photocopies of articles on Victorian excavations from the *Radnorshire Transactions*. And all the time, as he told Juliet with a wink, he was observing Stanley's colour, his breathing, his general demeanour. *Keeping tabs.*

She thought the man's style was wonderful: perfect preventative medicine. How different from the city, where a GP could barely spare one the time of day.

And Betty was rehearing Lizzie Wilshire: *'Dr Coll's been marvellous . . . such a caring, caring man.'*

Juliet Pottinger had said as much, without spelling anything out, to their most solicitous solicitor, Mr Weal, who was handling their purchase of a small strip of land – 'for a quite *ludicrous* amount' – from the Prosser brothers. How could she possibly repay Dr Coll's kindness?

Oh, well, said Mr Weal, when pressed, there *was* a certain local charity, to which Dr Coll was particularly attached. Oh, nothing *now*, he wouldn't want that, he'd be most embarrassed. But something to bear in mind for the future perhaps? And please don't tell Dr Coll that he'd mentioned this – he would hate to alienate a client.

It was two years later, while they were on holiday in Scotland – a particularly hot summer – that Stanley, exhibiting symptoms of what might be sunstroke or something worse, was whisked off by his anxious wife to a local hospital. Where two doctors were unable to detect a heart problem of any kind.

'Stanley died three and a half years ago of what, in the days before everything had to be explained, would have been simply termed old age,' said Mrs Pottinger.

'And did you ever take this misdiagnosis up with Dr Coll?' Betty was imagining Juliet waking up in the night listening for his breathing, monitoring his diet, being nervous whenever he was driving. It must have been awfully worrying.

'I took the coward's way out, and persuaded Stanley to move somewhere else, a bit more convenient. I said I was finding the village too claustrophobic, which was true. By then I'd discovered that Dr Coll had . . . well, *appeared* to have created a . . . dependency among several of his patients, and all of them, as it happened, incomers to the area. People who might be feeling a little isolated there, and would be overjoyed to find such a friendly and concerned local GP.'

'Making up illnesses for them, too?'

'I don't know. People don't like to talk about certain things. People are only too happy to praise their local doctor, to boast about what a good and caring GP they have. Perhaps ours was an isolated case. Certainly, some of them did die quite soon. One rather lonely elderly couple, childless and reclusive, died' – her voice faded – 'within only months of each other.'

'And did they by any chance leave money,' Betty asked her, 'to this . . .?'

'The Hindwell Trust. Yes, I rather believe there was a substantial bequest.'

'Did you never say anything?'

'Don't look at me like that,' Mrs Pottinger snapped. 'Was I supposed to go to the police? I'd have been a laughing stock. I believe Dr Coll even helped out as a police surgeon for some years. Yes, I

did, when we were about to leave the village, suggest to the Con-
nellys, who'd bought a rather run-down smallholding . . . but . . . No,
it was a waste of time. Dr Coll is a very popular man: he has five
children, he hosts garden parties at his lovely home on the Evenjobb
road. Even now, I don't necessarily believe—'

'What about the solicitor?'

'Oh, Mr Weal and Dr Coll go *right* back. Fellow pupils at the Old
Hindwell Primary School. In fact, Mr Weal administers the Hindwell
Trust – and its trustees include Councillor Gareth Prosser. You see?'

I see. Oh yes, I do see.

Such a caring, caring man.

Driving out of the hamlet of Kinnerton, Betty felt a rising panic,
an inability to cope with this news on her own. The Radnor Valley
was all around her, a green enigma. Abruptly, she turned into a lane
which she already knew of because it led to the Four Stones.

She stopped the car on the edge of a field beyond Hindwell Farm
– Hindwell, not *Old* Hindwell. Different somehow – placid and open
and almost lush in summer. She could see the stones through the
hedge. She loved this place, this little circle. She and Robin must
have been here ten or fifteen times already. It was still raining, but
she got out of the car and climbed eagerly over the gate. It felt like
coming home.

The Four Stones were close to the hedge, not high but plump
and rounded. Betty went down on her knees and put her arms around
one and looked across the open countryside to the jagged middle-
distant hillside where stood the sentinel church of Old Radnor. She
hugged the stone, surrendering to the energies of the prehistoric
landscape.

This was the religion – and the Radnorshire – that she understood.

The rain intensified, beating down on her out of a blackening
sky. Betty didn't care; she wished the rain would wash her into the
stone. When she stood up, she was pretty well soaked, but she felt
better, stronger.

And angry. Bitterly angry at the corruption of this old and sacred
place. Angry at the bloody *local people*, the level to which they
appeared to have degenerated.

She drove to the end of the lane and, instead of turning left towards Walton and Old Hindwell, headed right, towards New Radnor, against the rain.

Even if the woman's bungalow was strewn with copies of the *Daily Mail*, she would charm Lizzie Wilshire around to her side. She would ask her directly if the Hindwell Trust was mentioned in her will.

'Above all,' Max said, pouring himself a glass of red wine, 'we can challenge them intellectually.'

Max had this big, wildman beard. You could've lost him at a ZZ Top convention. But any suggestion of menace vanished as soon as he spoke, for Max had a voice like a one-note flute. He was a lecturer someplace; he liked to lecture.

'St Michael equates with the Irish god Mannon, of the Tuatha de Danaan. Mannon was the sea god, and also the mediator between the gods and humankind and the conductor of souls into the Otherworld. In Coptic and cabbalistic texts, you will find these roles also attributed to Michael. Therefore, every "Saint" Michael church is, regardless of its origins, in essence a pagan Celtic temple. Which is why this reconsecration is absolutely valid.'

Normally, even coming from Max, Robin would have found this amazing, total cosmic vindication. Right now he really couldn't give a shit.

Because it was close to dark now, and still Betty had not returned, had not even called.

He walked tensely around the beamed living room, which *they* had taken over, stationing candles in the four corners, feeding gathered twigs to a feeble fire they'd gotten going in the inglenook where the witch-charm box had been stored. When George and Vivvie had come down, the first weekend, Betty had stopped them establishing a temple in this room. But now, in her absence, they'd gone right ahead.

Altar to the north – some asshole had cleared one of the trestle tables in Robin's studio and hauled it through. Now it held the candle, pentacle, chalice, wand, scourge, bell, sword.

There had to be a power base, George said. There would be

negative stuff coming at them now from all over the country. It was about protection, George explained, and Betty would understand that.

If she was here. She'd never been away this long before, without at least calling him. Robin imagined the cops arriving, solemn and sympathetic and heavy with awful news of a fatal car crash in torrential rain.

Never, for Robin, had a consecration meant less. Never had a temple seemed so bereft of holiness or atmosphere of any kind.

'She'll be back, Robin.' A plump middle-aged lady called Alexandra had picked up on his anxiety. She'd been Betty's college tutor, way back, had been present at their handfasting. Her big face was mellow and kind by candlelight. 'If anything had happened to her, one of us would surely know.'

'Sure,' Robin said.

'I just hope she'll be happy we've come.'

'Yeah,' Robin said hoarsely. See, if she'd only called, he'd have been able to prepare her for this. He knew he should have held them off until he'd consulted with her. But when George had come through on the mobile, Robin had been already majorly stressed out, beleaguered, and it hadn't immediately occurred to him that they would have to accommodate a number of these people in the farmhouse, with sleeping bags being unrolled in the kitchen, and more upstairs.

And kids, too. Max and Bella's kids: two daughters and a nine-year-old son called Hermes – Robin had already caught the little creep messing with his airbrushes. At least *they* weren't gonna sleep in the house; the whole family were now camped in the big Winnebago out back. It had a pentagram in the rear window, the same place Christians these days liked to display a fish symbol.

Robin went over to the window again, looking out vainly for small headlights.

Sometimes suspicion pierced his anxiety. He wondered if this whole thing had been in some way planned. While George was into practicalities like dowsing and scrying, Vivvie was essentially political. For her, Robin sometimes thought, paganism might just as easily have been Marxism. And it was Vivvie who had accidentally, in the heat of the moment, let it out on TV. He never had entirely trusted Vivvie.

And now they were looking at a serious showdown with some seriously fanatical fundamentalist Christians. Two of the Wiccans, Jonathan and Rosa, had been down to the village to take a look, and had seen a gathering of people around a man in white. Ellis? This confrontation, Max said, must not be allowed to get in the way of the great festival of light. But George had grinned. George loved trouble.

'What is terrific about this,' Max piped, waving his wineglass, 'is that only two deities were directly filched from the Old Faith by Christianity. One was Michael, the other was the triple-goddess, Brigid, who became associated with Saint Brigid, the Abbess of Kildare – who was, in all probability, herself a pagan worshipping in an oak grove. So, as we know, Imbolc is the feast of Brigid, Christianized as Candlemas – the feast of *Saint* Brigid . . .'

Max beamed through his beard in the candlelight. There was no particular need for him to go on; they all knew this stuff, but Max was Max and already a little smashed.

'Therefore . . . it is absolutely fitting that this church should be reconsecrated on that sacred eve, in the names of both Mannon and Brigid, with a fire festival, which will burn away . . .'

Jesus. Robin stared out of the window into the uninterrupted night. He wondered if Betty, once away from here, had decided never to come back.

There was a green Range Rover parked in front of Lizzie Wilshire's bungalow, so Betty had to leave the car further down the lane, under the outer ramparts of the New Radnor castle mound, and run through the rain. It didn't matter now; this was the same rain that was still falling on the Four Stones.

When she reached the Range Rover, the clear, rectangular sign propped in its windscreen made her stop. Made her turn and walk quickly back to her car.

The sign said, 'DOCTOR ON CALL'.

She had to think. Was this a sign that she was supposed to go in there, tackle Dr Coll face to face?

Betty sat in the driving seat, thankful for the streaming rain obscuring the windscreen and her face from any passers-by.

She went over it all again in her head. Dr Coll, who was here. Mr Weal, the solicitor whose home was not so far from St Michael's Farm and whose wife had recently died.

'So how did Mr Weal become your solicitor?'

'He's simply there. He becomes everyone's solicitor sooner or later. He's reliable, it's an old family firm, and his charges are modest. He draw up wills virtually free of charge.'

'I bet he does.'

'I don't suppose any of this will affect you at all. You're too young: you'll see both of them out. It probably wouldn't have affected Major Wilshire, either. He was ex-regiment, a fit man with all his wits about him.'

Lizzie Wilshire: *'Bryan had a thing about the medical profession, refused to call a doctor unless in dire emergency. A great believer in natural medicine, was Bryan.'*

All his wits about him.

'... it was, unfortunately, entirely in character for Bryan to attempt such a job alone. He thought he was invulnerable.'

A light tapping on the rain-streaming side window made Betty jump in her seat. She was nervous again, and the nerves had brought back the uncertainty. She could be getting completely carried away about this. She hurriedly wound down the window.

'Mrs Thorogood?'

Betty was unable to suppress a gasp.

Raindrops glistened in the neat, pointed beard under his rugged, dependable face.

'I'm sure Mrs Wilshire wouldn't want you hanging around out here in the rain. Why don't you come into the house?'

'I didn't want to intrude,' Betty said. 'I was going to wait till you'd gone.'

'Nonsense,' said Dr Collard Banks-Morgan. 'As much as anything, I'd very much like to talk to you about the herbal medicine you so generously prepared for Mrs Wilshire.'

He held open the car door for her. He was wearing the same light-coloured tweed suit, a mustard-coloured tie. On his head was a tweed hat with fishing flies in it. He had an umbrella which he put up and held over her, guiding her briskly past his green Range Rover and up the path to the bungalow.

For a moment, it was almost like an out-of-body experience – she'd experienced that twice, knew the sensations – and she was watching herself and Dr Coll entering the porch together. As though this was the natural conclusion to a sequence of events she'd set in motion when she'd decided she had to leave Robin at the mercy of the media and seek out Juliet Pottinger.

She was now being led into a confrontation with Collard Banks-Morgan, in the presence of Mrs Wilshire. Bright panic flared, she was not ready! She didn't know enough!

But something evidently had taken over: fate, or something. Perhaps she was about to be given the proof she needed.

Betty could hardly breathe.

'Won't be a jiff.' Dr Coll stood in the doorway, shaking out his umbrella. 'Go through if you like. Mrs Wilshire's in the sitting room, as usual.'

Betty nodded and went through. Though it was not yet three o'clock, the weather had made the room dark and gloomy, so that the usually feeble-looking flames in the bronze-enamelled oil stove were brazier-bright, making shadows rise around Mrs Wilshire, in her usual chair facing the fireplace. She didn't turn when Betty came in.

'I'm sorry about this, Mrs Wilshire,' Betty said. 'I wasn't going to come over until the doctor had left.'

Mrs Wilshire still didn't turn round.

The shadows leapt.

The force of her own indrawn breath flung Betty back into the doorway.

'Oh, Jesus Christ!'

Not, *Oh, Mother!* which she only said, still self-consciously, at times of minor crisis.

Her hand went to her mouth. 'Oh no . . .'

There was a small click and wall lights came on, cold and milky blue.

'Go and look at her, if you like,' said Dr Coll. 'I think you ought to.'

He walked over to the fireplace, stood with an elbow resting on the mantelpiece.

'You aren't afraid of death, are you, Mrs Thorogood? Just a preliminary to rebirth, isn't that what you people believe?'

Betty found she was trembling. 'What happened to her?'

Dr Coll raised an ironic eyebrow. 'Among other things, it seems *you* happened to her.'

Betty edged around the sofa, keeping some distance between her and the doctor. When she reached the window, a movement outside made her look out. Another car had parked next to the Range Rover. A policeman and a policewoman were coming up the path.

Betty spun and saw Lizzie Wilshire, rigid and slightly twisted in her chair with a little froth around her bluing lips and her bulbous eyes popped fully open, as if they were lidless.

Dr Coll stepped away from the fireplace. He was holding up a round, brown bottle with a half-inch of liquid in the bottom.

'Is *this* your herbal potion, Mrs Thorogood?'

THIRTY-THREE

The Adversary

From Off, they were, nearly all of them, Gomer reckoned. He'd told Merrily he could never imagine too many local people sticking their heads above the hedge, and he was right. There were maybe fifty of them – not an enormous turnout under the circumstances – and the ones Merrily could hear all had English accents.

Two TV crews had stayed for this; they were pushing microphones at the marchers as they came to the end of the pavement, a line of lamps, moving on into the lane past Annie Smith's place, bound for the Prosser farm and St Michael's. Telly questions coming at them, to get them all fired up.

'But what are you really hoping to achieve here?'

'Do you actually believe two self-styled white witches can in some way curse the whole community?'

'Don't people have the right, in the eyes of the law, to worship whatever they want to?'

And the answers came back, in Brummy, in Northern, in cockney London and posh London.

'This is not about the law. Read your Bible. In the eyes of God they are profane.'

'Why are there as many as five churches around the Radnor Forest dedicated to St Michael, who was sent to fight Satan?' A woman in a bright yellow waterproof holding up five fingers for the camera.

There was a central group of hardcore Bible freaks. This was probably the first demonstration most of them had ever joined,

Merrily thought. For quite a number, it was probably the first time they'd actually been closely involved with a church. It was the isolation factor: the *need to belong* which they never realized they'd experience until they moved to the wild hills. And the fact that Nicholas Ellis was a quietly spoken, educated kind of fanatic.

'It's true to say,' a sprightly, elderly woman told HTV Wales, 'that until I attended one of Father Ellis's services I did not truly believe in God as a supernatural being. I did not have faith, just a kind of wishy-washy wishful thinking. Now I have more than faith, I have *belief.* I exult in it. I *exult.* I love God and I hate and despise the Adversary.'

For a moment, Merrily was grabbed by a sense of uncertainty that recalled her first experience of tongues in that marquee near Warwick. Whatever you thought about Ellis, he'd brought all these people to God.

Then she thought about his slim, metal crucifix.

Ellis himself was answering no questions tonight; gliding along, half in some other world, no expression on his unlined, shiny face. Self-belief was a great preserving agent.

Hanging back from the march, Merrily rang to check on Jane, walking slowly with the phone.

'It was on the radio,' the kid said. 'That Buckingham woman's probably dead, isn't she?'

'Not necessarily.'

'But if she is, you don't think she topped herself, do you?'

'That's something the police get to decide, flower.'

Jane made a contemptuous noise. 'The police won't do a thing. They don't have the resources. The only reason this area has the lowest level of crime in southern Britain is because half the crimes don't even get discovered, everybody knows that.'

'So cynical, so young.'

'I read the story in the *Mail.* Totally predictable right-wing stitch-up.'

'You reckon?'

'Yeah. Mum . . . Listen, the truth, OK? Have you spoken to Irene since we were in Worcester? Like, him telling you all about me conning him into taking me to *Livenight* by saying you knew all about us going and it would help his career. And then – like, in his role as a Welsh Chapel fundamentalist bigot – asking if you knew how seriously interested I was in alternative spirituality, and maybe that what I secretly wanted was to get to know some of those people – the pagans – and then you both agreeing that this was probably a spiteful teenage reaction against having a mother who was a priestess and into Christianity at the sexy end.'

The kid ran out of breath.

Merrily said, 'Was this before or after Eirion said to me, "Oh God, I'm so sorry, this is all my fault, what if she's got brain damage?" And I said, "No, it's all *my* fault, I should never have agreed to do the bloody stupid programme"? Was it *after* that?'

Jane said nothing.

'Look,' Merrily said, 'after the initial blinding shock of seeing you in the middle of the motorway, it didn't take a lot of creative mental energy to form what looked like a complete picture of how you and Eirion came to be in the neighbourhood of Birmingham anyway. Complete enough to satisfy me, anyway, without any kind of tedious, acrimonious inquest. I mean, you know, call me smug, call me self-deluded, but the fact is – when you really look at it – I'm actually not *that* much older than you, flower.'

Silence.

'Shit,' Jane said at last. 'OK, I'm sorry.'

'I know.'

'Er, might that have been the Long Talk, by any chance?'

'I think it might.'

'Phew. What time will you be back?'

'Hard to say.'

'Only, that nurse phoned.'

'Eileen?'

'Said whatever time you get back, could you ring her? She sounded weird.'

'Weird how?'

'Just not the usual "Don't piss me about or I'll take your bedpan back" voice. Kind of hesitant, unsure of herself.'

'I'll call her.'

'Yeah,' Jane said. 'Somehow, I would if I were you.'

When the procession reached the Prosser farm, Merrily saw two people emerge discreetly from a gate and join it without a word: Judith Prosser and a bulky, slab-faced man.

'That's Councillor Prosser, Gomer?'

'Impressive, en't he? Wait till you hears him talk. Gives whole new meanin' to the word orat'ry.'

'Not that you don't rate him or anything.'

'Prince among men,' said Gomer.

By the time the march reached the track to St Michael's Farm, a police car was crawling behind. That figured: even good Christians these days had short fuses. They walked slowly on.

'That reminded me,' Gomer said. 'Learned some'ing about the Prossers and this Ellis 'fore I left the Lion. Greg yeard it. One o' the boys – Stephen? – got pulled over in a nicked car in Kington. Joy ridin', 'e was. 'Bout a year ago, this'd be. Woulder looked real bad for a magistrate's boy.'

'It happens.'

'Not yere it don't. First offence, mind, so Gareth talks to Big Weal, an' they fixes it with the cops. Gareth an' Judy promises the boy won't put a foot out o' line again. Just to make sure of it, they takes him to the Reverend Ellis, gets him hexorcized . . .'

Merrily stopped in the road. 'I'm not hearing this.'

The mobile bleeped in her pocket. She pulled it out, hearing Judith Prosser's words: *Time was when sinners would be dealt with by the Church, isn't it?*

'Merrily?'

'Sophie!' She hurried back along the lane to a quieter spot.

'Is this convenient? I tracked down a Canon Tommy Long, formerly the priest in charge of St Michael's, Cascob. He was more than glad to discuss something which he said had been puzzling him for many years. Shall I go on?'

'Please.'

'Seems that, in the late summer of 1965, he had a visit from the

Reverend Mr Penney. A very odd young man, he said – long-haired, beatnik-type, and most irrational on this occasion – who suggested that, as Cascob was a remote place with no prospect of other than a slow and painful decline in its congregation, the Reverend Long might wish to seek its decommissioning by his diocese.'

'Bloody hell.'

'Once he realized this was far from a joke, the Reverend Long asked Mr Penney to explain himself. Mr Penney came out with what was described to me as a lot of nonsensical gobbledegook relating to the layout of churches around Radnor Forest.'

'St Michael churches?'

'In an effort to deflect it, the Reverend Tommy Long pointed out a folk tale implying that if one of the churches were destroyed it would allow the, ah, dragon to escape. Mr Penney said this was . . . quite the reverse.'

'Why?'

'Mr Long wasn't prepared, at the time, to hear him out and now rather wishes he had.'

'What happened then?'

'Nothing. Mr Long pointed out that the Church in Wales would hardly be likely to part with a building as historic and picturesque as Cascob, especially as it contains a memorial to William Jenkins Rees, who helped to revive the Welsh language in the nineteenth century. The Reverend Mr Penney went somewhat sullenly away and, some months later, committed his bizarre assault on St Michael's Old Hindwell.'

'When he went away, where did he go? Does Mr Long know?'

'There's no happy ending here, Merrily. Mr Long says he was told some years later that Terry Penney died in a hostel for the homeless in Edinburgh or Glasgow, he isn't sure which. The poor man had been a heroin addict for some time. I think I shall go home now, Merrily.'

Robin spotted some lights, but they were the wrong lights.

He saw them through the naked trees, through the bald hedge-row further along from the barn. They were not headlights.

George came to stand alongside him at the window.

'What do you want to do, Robin? Shall we all go out and have a few words with them – in a civilized fashion?'

Vivvie dumped her glass of red wine and came over, excited. 'Is it them?' She had on a long red velvet dress, kind of Tudor-looking, and she wore those seahorse earrings that Robin hated. The bitch was ready to appear on TV again. 'What I suggest is we—'

'What *I* suggest,' Robin said loudly, 'is *we* don't do a goddamn thing. This is still my house . . . mine and . . . Betty's.'

The whole room had gone quiet, except for the damp twigs crackling in the hearth.

'*I'm* gonna go talk to them,' Robin said.

George smiled, shaking his head. 'You're not the man for this, Robin. You tend to speak before you've thought it out, if you don't mind me saying so.'

'I *do* mind, George. I mind like *hell* . . .'

'And you're tired,' Alexandra said kindly. 'You're tired and you're upset.'

'Yeah, well, damn freaking right I'm upset. I've been accused by that bastard of being a manifestation of insidious evil. How upset would *you* feel?'

'That's not what I meant.'

Robin backed up against the window, gripping the ledge behind him with both hands. 'So, I'm gonna go out there on my own.'

'That's really not wise,' Vivvie said, appealing to the coven at large.

Max cleared his throat. 'What I would suggest—'

'Don't you . . .' Robin threw himself into the room. 'Don't any of you tell me what's wise. And you . . .' He levelled a shaking finger at Vivvie. 'If it hadn't been for you and your goddamn big mouth—'

'Robin . . .' George took his arm, Robin shook him off.

Vivvie said, 'Robin, I'll thank you not to use the expression *God-damned* . . .'

'Shut the fuck *up!*'

Robin saw that it had begun to rain again. He saw the lights curling into rivulets on the window.

He took off his sweater.

*

The gate to St Michael's Farm was shut.

Through the bare trees you could see lights in the house, you could see the black hulk of what seemed to be a barn. But you could not see the church. The itinerant congregation formed a semicircle around Nicholas Ellis at the gate. The two men with garden torches stood either side of the gate.

A white wooden cross was raised – five or six feet long, like the one in the bungalow garden on the road from Walton.

Merrily felt an isolated plop of rain. Umbrellas went up: bright, striped golf umbrellas. A cameraman went down on one knee on a patch of grass, as if he'd found God, but it was only to find a low angle, to make Ellis look more like an Old Testament prophet.

Disgracefully, Ellis responded to it. A kind of shiver seemed to go through him, like invisible lightning, and his wide lips went back in a taut grimace.

'My friends, can you feel the *evil?* Can you feel the evil here in this place?' And then he was crying to the night sky. 'Oh Lord God, we pray for your help in eradicating this disease. You who sent Your most glorious warrior, Michael, to contain the dragon, the Adversary, the Old Enemy. Oh Lord, now that this infernal evil has once again returned, we pray that You will help us drive out these worshippers of the sun and the moon and the horned gods of darkness. Oh Lord, *help us*, we pray, *help us!*'

And the chant was taken up. 'Help us! *Help us, Lord!*' Faces were turned up to the rain.

Merrily winced.

Ellis cried, ' . . . You who send Your blessed rain to wash away sin, let it penetrate and cleanse this bitter earth, this soured soil. Oh Lord, wash this place clean of Satan's stain!'

His voice rode the slanting rain, his hair pasted to his forehead, the hissing torchlight reflected in his eyes. *Until I attended one of Father Ellis's services I did not truly believe in God as a supernatural being.*

Now Ellis was spinning round in the mud, his white robe aswirl, and putting his weight against the gate and bellowing, 'Come out! Come out, you snivelling servants of the Adversary. Come out and face the sorrow and the wrath of the one true God.'

'Fuck's sake, Nick . . .'

Ellis sprang back.

The weary, American voice came from the other side of the gate. The TV camera lights found a slightly built young guy with long, shaggy hair. He wore a plain T-shirt as white as Ellis's robe, but a good deal less suited to the time of year. He was just standing there, arms by his side, getting soaked. When he spoke, the tremor in his voice indicated not so much that he was afraid but that he was freezing.

'Nick, we don't need this shit, OK? We never touched your lousy church. There's no dragon here, no Satan. So just . . . just, like, go back and tell your God we won't hold you or your crazy stuff against him.'

The man with the cross stood alongside Ellis, like a sentinel. One of the garden torches fizzed, flared and went out. There was a gasp from the crowd, as though the flame had been a casualty of demonic breath. To charismatics, everything was a sign. Merrily moved in close to the gate. She needed to hear this.

Ellis put on a grim smile for the cameras. 'Let us in, then, Robin. Open the gate of your own free will and let us – and Almighty God – be readmitted to the church of St Michael.'

He waited, his white habit aglow. 'Praise God!' a man's voice cried.

Robin Thorogood didn't move. 'I don't think so, Nick.'

He was watching Ellis through the driving rain – and fighting just to keep his eyes open. To Merrily, he looked bewildered, as if he was struggling to comprehend the motivation of this man who was now his enemy on a level he'd never before experienced. He finally hugged himself, bare-armed, his T-shirt soaked, grey and wrinkled, into his chest. Then, defiantly, he let his arms fall back to his sides, still staring at Nick Ellis, who was now addressing him sorrowfully and reasonably in a low voice which the TV people might not pick up through the splashing of the rain.

'Robin, you know that we cannot allow this to go on. Whether you understand it or not – and I believe you fully understand it – if you and your kind proceed to worship your profane, heathen deities in a temple once consecrated in His holy name, you commit an act of gross sacrilege. You thereby commend this church into the arms of Satan himself. And you curse the community into which you and your wife were innocently welcomed.'

'No.' Robin Thorogood shook his sodden hair. 'That is bullshit.'

'Robin, if you don't recognize it, I can't help you.'

The big cross was shaking in the air. One of the men screamed out. *'Thou shalt not suffer a witch to live!'*

Merrily tensed, expecting an invasion – when something struck Ellis in the chest.

THIRTY-FOUR

Kali

Jane agonized for a while, cuddling Ethel the cat, and then rang Eirion at what she always pictured as a grim, greystone mansion beyond Abergavenny. The line was engaged.

She went back to the sitting room, still holding the cat, and replayed the tape she had recorded of the Old Hindwell story on the TV news.

There was a shot of the church from across a river. The male voice-over commented, *'The last religious service at Old Hindwell Parish Church took place more than thirty years ago. Tomorrow night, however, this church could be back in business.'*

Cut to a shot of a dreary-looking street, backing onto hills and forestry.

'But the people of this remote village close to the border of England and Wales are far from happy. Because at tomorrow night's service, the ancient walls will echo to a different liturgy.'

Ancient black and white footage of naked witches around a fire, chanting, 'Eko, eko, azarak . . .'

'And to one local minister, this is the sound of Satan.'

Talking head (Eirion had taught her the jargon) of a really ordinary-looking priest, except that he was wearing a monk's habit. The caption read: 'Father Nicholas Ellis, Rector'.

This Nicholas Ellis then came out with all this bullshit about there being no such thing as white witchcraft. His voice was overlaid with pictures of candles burning in people's windows – *seriously* weird

– and then they cut back to Ellis saying, 'It's out of our hands. It's in God's hands now. We shall do whatever he wants of us.'

Over shots of their farmhouse, the reporter said that Robin and Betty – Betty, Jesus, whoever heard of a witch called Betty? – were in hiding today, but 'a member of their coven' had confirmed that the witches' sabbath would definitely be going ahead tomorrow at the church, to celebrate the coming of the Celtic spring.

'The Diocese of Hereford says it broadly supports Father Ellis, but seems to be distancing itself from any extreme measures.'

Then up came Mum: 'Personally, I don't care too much for witch-hunts.'

On the whole, Jane felt deeply relieved.

She called Eirion again. This time it rang, and she prepared to crawl.

Eirion's stepmother, Gwennan, answered – a voice to match the house, or maybe it just sounded that way because she answered in Welsh. Jane almost expected her to hang up in disgust when she found it was someone who could only speak English, but the woman was actually quite pleasant in the end.

'He's in his room, on the Internet. Seventeen years old and still playing with the Internet, how sad is that? Hold on, I'll get him.'

'OK. I'm sorry,' Jane said when he came on. 'I am so totally sorry. Everything I said . . . I'm brain-damaged. I make wrong connections. I don't deserve to live.'

'I agree, but forget that. Listen . . .'

'Charming.'

'Are you online yet?'

'No, I keep telling you. Mum's got the Internet at the office in Hereford. If there's anything I need, I look it up there. Too much surfing damages your—'

'I was going to give you a web site to visit.' Eirion sounded different, preoccupied, like something was really getting to him. 'I'd like you to see it for yourself, then you'll know I'm not making it up.'

'Why would I think that?'

'I mean, the Web . . . sometimes it's like committing yourself into this great, massive asylum.'

'Irene . . .?'

'I was checking out pagan web sites, trying to find out what I could about Ned Bain and these other people, OK?'

'Why?'

'Because I'm off school and I got fed up with walking the grounds contemplating the infinite.'

'And where did it get you?'

'To be really honest, into places I didn't think existed. You start off on the pagan web sites, which are fairly innocent, or at least they *seem* innocent afterwards, compared with the serious occult sites you get referred to. It's like you're into a weeding-out process and after a while it's kind of, only totally depraved screwballs need apply, you know? Like, you can learn, among other things, how to effectively curse someone.'

'What's the address for that one? Let me grab a pen.'

'Jane,' he sounded serious, 'take my word for it, when you actually see it on the screen it suddenly becomes less amusing. It's like getting into some ancient library, where all the corridors stink of mould and mildew. All these arcane symbols.'

'Sounds like Dungeons and Dragons.'

'Only for real. You start thinking, Shit, suppose I pick up some . . . I don't know . . . virus. And periodically you get casually asked to tap in your email address or your name and your home address . . . or maybe just the town. And sometimes you almost do it automatically and then you think, Christ, they'll know where to *find* me . . .'

'Wimp.'

'No. Even if you put in a false name, they can trace you, and they can feed you viruses. So, anyway, I got deeper and deeper and eventually I reached a site called Kali Three.'

'You mean, like . . .'

'Like the Indian goddess of death and destruction. *That* Kali.' Eirion paused. 'And that was where I found her.'

Found her? For some reason, Jane started thinking about Barbara Buckingham. A shadow crossed the room and she sat up, startled.

It was Ethel. Only Ethel.

Jane said, 'Who?'

'Your mum,' Eirion said. 'Merrily Watkins, Deliverance Consultant to the Diocese of Hereford, UK.'

'Wha—'

'She came up on Kali Three pretty much immediately. There was a picture of her. Black and white – looked like a newspaper mugshot. And then inside there was kind of a potted biography. Date of birth. Details of the parish in Liverpool where she was curate. Date of her installation as priest-in-charge at Ledwardine, Herefordshire. Oh . . . and "daughter: Jane, date of birth . . ."'

'Picture?' Jane said bravely.

'No. But there's a picture of your dad.'

'*What?*'

'Another black and white. Bit fuzzy, like a blow-up from a group picture. Sean Barrow. Date of birth. Date of . . . death. And the place. I mean the exact place, the flyover, the nearest junction. And the circumstances. All of what Gerry said at *Livenight* and more. It says "Sean and Merrily were estranged at the time, which explains why she afterwards retained the title Mrs but switched back to her maiden name." It says that "She is" . . . hang on, the print goes a bit funny here . . . yeah, that "she is still vulnerable" . . . something . . . "the death of her husband. Without which she might have found it harder to enter the Church."'

Jane exploded. 'Who *are* these bastards?'

'I don't know. There are several names, but I don't think they're real names. I think it'd take you a long time to find out who they are – if you ever could. They could be really heavy-duty occultists or they could just be students. That's the problem with the Net, you can't trust anything on there. A lot of it's lies.'

'But . . . why? What kind of . . .?'

'That's what scares me. There's a line at the bottom. It says, "The use of the word 'Deliverance' is the Church's latest attempt to sanitize exorcism. Having a woman in the role, particularly one who is fairly young and attractive, is an attempt to mask what remains a regime of metaphysical oppression. This woman should be regarded as an enemy.'

Jane felt herself going pale. 'Mum?'

'And there are all these curious symbols around the bottom, like runes or something – I've no idea what a rune looks like. But it – this is the worrying bit – it points out that "Anyone with an interest can see Merrily Watkins on the *Livenight* television programme", and it gives the date, and it says that the programme will be coming live from a new Midlands studio complex, just off the M5. So that's out of date now, but it must have been there before the programme took place, obviously. And it says that if anyone is interested in further information, they can get it from . . . and then there's a sequence of numbers and squiggles which I can't make any sense of, but I don't think it's another web site, more like a code, so . . . Jane?'

'Yeah.' A whisper.

'I'm sorry. I didn't want you to hear it like this, because I could be making it up, couldn't I? To support the stuff you were rubbishing this morning.'

'Irene . . . what am I going to do?'

'I don't know. What happened . . . happened to other people. It's not even a good coincidence. I mean, who believes in any of this crap?'

'*You* do.'

'I don't know whether I do or not. And anyway, I'm just a fundamentalist Welsh Chapel bigot.'

'Were there any other people mentioned on this web site, apart from Mum?'

'Probably. I didn't look, to be honest. What if there'd turned out to be a whole bunch of names and biographies of people and they were all recently dead or . . .? Shit, that's how it's supposed to work, isn't it? Preying on your mind?'

'Like, suppose there was this big hex thing and people . . . all over the country . . . the world . . . were being invited to, like, tune in and focus on Mum, the enemy, to put her off. Because, we both know how rubbish she was on that programme. I mean, she was fine on TV tonight, wasn't she? Kind of cool, almost. Suppose it wasn't just nerves that night. Suppose there were hundreds – thousands – of people sending her hate vibes or something. And then they all started focusing on that piece of road, where Dad . . . It's *horrible!*'

'It's also complete crap, Jane. We're just stretching things to fit the facts. We're playing right into their hands.'

'*Whose* hands?'

'Anybody who frequents the web site – including, presumably, Ned Bain, if he was the one putting it round about your mum. That doesn't mean he's behind any of it. It just tells us where he got his information.'

'It's still creepy.'

'It's meant to be creepy.'

'Can you tell when it was originally pasted on the site?'

'Somebody else might be able to, but not me. For all I know, somebody could have pushed it out *after* the show, to make it look . . . I don't know. It's all crap, and it makes me mad.'

'Irene, I'm going to have to tell her.'

'I think you should. I'll try and find out some more.'

'You're wonderful,' Jane said. *Whoops.* 'Er . . . how's the whiplash?'

'Well, it just kind of hurts when I look over my shoulder.'

Jane instinctively looked over hers and shivered, and it wasn't an exciting frisson kind of shiver. Not now.

THIRTY-FIVE

This is History

'A martyr?' The rain had eased. Merrily pushed back the dripping hood of her saturated, once-waxed jacket. 'With his chest all splattered. Perhaps that was what he wanted.'

When the police had gone in, she'd walked away from it all. Her first instinct had been to stay on Robin Thorogood's side of the fence, maybe go and talk to him, but now the cops were doing that. Journalists and cameramen were together in another group by the gate at St Michael's Farm, waiting for someone to emerge.

Ellis had been driven away in a white Transit van, the cross and the torches packed away in the back. His followers watched the white van's tail lights disappear along the end of the track, talking quietly in groups. There was an air of damp anticlimax.

'For just one moment,' Merrily said to Gomer, 'I thought—'

'Coppers thought that, too. Out o' their car in a flash.'

'It looked like blood.'

'Shit does, in a bad light.'

'It really was?'

'Sheepshit, or dogshit more like, stuck on a bloody great lump o' soil. He din't smell too fragrant then. Likely the real reason he's buggered off so quick.'

'Whoever threw it . . . that wasn't a great idea. Thorogood was winning their argument.'

'Young kiddie, it was. 'E had it on the end of a spade. Seen him come up behind the boy in the T-shirt.'

'Still look good in the press, though,' Merrily said glumly. 'On their pictures he *will* look like a martyr. I . . .' She glanced over the gate to where two police were still talking to Thorogood.

'Look out, vicar,' Gomer murmured.

Judith Prosser was heading over, without her Gareth. She wore a shiny new Barbour, a matching wide-brimmed hat.

'They've found Barbara's car, then, Mrs Watkins.' She spotted Gomer. 'Ah . . . I see you have your *informant* with you.'

''Ow're you, Judy?'

'Gomer. I heard your wife died. I'm sorry.'

'Things 'appens,' Gomer said gruffly. He shook his head, droplets spinning from his cap.

Judith nodded. 'So what about Barbara, Mrs Watkins? She down there, in Claerwen Reservoir, is it?'

'Well, I don't *know* those reservoirs, Mrs Prosser. But I think if Barbara's body was in there, they'd have found it by now. I reckon the answer to that mystery's much more likely to be found here.'

'Do you indeed?'

'Don't you?'

'You like a mystery, do you?'

'How's Marianne?' Merrily said.

'Mrs Starkey is quite well' – wary now – 'I assume.'

'Those lustful demons can be difficult to extract.'

The caution was suddenly discarded as Judith laughed. 'Don't you believe all you hear.'

'Like what?'

'All kinds of nonsense gets talked about, Mrs Watkins. Be silly for you to start passing on rumours, isn't it? I certainly haven't heard anything to upset me.'

She smiled; she had good teeth.

'In that case, you must have a strong constitution, Mrs Prosser,' Merrily said.

Left to himself, Robin would have kicked the kid's ass.

Hermes, nine years old, brother of Artemis, twelve, and of Ceres, six and a half.

Max and Bella did not kick Hermes's ass. They were not the

ass-kicking kind. They would, presumably, explain to him later, in some detail, what effect having tossed shit at the Christian priest might have on him karmically.

No hassle from the cops for Hermes, either. Soon as they found out this was a kid, and that they didn't get to lean on a grown pagan, they didn't hang around. Soon as the cops had gone, the media went off too, back to the Black Lion. None of them came to the house.

Robin peeled off his sodden T-shirt, towelled himself dry, stood in front of the cheery fire with a bath towel around his shoulders.

'They'll be back tomorrow night,' George said with a good lashing of relish, 'when we're in the church. And this time there'll be hundreds of them. It's going to get really, really interesting, man.'

Robin said, 'Did she call?'

'Betty? Er, no.'

'That car's old, Robin,' Vivvie said. 'Maybe it's just broken down.'

'I listened to the weather forecast,' George said. 'The rain's likely to have passed by morning. It'll get colder, but tomorrow looks like being dry, so we'll have all day to prepare the site.'

Robin shivered under the towel. 'You guys don't get it, do you? This is not gonna happen without Betty. If Betty doesn't come back . . . no Imbolc.'

'You're tired, man,' George said.

'She *will* come back,' Vivvie promised with intensity. 'She won't want to miss this.' Her eyes glowed. 'Imbolc . . . the glimmering of spring. This really is the start of an era. This is history. Like Max was saying while you were outside, it's going to be the biggest thing since the Reformation. But whereas that was just Henry VIII plundering the riches of the Catholic Church, this is about the disintegration and decay of pride and vanity . . . and the regrowth of something pure and organic in the ruins. This is so beautifully symbolic, I want to cry.'

'Well, I'll tell you,' Robin said. 'I'm starting not to give a shit.'

'You don't mean that. You did a terrific job tonight.'

'I most likely looked a complete asshole. I just wasn't gonna cringe in front of that creep in his monk's robes, was all. I was gonna look as white as he was.'

And maybe less pretentious. He wasn't gonna go out there

swinging a gold pentacle. He'd wanted to handle the confrontation with simple human dignity. Because what he'd really hoped for was that Betty would be out there watching – that she'd gotten home OK, but had been unable to come through the gate on account of the march, so was out there watching her *tactless, thoughtless, irresponsible* husband handling a difficult situation with some kind of basic human dignity.

And then fucking Hermes had blown it all away.

If you were looking for omens, you sure had one there. What kind of headlines were they gonna get tomorrow? 'Witches Hurl Shit at Man of God'. The perfect follow-through to Robin looking like a freaking cannibal that last time.

'Robin . . .' The motherly Alexandra smiled a tentatively radiant candlelight smile at him across the room.

'Sorry?'

'Robin, there's a small car just come into the yard.'

'Huh . . .?'

He shot to the window, the bath towel dropping to the flags. He shaded his eyes with his cupped hands, up against the glass, hardly daring to hope that he'd see . . .

A little white Subaru Justy.

Oh God. Oh God. Robin sagged over the big, wide window sill, staring down between his hands and working on his breathing until he no longer felt faint with relief.

He straightened up. 'Look, would you mind all staying here? I have to do some explaining.'

The Black Lion was packed, the air in the bar full of damp and steam, coming off journalists, TV people, even a few of the Christian marchers – all wet through, starved, in need of a stiff whisky. Greg was run off his feet. No sign of Marianne yet.

Gomer fetched Merrily a single malt and one for himself. There was nowhere to sit except in a tight corner by the window next to the main door. Whenever the door opened, they had to lean to one side, but at least they weren't overheard as Merrily told Gomer the plain truth about Marianne's exorcism.

Gomer didn't blink. He weighed it up, nodding slowly. He laid out a row of beer mats on the table – and, with them, Merrily's dilemma.

'Gotter be a problem for you, this, girl. Question of which side you're on now, ennit?'

'Yes.' Merrily lit a cigarette. She'd taken off her wet coat, but still had the scarf wound round her neck. She was still seeing Robin Thorogood there on his own, vastly outnumbered, not wearing anything witchy, not countering Ellis's talk of Satan and sacrilege with any pagan propaganda. It could have been an act, to appear ordinary in the face of all the cross-waving – and yet it was *too* ordinary to be feigned.

'What you gonner do, then, vicar?'

'Gomer, how could Judith Prosser and those other woman sit there and watch it? Can they really believe in him to that extent?'

Gomer took out a roll-up. 'Like I said, it's about stickin' together, solid. Ellis's helped the right people, ennit? Judy and Gareth with their boy. And who knows what else he done.'

'Oh my God.'

'Vicar?'

Merrily drank the rest of her whisky in a gulp.

'Menna,' she murmured. *'Menna . . .'*

Robin turned on the bulkhead lamp. It was no longer raining, but the wind had gotten up. A metal door creaked rhythmically over in the barn; it sounded like a sailing boat on the sea making him wish he and Betty were alone together, far out on some distant ocean.

Still naked to the waist, he stood on the doorstep and watched her park next to one of the Winnebagos. She stepped out of the car and into a puddle. The whole of the yard was puddles tonight.

She didn't seem to care how wet her feet got. Her hair was frizzed out by the rain, uncombed.

Oh God, how he loved this woman. He tried to send this out to her. *I take thee to my hand, my heart and my spirit at the setting of the sun and the rising of the stars . . .*

He saw her standing for a moment, entirely still, taking in the extra cars in the yard, the two Winnebagos.

Then she saw him.

He came out of the doorway, walked towards her. She still didn't move. If it was cold out here, he wasn't feeling it yet.

'Bets, I . . .'

He stopped a couple of yards from his wife. The back of his neck felt on fire.

'Bets, I couldn't stop them. It was either them or . . . or all kinds of people we didn't know. It had all gotten out. You just couldn't imagine . . . It was all over the Internet. We were getting hate faxes and also faxes from people who were right behind us – like, religious polarization, you know, over the whole nation? Or so . . . so it seemed.'

Betty spoke at last, in this real flat voice.

'Who are they?'

'Well, there . . . there's George and Vivvie, and . . . and Alexandra. And Stuart and Mona Osman, who we met at some . . . at some sabbat, someplace. And Max and Bella . . . Uh, Max is kind of an all-knowing asshole, but they're OK where it matters. I guess. And some other people. Bets, I'm sorry. If you'd only called . . .'

There was no expression at all on her face; this was what scared him. Why didn't she just lose her temper, call him a stupid dickhead, get this over?

'See, we always said there was gonna be a sabbat at Imbolc. Didn't we say that? That we were gonna bring the church alive with lights? A big bonfire to welcome the spring? So like . . . maybe this was destined to come about. Maybe there was nothing we could do to get in the way of it. Like it's meant to be – only with more significance than we could ever have imagined.'

Why did this all sound so hollow? Why was she taking a step back, away from him?

There was a splish in a puddle. Her car keys? She'd dropped the car keys. Robin rushed forward, plunged his hand and half his arm into the puddle, scrabbling about in the black, freezing water, babbling on still.

'Look . . . Ellis was here, with his born-again buddies. Chances are they're gonna be back tomorrow – only more of them. There was like this real heavy sense of menace. You and me, we couldn't't've handled that on our own, believe me.'

He hated himself for this blatant lie, but what could he say? He pulled out the dripping keys, hung on to them.

Betty said, 'Give me the keys, Robin.'

'Why? *No!*'

'I can't stay here tonight.'

'Please . . . you don't know . . . Bets, it's gotten bigger than us two. OK, that's a cliché, but it's true. What's happening here's gonna be . . .'

'Symbolic,' a voice said from behind him. He turned and saw Vivvie on the step. Vivvie had come out to help him. Vivvie alone.

The worst thing that could've happened.

'Symbolic of the whole struggle to free this country from two millennia of religious corruption and spiritual stagnation. He's right, Betty. We have to play our part. We have to reconsecrate the church and it has to be tomorrow night. It's why we're here.'

Betty started to shake her head, and the light from the bulkhead caught one side of her face and Robin saw the dark smudges, saw she'd been crying hard.

'Bets!' He almost screamed. 'Look, I know things haven't been right. I know you never connected with this place. Honey, please . . . once this is over we'll sell up, yeah? I mean, like, Jeez, from what I've been hearing there's gotta be about a hundred pagans ready to take it off our hands. But this . . . Imbolc . . . this is something we have to go through – together, yeah? Please let it be together.'

'Give me those keys.'

'I will not let you leave!'

'You will not stop me,' Betty said. 'And *she* certainly won't.'

She turned away, walked across the yard toward the track.

Robin ran after her, managed four paces before the cold, suddenly intense, bit into his chest and his breathing seemed to seize up. But that was nothing to the pain right dead centre of his heart chakra.

His eyes flooded up.

'Don't follow me,' Betty said. 'I mean it, don't take one more pace.'

THIRTY-SIX

The Atheist

'You're back home?' Eileen Cullen's relief was apparent, even over hospital corridor echo and clattering trays.

Merrily switched on the engine, turned the heater up all the way and shook a cigarette into her lap. 'I'm in my car on a pub car park in Old Hindwell, and wet and cold.'

'You're still *out* there? Oh hey, one of the porters saw you on the box tonight, said he fancied the hell out of you. Listen, you've heard about Buckingham? The car in the reservoir?'

'It doesn't mean she's dead, Eileen.'

'It's scary, Merrily. Civilized woman like that, if she wanted to do away with herself, why not a bottle of Scotch and a handful of pills?'

'I still can't believe she has.'

'Aye, well, sometimes you . . .' Cullen hesitated. 'Sometimes there's things you just don't want to believe, no matter what. What are the alternatives, after all? It's suicide, face it. And don't you go feeling guilty. There's nothing you could've done.'

'How can you say that?'

'Because, Reverend, that's the official motto of the National Health Service. Listen, will you be in town tomorrow?'

'Probably not tomorrow.'

'I need to talk to you.'

'Are we not talking now?'

'What I want to talk about, you don't on the phone. Well you don't at all if you've got any sense. I could come and see you . . . at your home.'

'Eileen?' Jane was right; Cullen, hard as a hospital potato, had never sounded less assured.

'Truth is . . . I've not been frank with you, Merrily – or with meself, come to that. There's things I ought to've said.' She dropped her voice to just above a whisper. 'About the night Menna Weal died. And I can't talk here, I'm on the public phone.'

'You've got an office, haven't you?'

'It's open house in there, so it is. Anyway, I *won't* talk in this place, and I don't get off now until the morning. You've got my home number, so call me when you can.'

'Eileen, don't . . . do *not* hang up. Let's just talk about Menna, OK? The stroke could have been brought on by stress, right? Severe emotional stress?'

'Hypertension due to emotional trauma. Distended arteries, then a clot gets shunted into the brain. What kind of trauma you thinking about?'

'Exorcism,' Merrily said.

'Oh, terrific,' Cullen said drably.

'The expulsion of an evil entity. *Intended* expulsion.'

'I know what it *is*, I was raised a Catholic. But, excuse me, Reverend, would not someone in your job be seeing it everywhere you bloody look?'

'Just . . . bear with me, OK? You get some ministers – of an evangelical or charismatic persuasion – who believe that demonic forces . . . and angelic forces, come to that . . . are all around us in all kinds of guises. Like there are probably a few in California who'd offer to exorcize me in order to expel the demon nicotine.'

'You mean eejits.'

'So here's poor Menna – withdrawn, maladjusted maybe, communication problems. OK, I won't go into details, but there's good reason to think she was abused by her dad.'

'Is that a fact.' Cullen who'd heard it all many times before.

'Probably over a long period. But not necessarily when she was a kid.'

'So you could be talking about more of an unnatural *relationship*.'

'If she was as naive and immature as I've been told, I think we're still talking about abuse.'

Merrily lit another cigarette and gathered her thoughts, staring out along the village street. From here, she could count candles in nine separate windows. The street lighting was so meagre and widely spaced that some of the candles seemed disproportionately bright through the rain-blobbed windscreen and unintentionally jolly, like Christmas lights.

She just wanted to air this stuff, to another woman.

'I don't want to speculate too much about the state of the Weal marriage . . . but it seems likely the obsessive love there was fairly one-sided. And Weal must have realized that – that the father was still very much in the background, even though dead.'

'You mean Weal's thinking he might be having a happier time altogether if he can remove whatever emotional block's been left behind in Menna by her having a sex beast for a father.'

'I doubt the concept of happiness means much to him, but yeah . . . And he wouldn't have her seeing a psychiatrist or a therapist because that's not the kind of thing you're seen to do in Old Hindwell. So, after a lot of agonizing and soul-searching, perhaps, he goes to the priest.'

'Who you say's not your regular kind of priest, yeah?'

'Mmm. At the funeral, Ellis disclosed that Weal and Menna were baptized *together*, not long before she died. I think *that* means she was exorcized. Historically, baptism's always been linked with exorcism. In the medieval Church, it was more or less believed that until it was baptized, a baby was the property of the Devil and if it died before baptism it would be consigned to the fires of hell.'

'No offence to you, personally,' Cullen said, 'but how I hate the Church.'

'So, suppose Weal believed that having Menna rebaptized into the faith would free her from the influence of her father . . . from the effects of her childhood. And suppose the ceremony – conducted in the privacy of their home – involved . . . well, something considerably more stressful than a sprinkling of holy water. And I *mean* more stressful.'

'Then, sure, you *could* be into stroke country.'

'That's what I thought.'

'And . . .' Cullen hesitated, 'as you've mentioned baptism, the anointing of the forehead with water, if we cast our minds back to a certain wee side ward . . .'

'Mmm.'

'I always thought any anointing of a corpse was down to the priest.'

'Me, too.'

Long silence.

'Possession is nine points of the law,' Merrily said. 'That was what Barbara Buckingham said.'

'Possession?' Cullen said.

'Possession of the dead by the living, was how she put it, ostensibly meaning the private tomb. But I think there were other things she wasn't prepared to put into words, maybe even to herself.'

'Ah, Merrily . . .'

'Pretty much like you, really. Why don't you just tell me the rest?'

Cullen said, 'This is a pressure job, you know? You get overtired, so you do.'

'And imagine things.'

'That's true.'

'Like?'

'Like things you don't believe in.'

'Did something happen when you went down to the morgue?'

Cullen sighed. 'Maybe.'

'He went along with you – which is not usual.'

'Not only that, he sent the porters away. He asked could he spend some time with her, say his goodbyes.'

'How long?'

'A clear hour. To cut a long story short, they sent for me, in the end, to exercise my fabled diplomacy on the man. When I get down there, I'm delighted to see he's finally leaving. Has on his hat and coat, a big dark solicitor's overcoat, like he's on his way to court. I didn't approach him, but I thought it was as well to follow him, to make quite sure he left the premises. So I did that. I followed him.'

Cullen broke off. There was the sound of someone calling from a distance, then Cullen said, 'Two minutes, Josie, all right?'

'Bloody hell,' Merrily said, 'don't stop now.'

'Ach, normal way of things you wouldn't get this out of me with thumbscrews. All right. Weal goes out by one of the back doors near the consultants' car park. You can get across the yard there to the temporary visitors' car park. It's the quickest way, if you don't mind there being no lights. Which I wish to God there had've been, then I could've said it was a reflection.'

Merrily revved the engine to blow more heat into the Volvo.

'I could still say it was,' Cullen said defiantly. 'I can say any damn thing I want to, as I'm an atheist. I do not believe in God, I do not believe in angels or demons.'

'And you don't believe what you saw. A lot of people say that. That's OK.'

'Feel free to be patronizing, Reverend. I've woken up about seven times in the night since then. Gets into me fockin' dreams, the way you get a virus in your computer. And everything freezes on you.'

'I know.'

'Oh, *you* know everything, so you do!'

'I'm sorry.'

'I'm standing in the doorway, just the other side of the big plastic doors, and I'm watching him walk across to the visitors' car park, which is all but empty now. Nobody about but him and this . . . Jesus.'

Merrily's eyes turned this way and that, determinedly counting nine candles in nine windows, banishing all wildly flickering thoughts of the old rectory garden, while Cullen kept her waiting.

Until, at last, over the sound of footsteps in the hospital corridor and a woman squealing, she whispered, 'Just a hovering thing, you know? Like a light. Not a bright light . . . more kind of greyish, half there and half not. That's as best as I can tell you. You could see it and then you couldn't. But you knew . . . you bloody *knew*. I went very cold, Merrily. *Very* cold, you know?'

'Mmm.'

'And him . . . Oh, he knew it was there, all right. I swear to God he knew it was there. Twice, he looked back over his shoulder. I . . . Aw, hell, I can't believe I'm saying this out loud. It made me go cold, you know?'

'I *do* know,' Merrily said.

THIRTY-SEVEN

Night Hag

Gomer was standing up at the bar with Greg Starkey, talking to him between other customers buying drinks. Greg glanced at Merrily through bloodshot eyes, trying to keep his voice muted, not succeeding.

'I'm on eggshells, trying to run a boozer, while she's up inna bedroom, sitting on the edge of the bed, staring into space. If I put a hand on her it's like I've hit her, you know? Like she got no skin? That's what it does to them, is it? A blessing?'

A *blessing*? 'How much did she tell you about it?' Merrily asked.

'Not a lot. I fought it was all gonna be "Praise the Lord" and that. I was geared up for that. Woulda been better than the battered wife routine. Who's that bastard fink he is?'

'Thinks he's St Michael,' Merrily said soberly. 'Greg, do you think she'd talk to *me*?'

'I just told Gomer I'll put it to her. Soon's I get a minute, which could be closing time. How long you got?'

'As long as it takes.'

'I'll do what I can. *Yes*, sir . . . Carlsberg, is that?'

Merrily beckoned Gomer back to the cold place nobody else wanted, near the door. She told him what she'd discussed with Eileen Cullen, about the reasons they figured J.W. Weal might have wanted Menna cleansed.

Gomer said shrewdly, 'You reckon Barbara Thomas knew?'

'About the baptism? It's possible, isn't it?'   ✦

The steamy light pooled in Gomer's glasses. 'Likely what Barbara Thomas found out got her killed then, ennit?'

'Good God, Gomer!'

Gomer sniffed. 'Reckoned I'd say it 'fore you did. Mind your back, vicar.'

A young woman had come in alone. She stood on the mat, shaking back wild, corn-coloured hair that somehow looked not only out of place in Old Hindwell, but out of season. She drew a breath, scanned the crowd in the bar and then walked through.

'Until there's a body,' Merrily said, 'she hasn't been killed. Until there's a body she isn't dead.'

'Who you got lined up for it, then? Big Weal hisself?'

'Shhhh!'

Gomer looked around, unconcerned. 'He en't yere.'

'OK,' Merrily whispered, 'considered objectively, it seems ridiculous. I mean, if Barbara found out Weal arranged to have his wife exorcized by Ellis, as some kind of primitive pyschological therapy . . . well, he might not want that out in the open, but it's only slightly dirty washing. And it *is* Christianity, of a sort. It's no reason to kill somebody. And would he really expect to get away with it in a place like this?'

Gomer threw up his hands. 'Place like *this*? Nowhere bloody easier, vicar! Local people protects local people. Might keep any number o' secrets from each other, but if they gets a threat from Off, they'll close in real tight till it's over and gone. They thought1jyWeal *had* done it, they'd be happy to shovel shit over his tracks, ennit?'

'The other thing that struck me,' Merrily said, 'is that the doctor who kept prescribing all that oestrogen that sent Menna's blood pressure up . . .'

'Dr Coll, eh? Now *there's* a respected man.'

'If Menna did develop dangerously high blood pressure, furred arteries, serious danger of fatal clotting, why didn't he warn her? Why wasn't he monitoring her? If she was on the Pill for . . . I don't know, twenty years or more . . .'

Gomer said, 'What you wanner do is you wanner talk to Judy.

Proper, though. None o' this circlin' round each other. Talk to her straight.'

'Tonight?'

'As well as Mrs Starkey? Busy ole night you got lined up there.'

'OK, tomorrow.' She pulled out her cigarettes and then put them back. 'I don't know why I'm doing this. Why am I doing this, Gomer?'

'Because . . . 'ang about.' Gomer turned towards the bar. Merrily saw Greg Starkey frantically beckoning them over. 'I think the boy wants you,' Gomer said.

Greg opened the solid wooden gate in one side of the bar, to allow Merrily and Gomer through.

'Just walks in like noffink's happened, asks for a room for the night. Well, I've only got two rooms, ain' I, and they've both gone to reporters. I can't turn her away, but what if the wife comes out, nursing her Bible, and finds the bleedin' spawn of Satan under a blanket on the settee?'

'Gomer,' Merrily said, 'just don't call me vicar in front of her, OK?'

Greg led them into the well-fitted kitchen with the tomato-red Aga. A woman stood next to it, gripping the chromium guard rail, as though she was on the deck of a small boat in a gale.

The night hag.

Couldn't be more than late twenties. Pleated skirt, dark sweater, ski jacket, all that blond hair.

'This is my friend,' Greg said, 'wiv the accommodation. Merrily Watkins.'

Merrily watched the young woman's eyes. No recognition at all. Clearly not a *Livenight* viewer, not even that particularly relevant edition.

'*OK,*' she'd said to Greg, in a snap decision, '*just tell her I'm someone with a big house who does B and B sometimes.*'

B and B? Sanctuary? What a vicarage was for.

Good Samaritan. The good Samaritan, who went to the aid of someone from a different culture, a different ethos.

'It's only for one night,' Betty Thorogood was saying. 'Probably.'

'And this is Gomer Parry,' Greg said.

''Ow're you?' Gomer flashed the wild-man grin.

Gotter be a problem for you, this, girl. Question of which side you're on now, ennit?

Part Four

When people experience the outpouring of the Holy Spirit
and the reality and presence of God in their lives, they also
become more aware of the power of evil.

Deliverance (ed. Michael Perry)
The Christian Deliverance Study Group

THIRTY-EIGHT

The Real Thing

Merrily flashed her headlights twice and then pulled out to the end of the car park and waited for the young woman to come over.

'Funny how things turns out, ennit?' Gomer said mildly, from the back seat.

'You think this is a terrible mistake?'

'Bit late to worry 'bout that, vicar.'

The blonde came warily out of the short alley leading to the Black Lion's yard, and got into the Volvo. Merrily eased the car into the main street, glancing into her wing mirror; nobody was following them.

'Just put my mind at rest,' Betty Thorogood said. 'You're really *not* from the media, are you?'

'I'm really not.' Merrily felt deeply uneasy about this now but, at the same time, curiously elated. She drove carefully along the village street, past all the little candles glowing brightly. 'Actually, Betty, it's much worse than that.'

She was getting uncomfortable, anyway, driving with the scarf on.

Jane had called Eirion back. 'I'm getting obsessed about this. The more you think about it, the more things occur to you.'

'Then stop thinking about it. Go to bed.'

'I'd just lie awake, getting spooked. I keep thinking how keen they were to get Mum on that programme, all those calls from Tania.

Why *would* they go to all that trouble for just one person who's not very controversial.'

'Nice legs, nice face – tabloid television?'

'But they told Bain about her – or somebody did – well before-hand. So they'd have plenty of time to prime Kali Three.'

'I doubt anyone at *Livenight*'s even heard of Kali: the web site *or* the goddess. When you're putting a programme together you must make all kinds of deals to get people to come on. I don't really think we're looking at any kind of big conspiracy – it's just the way things turned out. However . . .'

'What?'

'Just I hit on another site. It's called Witchfinder. It's for people who want to contact a coven. Wherever you are in Britain, it'll put you in touch with your nearest group: email addresses mainly.'

'Any around here?'

'Loads . . . well, two. But that's not the point. From Witchfinder, I clicked on another site, which was a kind of pagan *Who's Who?*'

'The *Which Witch* guide?'

'Very good, for somebody with brain damage.'

'It's *because* of the brain damage. Normally I'm serious and pedantic.'

'I got it to search for Ned Bain. Turned up a surprising amount. I assume it's true, but anybody can put anything on the Net.'

'Unflattering stuff?'

'Not particularly. Biographical stuff, mainly. He's a writer and publisher, now in charge of Dolmen Books, the New Age imprint at Harvey-Calder. Been married twice, high priest of top people's coven in Chelsea. A champagne pagan, that's what he gets called.'

'Sham-pagan?'

'I wouldn't say that, since he's been into it a long time – since he was at university and possibly before. But what's really significant is that we suddenly have an explanation of why he hates the Church so much.'

'He never *said* that,' Jane said crossly. 'He insisted his lot were an alternative to Christianity. He didn't say anything about—'

'Well, it's pretty obvious, when you read about his background.

His father was an academic – a professor of English literature at Oxford, and also a fairly acclaimed poet, though I've never heard of him. Edward Bainbridge?'

'Bain*bridge*?'

'That's also Ned's real name. His father died back in the mid-'70s. He was . . . I wish you could see this stuff. I don't want you to think I'm jumping to the wrong conclusions.'

'Just tell me.'

'It's just that his father was stabbed to death.'

Jane gripped the phone. 'Ned Bain's father was *murdered*?'

'It's complicated.'

'Spill it. No, hang on a sec.' She pulled the phone from her ear. Sound of a car in the drive. 'Mum's here. I'll call you back – if not tonight, first thing tomorrow.'

'I'll go back online,' Eirion said. 'See what else I can discover before midnight.'

'Anorak.'

'Don't lie there getting spooked, Jane. Think of me, think of my strong body.'

'In your dreams, Welshman.'

The headlights exposed Ethel trickling across the lawn – a black cat, witch-friendly, crossing the beam of the sensor which then activated the lantern on the porch, spraying light up the 400-year-old black and white facade of Ledwardine vicarage.

Merrily switched off the engine. How would Nicholas Ellis react if he could see her giving sanctuary to the spawn of Satan, a child of the dragon, a worshipper of profane, heathen deities . . . filth, scum, spiritual vermin. How, come to that, would the bishop react? *'The pagans'll have you down as a jackboot fascist, while Ellis is calling you a pinko hippy doing the tango with Satan.'*

The elation was long over. Merrily's head was choked with contradictions. The twenty-five-minute journey through deserted country lanes had been, at best, awkward, their conversation sparse and stilted. It was evident that there was far more wrong in the life of Betty Thorogood than Nicholas Ellis and the *Daily Mail*, but very little had come out. What was she supposed to say to this woman: '*Trust me, I'm a priest*'?

Gomer, sensing the tension, opened his side door. 'How 'bout you gives me your key, vicar? I could put the ole kettle on, and explain a few things to young Jane first, if she's still up.'

'Brilliant.' Gomer could be uncannily perceptive.

They watched him let himself into the vicarage. When he opened the door, a light came on in the hall.

'I promise I won't be sick as I walk in,' Betty Thorogood said drily.

Merrily leaned her head on the back of her seat. 'Is it that obvious?'

'I can tell you're having second thoughts.'

'Being psychic.'

'I'm not psychic that way.'

At the first sight of the dog collar, Betty Thorogood had not screamed or hurled herself at the passenger door. This was not a Hammer film. This was not *Livenight*.

'I'm sorry,' Merrily said. 'It was a stupid remark.'

'Aye, well. Nearly as stupid as mine about being sick.' Something – tiredness, probably – had brought out a Northern accent. Yorkshire? 'Look, I realize what you did was a spur-of-the-moment thing. You couldn't have known I'd walk into that pub.'

Merrily said, 'What actually brought you there?'

'Couldn't go back home.' Mirthless laugh. 'Place was full of witches.'

The porch light went out. Merrily could no longer see Betty's face.

'Also,' Betty said tonelessly into the darkness, 'I'd just been virtually accused of murder.'

Despite *Livenight*, Jane still always thought of *them* as dark-haired, dark-complexioned. Celtic. But this was an English rose, and a wild rose at that. She had a subdued energy about her. Or maybe that was just a subjective thing, because, thanks to Gomer, Jane *knew*.

Wow!

'This is Betty,' Mum had said casually. 'She's staying the night. This is my daughter, Jane. Brew some tea, flower. We'll be down in a few minutes.'

Under normal circumstances, this would have been an ultra-cool moment, a significant chapter in the liberalization of the Anglican Church.

But the chances that the Thorogood woman was *not* involved with Ned Bain were pretty remote. Pagans stuck together, so clearly Mum could have invited in more than she knew.

'We keep a room *fairly* ready,' she was saying. 'It's not very grand, but the bedding should be aired.'

'Anything, please,' Betty Thorogood said.

Jane forgot about the tea, followed them upstairs. The blonde, it had to be admitted, did not *look* like a threat. Instead she looked done in. By now, most people who'd never been here before would be commenting on the atmosphere and the obvious antiquity of the place – the twisting black beams, the bulging walls, the tilted ceilings. This woman might have been climbing the stairwell of a concrete apartment block.

Mum said, 'If you need a change of clothes I'm sure we can sort something out. I'm a bit on the stunted side, but Jane's got a lot of stuff from the days when you were supposed to buy everything a couple of sizes too big.'

The self-styled witch and Mum were standing on the landing, near the second staircase leading to Jane's apartment. 'Bathroom's that one.' Mum indicated the one door that was slightly ajar. 'It's bleak and cold and horrible, but one day, when we get the money . . .' She broke off.

From six stairs down, Jane witnessed this clearly. Betty Thorogood quivered for just an instant before tossing back her mass of hair and, almost absently, shaking out a word.

'Apples?'

Mum froze; Jane saw her eyes grow watchful.

Mum said, 'I'm sorry?' As though she hadn't heard, which of course she had.

She and Jane both had. And they knew what it meant. For a moment, the air up here seemed almost too thick to breathe.

'I'm sorry,' Betty said. 'I just . . . you know . . . Sorry.'

Jane marched up four steps. 'You had a feeling of apples?'

Mum frowned. 'Jane . . .'

'What kind of apples?'

'I . . .' Betty shook her head again, as if to clear it, her hair tumbling. 'I suppose not apples as much as blossom. White, like soft snow.'

'Oh, wow,' Jane breathed.

'I'm sorry,' Betty said. 'It just came out.'

Mum bit her lip.

Jane said, 'And we thought Wil had *gone* . . .'

Mum started flinging lights on. 'Betty, if you want to just check out your room . . .'

Betty Thorogood nodded and followed her.

She wasn't getting away that easily.

'Wil was our ghost,' Jane called after them. 'Wil Williams, vicar of this parish. Found dead in the orchard behind the church in 1670. Hanging from an apple tree – when the blossom was out.'

'I'm sorry,' Betty Thorogood said again. 'It's a problem I have.'

'Wow,' Jane said, in serious awe. Nobody knew about the apple blossom. Not even Kali Three. 'You're the real thing, aren't you?'

THIRTY-NINE

Witches Don't Cry

The kid brought them tea at the kitchen table and then started filling the kitchen with the seductive scent of toast. It was ten thirty. As far as Jane was concerned, Betty Thorogood had proved herself.

Merrily had stopped agonizing about this stuff. Where sensitives were concerned, seeking the cold, earthly, rational explanation could be wastefully time-consuming. Life was too short to question it too hard; it just *was*. It would have been less impressive in Betty's case if she hadn't, in other respects, appeared defeated, demoralized, broken. As though she'd looked into her own future and seen black water.

'Is Wil still here?' demanded Jane, galvanized – knowing nothing about the death of the elderly woman, Mrs Wilshire. 'I mean as a spirit, not just an imprint?'

'I don't know,' Betty said. 'Sometimes it's hard to qualify what I feel. I just get images sometimes. Fragments, incomplete messages.'

The apple blossom. Last year, when they'd first moved in, Merrily had been sensing an old distress locked into the upper storeys of the vicarage, the timeless dementia of trapped emotions. Jane, under the influence of Miss Lucy Devenish, folklorist and mystic, claimed to have actually smelled the blossom, felt it on her face like warm snow.

It was this undismissable haunting and the Church's general disinterest which had prodded Merrily in the general direction of Deliverance. There needed to be someone around to reassure people that they weren't necessarily losing their minds.

Jane was saying, 'Were you like sensitive *before* you became a witch?'

Betty looked uncomfortable. 'It's why I became one. If you exclude spiritualism, Wicca's one of the few refuges for people who are . . . that way. My parents are C of E, which doesn't encourage that kind of thing.'

An apologetic glance at Merrily, who also caught a triumphant glance from Jane, little cow, before she went greedily back into the interrogation. 'But, like, who do you actually *worship?*'

'That's probably the wrong word. We recognize the male and female principles, and they can take several forms. Most of it comes down to fertility, in the widest sense – we don't need more people in the world, but we do need expanded consciousness.'

'And you, like, draw down the moon?' The kid showing off her knowledge of witch jargon. 'Invoke the goddess into yourself?'

'Kind of.'

Betty was reticent, solemn in the subdued light of the big, cream-walled kitchen. Maybe having a vicar in the same room was an inhibiting factor, but this woman was certainly not *Livenight* material. Merrily sat down at the table and listened as Betty, pressured by Jane, began explaining how she'd actually got into Wicca, at teacher training college, before dropping out to work for a herbalist. How she'd saved up to go with a friend to an international pagan confer-ence in New England, where she met the American, Robin Thorogood, making a film with some old art school friends. So Robin had found Betty first, and *then* Wicca, in that order. Betty's face momentarily shone at the memory. Her green eyes were clear as rock pools: she must literally have bewitched Robin Thorogood.

The phone rang. Jane dropped the cheese grater and carried the cordless into a corner.

'You have a disciple,' Merrily said softly.

'Kids only find Wicca exotic because it's forbidden. When it becomes a regular part of religious education they'll find it just as boring as . . . anything else.'

'Don't feel you have to talk it down on my account.'

'Merrily' – Betty pushed back her hair – 'there doesn't need to be conflict. There's actually a lot of common ground. Spiritual people

332

of any kind have more in common than they do with total non-believers. In the end we want the same things, most of us. Don't we?'

'Maybe.'

Jane said loudly, 'No, I'm sorry, she's not here. I was kind of expecting her back, but in her job you can't count on anything. Sometimes she spends, like, whole nights battling with crazed demonic entities and then she comes home and sleeps for two days. It's like she's in a coma – really disturbing. Sure, no problem. Bye.'

'Flower,' Merrily said, 'you do realize that little exercise in whimsy might be lost in the transition to cold print.'

'In the *Independent?*'

Merrily nodded. 'So just don't say it to the *Daily Star.*'

She went over to switch on the answering machine. When she came back Betty was saying, 'In Shrewsbury, we were members of a coven containing quite a few . . . pagan activists, I suppose you'd have to call them. Teachers, mainly. They're good people in their way, but they'd be more use on the council. They're looking for organized religion, for structure.'

'These are the people who've moved in on your house?' Merrily asked her.

'Some of them. It's what I wanted to come down here and get away from. You don't *have* to work in a coven. The only structures I'm really interested in now are the ones you build for yourself. But Robin will go along with anybody, I'm afraid.'

'Why don't you phone him?'

'I will. I just don't want to speak to any of the others. We came down here to work alone. At least, I did. Robin just wanted to live somewhere inspiring and to show it off to his friends. He'd tell you we were sent here because of a series of omens. All that was irrelevant to me.'

Interesting. What was slowly becoming apparent to Merrily was that Betty had come to Old Hindwell in a state of personal spiritual crisis. She'd been drawn into witchcraft by the need to understand the psychic experiences she'd been having from an early age. But maybe paganism hadn't come up with the answers she'd sought.

'Omens?' Merrily brought out her cigarettes. To Jane's evident disgust, Betty accepted one.

'Estate agent particulars arriving out of the blue, that kind of thing. When Robin saw the church, he was hooked. Just like Major Wilshire.'

'Tell me about *Mrs* Wilshire again,' Merrily said.

The police had questioned Betty for almost an hour at Mrs Wilshire's bungalow. A detective constable had arrived who probably had never had a suspicious death to himself before.

'I'd no idea she suffered angina,' Betty had told them. 'I just concocted something harmless for her arthritis.'

No, she could not imagine why Mrs Wilshire would stop taking the Trinitrin tablets prescribed for her angina, a full, unopened bottle of which had been discovered by Dr Banks-Morgan. No, she would never in a million years have advised Mrs Wilshire to stop taking them. She had only suggested a possible winding-down of the steroids if and when the herbal remedy had any appreciable effects on the arthritis.

'She told me Dr Coll knew all about me, and he was very much in favour of complementary medicines for some complaints.'

'You know that's not true, Mrs Thorogood,' the CID man had said. 'Dr Banks-Morgan says he has no respect at all for alternative medicines and he makes this clear to all his patients.'

It got worse. If Mrs Wilshire was not becoming unduly influenced by Mrs Thorogood and her witch-remedies, why would she tell Dr Banks-Morgan he needn't bother coming to visit her again?

Betty could not believe for one minute that Mrs Wilshire had told her caring, caring GP not to come back. But she knew which of them was going to be believed.

'What a bastard,' Jane said. 'He's trying to fit you up.'

'Where did they leave things?' Merrily said. 'The police, I mean.'

'They said they might be in touch again.'

'They probably won't be. There's nothing they can prove.'

Betty said, 'Do you believe me?'

'Course we do,' Jane said.

'Merrily?'

'From what little I know of Dr Coll, I wouldn't trust him too far. Gomer?'

Gomer thought about it. 'Smarmy little bugger, Dr Coll. Always persuading folk to 'ave tests and things for their own good, like, but it's just so's he can pick up cash from the big drug companies – that's what Greta reckons.'

'Then I'll tell you the rest,' Betty said.

And she told them about Mrs Juliet Pottinger and what she'd said about the Hindwell Trust.

'En't never yeard of it,' Gomer said when she'd finished.

Merrily didn't find that too surprising if the trust was administered by J.W. Weal.

'Lot of incomers is retired folk,' Gomer confirmed. 'Like young Greg says, they comes out yere in the summer, thinks how nice it all looks and they're amazed at how low house prices is, compared to where they comes from. So they sells up, buys a crappy ole cottage, moves out yere, gets ill . . .'

'Fair game?'

'Like poor bloody hand-reared pheasants,' Gomer said.

Merrily asked Betty, 'Is it your feeling Mrs Wilshire's left money to the Hindwell Trust?'

Betty nodded.

'This stinks,' Merrily said.

'Works both ways, see,' said Gomer. 'Patient needs their will sortin', mabbe some poor ole biddy goin' a bit soft in the head, and Dr Coll recommends a good lawyer, local man, trust him with your life. Big Weal turns up, you're some little ole lady, you en't gonner argue too much. 'Sides which, it's easy for a lawyer to tamper with a will, ennit? Get the doctor to witness it. All local people, eh?'

Betty explained why she'd gone to see Mrs Pottinger in the first place. Talking about that particular atmosphere she'd perceived in the old church, but hesitating before finally describing the image of

335

a stricken and desperate man in what might have been a stained cassock.

'Wow,' said Jane.

Merrily tried not to react too obviously, but she was becoming increasingly interested in the Reverend Terence Penney. 'What year was this, again?'

'Sixty-five,' Betty said. 'He seems to have been turning into a hippy.'

Gomer looked up. 'Loads o' hippies round yere, late sixties. You could get an ole cottage, no electric, for a few 'undred, back then, see, and nobody asked no questions. More drugs in Radnor them days than you'd find the whole o' Birmingham.'

'But you never actually ran into Penney yourself?' Merrily lit another cigarette.

'No, but I been thinkin' of Danny Thomas. That boy knew all the hippies, see. Most locals they didn't have nothin' to do with 'em, but Danny, 'e was right in there. Up in court for growin' cannabis, the whole bit. You want me to get Danny on the phone?'

'It's a bit late,' Merrily suggested.

'Boy don't keep normal farmin' hours,' Gomer said.

Danny Thomas had now turned down the music. In Danny's barn there were speaker cabinets the size of wardrobes, all covered with chicken shit. Gomer also recalled an intercom on the wall. Bawling down it at Danny when he was wanted on the phone was how most folk reckoned Greta's voice had reached air-raid siren level.

It must be cold tonight out in Danny's barn, but Danny would jump around a lot to the music before collapsing into the hay with a joint. Gomer pictured him sitting on a bale, straggly grey hair down the back of his donkey jacket, with Jimi at his feet – Mid-Wales's only deaf sheepdog.

Gomer sat on the edge of the vicar's desk and waited while Greta had summoned Danny back to the farmhouse.

'What's goin' down, Gomer, my man? You become a private eye, is it? Every bugger I meet these days, they just been grilled by Gomer Parry.'

'All right, listen to me, boy,' Gomer said. 'Give your ole drug-raddled memory a rattle on the subject of Terry Penney.'

A few seconds of quiet. Bit of a rarity around Danny unless he'd had a puff or two.

'Poor bugger,' he says at last.

'Come to a sad end, what I yeard.'

'I liked ole Terry.'

'You go to 'is church?'

'Din't like him *that* much. But he was all right. He lent me his Dylan albums.'

'When?'

'Sixty-four, sixty-five. This to do with that bugger Ellis? Tricky bastard, he is. Blew poor ole Gret's mind. Gets 'em all in a bloody trance.'

'Why'd he do it, Danny? Why'd Penney fill up the ole brook with good pews?'

'Dope, ennit?'

'Ar, well, that's what they all says. Don't mean bugger all.'

Danny went quiet again.

'What you know about Penney, Danny? What you know about Penney you en't sayin'?'

'Long while back, Gomer. Terry's dead. Let the poor bugger lie.'

'Can't.'

'It's that vicar o' yours, ennit? Diggin' the dirt.'

'We needs to know, boy.'

'Gimme a day or so to think about it.'

'Can't. C'mon, Danny, who's it gonner harm?'

'Me.' Danny's voice went thin. 'I'm as guilty as any bugger, Gomer. It was me got Terry into it. Well . . . me and Coll.'

'Dr Coll?'

'*Me* and Dr Coll,' Danny says. 'And the bloody sixties that promised us the earth. And here we all are nigh on forty year later and further in the shit.'

'Stay there,' Gomer said. 'Don't move.'

*

When Betty Thorogood started to cry, it turned everything around.

Until now, talking about a world she knew, she'd been cool and assured. The otherworldly – visions and gods and archetypes – did not scare her, any more than neuroses scared a psychologist. In the everyday world, implicated in the death of a harmless widow, Betty came apart.

'I just wanted to help her. I was *sorry* for her . . . that's all there was to it.'

Jane had moved her chair back, appalled. Witches don't cry! Merrily leaned across the table, put a hand over Betty's.

Betty parted her hair, peered at Merrily through her tears. 'What if their tests show up something nasty in that potion I gave her? Something I didn't put there.'

'What are they going to find? Henbane? Deadly nightshade? Rat poison? He doesn't need all that. He's got natural causes, apparently hastened by her overreliance on you.'

'I just don't understand why she would stop taking the pills he'd prescribed. She thought he was wonderful. She thought . . .' Betty's eyes filled up again. 'She thought *everyone* was wonderful. Everyone who tried to help her. The local people were *so good*. Because she was from Off, anyone local who didn't actually spit on her front step seemed wonderful and caring. I was so sorry for her. And dying there, in her chair, in front of that lukewarm fire . . . Perhaps he *is* telling the truth. Perhaps poor, fuddled Mrs Wilshire thought my little herbal remedy, bottled under the moon, was some sort of cure-all.'

'There's an experienced nurse I know,' Merrily said. 'Perhaps I'll give her a call.'

She stopped as Gomer returned. His glasses shone like twin torch-bulbs.

'Come and talk to Danny, vicar.'

FORTY

Key to the Kingdom

As Danny talked, the picture formed for Merrily in ragged, fluttering colours. Radnor Forest in the 1960s: hippy paradise.

The flower children had wandered in from Off and settled in this border country in their hundreds because it was cheap and remote. They rented or even bought half-ruined cottages far from the roads. Thin boys in yellow trousers chopping wood from the hedges. Beautiful, long-haired girls in ankle-length medieval dresses fetching water from the well.

In spite of the electricity supply being at best intermittent, they brought the new music – why, The Incredible String Band even lived for a while near Llandegley towards the north-western end of the Forest.

And the dope. The hippies also brought the dope.

The local people were amused rather than hostile – the hippies didn't do any damage and they were always a talking point.

And for some – like Danny Thomas, dreamy, faraway farmer's boy – this was what they'd been waiting for all their lives. When it was really happening Danny was good and ready; he figured he must've been born a hippy – growing up on Elvis, then the Beatles, popping purple hearts to groove all night and still be awake in time to milk the cows.

Merrily smiled.

And then cannabis. Danny had acquired his first joint at a dance in Llandod in 1963, with another to smoke in the top field after sunset. He did a bit of dealing for a while, but he was never much good at that and, besides, there was a much more reliable dealer emerging in the area. Better just to grow the stuff – nice, sheltered spot, in Bryncot Dingle – and then give it away. Danny was so excited by the dawning of this incredible new world that, by the summer of 1965, he was wanting to turn on the whole Forest.

'Who was this "more reliable dealer"?' Merrily asked. 'Can I take a guess?'

Danny was talking freely now, his voice hoarse but liquid, like wet ash. Dr Coll had been the son of a surgeon at Hereford Hospital with a house in New Radnor. Still a medical student back then, in need of a few quid, like all your students. 'Medical students always got their sources, ennit?' Danny said.

'He was a hippy, too?'

'Lord, no. Dr Coll en't never been a hippy, not even as a boy. Just a feller with a eye to a few quid. Course when he qualified as a doctor, that all come to an end. Gotter keep 'is nose clean. Or at least keep it *lookin'* clean.'

And there would have been better ways of making money by then, Merrily thought. 'What about Terry Penney? When did he appear?' From what Betty had learned from Mrs Pottinger and from what Sophie had passed on to Merrily, Penney had emerged as a bright boy, but impressionable, and not too well-off. But what Danny was saying produced a different picture: Terry was an upper-middle-class radical with a posh, wealthy girlfriend who everyone thought was his wife, until she found life in Radnor seriously lacking and went back to the Smoke, leaving the vicar of Old Hindwell to grow his hair and smoke dope with the likes of Danny Thomas.

Terry, like Danny, was finding the sixties life-enhancing and life-changing. But Terry also saw it from a religious perspective: drugs opening the doors of perception, the gates of the soul. Terry was a fan of the seventeenth-century poet, Thomas Traherne, who had found secrets of the universe in Herefordshire meadows.

The dope had certainly elevated and coloured Terry's faith in God. Today, perhaps he'd be all happy-clappy and singing-in-tongues, like Ellis, and perhaps the drugs would have represented a passing phase. But it was a never-ending inner journey, then. Terry and Danny, untroubled by the law, would smoke dope supplied at very reasonable rates by young Dr Coll, and Danny discovered that he loved the whole world and Terry loved the world and God. Terry believed that the time was coming when all mankind would be herbally awakened to the splendour of the Lord.

Then Dr Coll brought the acid along.

'What you gotter remember,' Danny said, 'is that this was before the Beatles was admitting to doin' drugs. En't nobody hardly'd yeard of LSD, 'specially in Radnorshire.'

Merrily nodded. Acid had been something different. Not just another drug, but the key to serious religious experience, a direct line to God. To Aldous Huxley, Timothy Leary, all those guys, LSD was the light on the road to Damascus, and anyone could get there.

So, one fine, warm day in the summer of 1965, Terry Penney and Danny Thomas and Dr Coll had found a shady corner of a Radnor Valley field, overlooking the Four Stones. They had their lumps of sugar and Dr Coll brought out the lysergic acid. An experiment, he said. He wouldn't take any himself; he'd supervise, make sure they came to no harm.

Danny's trip lasted for ever. Under the perfumed, satin sky, he went through whole lifetimes in one afternoon. He found that the Radnor Valley was in his blood . . . *really in his blood* – the whole landscape turning to liquid and jetting through his veins. When he looked at the inside of his wrist he could see through the skin and into that fast-flowing land. He *was* the land, he was the valley, he was the forest. He walked through the silken grass down to the Four Stones, which he now understood to hold the mind of the valley, and Dr Coll said afterwards he had to stop Danny beating his head on the prehistoric stones to get inside them because the stones knew the secret.

The Reverend Penney, meanwhile, came to believe he'd been granted access to the very kingdom of heaven.

He saw an angel, a giant angel with his feet astride the valley. Merrily imagined a great William Blake angel with the red sun in his wings and a raised sword which cleaved the hills.

Life was never going to be the same again for either Terry or Danny. Danny was still tripping when he got home to the farm and he walked down the yard and saw the depth of sorrow in the eyes of the beautiful pigs and realized how much he loved those pigs. To this day, Danny Thomas said, he wouldn't see a pig ever killed.

He and Terry took four more trips together. Terry told Danny that he knew now that he had seen the Archangel Michael, who had been appointed to guard the forest and the Radnor Valley, because this was a great doorway through which you could enter the kingdom. Terry found a book by the Reverend Parry-Jones who'd been vicar at Llanfihangel Rhydithon back in the 1920s and he too thought the Forest was special, but he also mentioned a dragon that you could hear breathing in the night, and Terry said this was no surprise because places of great spiritual power were equally attractive to devilish forces.

Terry considered it no accident that he had been brought here, now, at this time of spiritual awakening, to be the priest of one of St Michael's churches. He had told Danny he was going to call a meeting of all the other St Michael clergy around the Forest because they were destined to work together. But this never happened, because the other ministers had all heard about Terry Penney.

Still Terry insisted he was being groomed by God for the Big Task. Every day, before dawn, he'd kneel before his altar in Old Hindwell Church and beg God and St Michael that his mission might be revealed to him.

But God held out on him.

Terry decided he was not yet worthy, did not yet know enough, was not yet pure enough. He stopped smoking cannabis and concentrated on reading the Book of Revelations a hundred times. He wrote out important verses from it on sheets of white card and hung them around his room at the old rectory. His sermons became impenetrably apocalyptic. He began to research St Michael and the lives of those saints and mystics who had become obsessed by the warrior archangel. He made solemn pilgrimages to all the St Michael churches around Radnor Forest . . . approaching each from the direction of the last, walking the final mile barefoot after a day's fasting.

'Local people was startin' to go off him in a big way,' Danny said. 'Local people don't like it when their vicar gets talked about in other parishes.'

Terry Penney had walked barefoot across the bridge to the church of St Michael, Cefnllys – an awesome setting, where an entire medieval town had been laid out under its castle. Then Terry had hiked unshod across the bleak Penybont Common to Llanfihangel Rhydithon. Next, he'd come down from the Forest to the yews encircling the rebuilt roadside church at Llanfihangel nant Melan. And finally he'd tramped on callused feet along the sombre, narrow road to Cascob, where he'd stood before the old *Abracadabra* charm.

It was three weeks after this that Terry had that visit from Councillor Prosser, wondering why he hadn't applied for a grant towards the upkeep of the old building.

Two weeks later, Terry trashed the church.

What had happened, Danny said, was that one night Terry came to the conclusion that God wanted him to go alone into St Michael's, Old Hindwell, and open himself to revelation.

In fact, drop some acid.

Danny had obtained the LSD for Terry from Dr Coll. The price had gone up by then, acid being in demand, but Terry didn't care. In fact, the idea of the priest taking a trip in his own parish church bothered Danny more than Terry.

'This would be about the time,' Merrily said, 'that Timothy Leary first promoted acid as a religious experience.' She'd once done a paper on that at college.

'A great religious man, vicar,' concurred Danny. 'Studied the use of peyote in the ole American Indian churches.'

'What about the Old Hindwell Church experiment?' she probed.

'Well,' said Danny. 'For starters, he wouldn't 'ave nobody with him. Dr Coll was back home at the time, but Terry wouldn't 'ave him to supervise – nor me. Had to be just him an' God, see. Terry reckoned nothin' bad was gonner happen to him in the house of God. But me, I wouldn't've gone in there alone at night in a million year, with or without drugs – creepy ole place like that.'

'Bad trip?'

'Had a bad one meself, few months later,' Danny said. 'Kept gettin' flashbacks for bloody weeks. Scared the shit out o' me. Anyway, the next time I seen Terry, the boy was a mess. Hadn't shaved, din't smell too good. Smelt of *fear*, you know?'

'Yes.'

'*I* don't know what 'appened to Terry Penney that night. I just sits in yere, hammering buggery out o' the ole Les Paul and I remembers the good times.'

'You must have asked him about it?'

'Terry din't wanner talk about it at all, vicar. Kept 'isself to 'isself. And then they finds bits o' church floatin' down the brook, and Terry's gone. I used to wonder whether the boy seen the carvings on the wood screen come alive, or whether he seen . . . I dunno . . .'

'The dragon?' Merrily said.

'He seen St Michael out in that field. Mabbe 'e seen the dragon in 'is own church?'

Merrily recalled the William Blake print in Nick Ellis's war room. *The Great Red Dragon and the Woman Clothed with the Sun* – relating to an image from Revelations about the dragon waiting for the woman to give birth so that it could devour the child. The dragon was said to have seven heads and ten horns. It was not a nice dragon, and Blake's painting throbbed with a transcendent evil.

'I don't know how much of this Ellis knows,' Merrily said, telling them as they sat around the kitchen table, 'but it would account for a lot. If he believes Penney had a black vision of the dragon inside that church – Satan rising, or in his view paganism rising – and if we believe what he told me about being the subject of some kind of hate campaign, forecasting a return of the dragon . . .'

Poison-pen letters for months. And phone calls – cackling voices in the night. Recently had a jagged scratch removed from my car bonnet. Series of chevrons . . . like a dragon's back.

' . . . then, to him, Betty, you and Robin are the embodiment of something that already exists in those ruins on a metaphysical level.'

'It's not true, though,' Betty said. 'We didn't know anything about Penney. We didn't even know for certain that the church had been built on an ancient site until we'd bought it.'

'How do you know that now?'

'Well, after we learned about all the prehistoric archaeology in the area, it seemed like it was on the cards. Also – this probably won't cut much ice with you – a friend of ours went round with a dowsing rod and pendulum.'

'Jane, do we have an Ordnance Survey map handy?'

'Brilliant!' Jane leapt up.

Mr Penney came out with what was described to me as a lot of nonsensical gobbledegook relating to the layout of churches around Radnor Forest.

Betty said that Robin had tried to work out a pattern on the map, but they had been aware of only three St Michael churches at the time.

'OK.' Jane had returned with the map, spread it out on the table. 'You'll have to help me out here, Gomer. Where's Cascob?'

Gomer found it after a bit of peering. He also found St Michael's, Cefnllys, then Llanfihangel Rhydithon and Llanfihangel nant Melan. Jane encircled them – along with Old Hindwell (ruins of).

'Five now.' Jane drew a ring round the last one. 'And they do go right around the Forest.'

Betty was silently contemplating the map. 'It's too big, this,' she said at last. You wouldn't have anything smaller scale?'

'Only a road map.' Jane bounced up again. 'I'll get it.'

'And some paper?' Betty said.

Neither Cascob nor Cefnllys was marked on the road map, but she put circles on the approximate spots, and pushed the map and the paper and a pencil towards Betty.

Betty copied the pattern onto the paper. 'It's not perfect, but it's there.'

'It's a five-pointed star,' Merrily said. 'A pentagram.' She looked at Betty. 'Can you explain?'

Betty swallowed. 'Could I have another cigarette?'

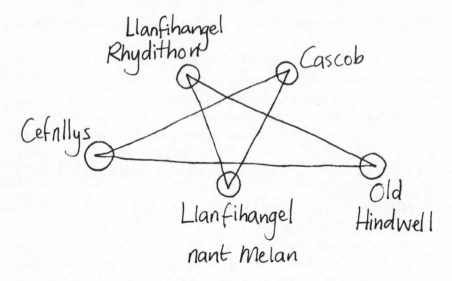

Merrily lit it for her. Betty was now looking uncertain, perhaps worried.

'If these churches were built to form not a circle but a five-pointed star, that would represent a defensive thing, OK? The pentagram's a powerful protective symbol. It's used in banishing rituals. Like if you're faced with . . . an evil entity . . . and you draw a big pentagram in the air, it ought to go away. So the medieval Christians might have wanted to enclose Radnor Forest in a giant pentagram of St Michael churches for the purpose of containing the dragon. Or whatever the dragon represented for *them*.'

'It's hardly a perfect pentagram,' Merrily pointed out. 'It could be purely coincidental.'

But then, she thought, in Ellis's ministry, nothing is coincidental.

'There's another connection here,' Betty said, 'with Cascob. The word "abracadabra" is used in a charm – an exorcism – which was found buried in the churchyard. The word "abracadabra" has become devalued because of all those stage conjurors using it, but it's actually very, very old and very powerful, and it's believed to represent the pentagram because it contains the letter "A" five times. And if you put the "A"s together . . .' Betty pulled Jane's pencil and paper across and drew:

'Cool,' Jane said.

'Actually, it's not,' Betty said soberly. 'The defensive, white magic pentagram has the point at the top. What you've just found on the map is an *inverted* pentagram.' She put down the pencil and looked at Merrily. 'I don't think I need to explain what that means.'

'No.' Merrily pulled out a cigarette. 'Probably not.'

Jane looked mystified. 'You mean it's like an aggressive thing?'

Betty said, 'It tended to be used in black magic. See the horns? Even pagans accept that horns are not *invariably* a good sign. Look . . . I went to Cascob the other day. That exorcism's displayed on the wall, in a frame. It dates back to about 1700, and was used to purge a woman called Elizabeth Loyd of evil spirits and alleged assaults of the Devil. I . . . got a bad feeling from it.'

'In what way?'

Betty looked embarrassed.

'You mean the exorcism itself?'

'I don't know. My first thought was that Elizabeth Loyd was just some poor epileptic or schizophrenic girl who somebody decided must be possessed. Then I . . . got the feeling that maybe she did have something . . . satanic . . . inside her. I don't know. The wording was a mixture of Roman Catholic and pagan and cabbalistic references.'

'Oh?'

'A combination of religion and magic, therefore. I suppose what really scared me was that the words were so very similar to the ones used in a charm that was found in a box concealed in an old fireplace at our house. And that one was dated over a century later. Nothing had changed.'

Nothing had changed.

Nothing changes. Merrily tried to focus. There was something very important here.

'*You* found this charm?'

'No, it was delivered to us. The box was placed on our doorstep just after we moved in. It spooked us quite a bit, because it was a charm against witchcraft. It seemed to be saying, "We know what you are and we know how to deal with you." There was a note with it, signed "The Local People".'

'Nasty,' Jane murmured.

'The wording of this exorcism,' Merrily said, 'do you remember how it went?'

'It invoked God and the Trinity. It said it would deliver Elizabeth Loyd from all witchcraft and spirits and hardness of heart. It had Roman Catholic stuff, kind of Ave Maria, and it used these cabbalistic names of power – Tetragrammaton, the mighty name of God.'

'Did it really?'

'That means something?'

'I don't know. OK, something else . . . Cascob. Apparently, Penney approached the then vicar or rector of Cascob and suggested he get his church decommissioned. He talked about the St Michael churches around Radnor Forest. The vicar reminded him of a folk tale implying that if one of those churches were destroyed it would allow the *dragon* to escape.'

'Right.'

'Penney said it was . . . quite the *reverse*.'

'Wow,' Jane said, 'like the reverse pentagram. I don't get it.'

'Nor me.' Merrily stared at the irregular star of churches. 'Whether the churches were intended to be a circle and just happened to fall into this rather vague star shape . . . or whether it's all complete coincidence. And, when you think about it, if you turn the map upside down, it's not inverted any more, is it?'

'*Wrong!*' Jane cried. 'Because pagans always work to the north, right, Betty? Their altars are *north-facing*. The two prongs, the horns, are pointing north.'

Merrily nodded, with reluctance. 'Yeah, OK. I think it's at least fair to say that Penney became convinced this was bad news. If his LSD experience – and in those days, the early Leary days, the feeling was that this wasn't just another drug – if his experience convinced him that the unfortunate layout of the churches invited the old serpent to slither in ... then that would explain why he was so determined to destroy the pattern by taking out one of the churches.'

'I wonder how much of this Ellis knows?' Betty said.

Possibly quite a lot, Merrily thought. She was considering the distinctly medieval aspects of Ellis's unnecessary exorcism of Marianne Starkey.

She dreamed, through most of that night it seemed, in colour.

Deep velvet purples and wild, slashing yellows. Abstract images, and then the church at Old Hindwell, vibrating blue against a pink evening sky. White-clad Ellis and his followers walking like pilgrims through the woods with their Bibles and bottles of holy water to exorcize the pagan place by night. Betty, in a robe of pale mauve.

Jesus Christ screaming on the cross.

Fire sizzling. Yellow fire in the kindling. The robe shrivelled and blackened. Betty's golden hair alight.

At the foot of the cross, Marianne Starkey in a torn white night-dress, blood-flecked.

Out of a dream full of savage heat, Merrily awoke into the cold. The sizzling became the metallic rattle of night hail on the bedroom window. Merrily wrapped herself in the too-thin duvet and prayed for the blue and the gold, but they wouldn't come.

FORTY-ONE

The Kindling in the Forest

It was dawn.

Max led Robin out, through his own house, through the mingled aromas of incense and marijuana, out through the kitchen, past the Rayburn on which sat the remains of a pot of fragrant stew tended last night by Alexandra, past sleeping people in sleeping bags.

Robin, as if sleepwalking, his mind disconnected.

He followed Max across the cold yard, in between the oily pools, past the barn, five cars as well as the Winnebagos parked in front of it now, including the Subaru Justy. There was an intermittent sleet.

'I thought it was meant to be cold and sharp and fine.'

'Give it time,' said Max.

In fact, the sky was not so dark: there was a curdled-milk moon under thin cloud and a pale, muddy glow in the east. It was February, and the blackest night of Celtic winter was supposed to be over.

The fuck it was over. Robin stared, for the first time with resentment, at the church: big and bare. The tower was lamp black. The sky in the north and west was burnt umber.

Robin had spent the night in his studio, but had hardly slept. He hadn't shaved for two days. He didn't want to be here any more, not without Betty. Without Betty there could be no light.

A short while ago, he'd been aroused from a miserable doze by a tapping on the door, and there was big, beardy, flutey-voiced Max, and he said, 'Oh, Robin, I'm sorry to disturb you so early, but we have to discuss tonight.'

'Max, how many ways can I say this? If there was *no* tonight, I would not be awfully gutted.'

Max was nodding solemnly, the asshole. 'I understand. I do understand, Robin. I would give anything to have Betty back, but if she has a problem with all this, it's perhaps as well she stays away, and she probably knows that.'

'Oh, that's what you think, is it?'

Betty had to be someplace close. She couldn't have gone far, unless she'd called for a cab. And then where? Back to Shrewsbury? Back to her parents in Yorkshire, who'd barely spoken to her since she gave up her career for the Craft? Maybe she was staying with the widow Wilshire.

He'd thought she would at least've phoned. He'd had the phone and the answering machine in his studio all night, but all he heard were good wishes from supporters he didn't know, threats from enemies he didn't know, offers from media people – even one call from some private TV production company suggesting the Thoro- goods might like to discuss the possibility of a docusoap series about the day-to-day lives of witches. What did these guys think their average day was like, for Chrissakes – they had breakfast in their cere- monial robes, went down to the shops hand in hand, skyclad, then sang 'The Witches' Rune' together in the tub before having tantric sex in front of an open fire?

Max was bleating on, ' . . . *would* have been a problem with numbers but, as usually happens when something is meant, it's been solved.'

'Solved?' Robin said vaguely.

'I want you to come and meet someone.'

A Tilley lamp stood on one of the old tombstones in what had been the chancel, about where the Christian altar was originally located. Presumably the Reverend Penney had hurled the altar in the creek with the rest of the stuff – or had he baulked at that?

When Max and Robin walked into the nave, George Webster was

saying to someone, 'Yeah, I see your point. The problem is, this whole building, being Christian, is oriented on the east. We can either go with that or we can just pretend the building isn't here at all and work with the site geophysically. You know what I mean?'

'So which do *you* think, George?' A man's voice, smooth. 'You're the geomancer.'

'I think there's got to be a compromise somewhere.'

'No,' the man said firmly. 'Oh no, no compromise. We either use their altar and change the current, or we build our own to the north and work, as you say, with the site'

'Ah . . . Ned.' Max sounded like a hesitant owl. 'I've brought Robin Thorogood.'

Ned Bain, pagan publisher, king-witch in all but title, came out into the lamplight. Robin had never seen him before. His face looked white in the gaseous Tilley light, but it was strong and lean and kind of genial. His hair was tight and curly. He had on a dark suit with a dark shirt underneath, kind of priesty – like *church* priesty.

'Hi.' He gripped Robin's arm.

'Hello.'

'I do like your name. It evokes Robin Goodfellow, the hobgoblin. Is it your given name?'

'Sure.'

'Someone's prescience? And I very much like your work.'

'Well, uh . . . thanks.' Despite the temperature, Robin's arm felt warm all the way to the shoulder, even after Bain let it go.

'This place inspires you?'

'I guess.'

'It should do. It's an important site. It's an axis.' Bain's voice was one peg down from smooth and refined, maybe a tad camp, but not enough to deter the ladies, Robin guessed. He felt faintly uncomfortable about the heat in his arm.

'Listen, Robin, I'm grateful for what you're doing. I know this has *got* to be a strain. I mean physically, psychically, domestically.'

'Uh . . . yeah, domestically, sure.'

'But I can't tell you how important it is, mate.' Bain was standing on the tombstone next to the lamp, casual, on someone's grave. His eyes found Robin's. Couldn't see those eyes but they'd found him and they held him. 'This *is* our religion. We *are* the religion of the British Isles. All these church sites are *our* sites.'

'Right. Uh, I've been kind of out of it . . . You just drive over here or were you here last night?'

'No, I was in a hotel last night. I think you were already crowded enough, weren't you? I drove over this morning. I wanted to watch the sun rise here. And to see the place in the dark. I'm sorry, I should've asked your permission.'

'Uh, no, that's . . .'

Max said, 'The point is, we have to get this right. Old Hindwell's a crucial test case, and if we're seen to back down before this man Ellis, it'll set the Craft back years . . . decades, even.'

Robin glanced at George. George was looking up over the walls of the nave towards the moon. Robin guessed George had told Ned Bain all about Betty walking out and Robin coming to pieces. He'd been set up for a pep talk. Trouble was, it was working. Bain had magnetism, even in the dark – maybe especially in the dark. Also he had a certain instant gravitas: when Max talked, you thought *bullshit*, but if Ned laid something on you, you were inclined to accept its importance.

'You've done Imbolc before, of course, Robin?'

'Sure.'

'It *is* very appropriate.' Ned picked up the Tilley lamp by its wire handle. He looked like a modern, clean-shaven Christ out of Holman Hunt's *The Light of the World*. 'It's the first fire festival of the year. The kindling in the forest of winter.'

'Like, the winter of Christianity?'

'Well perceived,' Bain said very softly. Robin felt stupidly flattered. 'It *is* the winter of Christianity.'

'And Ned's devised a rite reflecting that,' George said.

'Didn't take many modifications. Which shows how essentially right it is.' Ned Bain raised the lamp so that there was a core of light in the centre of what had been the chancel. 'For instance, when we chant, "Thus we banish winter, thus we welcome spring", we'll be banishing rather more than winter. Or, in this case, a spiritual winter which has lasted 2,000 years. And we'll be welcoming, into this temple, a new light stronger than any one spring.'

'Right,' Robin said.

The lamp sputtered. Around Ned, as he lowered it, shadows grouped and divided again.

'What I'm saying, Robin, is that for the duration of our rite, Old Hindwell will be the centre of . . . everything.'

Robin was awed, no longer reluctantly.

George said, 'She'll be sorry she missed out on this.'

'Betty?'

'Yeah. Can't you get her back, man? She's the priestess for this. She's got more' – George opened his hands like he was letting out a cloud of smoke – 'than any of us.'

'I *was* very much looking forward to meeting her,' Ned Bain said. 'Word gets around.'

'Well, uh . . .' Robin looked down into the dark around his feet. 'I guess the pressure got too much, is all. Things haven't been going so very right for either of us.'

'Yes. I heard about Blackmore.'

Robin looked up.

'He's an awkward sod.' Ned shrugged. 'But personally . . . you know . . . I *liked* that design.'

'You did?'

'A lot. I mean . . . Well, I still think Kirk could be persuaded to listen to reason.'

For Robin, the volatile light seemed to leap up the walls. 'Even at this stage?'

'The central motif's there, isn't it?'

'Well, sure, I . . . I could have all seven covers . . .' Robin's heart raced. 'I mean I could have them completed inside a month.'

'Well, you know, I can't make any promises. Except to talk to him. But we go back quite a long way.'

'There you are, man,' George said. 'Ned talks to this Blackmore, you talk to Betty.'

Robin breathed out ruefully. 'My part is not gonna be easy.'

'Do your best.' Ned Bain clapped Robin on the back. That heat again. Bonding. 'We're going to need all the psychic energy we can produce.'

Robin was elated. The electricity of fate. After the blackest night, the last night of winter, his personal lowest point for years, this guy just shows up without warning and things start coming together. Holism? Interconnection? The central premise in Wicca.

There was some kind of psychic energy here today all right. The kindling in the dark forest. Robin's inner vision projected it onto the church walls like the airbrush mist around Lord Madoc. He could see it all coming together, like a beautiful painting. Betty would inevitably be drawn back. It was how these things worked.

Imbolc: it would be *their* rebirth, too. Robin tried to conceal some of his delight. He mustn't look naive.

'Well . . .' He grinned. 'I guess the whole thing would be easier if Ellis and his . . . flock . . . Like, if he just gave up and left us alone.'

George glanced at Ned Bain.

Ned Bain smiled broadly, shaking his head.

George felt it was safe to laugh.

Max said, 'I don't think you quite get this, do you, Robin? This *is* the energy. The surrounding hostility, the negativity from the village, all helps to create a rather special kind of tension. What you have is the whole struggle in microcosm. With those fanatical, fundamentalist Christians the other side of the gate singing their simplistic hymns, throwing everything at us, everything they've got left.'

'Friction, man.' George Webster rubbed his hands together and then did that smoke thing. 'The combustion. It's a fire festival. The dragon rises.'

FORTY-TWO

Raising the Stakes

'Christ be with me, Christ within me, 'Christ behind me, Christ before me . . .'

In the not-quite-silence of Ledwardine Parish Church, amid dusty skitterings at mouse and bat and early-bird level, Merrily was kneeling near the top of the chancel steps, asking for clarity of mind, clearance of all nightmares. Murmuring the ancient Celtic prayer, 'St Patrick's Breastplate'.

'I bind unto myself the Name,
The Strong Name of the Trinity . . .'

Today was Candlemas – known to pagans as Imbolc. It concerned the quickening of life in Mother Nature's belly. The Catholic Church blessed its candles on this day. The Church of Nicholas Ellis kept them in its windows to ward off witchcraft.

When the 'Breastplate' was around her, Merrily went and sat in the front pew. She was wearing jeans and a sweater and Jane's duffel coat. She was still recalling details of Ellis's exorcism of Marianne Starkey.

'*Cursed dragon, we give thee warning in the names of Jesus Christ and Michael, in the names of Jehovah, Adonai, Tetragrammaton . . .*'

In the half-light, she was granted clarity. What became clear was that Ellis was following a tradition of exorcism accepted there on the border for many centuries. Betty had written out for her what she could remember of the charm found in the fireplace at St Michael's farmhouse and also the one in Cascob Church: a mongrel exorcism, a cunning cocktail of Catholicism, Anglicanism, paganism and ritual magic. Precisely what you would expect to find in an area where cultures and languages and religions overlapped and survival often depended on juggling in the dark. This litany of names of power and magical repetition, was a blunt instrument, a club. Merrily imagined Elizabeth Loyd 300 years ago, kneeling cowed and emptied on the stone flags of St Michael's Cascob.

When you found an adversary or an obstacle, you demonized it and then, powered by the sacred names, you beat it into the stones. Hard, practical . . . tested over centuries. *'Father Ellis doesn't do a soft ministry.'*

'It's hardly Jeffery Weal, is it?' Barbara Buckingham had said of Ellis's happy-clappy evangelism. Hardly. But happy-clappy was only the surface of it. Happy-clappy could unite the population, ensnaring the hearts and minds of local and incomer alike.

But under the surface, as Judith had said, Ellis suited the village. A quiet evangelist, neither ebullient, nor charismatic in the popular sense, but practical – dressed like an army chaplain. And he could, when required to, put the fear of God into people: the councillor's boy who took a car, threatening to bring dishonour to his respected family . . . the kid with a pocketful of Ecstasy . . . the repressed solicitor who only wanted his love for his wife to be reciprocated . . . the bored and lascivious licensee's wife who, sooner or later, might tempt a *local* man.

Ellis had earned his support by dealing with ripples on the normally dark and stagnant waters of Old Hindwell, while focusing, beyond them, on some bigger, darker, more nebulous objective. In the village hall, he had been rooting out some imagined, petty demon of desire. But also, through Marianne, attacking Robin Thorogood and what he represented.

But what *did* he represent? The Thorogoods had made no threats, taken no particular stance – Betty even appeared unsure that witchcraft was the right and only way for her. Yet Ellis had lost no time in demonizing them.

'Gotter be a problem for you, this, girl. Question of which side you're on now, ennit?'

Merrily stood and approached the altar. The stained-glass windows were coming alive with the dawn. She spoke the last verse of the 'Breastplate', the address to Jesus.

'Let me not run from the love that you offer
But hold me safe from the forces of evil.
On each of my dyings shed your light and your love.
Keep calling me until that day comes
When with your saints I may praise you for ever.
Amen.'

Merrily walked, blinking, out of the church. It was going to be a cold, bright, hard day.

When she got home, Jane had breakfast ready. The radio was turned to 5 Live, the news station.

'Mum, they've just trailed a report from Old Hindwell. It's coming up within the next ten minutes. That was about five minutes ago.'

'Better turn it up then.'

'And . . .' Jane cleared her throat, 'there's some stuff I need to tell you.'

'Any chance it could wait? It's just I seem to have got more to think about than at any time since my A levels.'

'No,' Jane said, 'it can't wait. It's about a web site, called Kali Three. Kali as in the goddess of death and destruction?'

'Not one of ours.' Merrily helped herself to a slice of toast. She was thinking about how best to approach Marianne Starkey. Marianne was crucial now, if Merrily was going to restrain Ellis. 'Not even one of Betty's.'

'Are you listening?'

'Sure. Sorry.'

'There's this obscure web site. A really heavy occult thing. A kind of like a hit list of people who are considered a threat to the, er . . . to, like, the expansion of human consciousness through magic, that kind of thing. Anyway, you're included on it.'

'You're kidding! Still . . . shows I must've got something right.'

Jane said, 'Sometimes you just make me sick, you know that?'

Merrily put down her toast. 'Jane, any other time I might be mildly affronted to think a bunch of loonies had put out a fatwa on me on the Internet, but right now . . . hold on, turn it up.'

Jane angrily turned up the radio far too loud. A woman said, ' . . . *remote Welsh border village of Old Hindwell, where the local rector has declared holy war on a community of witches occupying a one-time parish church. In Old Hindwell is our reporter, Tim Francis. Tim, what's happening there?'*

'Well, not too much at the moment, Melissa, but I suspect this is merely the calm before the storm, because tonight is when the witches are proposing to actually reconsecrate this former Christian church to their own gods. Tonight is, in fact, the pagan festival known as Imbolc – I think I pronounced that right – which is apparently the first really important witches' sabbath of the year.'

'Gosh, that sounds rather sinister.'

'Well, apparently it commemorates the start of the Celtic spring, which is not terribly sinister . . . However . . . what is seen by the rector, Nick Ellis, as a provocative gesture is the witches' intention to celebrate that festival tonight inside the former St Michael's Church, which in effect will make it into a pagan temple again.'

'And are they going to dance in the nude, Tim?'

'God,' said Jane, 'this woman is so sad.'

'I would say that is, um, a strong possibility. Now, last night we saw the new owner of the church, Robin Thorogood, clearly trying to calm down the situation when he confronted Nick Ellis here at the entrance to his farm, also leading to the church.'

Clip of Robin Thorogood over rain: *'We never touched your lousy church. There's no dragon here, no Satan. So just . . . just, like, go back and tell your God we won't hold you or your crazy stuff against him.'*

Tim said, *'However, Melissa, last night's placatory attitude was to be short-lived. We believe about a dozen witches are now residing at the farm here, and their leader, the latest to arrive, is a former official of the British Pagan Federation and an outspoken proponent of pagan religion. That's Ned Bain . . .'*

Jane gasped.

'. . . who joins me now. Ned Bain, the impression we all get is that you're raising the stakes here. The very fact that you, a leading pagan activist, have come all the way from London—'

'I think, Tim, that the stakes have already been raised enormously by Nicholas Ellis. He's a driven man, a fanatic, who's made life hell for two people who just wanted to be left alone to practise their religion.'

'In a Christian church.'

'In an abandoned church built on a site of ancient worship. Nicholas Ellis made the preposterous suggestion last night that he and his cronies should be allowed access to the site to carry out what amounts to an exorcism. Well, let's not forget this land now belongs to Betty and Robin Thorogood. They've been faced with an army of militant Christians who've promised to turn up in even greater numbers. We're here to support the Thorogoods.'

'And you'll be welcoming the Celtic spring with them tonight.'

'Indeed.'

'At the church itself?'

'At a site of established ancient sanctity.'

'And how many of you will be involved in that?'

'A full coven. Thirteen members.'

Melissa said from the studio, *'Ned, you going to be dancing in the nude?'*

'We shall probably be skyclad, yes, unless the weather is particularly inclement.'

'You'll be freezing!'

'Melissa, our beliefs will keep us warm.'

'Well, rather you than me. Thank you, Ned Bain, and Tim Francis. And we'll keep you up to date with whatever happens. Now, here on 5 Live . . .'

Jane switched off. When she turned round, her face had darkened. 'They're not taking any of it seriously.'

'Vicars and witches? What did you expect?'

'How can you *sit* there and—'

'Because I'm used to it. It's a secular society and we've become a quaint anachronism. Of course they're not taking it seriously.'

Unfortunately, they would do soon, if it came out that the police had interviewed Betty regarding Mrs Wilshire.

Jane pulled out a chair and sat down directly opposite Merrily. 'You have *got* to listen to me, do you understand?'

'I'm listening.'

'Ned Bain—'

'He's a smooth operator. A clever man.'

'It goes deeper. Up in the gallery, at *Livenight*, we found the researcher already knew all about you and Dad and how Dad died and where it happened and everything, and he told Irene he got that information from Ned Bain, and it's all there on the Kali Three web site with suggestions that you should be regarded as an enemy, like, by pagans and occultists everywhere.'

'How do you know all that?' The kid had her full attention now.

'Because Irene spoke to Gerry, the researcher, afterwards.'

'About your dad? They had all *that?*'

For an awful moment, she was back in that stifling, oppressive studio, dry-mouthed, with Bain lazily watching her through what appeared, for just a moment, to be Sean's eyes.

'Everything,' Jane confirmed.

And earlier that man smiling Sean's pained, 'Isn't it all so tedious?' smile. All of it following a Sean-haunted drive up the M5, and then, when returning home, on that same stretch of motorway, on the way back.

'What we figured it means,' Jane said, 'is that people all over the world were probably sending you ill will at that point.'

'Down their computers?'

'Don't try and laugh it off. You were *crap* on telly.'

'Thanks.'

'Maybe that wasn't all your fault, you know? There's a lot of really heavy people out there. They knew your weaknesses: your guilt trip about Dad and the Church.'

'That's . . . silly.'

'And now Ned Bain's in Old Hindwell.'

'OK, not good.'

Two religious fanatics facing each other across the ruins of a church that was spiritually suspect. Both sides raising the stakes.

*

Betty Thorogood came down, wearing a sloppy old baseball sweater of Jane's. She declined an egg, but accepted toast and honey.

She'd heard the radio report from upstairs.

She said she was going back to St Michael's.

'I don't want that church reconsecrating – not in anybody's name. I'm not forecasting some apocalypse scenario, I just don't want it to happen. I'm stopping it.'

'You've got thirteen people to persuade. All determined to celebrate Candlemas.'

'They can bloody well do it somewhere else,' Betty said flatly.

Merrily brought coffee. 'Tell me exactly what happens at Candlemas.'

'It's the festival of Brigid, the triple goddess.'

'Three stages of womanhood,' Jane translated, 'maiden, mother, hag.'

'Imbolc means belly. It's about Mother Earth giving birth to spring, so in Wicca we put the emphasis on the mother. Three women are involved in the rite, but the mother wears the crown of lights . . . that's a headdress of candles. This is a festival of light and new awakening. Of all the sabbats, it's probably the one closest to Christianity, I'd guess.'

Merrily nodded.

'Normally, it would be an especially good time to consecrate a church or temple, simply because it's coming out of a long period of darkness, reawakening to spring.'

'Everything perfect, then,' Merrily said neutrally, 'for giving back Old Hindwell to the old gods.'

'No, everything's utterly wrong – take it from me. If there were good omens before, it all reversed when we moved in. I've become snappy and irritable and . . . alienated from Robin. We've hardly even, you know, touched each other since we arrived. And even regarding money. Robin had the possibility – almost the *certainty* – of a very lucrative contract, to do seven book covers for Kirk Blackmore, the fantasy writer.'

'Wow,' Jane said. 'I used to read his stuff, when I was a kid.'

'And then the rug seems to have been pulled. Blackmore's

decided he doesn't like Robin's concept, and it's Blackmore calls the shots. That's just the latest thing to go wrong.'

Jane said, 'Maybe *you* need the new light.'

Betty shook her head. 'There won't be any. We won't bring that place out of the darkness; it'll suck us in.' She looked vaguely around, from face to face. 'Whatever you may think about this, I've called out to the goddess in the night, and the goddess won't come to me. I'm not being emotional or hysterical about this. I just don't see a good future.'

'OK, so you go back,' Merrily said, 'and you try to stop it. How do you do that?'

Betty shrugged. 'If necessary I can just tell them all to get out. It'll cause another row with Robin, but the house is half mine. That's only a last resort. If I play along for a while, something subtler might occur. I don't want to create negative vibrations, if possible. What about you?'

'I'm going to have to try and cool Ellis. One or two ideas occur. Well, one anyway.' Merrily's throat was dry from too much smoking, not enough sleep. 'Maybe we can meet somewhere, late afternoon, and see where we stand.'

'There's a footbridge,' Betty said, 'that leads from the church to the other side of the brook.'

'I know it. Four o'clock?' Part of her was saying this was whimsy, that the only really important things were to, first, find Barbara Buckingham, and second, persuade the police to investigate the Hindwell Trust. 'Betty, what do you think, seriously, is likely to happen if we can't stop this tonight?'

Betty shook her head quickly, non-committally.

'The dragon gets out,' Jane said, 'whatever that means.'

'I've been thinking.' Betty looked at Merrily. 'The problem with this place is nothing really to do with us. But it *is* to do with you, I suspect – with what you do. Ellis thought it needed exorcizing. I'm not sure he was wrong.'

'But not by him.'

'No,' Betty said, 'not by him.'

'You mean . . . by me?' Merrily felt obscurely honoured and immediately guilty about that.

'I wondered about tonight,' Betty said. 'Candlemas is Candlemas. I suppose it's a good time, wherever you stand. I mean, I'd go in *with* you, if you thought that would help. Or, if you thought that would be spiritually wrong, I'd stay out of the way.'

'I don't know.'

'Would you think about it, Merrily? It's become kind of central to everything, hasn't it?'

'But . . . exorcizing a church . . .'

'Like you keep saying,' Jane said, 'it isn't a church any more.'

'All right, I'll talk to the bishop.'

'Please don't do that,' Betty said. 'He might suggest you have other priests along. That would bother me. I don't want it to look like a *formal* sellout.'

Merrily nodded. 'OK.'

'Wow,' Jane said.

FORTY-THREE

Mitigating Circumstances

Jane had called Eirion at the rotting mansion and there was no answer. Well, there *was* an answer . . . on a machine, and in Welsh.

Like she wasn't already feeling excluded enough. Gomer had collected Betty and taken her back to Old Hindwell, Mum had gone off on her own. Little Jane had been given the really important job of relaying any messages to Mum on her mobile.

Bastards!

'I can't *speak* bloody Welsh!' she howled over the message. 'Just tell Irene . . . Eirion . . . to call me. It's very urgent. It's Jane Wat—'

She shut up. The message was being translated.

'Dafydd and Gwennan Lewis are unable to take your call. Please leave your message after the tone. Diolch yn fawr.'

'OK. Please, please, tell Eirion to ring me. It's Jane Watkins. It's very urgent. Please?' Realizing she'd ended on a kind of strangled sob. Maybe that would underline the urgency, or maybe just the existing suspicions of the wealthy and powerful Dafydd Lewis about the hysterical English. It was not bloody *fair*, because she now had, like, *masses* of new data to lay on Eirion. He could hit the Net, and they could crack this thing wide open.

Jane paced the kitchen. Actually, she was quite proud of Mum this time, agreeing to undertake an exorcism on behalf of a witch. Like, it was a really heavy decision to have to make. But had she accepted the significance of Kali Three? It really was a pity they hadn't got a decent computer.

Ah!

365

Jane went rapidly round the house, doing what had to be done – laying a fire in the drawing room, putting out dried cat food for Ethel, and all the time thinking hard. She didn't need Irene; she just needed an on line computer.

Sophie!

Sophie had one in the Deliverance office. It was only right that the diocese should pay for this research.

There should be a bus to Hereford passing through Ledwardine within the hour. Jane ran a brush through her hair, tugged on her fleece coat and was out of there. There'd be some resistance from Sophie, sure, but nothing Jane couldn't handle with the usual combination of pathos and rat-like cunning.

She bought a Mars bar from the Eight-till-Late and stood on the square munching it, relishing the freedom to *do* things. Back at bloody school next week, with dismal GCSEs looming. Although the public school system was this, like, totally disgusting anachronism, she wished she was at the cathedral school with Eirion; at least it was in the middle of town.

It was bright but unexpectedly cold on the square. Jane chewed and stamped her feet on the cobbles. A silver BMW went past, then slowed suddenly and backed up and stopped on the edge of the square. The window glided down on the passenger side. Some sex beast wondering if she was in need of a lift.

'Excuse me, little girl.' Creepy voice sibilating from the bourgeois, tinted interior. Eyes narrowing, Jane pocketed the Mars bar and sashayed over. 'Looking for somewhere, I am, see?' he oozed. 'Wonder if you can point me in the right direction. Little place called . . . if I can just see it on the map . . . Ah, got it . . .' The passenger door was thrown wide open. '*England!*'

Jane glared in delight. 'You bastard!'

'Good morning, Eirion,' Eirion said. 'How's the whiplash? Well, it's quite a bit more comfortable, thank you, Jane.'

Jane got in. The leather seat creaked luxuriously. 'Where'd you steal the flash Kraut wheels?'

'Gwen's, it is. She owes me. Don't ask. Are you doing the decent thing and going to school?'

'Well, I *was*, naturally. But, on second thoughts, I think we'll go to Hereford Cathedral. I can show you the Deliverance office, in the gatehouse.'

'Jane . . .' Eirion snatched off his baseball cap and his dark glasses. 'Half the school goes past there.'

'You won't be spotted, you'll have your head bent over a keyboard. By lunchtime your eyes will be so terminally weakened you'll be regretting you ever left the land of Druids and sad male voice choirs.'

Eirion sighed and let out the clutch. He handed her a brown A4 envelope. 'Read this.'

'What is it?'

'What do you think it is?'

Jane pulled out a thin sheaf of printouts.

'Kali Three.'

She read about her mother and her father.

At home with a young child, Merrily Watkins was horrified to discover that her husband was 'representing' Gerald McConnell, a West Midlands businessman who would later be jailed for four years for fraud and money-laundering. It was this . . .

Jane looked across at Eirion. She felt embarrassed.

Eirion drove serenely on. 'There but for the grace of God, Jane. When my father was on the board of the Welsh Development Agency . . . Never mind, he'd have been out by now even if the charges had stuck.'

'You're just saying that to make me feel better.'

'I wish. Read the other stuff, on Bain and his old man. Start at the top of page five.'

Jane read:

Ned was ten years old when his mother, Edward Bainbridge's

first wife, Susan, walked out on her husband. They were quietly divorced and, soon afterwards, Bainbridge formed a relationship with Mrs Frances Wesson, the widow of a chaplain at his college. Mrs Wesson had remained a strong, even fanatical Christian, although the extent of this did not become apparent to Bainbridge or his son until after the marriage.

Strange how formally this was written. Like out of a real biography, not the usual chatty crap you got off the Net. It drew you into what, even though it was then the mid-1970s, seemed like a Victorian kind of world.

Thus Ned entered his teenage years in a stifling High Church household dominated by the beautiful but austere Frances Wesson, whose own two children seemed to be accorded special privileges. To please his new wife, Bainbridge, hitherto a lukewarm Christian at most, began to attend church services twice every Sunday. Ned was soon glad to be sent away to public school, where he was free to pursue an interest in subjects which would certainly have been forbidden at home.

During school holidays, he became aware of his father's slide into depression. Edward Bainbridge had given up writing poetry after his latest volume had been derided as maudlin, self-pitying and, indeed, pitifully inept. Unsurprisingly, his academic reputation was crumbling and his drinking had become a problem. All of this was concurrent with the dissolution of the Bainbridge marriage, with the couple living increasingly separate lives. If Edward now no longer attended church, his wife had inflicted all its trappings and symbolism on what remained of their domestic life. The house in Oxford had become heavy with icons and crucifixes; its drawing room had a constant and pervading smell of incense, and Frances had even set up a private chapel in a pantry next to the kitchen.

The summer of 1975 brought a severe and life-changing shock for Ned. Edward Bainbridge's brother, David, arrived at the school to break the news that his father was dead. Ned learned, to his horror, that his father had bled to death on the floor of the private chapel, and that his stepmother had already been charged with murder.

Some days later, to the eighteen-year-old Ned's outrage, the charge was reduced to manslaughter, to which Frances Bainbridge had agreed to plead guilty. There was, she had claimed, a strong element of self-defence. According to Mrs Bainbridge, her husband, who had been drinking heavily for most of the day, had come hammering on the door of the chapel while she was at prayer and, when she refused to admit him, had kicked in the door, burst into the tiny chapel and proceeded to tear down drapes and overturn the altar. When she screamed at him to get out, he began to slash viciously with a kitchen knife at a Victorian picture of Christ, until he stumbled and dropped the knife – whereupon Mrs Bainbridge snatched it up. Edward Bainbridge then attacked his wife, tearing at her dress, and in her struggle to get away she stabbed him fatally in the throat.

The original murder charge was reduced to manslaughter after Frances Bainbridge's description of the events – somewhat unconvincing to Ned – was supported by her son Simon, aged fifteen, and her twelve-year-old daughter Madeleine, both of whom said they had witnessed the struggle. Frances Bainbridge pleaded guilty to manslaughter, but walked free from the court after being given a two-year suspended sentence because of the mitigating circumstances.

Ned Bainbridge returned to school to sit his A levels before going up to Oxford, to his father's old college where, with fellow students, he formed his first coven.

Eirion drove into Hereford via Whitecross. 'Quite a significant family skeleton, isn't it?' he said. 'You can understand that guy not being over-fond of the Church.'

FORTY-FOUR

Feel the Light

Greg had shaved. He wore a clean shirt. He stood in the back doorway at the end of the yard and made rapid wiping movements with his arms.

'No, no, *no*.'

Merrily stopped about four yards away. 'She's worse?'

'She's better,' Greg said. 'That's the point, innit? I'm grateful for you taking the witch away and everyfing, but I'm not having you upsetting my wife.'

The day, like Greg, had hardened up. Merrily dug her hands into the pockets of Jane's much-borrowed duffel coat. She nodded, resigned, looking down at all the crushed glass ground into the pitted concrete yard.

'I'm sorry, Reverend,' Greg said. 'I said I'd ask her if she'd talk to you, but I didn't in the end. I don't want noffink bringing it back. These past two days – bleedin' nightmare. You understand, don't you?'

'You think she's coming out of it?'

'She's talking to me. That's enough for now.'

'Right, well . . .' Merrily shrugged. 'Thank you. I'll see you, Greg.'

It was nearly 11 a.m. Martyn Kinsey, of BBC Wales, had spotted her going into the yard, and given her a conspiratorial wink. Martyn was going to be her last resort, if she got nowhere with Marianne Starkey. Martyn Kinsey and a big, unchristian lie: *Entirely off the record, the diocese has received two complaints, of a very serious nature, against Father Nicholas Ellis. Yes, of course from women.*

Last resort, though.

Merrily had reached the entrance to the alley which led from the Black Lion yard to the village when she heard the wobble and slide of a sash window. 'Who's this?' a woman called down.

''S all right,' Greg rasped. 'I dealt wiv it. Just go back and siddown, willya?'

'Hey!' Marianne leaned out of the upstairs window. 'I saw you, din' I?'

Merrily paused. *Please, God . . .*

'Inna toilets,' Marianne said, 'with Judy Prosser. 'Cept you was wearing a . . . whatsit round your neck.'

Merrily put a hand to her throat. 'Day off today.'

Greg said nervously, 'Marianne, just leave it, yeah?'

'You wanna cuppa tea, love?'

'That would be really very nice,' Merrily said. 'It's quite cold again today, isn't it?'

Greg hung around, restive, breathing down his nose. Marianne waved him away. 'It'll be OK. You go and replace your kegs.'

They were upstairs in the living room of the flat above the pub. The furniture looked inexpensive, but it was all newish, as if they'd ditched all their old stuff when they moved here. For a bright new start.

Greg waved a finger at his wife. 'You just say what you wanna say.'

Marianne was in a cream towelling robe, and she wore no make-up. She slid back into a big lemon sofa opposite the television. The sound was turned down on two young women ranting at Robert Kilroy-Silk.

'Slept late,' Marianne said. 'Must have a clear conscience.'

'Good.'

'You reckon it can really do that? Wipe the slate clean?'

'Why not?'

'Siddown . . . please.' Marianne picked up a cigarette packet from the sofa. 'Ain't taken everything away, mind. I still need these. Don't suppose you do?'

'Actually . . .' Merrily slipped off her coat, let it fall to the carpet. She sat on the edge of an armchair beside the TV, and accepted one of Marianne's menthol cigarettes.

'Blimey, you'll go to hell, love. In spite of it all.'

'I prefer to think I'll just go to heaven a bit sooner. How do you feel now, Marianne?'

'Bit weird. Bit hollow.'

'All happened kind of suddenly, hasn't it?'

'Can't believe it. I feel like a little girl. All nervous. Need me hand held.'

Probably why she'd been so glad to see Merrily. A lady priest. Someone who would know, would understand.

'I mean, you shouldn't be feeling like that at someone's funeral, should you?' Marianne said. 'Ain't right.'

'You mean feeling good?'

'Yeah.'

Merrily lit their cigarettes. 'Finding yourself joining in the singing?'

'The singing. Sure.'

'Mmm. I know what that's like.'

'I should think you do, Reverend.'

'Merrily.'

'Nice name. Yeah, that's what happens, Merrily. I only went along for a laugh. No, not a laugh, I was hacked off with everybody, with this place, with Greg. Like, Greg's sayin', one of us oughta go, put in an appearance. It's the way they are, the locals, innit? God-fearing? So, yeah, OK, I'll do it – 'cos they all reckon I'm a slapper – I'll be down that hall with me hat on and I'll put on a real show for 'em.'

Merrily smiled. 'And in the middle of the show . . . wow, it turns into the real thing.'

'Cloud nine, love. Like after half a bottle of vodka? Nah, not really. I mean, I was so ashamed. Joyful, yet ashamed. Ashamed of *me*. I was horrified at me – what I was, what I'd been. I wanted . . . what's the word . . .?'

'Redemption?'

'That's a bleeding big word.'

'Big thing.'

'Do you know, I went out the back afterwards, and I was sick over the fence? Sick as a dog, with all that hating of meself pouring out. After that, I felt very . . . light, you know? Cut loose. Then this lady come over, I don't know her name, but she lives in a bungalow on the road out of here, and that's where we went. Some other ladies come too, and they was all really kind. I cried most of the time.'

Merrily smoked and nodded. It was difficult to believe it could happen so quickly until you encountered it, but it did happen. It happened particularly to people in crisis, depressed people and – unexpectedly – to angry, cynical people.

'Found I could talk to them. Talked about stuff I never talked about since I left London. Personal stuff, you know? One of the ladies, she says, "I knew you was in trouble when I seen you and that feller."'

'Robin Thorogood.'

Marianne shivered. 'I thought it was *me* invited *him*. But he was playing with me. He's a dark person, he is, Merrily. He brought out the bad and lustful part of me.'

'Who told you he was a dark person?'

'In the paper, wannit? They come round with the paper . . . yesterday.'

'Who did?'

'Eleri, from the post office. And Judy Prosser. I'd been to church – to the hall – on Sunday, and it was wonderful, I was blown away all over again, really. And afterwards I was introduced to Father Ellis, and he's like, "I can tell you been deeply troubled. I feel you been exposed to a great evil." And it sets me off crying again, and he takes my hand and he says, in this lovely soft voice, he says, "You come back to me when you feel ready to have the disease taken away." And the next day Eleri come round with the paper, and there *he* is, that Robin, his face – like I never seen it before, I mean you could *see* the evil in him, snarling, vicious. I went a bit hysterical when I seen that picture. He was like they said he was.'

'What happened then?'

'They took me up the hall. Father Ellis was there.'

'Did they tell you *why* you were going to the hall?'

'What?'

'Doesn't matter. Father Ellis . . .?'

'He was dressed all in white, as usual. He was like a saint, and I felt so comforted. I felt I was in the right hands, the hands of a living saint. And we sits down and Father Ellis explains about the demon what Robin had put inside of me.'

'Those were his words?'

'Once he'd given me the demon, he didn't wanna know me no more, he just pushed me away.'

'Robin?'

'Pushed me away, and I fell down in the street. The demon did that. That was the demon. After the pub closed, Greg and me, we had this terrible ding-dong. I'm insulting him, I'm like *belittling* him, you know what I mean? I'm screaming, "Go on, do it to me, you got any bottle." Poor Greg. Turns him off like a light, you talk dirty. But that wasn't *me*. I know now that wasn't me. That was the *demon*.'

'Is that what Father Ellis said?'

'He said he could take it away, but it wouldn't be easy, and it was not to be gone into lightly and I would have to understand that I would be giving myself to the Holy Spirit. He said it was a foul entity, the demon, and it was gonna have to come out . . . like a rotten tooth.'

Merrily said. 'You mean . . . out of your mouth?'

Marianne's eyes narrowed, lines appeared either side of her mouth. She looked accusingly at Merrily. 'Judy said you come to spy on Father Ellis.'

'I was sent to support him,' Merrily said. 'From the bishop, remember? The bishop thought he needed some help.'

Marianne looked confused. 'That Judy, she took you outside, din't she? I was glad when she did that.'

'We hadn't met before. I think she was a bit suspicious of me.'

'She took you outside,' Marianne said. 'I was very glad.'

'We had a good chat,' Merrily assured her. 'We worked things out. Marianne, do you remember what Father Ellis did . . . to exorcize the demon of lust?'

Marianne blinked, affronted. 'He said the Church has strict rules about the exorcizing of demons. They don't just *do* it. You could wind up exorcizing someone who was mentally ill, couldn't you?'

'Er . . . yes. Yes, you could.'

Ellis told her this? Merrily's heart sank a little. This was established Deliverance procedure. You didn't even contemplate exorcism until all the other possibilities, usually psychiatric, had been eliminated.

'Don't get me wrong, love, he could've done what he liked without a word, the way I was feeling, long as he took it away. But he explained it was a *disease*. I needed checking over by a doctor, and what he was doing should be medically supervised.'

'He *said* that?'

'Dr Banks-Morgan was there for the whole thing,' Marianne said. 'That's the kind of man Father Ellis is.'

The male figure in the doorway.

She sat in her car for a while.

Then she rang Hereford Police, asked for Mumford. He was out, so she rang Eileen Cullen at home, hoping she wasn't asleep. A man answered; Merrily realized she knew nothing about Cullen's domestic situation. When she came on the line, she sounded softer, a bathrobe voice.

'Before you say a word, Merrily, there is one incident I will never talk about again, not to you, not to anyone.'

'Angina,' Merrily said.

'Ask away,' Cullen said.

'The pills you take for angina. Tri-something?'

'Trinitrin. You feel it coming on, you stick one under your tongue.'

'Becomes automatic?'

'Long-term sufferers, they practically do it in their sleep.'

'Take a hypothetical case. Person on Trinitrin for angina becomes converted to herbal remedies. Says I'm going to stop filling myself up with these nasty drugs. Then she feels an attack coming on, so what does she do?'

'Reaches for the Trinitrin. Says I'll stop fillin' meself up with these awful drugs *tomorrow*.'

'All right.' No time for the subtle approach. 'Hypothetically, if, in circumstances like this, a doctor saw an opportunity to do away with a patient in a way which might throw blame on someone else, say for instance the herbalist . . . how would he go about it?'

'Jesus, Merrily, what *is* this?'

'It's, er . . . a question. Just a question.'

'Well here's your answer – a hundred ways. Could casually swap her Trinitrins for blanks, for starters. Who's gonna know? It's easy for a doctor. Always has been.'

Robin had been gazing from his studio window when he saw her walking, like some grounded angel, across the yard, and he'd gone running wildly through the farmhouse, like some big, stupid kid, knocking a bowl of cornflakes out of the hands of a mousy, pregnant witch from Gloucester, called Alice.

Now he held Betty's hand, and he was breathing evenly for the first time in many hours. They shared this big cushion they used to have in their previous apartment. Only now it was on the floor of the parlour, the room with the inglenook which was now the house temple.

They'd been left alone in here, just Robin and Betty and the altar and the crown of lights.

The kindly, mature witch, Alexandra, Betty's one-time tutor, had made it. Alexandra was a twig-weaver, or whatever you call it, and this was a tight wreath of hedgerow strands, like a crown of thorns without the thorns. Across the top of the wreath was shaped a kind of skullcap made out of one of those foil trays you got around your supermarket quiche. The candles which ringed its perimeter were the kind you had on birthday cakes, though not coloured.

'A *Blue Peter* job,' Betty had said with a wistful smile, referring to some TV show she used to watch as a kid, where you were taught how to make useful artefacts from household debris. Foil trays apparently featured big.

'I love you,' Robin said. 'I want you to wear it tonight.'

Outside on a calm night, with all the candles lit around the head of a beautiful woman, the crown of lights looked awesome.

'It's the mother wears the lights,' Betty said.

'This is special.'

'What would Ned say?'

'He'll be cool.'

Everything was cool, coming together, happening just like he'd known it would. He hadn't asked where she'd spent last night. That didn't matter. She sometimes needed time to think things out. He recalled how one moonlit night she'd gone out walking from Shrewsbury into the countryside, hadn't returned until dawn, had covered maybe twenty miles and hadn't noticed the time go by. He'd been frantic, but she was her own person. She was his priestess. He would trust her for ever, through life after life after life.

'Ned's even gonna fix things with Kirk Blackmore, I tell you about that?'

'Yes,' Betty said, 'I'm sure he will.'

'Bets, things are really turning around. It's Imbolc. I can feel the light coming through.'

'Yes,' Betty said.

Down the hill, into the forestry land, until she came to the point where there were farm buildings either side of the road and a Land Rover with a 'Christ is the Light' sticker. Oh, he had his uses, did Jesus Christ: the very name served as a disinfectant.

Merrily turned in to a rutted track between two stone and timbered barns, and there was the farmhouse, grey brown, black windows. No garden, just a yard of dirt and brown gravel, where she parked the Volvo. There was a glazed front porch, its door hanging ajar. She saw the interior door swing open before she was even into the porch, and Judith Prosser standing there, cool and rangy in her orange rugby shirt.

'You're late, Mrs Watkins. Had you down for an early riser, I did.'

The banter was wrapped around Judith's need always to be ahead of the situation. This visit must, on no account, be seen as a surprise.

'Late night, Mrs Prosser.'

'I've coffee on.'

'That would be good . . . Erm, I felt there were things left in the air from last night.'

'No bad thing, sometimes,' Judith replied swiftly. 'Left in the air, they have a chance to blow away.'

'But sometimes they stick around and the air goes sour, and that's not a good thing in my experience.'

'Oh, *your* experience.' Holding open the door for Merrily. 'Profound today, is it, Mrs Watkins?'

'You have a problem with profound?' Merrily blinked. It was dark inside and the hulking furniture made it darker.

'Life's too short to tolerate problems.'

'Life's too short for cover-ups, Mrs Prosser,' Merrily said.

Judith turned to face her. They were standing in a square hall dominated by a huge, over-ornate chair with a nameplate on the back. It looked like the seat of a council chairman or a presiding magistrate. Judith leaned an elbow on one of its carved shoulders.

'As I said last night, it would be stupid for you to react to silly rumours.'

'Here's the situation,' Merrily said. 'I was there, I saw the whole thing: the cross, the petroleum jelly. Also Dr Coll standing in the doorway – and didn't *that* explain why a bunch of local matrons were able to sit there and watch Ellis violate a woman with a metal cross? Because there was a *doctor* present. This, of course, makes everything all right, above board, entirely respectable, clinically proven.'

Judith Prosser flicked a speck of dust or ash from the point of the chairman's chair.

'I'm not sure how far from being a police matter this is,' Merrily continued, 'but we're very close to finding out.'

FORTY-FIVE

Stupid Wires

Jane typed in the word 'charismatic'. The usual, mainly irrelevant list appeared. She grabbed the mouse, dithered over 'Charismatic Q and A'.

'Try it,' Eirion suggested. 'Might lead somewhere better.'

On the screen: 'The Charismatic Movement: what in the name of God is it all about?'

'Click,' Eirion said.

> The Charismatic Movement (from the Greek *charismata*, meaning 'spiritual gifts') developed in the 1950s and '60s from the Pentecostal movement, crossing over the denominations, embracing the sphere of angelology and the gifts of healing, prophecy, speaking in tongues and power-prayer. It reached a new peak worldwide in the 1990s ...

There was a list of options. Jane clicked on 'Yes, I want to talk to God.'

They needed all the help they could get.

Sophie had said she shouldn't be allowing this, before shutting them in the Deliverance office with the computer.

And she wanted copies of anything they found.

Jane had said, 'This is awfully good of you ... Mrs Hill.'

Collecting a contemptuous frown and, 'Jane, you are not among the people with whose patronage I can cope. Try "evangelism".'

On the way here, Jane had told Eirion virtually everything she'd learned so far – about Terry Penney, about pentagrams . . . The poor little Chapel boy had seemed unnerved, regaining his cool only when he saw the computer. Smiling his famous smile at Sophie, who wore a checked woollen skirt with a grey twinset and pearls – Sophie, who might one day be the last person in the entire universe still wearing a twinset and pearls.

Jane clicked again, losing enthusiasm for talking to God. When it was working fast and well, the Internet could give you the illusion of *being* God – you could imagine Him operating like this, constructing human situations with a click of the mouse, running programmes, consigning icons to the dumpbin.

'Evangelism', though, had been a bummer. There were background articles on St John the Evangelist. There were four web sites about some kind of computer sotftware with that name. There were no obvious links into crank preachers in the American South who might have known Nick Ellis; and 'Charismatics' proved little better.

'I could try "Bible Belt",' Eirion offered.

'You'd probably get suppliers of religious fashion accessories,' Jane said gloomily.

'"Cults?"'

'No chance. People never think of themselves as being in a cult. "Just off to the cult, don't wait up" – doesn't happen.'

'What we need is a Christian search engine.'

'What we need is divine intervention.' Jane walked over to the window which overlooked the forecourt of the Bishop's Palace. No good searching for it out there.

'OK,' Eirion said. 'What are we *really* asking for?'

'Some big, rattling skeleton in Ellis's vestment closet. Something that maybe caused him to leave America, come back here in a hurry. When you think about it, most Brits who go over to the States tend to stay there, making piles of money. So it's reasonable to think Ellis came back because something happened to make him kind of persona non grata. Like he was the leader of a mass suicide cult who contrived not to go down with the rest.'

'We'd have heard about it.'

'We're stuffed.' Jane angrily keyed in 'loony fundamentalist bastards', and the Web found, for some no doubt entirely logical reason, a bunch of science fiction and fantasy writers including David Wingrove, David Gemmell and Kirk Blackmore.

'We're just not asking the right questions.'

'Kirk Blackmore . . . where did I hear that?'

Sophie came in then, with a piece of paper, a name written on it. 'Try this.'

'Ah,' Jane said, as Blackmore came up on the screen. 'This was the guy whose covers Robin Thorogood was going to design, but they pulled the plug.'

Eirion was staring up at Sophie, bewildered.

'I used the telephone.' Sophie inclined her neck, swan-like. 'It's rather old-tech, it involves the less-exact medium of human speech, but it does tend to be more effective when dealing with the clergy.'

'"Marshall McAllman",' Eirion read.

'Before the Reverend Nicholas Ellis came to New Radnor and then Old Hindwell, he was a curate for just over a year at a parish outside Newcastle-upon-Tyne. I've talked to his former vicar, the Reverend Alan Patterson, who only found out after the Reverend Mr Ellis had been with him for several months that he'd previously been a personal assistant to the Reverend Mr McAllman – which did not entirely please him.'

'Let's put it in, Jane.' Eirion keyed in the name, while the computer was still showing:

KIRK BLACKMORE ORACLE.
The reclusive Celtic scribe returns with a
remarkable new Lord Madoc novel which . . .

'Found,' Eirion said, after a few seconds. '"The Mobile Ministry of Marshall McAllman".'

He clicked. Kirk Blackmore vanished.

'There you are.' Sophie peered. '"Angelweb Factfile. The journeys of Reverend Marshall McAllman were directed by the Will of God and took him from Oklahoma . . ."'

' " . . . to South Carolina",' Eirion read from the screen, '"via Arkansas and Tennessee, dispensing a low-key but extremely potent evangelism effectively tailored to the needs of small towns and simple folk. He developed a loyal following after several witnessed instances of prophecy, divine inspiration and angelic" blah blah blah . . . "Reverend McAllman retired in 1998, a disillusioned man, after surviving a campaign by an unscrupulous journalist on a Tennessee newspaper, the *Goshawk Talon*. Although there remains considerable debate about Reverend McAllman's ministry, his name is still revered in" blah, blah—'

'There you have it, then,' Sophie interrupted. 'Your next port of call must surely be the, ah, *Goshawk Talon*.'

'Does that mean it's in a place called Goshawk?' Jane wondered.

'Doesn't matter, let's just put it in,' Eirion said. 'This is very fast, Mrs Hill, are you on ISDN?'

'I wouldn't know. It's all stupid wires to me. Go *on*.'

'"Found". Some stuff on birds of prey. And . . . "The *Goshawk Talon* and Marshall McAllman" . . . OK.' Eirion clicked, waited. 'Oh.'

The file you are seeking is unavailable.

Jane's face fell. 'What do we do now?'

'A technical brick wall.' Sophie sighed. 'Hard to imagine how we survived for so long without all this.' Then she did something most un-Sophie-like – stamped her foot. '*Phone* them, child! They presumably *have* telephones in Goshawk, Tennessee. If this publication still exists, it shouldn't take long to find the number. If it doesn't, we shall have to think of something else. Get onto international directory enquiries.'

'I don't know how.'

Sophie sighed in mild contempt. 'Leave it to me.' She stalked out.

'Wow,' Jane said. 'The turbo twinset.'

Eirion smiled his Eirion smile. It did things to her, but this was not the time. There never seemed to be a time. The sudden urgency manifested by Sophie made Jane quite tense. What if someone was ringing home with information far more important than anything they could hope to find on the Net, and she wasn't there to relay it. Paranoid, she rang the vicarage answering machine. One message for Mum to call Uncle Ted. *Sod that.*

'We seem to be drifting a long way from Kali Three,' Eirion said. He started to key it in.

'No, don't.' Jane leapt up and stood at the window, staring down at the wood pile below. There was a sense of being very close to something, but it was too indistinct, ghostly. She felt that invoking Kali Three would somehow bring bad luck. She turned back to the room.

'We have to go there.'

'Old Hindwell?' Eirion said. 'I'm not sure about that. Why?'

'We just *do*.'

'Absolutely not.' Sophie was in the doorway.

'Sophie, there's some really heavy—'

'Don't you think your mother has enough to worry about? Sit down and speak to the man from the paper. Or would you prefer me to do it? Perhaps it might be better if I did.'

'She's right,' Eirion said. 'She's going to sound so much more authoritative than either of us. Especially to Joe-Bob McCabe, of the *Goshawk Talon*.'

'Ah sure lerve your *a*ccent, ma'am,' said Jane. The only person from Tennessee she'd ever heard talk was Elvis.

'The man's name,' said Sophie, 'is Eliot Williams. He's busy at the moment, but his editor's getting him to call me back. I think he rather senses a story.'

'Wow,' Jane said, 'you're, like, incredible.'

But Sophie had already returned to her office, where the phone was ringing.

FORTY-SIX

Nine Points

A dark, Victorian living room. Merrily imprisoned in the lap of a huge, high-sided leather armchair, coat folded on her knees, cup and saucer on top of that.

Judith Prosser was adept at disadvantaging her visitors.

'And since when is religion a matter for the police, Mrs Watkins?'

'When it's sexual assault.' Merrily drank some of the coffee. Perversely, it was good coffee.

'Do you know what I think?' Judith's own chair put her about a foot higher than Merrily. 'I've been enquiring about you, and do you know what I think? I think that Father Ellis has dared to intrude into what you consider to be your back yard. He is doing what you think only you should be doing.'

'You think *I'd* do—?'

'How would I know *what* namby-pamby thing you would do these days, when the Church is like a branch of the social services?' A withering contempt for both.

'Now we're getting to it,' Merrily said.

'*Are* we, Mrs Watkins?'

Merrily tried to sit up in the chair. She felt like a child. Around the walls were dozens of photographs, mostly of men wearing chains of office, although a group of more recent ones showed boys with motorbikes and trophies.

'What *are* "we" getting to?' Judith leaned back, arms folded.

'The question of Old Hindwell preferring to do its own thing. Which is kind of admirable in one sense, I suppose.'

Judith reared up. 'It is *entirely* admirable, my girl. This is an independent part of the world. What do we need with the mandarins in Cardiff and London and Canterbury? The English. Even the Welshies . . . they all think they can come out yere and do what they like. When Councillor Prosser was on the old Radnor District Council, they used to have to employ young officials, trotting out their fancy ideas – hippies and vegetarians, half of them. It was, "Oh, you can't build *there* . . . you have to use *this* colour of slate on your roofs . . . you can't do *this*, you can't do *that*." Well, they were put in their place soon enough. The *local* people, it is, who decides. *We* know what's needed, *we* know what works. And Father Ellis, even though he's not from yere, is a man with old values and a clear, straightforward, practical approach, based on tradition. He *understands* tradition.'

Merrily was tired of this. 'How many people has he exorcized so far?'

'I can tell you that all of them have come freely to him and asked for it to be done.'

'Like your son?'

A pause. 'Gomer Parry again, I suppose.'

'Doesn't matter where it came from. I just wondered if your son actually went along to Ellis and asked to be cleansed of the taking-and-driving-away demon.'

'His parents took him.' Judith scowled. 'Another problem in today's world is that parents don't take responsibility. *We* took him to Father Ellis, Councillor Prosser and I. It was our duty.'

'And you really think he had a demon inside him that demanded the full casting-out bit?'

'Oh . . . Mrs . . . Watkins . . .' Exasperated, Judith stood and went to lean an arm on the high mantelpiece. 'They *all* have demons in them, whether it's mischievous imps or worse. In the old days, the demons were beaten out of them at school. Now, if a teacher raises a hand to a child, he's in court for assault, and nothing the poor magistrate can do to help him.'

'I see.' There was an awful logic to this: exorcism as a tool of public order. Evidently the local women had decided that the wanton demon in Marianne Starkey – which perhaps made some local men a little restless, a touch frisky – should be eradicated before it led to trouble. Marianne's reaction to the male witch adding a piquantly topical flavour to the exercise.

'Menna,' Merrily said. 'What about Menna?'

Judith brought her arm slowly down to her side, stiffening ever so slightly.

'Judith, did Menna herself go to Father Ellis and beg for exorcism, to get rid of the molesting spirit of Mervyn Thomas?'

Judith was silent.

'Or was it J.W.'s idea? In his role as husband. And father figure.'

Judith said, eyes unmoving, 'How do you know she was cleansed?'

'Wasn't she?'

'Is that any business of yours or mine?' First sign of a significant loss of cool. 'What would *I* know about the private affairs of Mr and Mrs J.W. Weal? Was I supposed to be her guardian and her keeper *all* her life?'

'You were obviously still concerned about her. You went to visit her regularly. You were still, by all accounts, her only real friend. You were the best person to realize she was . . . still a victim.'

'He loved her!'

'He *suffocated* her, Mrs Prosser. When she was in hospital, he tended her, he washed her, hardly let the nurses near her. I saw him with a bowl of water, as if he was baptizing her all over again. As if he was somehow confirming and reinforcing what Father Ellis had done.'

'You see everything, don't you?'

'Look, I just happened to be there, with Gomer the night his Minnie died. J.W. was like a priest, giving his wife the last rites. But she was already dead. Ellis said at the funeral that he'd baptized them together. Was that a public thing? Were you present?'

Judith came away from the fireplace. There was a large, iron coal stove in it, closed up. She walked to the small window and stood looking out. She was thinking. And she evidently did not want Merrily to see her thinking.

'No,' she said eventually. 'No, I was not there, as such.'

'Am I right in thinking that Menna was still felt to be . . . possessed, if you like, by her father?'

'He was not a pleasant man,' Judith said.

And did you get Menna on the Pill from an early age because you were afraid that what happened to Barbara might happen to her, too? Merrily didn't ask that. It perhaps didn't need asking, not right now.

'You couldn't *really* be sure that Merv was leaving her alone, could you?'

Judith didn't reply.

'And whatever he was like, she was still dependent on him. Dependent on a strong man? Which Weal realized, and lost no time in exploiting.'

Judith kept on looking out of the window. 'He was too old for her, yes. Too rigid in his ways, perhaps. But she *was* a flimsy, delicate thing. She would always need protection. She was never going to have much of a life with Jeffery, but she would at least be protected.'

'Like a moth in a jar,' Merrily said – and Judith turned sharply around. Merrily met her clear gaze. 'When exactly did you begin to think that J.W. Weal, in his way, might be as bad for Menna as her father had been?'

'It was not my business any more.'

'Oh come on, you'd known that girl all her life. Did it really not occur to you that Weal might think he was somehow still in competition with the dead Mervyn Thomas for Menna's affections? If that's the right word? That maybe he didn't think he was getting . . . everything he was entitled to.'

Judith came back to the fireplace. 'Who is this going to help now?'

Merrily thought back to Barbara Buckingham. *'Possession is nine points of the law.'* Perhaps there was still a chance to help Barbara.

But that wouldn't matter much to Judith Prosser.

'Menna,' Merrily said softly. 'Perhaps it will help Menna.'

And so it came out.

The big room at the back of the house. The dining room in which probably no one ever dined. The bay-windowed room with rearing shadows. The room facing the mausoleum.

'This was where it was actually done?' Merrily said. 'How do you know that?'

'Because I watched, of course. I stood in the garden and I spied, just as you did on the night of Menna's funeral. I was in our yard when I saw Father Ellis's car go past slowly. I followed on foot. I saw him enter the old rectory with the medical bag he carries for such occasions. It was towards evening. I saw Menna dressed in white. I saw Father Ellis. I did not see Jeffery.'

Something had snapped. Something had fallen into place. Perhaps something which, even to a *local person*, was no longer defensible.

Merrily said cautiously, 'And did what happened bear comparison with what took place at the village hall yesterday?'

'I don't know,' Judith said. 'It was not possible to see what was happening below the level of the window.'

Merrily's palms were damp. 'You're saying she was on the floor at some point?'

'I'm saying she wasn't visible.'

'When was this?'

'About three . . . four . . . weeks ago? I can't remember exactly.'

'Not that long before she had her stroke, then.'

'I'm making no connection, Mrs Watkins.'

'Do you believe she was possessed and needed exorcism?'

'I think she needed help.'

'Was Dr Coll there?'

'I have no reason to think so.'

'So just Ellis and Menna.'

'I imagine Jeffery was somewhere in the house. His car was there anyway.'

'But you didn't see him in the room?'

'No. What do you want, Mrs Watkins? How can *you* knowing any of this possibly help Menna now?'

'She haunted Barbara,' Merrily said.

'Haunted?'

'I'm using the word loosely. Like memories haunt, guilt haunts.'

'Yes, we know all about that.'

'And spirits haunt.'

'Do they really?' Judith said. 'Do you seriously believe that?'

'Wouldn't be much good in this job if I didn't.' What did Judith herself believe? That Ellis was an effective psychologist or an effective and useful con man?

Merrily said, 'Barbara wanted me to do a kind of exorcism in reverse, to free Menna's spirit from Weal's possession. Possession of the dead by the living.'

'Do you seriously believe—?'

'*She* believed. And *I* believe we may have a tormented and frantic . . . essence which can't find peace. Like a moth in a jar, except—'

'A moth in a jar doesn't live long.'

'Exactly. That's the difference.'

'And how would you deal with this, Mrs Watkins?' Judith placed her hands on her narrow hips. 'How would you deal with it *now*? How would you go about it? Explain to me.'

'Well, it wouldn't be an exorcism, because this is not an evil spirit. If we think of her perhaps as still a victim, needing to be rescued. Which is normally done by celebrating a Requiem Eucharist in the appropriate place, in the company of people close to the dead person. In this case it could be you. And Mr Weal, obviously.'

'Then it will never be done, will it?'

Merrily heard Eileen Cullen, with the echoes of hospital clatter. *'Swear to God he knew it was there. Twice, he looked back over his shoulder.'*

'He *won't* let her go.' She sank into the chair, clutching the bundled coat to her chest. 'That's what this is about: possessing her in death as he never fully did in life. And knowing that . . . how can I let it go on?'

'Suppose . . .' Judith's voice had risen in pitch. 'Suppose I could get you into that house, into that room – or into the tomb – to perform your ceremony? You wouldn't be doing it with his compliance, but you wouldn't be doing it against his will either, since he wouldn't know about it. Wouldn't that be better than nothing from your point of view, Mrs Watkins?'

'How could you fix that?'

'I have keys, see – keys to the house and also to the tomb. Menna was often taken unwell, so Jeffery gave me a key to get in and attend

389

to her. When she died, he needed someone to let the masons in, to work on the tomb.'

'Why would you want to risk letting *me* in?'

'Perhaps,' Judith said, 'it's a question of what is right – the right thing to do. I cared for Menna when she was alive. Perhaps it's the last thing I can do for her.'

'But it's not right for *me* to go into someone's house without permission.'

'Well . . .' Judith shrugged. 'That's your decision, isn't it?' She bent over and released a valve on the iron stove; there was a rush of air and a slow-building roar of fire. 'I was about to say, Mrs Watkins, that Jeffery won't be there tonight. It's his lodge night. He never misses it, unlike Councillor Prosser. It'll be even more important to him now. Always a great comfort to a man, the Masons.'

Merrily said, 'Perhaps it's a job for Father Ellis instead.'

Judith looked at her with severity. 'Does that mean you are afraid, Mrs Watkins?'

Part Five

When I looked for good, then evil came unto me;
and when I waited for light there came darkness . . .
I stood up and I cried in the congregation . . .
I am a brother to dragons and a companion to
owls.

Book of Job, Chapter 30, v.26–9

FORTY-SEVEN

Breath of the Dragon

Merrily had arranged to meet Gomer in the Black Lion for a sandwich around two thirty. She was early, but the pub was already filling up with those civilized rambling-club types – anoraks and soft drinks – who seemed to constitute Ellis's core congregation.

More of them today, substantially more. You looked at them individually and they seemed worryingly genuine: young people with a vision of a new day, elderly people with a new and healthy approach to the evening of the day. There was a buzz of energy in the dispirited, part-painted Black Lion bar, each hug, each 'Praise God' passing on a vibration.

Merrily found herself standing next to a white-bearded man of about sixty, one of the few with a glass of beer. She asked him where he was from. Wolverhampton, he said, West Midland Pentecostal.

'How far've you come, sister?'

'Oh, just from Ledwardine, just over the border. How many of you are there?'

'About ... what, fifty-five? Hired ourselves a coach. Luckily, there's a lot of retired people in our church, but quite a few young-sters've taken a day off work.' He grinned, relaxed. 'It's a question of whose work you put first, isn't it? We're going to walk down to this satanist place after lunch and hold some Bible readings outside the gate. I've not actually seen Father Ellis yet, but I'm told he's a very inspiring man.'

'So they say.'

'Praise God,' said the man from Wolverhampton.

Merrily saw Gomer coming in and pointed to the table near the door. She ordered drinks and cheese sandwiches at the bar. Greg Starkey avoided her eyes.

Gomer was wearing his bomber jacket over a grey sweatshirt with 'Gomer Parry Plant Hire' on it in red.

'Three bloody coaches on the car park, vicar.'

'Mmm. It's what happens these days – everything goes to extremes. Fastest growing movement in the Church and, hey, they're going to prove it.'

'En't the only ones. Bunch of ole vans backed into a forestry clearing up towards the ole rectory. Lighting camp fires, bloody fools.'

'Travellers?'

'Pagans, they reckons.'

Merrily sighed. 'All we need.'

'Two police vans set up in the ole schoolyard – Dr Coll's surgery. Another one in Big Weal's drive – the ole rectory. Makes you laugh, don't it? Two biggest bloody villains in East Radnor, both well in with the cops.'

Merrily dumped her cigarettes and lighter on the table. 'You find out some more?'

'Been over to Nev's.'

'Your nephew, yes?'

'Ar. Drop in now and then, make sure the boy's lookin' after the ole diggers. Anyway, Nev's with a lawyer in Llandod, plays bloody golf with him. He gave him a ring for me, off the record, like. Word is Big Weal's favourite clients is *ole* clients, specially them not too quick up top n'more.'

'Going senile?'

'Worries a lot about their wills when they gets like that, see. Who's gonner get what, how it's gonner get sorted when they snuffs it. What they needs is a good lawyer – and a good doctor. Puts their mind at rest, ennit?' 'Specially folk as en't had a family lawyer for generations, see.'

'Incomers? Refugees from Off, in need of guidance?'

'Exac'ly it, vicar. This boy in Llandod, he reckons Weal gets a steady stream of ole clients recommended by their nice, kindly doctor. That confirm what you yeard, vicar?'

'Fits in. And if we were to go a step further down that road, we might find a nice kindly priest.'

'Sure t'be,' Gomer said. 'Church gets to be more important, the nearer you gets to that big ole farm gate.'

Two bikers came in. One wore a leather jacket open to a white T-shirt with a black dragon motif. The dragon was on its back, with a spear down its throat. It was hard to be sure which side they represented.

At four o'clock, the ruined church of St Michael looked like an old, beached boat, waiting for the tide of night to set it afloat.

'Going to be lit up like a birthday cake,' Betty said with distaste. 'You can't spot them from here, but there are clusters of candles and garden torches all over it. In the windows, on ledges, between the battlements on the tower. It'll be visible for miles from the hills.'

'Making a statement?'

'Yeah. After centuries of holding ceremonies discreetly in the woods and behind curtains in suburban back rooms, we're coming out.'

They'd met in the decaying copse, Merrily walking from the old archaeological site, where Gomer had parked, Betty coming across the bridge from the farmhouse and joining the footpath.

The sky had dulled, low clouds pocketing the sunken sun, and you could feel the dusk, carrying spores of frost. Betty looked cold. Merrily tightened her scarf.

'Bain still wants to do it naked?'

'Possibly. They'll light a small fire inside a circle of stones in the open nave. Dance back to back with arms linked behind. Not as silly as it sounds. After a while you don't feel it. You're aglow.'

Like singing in tongues, Merrily thought. A long, flat cloud lay over the church now, like a wide-brimmed hat. From the other side of the ruins, beyond the pines and the Sitka spruce, they could hear the sounds of a hymn: straggly singing, off-key. The Christians at the gate.

'They're going to keep that up all night long, aren't they?' Betty said.

'You've heard nothing yet. There are scores more in the village now.'

'Bad.' Betty shivered. 'Ned believes the spiritual tension will fuel the rite. He says we can appropriate their energy. That is way, way out of order.' She shook herself. 'I need to get them out of here, lock the gates and . . . try and save my marriage.'

'Will you stay here . . . afterwards?'

Betty shook her head. 'We won't survive this. We'll lose everything we've got with that house, but I don't care if we're destitute. Only problem is, I'm going to feel guilty about anyone else living here. I wish we could sell it to a waste disposal firm or something.'

'But we're going to deal with that,' Merrily said firmly.

'No. It was very stupid of me to ask you.' Betty looked at her, green eyes sorrowful, without hope. 'I wasn't thinking. This is part of a prehistoric ritual complex. We don't know who or what those original inhabitants were, but they chose their sites well. They knew all the doorways. Can't you feel the earth and the air fusing together as it gets dark? This is a place that knows itself – but we don't know it. Can't you hear it?'

'Just the singing,' Merrily admitted.

'I can hear a constant low humming now. I know it's in my head, but it's this *place* that's put it there. We don't know what went on here, nobody does. There are no stones left standing, only the holes where they were . . . and that church. And whatever – metaphorically, if you like – is underneath that church. And whatever it is, it's much older than Christianity.'

'And much, much older than Wicca?' Merrily said.

'Sure. We were invented in the fifties and sixties by well-meaning people who knew there was no continuous tradition. Most of Wicca's either made up or culled from Aleister Crowley and Dion Fortune. It has no *tradition*. There. I've said it. Is that what you wanted?'

The singing was already louder; more Christians had arrived.

'There's a tradition here,' Merrily said, 'of sorts. A strand of something that goes back at least to medieval times. Unfortunately, it seems to have been preserved by *my* lot.'

'Yeah. You can certainly feel it in Cascob. Oh, and St Michael's, Cefnllys. I meant to tell you – I looked this up – that when they eventually built a new church at Llandrindod the rector had the roof taken off Cefnllys Church to stop people worshipping there.'

'He did?'

'It was in a book. I suddenly remembered it from when I was a kid in Llandrindod. So I looked it up. I mean, was *he* thinking like Penney? Did they both feel the breath of the dragon? Probably didn't understand any of it, but something scared them badly. Now people like Ned Bain are coming along and saying: it's OK, it's fine, its cool . . . because *we're* the dragon. Do you still want to go in there with your holy water?'

'What time?'

'Any time after . . . I dunno, nine? If you don't come, I'll understand. Who's that?'

It was a vehicle, creaking over the footpath, where it had been widened by the archaeologists. Merrily ran to the edge of the copse. She could see Gomer's ancient Land Rover parked the other side, with Gomer leaning on the bonnet, smoking a roll-up, watching the new vehicle trundling towards him. It was Sophie's Saab.

FORTY-EIGHT

Black Christianity

No candles? The candles had gone from the windows. Not just gone out, but *gone*: the trays, the Bibles, everything.

At first, it seemed an encouraging sign, and then Merrily thought, It isn't. It isn't at all. In the face of the invasion, the local people had withdrawn, disconnected; whatever happened tonight would not be their fault.

It was about 5.50 p.m. The post office and shop had closed, there were few lights in the cottages. Only the pub was conspicuously active; otherwise Old Hindwell, under dark forestry and the hump of Burfa Hill, had retracted into itself, leaving the streets to them from Off.

The multitude!

In the centre of the village, maybe 300 or 400 people had gathered in front of the former school. They had Christian placards and torches and lamps. They were not singing hymns. They seemed leaderless.

Gomer put the Land Rover at the side of the road, in front of the entrance to the pub's yard, where it said 'No Parking'. The car park was so full that none of the coaches would get out until several cars were removed. Two dark blue police vans lurked inside the school gates. Four TV crews hovered.

The minority of pagans here seemed to be the kind with green hair and eyebrow rings. Maybe twenty of them, in bunches – harmless probably. One group, squatting outside the pub, were chanting 'Harken to the Witches' Rune', to the hollow thump of a hand drum.

'Sad,' Jane commented. She and Eirion were in the back of the Land Rover; Merrily sat next to Gomer in the front. 'They're just playing at it, just being annoying.'

'You'll be joining the Young Conservatives next, flower.'

'But those so-called Christians *really* make me sick. They're tossers, holier-than-thou gits.'

'Phew,' Merrily said. Through the wing mirror, she saw Sophie's Saab pulling in behind them. Sophie didn't get out.

Eirion said, 'What do you want us to do, Mrs Watkins?'

'Just stay with Gomer and Sophie. Perhaps you could get something to eat in the pub?'

Jane was dismayed. 'That's all the thanks we get? A mouldy cheese sandwich and a can of Coke?'

'Don't think I'm not *immensely* grateful for what you two and Sophie've uncovered. Just that I need to put it to Ellis by myself. If there are any witnesses, he won't even talk to me.'

They'd talked intently for over an hour in the Land Rover, listened to a cassette recording of a phone call involving Sophie and some journalist in Tennessee, and then Merrily had watched as Betty, now armed with many things she hadn't known about Ned Bain, had walked away into the last of the dusk, not looking back.

Merrily leaned against the Land Rover's passenger door, and it opened with a savage rending sound.

'How long will you be?' Jane asked.

'As long as it takes. He hasn't even shown yet. An hour and a half maybe?'

'And then we come looking for you?'

'And then do whatever Gomer tells you.'

The crazy violence seemed to start as soon as Merrily's feet touched the tarmac: lights flaring, a woman's scream, a beer can thrown. A black cross reared out of a mesh of torch beams amid a tangle of angry voices.

' . . . *finished*, you fuckers. Had your time. Christ was a wanker!'

' . . . your level, isn't it? The gutter! Get out of my—'

Sickening crunch of bone on flesh. Blood geysering up.

399

'Oh dear God—'

'So why don't you just fuck off back to your churches, 'fore we have 'em *all* off you?'

'Stand back!'

'Reverend?' A hand pulling Merrily back, as the police came through.

'Marianne?'

She was pushed. 'Stand back, please. Everybody, back!'

Headlights arriving. Then Collard Banks-Morgan with his medical bag. Next to him, a man in a dark suit. *Not a white monk's habit, but a dark suit.*

A woman shrieked, 'You'll be damned for ever!' and started to cry.

'Listen, Reverend,' Marianne said calmly. 'I'm better now.'

'Good.'

'Things you oughta know.' She pulled Merrily into the yard.

She followed when they took the man with the broken nose into the surgery. A woman too, spattered with his blood, wailing, Ellis's arm around her. 'He's in good hands, sister. The best.'

In the waiting room, the lighting was harsh, the seats old and hard, the ceiling still school-hall high, with cream-painted metal girders. A woman receptionist smiled smugly through a hatch in the wall. 'Come through,' Dr Coll sang, voice like muzak. 'Bring him through, that's right.'

Doors slammed routinely. There were health posters all over the walls: posters to make you feel ill, paranoid, dependent. No surprise that Dr Coll had taken over the school, a local bastion of authority and wisdom.

'I'd like to talk to you,' Merrily said to Ellis.

'I'm sure you would, Mrs Watkins,' he said briskly, 'but I don't have the time or the interest to talk to you. You're a vain and stupid woman.' Under his suit he wore a black shirt, no tie, no clerical collar.

'What happened to your messiah kit?'

'Libby, tell Dr Coll I'll talk to him later,' Ellis said to the receptionist.

Merrily said, 'There's going to be trouble out there.' She waited as Ellis dabbed with a tissue at a small blood speck on his sleeve. 'Are you going to stop them marching to the church?'

'Who am I,' he said, 'to stop anyone?'

'You started it. You lit the blue touchpaper.'

'The media started it. As you say, it's already out of hand. It'd be highly irresponsible of me to inflame it further. Now, if you don't mind . . .'

'You *could* stop them. You could stop it *now*. It isn't worth it for a crumbling old building with a bad reputation.'

'I'd lock the door after us if I were you, Libby,' Ellis said to the receptionist.

'I'll do that, Father.'

Ellis held open the main door for Merrily, looking over her head. 'After you.' She didn't move. 'Don't make me ask the police to come in,' Ellis said.

'Could you clear up a few points for me, Nick?'

'Good*night*.'

She had no confidence for this, still couldn't quite believe it.

'"I am a brother to dragons",' Merrily said.

'Go away.' He didn't look at her, opened the door wider.

'Book of Job.'

'I do *know* the Book of Job.'

The sounds of the street outside came in, carried on cold air, sounds alien to Old Hindwell – shouts, jeers, a man's unstable voice, on high, *'May God have mercy on you!'*

'I think your real name is Simon Wesson,' Merrily said. 'You went out to the States with your mother and sister in the mid-'70s, after the death of your stepfather. Over there, your mother married an evangelist called Marshall McAllman. You later became his personal assistant. He made a lot of money before he was exposed and disgraced and your mother divorced him – very lucratively, I believe.'

She couldn't look at him while she was saying all this, terrified that it was going to be wrong, that Jane and Eirion had found the wrong person, that the journalist whose voice Sophie had so efficiently

401

recorded was talking about someone with no connection at all to Nicholas Ellis.

'McAllman concentrated on little backwoods communities. His technique was to do thorough research before he brought his show to town. He'd employ investigators. And although he would appear aloof when he first arrived . . .'

'None of your good-old-boy stuff from Marshall,' the journalist had told Sophie on the tape. *'Marshall was cool, Marshall was laid-back, Marshall would target a town that was hungry and he'd spread a table and he'd check into a hotel and sit back and wait for them to come sniffing and drooling . . .'*

' . . . his remoteness only added to his mystique. They came to him – the local dignitaries, the civic leaders, the business people – and he passed on, almost reluctantly, what the Holy Spirit had communicated to him about them and their lives and their past and their future . . . and he convinced them that they and their town were riddled with all kinds of demons.'

Merrily focused on a wall poster about the symptoms of meningitis. She spoke in a low voice, could see Libby the receptionist straining to hear while pretending to rearrange leaflets behind the window of her hutch.

'Time and time again, the local people would pull Marshall into the bosom of the community, everyone begging him to take away their demons, and their children's demons . . . especially the daughters, those wayward kids. A little *internal ministry* . . . well, it beats abortion. He was a prophet and a local hero in different localities. He only went to selected places, little, introverted, no-hope places with poor communications – the places that were gagging for it.'

The print on the meningitis poster began to blur. She turned at last to look up at Ellis, his nose lifted in disdain, but she could see his hand whitening around the doorknob.

'He taught you a lot, Nick, about the psychology of rural communities. And about manipulation. Plus, he gave you the inner strength and the brass neck to come back to this country and finally take on your hated, still-vengeful stepbrother.'

She stood in the doorway and waited.

Ellis closed the door again.

*

In the Black Lion, Jane saw Gomer was talking at the bar to a fat man of about thirty in a thick plaid shirt that came down halfway to his knees. At their table by the door, Sophie gathered her expensive and elegant camel coat over her knees to protect them from the draught.

'I'd take you two back to Hereford with me, if I thought you'd stay put in the office.'

'No chance.' Jane ripped open a bag of crisps, stretched out her legs.

'Nothing's going to *happen* here, Jane,' Sophie said. 'The whole thing comes down to two obsessive men settling a childhood grudge.'

'But what a grudge, Sophie. Serious, *serious* hatred fermenting for over a quarter of a century. A fundamentalist bigot and a warlock steeped in old magic. A white witch and a black Christian.'

'Jane!'

'He *is*. If you, like, *subvert* Christianity, if you use it aggressively to try and hurt or crush people of a different religion . . . or if you go around exorcizing demons out of people who haven't actually got demons *in* them, just to get power over them – like this guy McAllman – then you're using Christianity for evil, so that's got to be *black* Christianity.'

'I wouldn't exactly call Bain a *white* witch, either,' Eirion murmured.

Sophie said, 'Jane, your grasp of theology—'

But Gomer was back with them, thoughtfully rolling and unrolling his cap. 'That's Nev,' he said, watching the man in the plaid shirt go out. 'My nephew, Nev, see. Er, some'ing's come up, ennit? Mrs Hill, if there's a chance you could stay with these kids till the vicar gets back . . .'

'Uh-huh.' Jane shook her head. 'Mum said to stick with Gomer.'

Gomer sighed. He opened the pub door, peered out. Jane got up and leaned over his shoulder. There were still a lot of people out there and more police – about seven of them. Also, the guy in the plaid shirt standing by a truck. In the back of the truck was a yellow thing partly under a canvas cover.

'What's that?' Jane demanded.

'Mini-JCB.'

PHIL RICKMAN

'Like for digging?'
'Sure t'be,' Gomer admitted gruffly.

Ellis took her into the second surgery: a plain room with a big, dark desk, Victorian-looking. Authority. A big chair and a small chair. Ellis sat in the big chair; Merrily didn't sit down. She was thinking rapidly back over the history of her faith, the unsavoury aspects.

In the Middle Ages, Christianity was still magic: charms and blessings indistinguishable. The Reformation was supposed to have wiped that out but, in seventeenth-century Britain, religious healers and exorcists were still putting on public displays, just like modern Bible Belt evangelists. And when it was finally over in most of Britain, here in Radnorshire – inside the inverted pentagram of churches dedicated to the warrior archangel – it continued. In a place with a strong tradition of pagan magic, the people transferred their allegiances to the priests . . . the more perspicacious of whom took on the role of the conjuror, the cunning man.

Few more cunning than Nicholas Ellis, formerly Simon Wesson. His face was unlined, bland, insolent – looking up at her but really looking down.

'Where's your mother now, Nick?'
'Dead. Drowned in her swimming pool in Orlando, four years ago. An accident.'
'Your sister?'
'Still out there. Married with kids.'
'You came back to Britain because of what happened over Marshall McAllman and this Tennessee newspaper?'
'I've told you I *won't* discuss that.' He brought a hand down hard on the desk. He was sweating. 'And if you say a word about any of this outside these walls, I shall instruct my solicitor to obtain an immediate injunction to restrain you and make preparations to take you to court for libel. Do you understand?'
'This is Mr Weal, is it?'
'Never underestimate him.'
'I wouldn't. He'll do anything for you, won't he? After what you did for him. And for his wife – before she died.'

404

Ellis kept his lips tight, his face uplifted to the lights and shining.

'You must have investigated this parish pretty thoroughly before you applied for it. Or were you looking specifically for a parish that suited your kind of ministry? Or was it just luck?'

'Or the will of God?'

'From what I gather, your mother was into a particularly mystical form of High Church—'

He turned his chair away with a wrench. 'No. No. *No!* I will *not.*'

'Perhaps *she* found the connections. Perhaps she was a particular influence on McAllman's ministry.' Merrily stood with her back to the door. 'Any point in asking you if you *did* actually help to cover up a less-than-hot-blooded murder?'

His eyes burned.

'All that matters is Ned Bain thinks you did,' Merrily said.

'Edward is a despicable nonentity.'

'Not in pagan circles he isn't. I mean, I suppose it's easy to say that's *why* he became a pagan. It's rough, natural, wild . . . very much a reaction against your mother's suffocating churchiness.'

He rose up. 'Blasphemer!'

Merrily lost it, bounced from the door. 'Do you know what *real* blasphemy is, Nick? It's a man with a nine-inch cross.'

'I will *not*—'

'Do you sterilize it first?'

'May God have mercy on you!'

'Only, I was there when you exorcized Marianne Starkey. Who . . .' Merrily prayed swiftly for forgiveness. 'Who's now prepared to make a detailed statement.'

A lie. But she had him. He stared at her.

'We've prepared a press release, Nick. Unless she hears from me by seven o'clock, my secretary's been instructed to fax it to the Press Association in London.'

Ellis folded his arms.

Merrily looked at her watch. 'I make it you've got just under an hour.'

'To do what?' He leaned back, expressionless.

'Put on your white messiah gear,' Merrily said. 'Get out there

405

and tell them it's all over. Tell them to go home. Or lead them all up to the village hall and keep them there.'

Ellis spread his hands. 'They'll be there, anyway. The police wanted them off the streets. I believe the Prossers have taken them to the hall.'

'Keep them there then. Tell them you don't want to risk their immortal souls by having them stepping onto the contaminated ground of St Michael's.'

He shrugged. 'OK, sure.' He leaned back, two fingers along the side of his head, curious. 'But I don't understand. Why do you care?'

She didn't follow him. She stayed on the edge of the schoolyard, near the police vans, and saw lights eventually come on in what she reckoned was Ellis's house. Dr Coll came out of the surgery, but didn't so much as glance at her. Perhaps Judith hadn't told him. At the same time, two policemen went in, presumably to obtain statements from the injured man and his wife. Merrily resisted an impulse to yell at Dr Coll, 'Why did you kill Mrs Wilshire?' in the hope that some copper might hear.

The village was comparatively quiet again. The lights were still few and bleary. Or maybe it was her eyes. Was there more she could have done? If there was, she couldn't think what it might be. She was tired. She prayed that Ellis would see sense.

A few minutes later, she saw him coming down from the council estate, a Hollywood ghost in his white monk's habit. He walked past the school and didn't turned his head towards her. Leaving twenty or thirty yards between them, she followed him to the hall. A cameraman spotted him and ran ahead of him and crouched in the road, recording his weary, stately progress to his place of worship. A journalist, puffing out white steam, ran back to the pub to alert the others. Merrily prayed that they were all going to be very disappointed. Like the Christians.

*

'With respect, Father, what was the point of us coming at all?'

One man on his feet in the crowded hall. It was the biker with the black dragon.

Ellis brought his hands together. 'You came here because you were moved by the Holy Spirit. We must all obey those impulses which we recognize as a response to the will of God.'

'But,' the man persisted, 'what does God want us to *do*?'

Ellis let the question hang a while, then he said softly, 'You all saw what happened earlier to our brother. I can tell you that two men have been charged with assault causing actual bodily harm. That will be the least of *their* punishment. But, in allowing that to happen, God was telling us that a public demonstration is no longer the answer. The answer is prayer.'

'Praise God,' someone cried, but it was half-hearted. They wanted . . .

Blood? Merrily sat the back, demoralized even in victory.

'There will be no more . . . violence.' Ellis emphasized it with open hands. There was desultory applause. 'But our task is still far from over.'

He told them they must pray for the intervention of St Michael to keep his church out of the hands of Satan, out of the red claws of the dragon. And if they prayed, if their faith in God was strong enough, the Devil would fail tonight. The Lord would yet intervene.

A frisson went through the hall; there were tentative moans.

'God' – Ellis's arms were suddenly extended, ramrod stiff – 'arises!'

A man arose from the floor, his own arms raised, a mirror image of the priest. Others followed, with a squeaking and scraping of chairs.

Hundreds of arms reaching for the ceiling.

A woman began to gabble, 'God, God, God, God, God!' orgasm-ically.

Soon, Merrily found she was the only one seated and was obliged to scramble to her feet. She looked up and saw that Ellis – who must surely know that this was as good as over, that there would be no more generating paranoia, no more wholesale exorcism, no more *internal ministry* – was aglow again, his eyes like foglamps, and they

were focused, through the wintry forest of stiffened arms . . . focused
on her.

'*God arises!*' Ellis snarled.

Merrily left the hall. He was showing her that even in defeat his
power was undiminished. That the Holy Spirit was with *him*.

'A remarkable man, Mrs Watkins,' said Judith Prosser.

She was standing in the porch, in her long black quilted coat.

'Yes,' Merrily admitted.

Judith gently closed the doors on the assembly. She contemplated
Merrily with a wryly tilted smile. 'I take it,' she said lightly, 'that
you've made your decision.'

'I'm sorry?'

'Your "exorcism in reverse"' Judith said. 'The laying to rest of
the poor moth in the jar.'

'Oh. Yes.'

'Jeffery will have left now, for his lodge. But perhaps this was not
such a good idea.'

Inside the hall, a hymn was beginning. It would end in tongues.
Ellis and his followers were, for the time being, contained. Jane, too,
by Gomer and Sophie. Merrily had a couple of hours yet before she
was due at St Michael's. She walked out into the cold and looked
down on the meagre glimmer of the village. She shivered inside Jane's
duffel coat.

'All right,' she said. 'Let's go and do it.'

FORTY-NINE

Cashmere and Tweed

Jane had never seen Gomer quite like this before, although she'd
heard the tales. The legend.

Ciggy glowing malevolently in the centre of his teeth, like a ruby
in the face of some Indian idol, he rode the mini-JCB into the middle
of the field to where the earth was banked. The digger was the
size of a heavy-duty ride-on mower. A big yellow Tonka toy. Nev's
truck was parked a few yards back, engine running, headlights full
beam. Next to it, at a slight angle, was Gomer's Land Rover, with
Sophie inside.

In any other situation, Jane would have found this deeply, shock-
ingly thrilling, but tonight she only wanted to get it over with, and
find Mum.

This was Prosser's ground, turned over to the archaeologists
who'd dug trenches all over the place, and then paid fat Nev to
replace the tons of removed soil. Up here with Mum yesterday,
Gomer had noticed a part that was not professionally finished. Not
how he'd taught Nev to do it. Not seeded, but clumsily planted with
turf. Not made good to Gomer Parry Plant Hire standards.

Gomer had taken it up with Nev. Nev had been offended. Nev
said he'd left a bloody perfect job, banked up and seeded tidy.

Now, it could be that Gareth Prosser had buried some sheep
here, but no sheep grazed this area, and it was a long way to come
for a dull, lazy bugger like Gareth.

'Eirion!' Gomer yelled. 'Do me a favour, boy, back the ole Land
Rover up a few feet, then we can see the top o' the mound.'

'OK.' Eirion ran through the mud.

'Jane!' Sophie called from the truck. 'Either you come in here, or I'm coming out for you.' Knowing Jane was quite keen to sneak away and snatch a look at the ruins of the church across the brook, to see if they were all lit up.

'Oh, Sophie, Gomer might need some help.'

'Very well.' The truck's passenger door creaked open. There was a squelch. 'Blast!'

Jane grinned. Sophie was not the kind to carry wellies in the boot.

The bucket of the little digger went into the soft bank like a spoon into chocolate fudge. Gomer had thought this mini-JCB might be more appropriate than a big one, in the circumstances, and also less conspicuous. It couldn't be an awful lot less conspicuous, with all the noise Gomer was making.

'This is quite ridiculous.' Sophie was now limping across the field, serious mud-splashes on her camel coat. 'I don't know how I ever agreed—'

'You didn't agree. We dragged you along. I'm sorry, Sophie. You've been, like, really brilliant today.'

'Shut up, Jane.'

'We could have told the police, I suppose, but they probably couldn't have done anything without going to a magistrate for a warrant or something, and that would have meant tomorrow.'

'Mind yourselves!' Gomer bawled. The arm of the digger swung, the bucket dipped with a slurping, sucking sound. Jane wondered if Minnie's exasperated spirit was watching him now.

The bucket clanged and shivered. '—*ucking Nora!*' Gomer snarled. The digger's hydraulic feet gripped at the slippery earth, the whole machine bucked and Gomer rose from the seat like a cowboy. He turned and spat out his cigarette end. 'Eirion! Can you get the ole torch to that, see what we got there?'

But it was a just a big rock, too big for the digger to shift. Gomer and Eirion had to manhandle it out of the way. It took ages; they both got filthy.

*

After about half an hour, there was a new bank of earth, three feet high, at right angles to the one they were excavating. It was like some First World War landscape. Jane wandered over to the digger.

'Gomer, look, suppose Sophie and I go back and see what's happened to Mum? Is that OK?'

'Sure t'be.' Gomer sat back in the headlight beams, his glasses brown-filmed. 'We en't gettin' nowhere fast yere. Bloody daft idea, most likely. Gotter put all this shit back, too, 'fore we leaves.'

'It was worth a *try*, Gomer. You aren't usually wrong. OK, look, we'll get back just as soon as we—'

'Mr Parry!' Eirion's face turned round from the gouged-out bank. 'Ar?'

'Oh bloody hell, Mr Parry.' Eirion slurped desperately out of the clay. He dropped the lamp and his muddy hands went to his mouth. Jane heard him vomiting, the sick slapping into the mud.

Gomer was out of his seat, grabbing the hand lamp from where it had rolled. 'Stay there, Jane. Bloody *stay* there!'

Jane froze where she was, in the clinging mud. All those crass remarks she'd made to Mum after Mumford had been, after the radio reports. It should have been her, not Eirion. She deserved to face this horror.

Sophie was hopping towards her. 'What is it?'

'They've found something.'

'Then let's call the police.'

'He needs to make sure, Sophie.'

Realizing, with a horrible, freezing feeling that Gomer wasn't in any position to make sure of this. Only *she* was.

She would *have* to face it.

'Sorry.' Eirion came back. His baseball cap had gone. His face gleamed with greasy clay and sweat. There were touchingly childish mud streaks around his mouth where he'd wiped it with his hand. 'That was inexcusable.'

'Irene . . .?'

'It was the smell, I suppose.' He shuddered. 'I just put my hand

411

down this kind of fissure and this whole wall of stuff came down and like . . . Oh God.' He turned away, pushing slimy fingers through his hair.

Gomer came back for the spade.

'Is it?' Jane was shocked at the weakness of her own voice.

''Ang about,' Gomer said non-committally.

Sophie said, her voice dry and clipped, '*Is* it, Mr Parry?'

'Well . . . likely.'

'Oh, for heaven's sake, give me that torch!' Sophie snatched the rubber-covered lamp from a caterpillar of the mini-JCB and stalked off into the murk.

Gomer followed her with the spade, called back over his shoulder, 'Better stay there, girl. En't nothin' you can do.'

'I kind of think there is, actually,' Jane said sadly. She slithered after him towards the bank. Eirion plunged into the mud, grabbed her.

'No . . .'

'Irene, I'm the only one of us who's actually seen her.'

'Jane, believe me . . . that is not going to help you.'

'What?'

Even over the clatter of three engines, she heard Sophie's moan. Ahead of her, the newly unearthed soil and clay was shining almost white in the intersecting beams, and had that multihued, stretched look, like when you bent a Mars bar in half. Sophie came back, slapping dirt from her hands.

'Go back. Now!'

'Sophie . . .?'

'It's a woman.'

'Could it be Barb—?'

'Cashmere and tweed,' Sophie said. 'She's wearing cashmere and tweed.'

'What does she look like? I've seen her, you see. When she first came up to Mum at the funeral . . .'

'Come on, Jane.'

'I'm not a little kid, you know. Let me just—'

'Jane.' Eirion took her hand in his mud-encrusted paw. 'We don't know *what* she looks like.'

Sophie said coldly, 'Someone seems to have hacked her face to pieces before they buried her.'

Sophie's camel coat was ruined.

FIFTY

Scumbag

Alone in the yard, Robin looked back at the farmhouse, lit by the underfed porchlight, and it was like he was finally waking up.

Here were the once-white walls, stained and crumbling to reveal rubble underneath. There were the four front windows, small and sunken, like squinting eyes.

Then it just, like, hit him in the gut: *What a dump!* What was he doing here, stranded in this squalid hovel, with a coughing stove and a pile of wet wood, and his wife coming and going like some kind of elemental spirit, and his portfolios coming back marked 'Piece of shit', this whole godforsaken place rejecting him?

All day he'd felt a madness around him, wild fluctuations of mood, chasms of disaster opening up at his feet, like the potholes in the yard . . . and then the sun suddenly breaking out again, the puddles streaked with rainbows.

'I still think Kirk could be persuaded to listen to reason.'

The elegant and cultured Ned Bain could change it all about, even though Bain was doing this not for Robin, whom he didn't really need, but for Betty, whom he apparently did. Whom everyone did.

Even witches talked in hushed tones about Betty. There were all kinds of people in Wicca, and the ones you needed to be most wary of tended to be the men – guys who'd read about group sex and ritual flagellation, guys who'd heard you could learn to magic your dick into staying hard all night long. Every coven attracted a few of these, and they never stuck it long, and they were the trash end of the

Craft. And at the other end were women like Betty, about whom even witches talked in hushed tones. *'I was very much looking forward to meeting her,'* Ned Bain had said. *'Word gets around.'*

And yet, since Betty had returned home, she and Bain seemed hardly to have spoken, as though neither wanted the other to read their private agenda. Because there sure as hell *were* private agendas here, even stupid and decidedly unpsychic Robin could sense that. Maybe – like high priest and high priestess – Bain and Betty were communicating without words. Robin's fists tightened. He couldn't bear the thought of that.

The night was as cold as you could get without inches of snow on the ground, but it was bright, with a last-quarter moon and a scattering of stars. So what, in the names of all the gods, were they waiting for?

The church itself was primed for its reversion to the Old Religion. A hundred fat candles were in place, plus garden torches and sconces and fireworks for when it was all over. There was a purposeful silence around the place, unbroken even by crazy Vivvie and fluty-voiced Max. Even the goddamned Christians had cooled their hymn-singing.

Robin had had to get out of the house; he couldn't stand the tension, had kept getting up and walking around, irritating the witches who were sitting in the parlour, hanging out, waiting, their robes – in view of the extreme cold, they were at least starting this one robed – stowed in bags at their feet, and the crown of lights ready in the centre of the room. But whose house was this anyway? He'd wanted Betty to come outside with him, confide in him. She was a great priestess but she was still his wife, for heaven's sake.

But Betty had avoided his eyes.

Was there something she didn't want him to know? Something secretly confided to her by Bain? He who would later join with her in the Great Rite – simulated. *Simulated, right?* Robin's nails dug into his palms. Bain was a handsome and, he guessed, very sexual guy.

Usually – invariably, in fact – the hours before any sabbat were lit with this gorgeous anticipation. Tonight was *the* sabbat. An event likely to be more resonant, in Robin's view, than the collapse of the Berlin Wall, than the return of Hong Kong to the Chinese. This should be the finest night of his life. So how come, as he walked back toward the house, all he felt was a sick apprehension?

The pub car park, the point where the village streets come together, is full of nothing much. Coppers and reporters, yes – but where were all the funny Christians, then?

Gomer leaves the truck on the double-yellows outside the school, and that boy Eirion brings the Land Rover in behind him. Eirion's going along with Mrs Hill to tell the coppers what they've dug up. Better coming from somebody cultured, see, so the cops move faster. Besides which, Gomer and young Jane need to find the vicar in a hurry, on account of there's somebody out there has done for Barbara Thomas, then took what Gomer judges to be a log-splitter to her face, before her was planted in Prosser's ground.

One of the telly cameramen is pointing his lens at the mini-JCB. A bored-looking woman reporter asks, 'What have you been digging?'

'Sprouts,' Gomer tells her. He's spotted a light in the old school that's now become Dr Coll's surgery. 'Why don't we give this a try, girl?' he asks Jane. 'Vicar was in yere earlier, we knows that.'

They walk into the yard. Don't seem two minutes since this old place was a working school. Don't seem two minutes since Gomer had *friends* went to this school. That's life, too bloody short. Too short for bloody old wallop and bullshit.

So, who should they meet but Dr Coll himself in the doorway, coming out. Gomer stands his ground, and Dr Coll's got to take a step back into the building. Has to be a reason, going way back, that Gomer don't care for doctors, but he bloody don't, and that's the only mercy about the way Minnie went: no long years of being at the mercy of no bloody doctors.

'Look, I'm afraid surgery's long over.'

'It bloody en't, pal.' Gomer lets the youngster in, and then slams the door behind them all.

'I know you, don't I?' Dr Coll says, with a vague bit of a smile. Must be close on sixty now, but he never seems to change. Dapper, the word is. Beard a bit grey now, but never allowed to go ratty.

'Gomer Parry Plant Hire,' Gomer says.

'Ah, yes.'

'Never goes near no bloody doctors meself, but you might recall as how you used to peddle drugs to a friend o' mine, Danny Thomas.'

'I really don't think so.' The smile coming off like grease on a rag.

'And Terry Penney, remember? But that's all water up the ole brook, now, ennit?'

'If you're trying to tell me,' Dr Coll says severely, 'that you're hoping I'll supply you with proscribed drugs, I think you should decide to leave very quickly. In case you didn't notice, there's a police van parked directly outside.'

'Shows what kind of a bloody nerve you got then, ennit, Doc?'

'Mr Parry—'

'Them coppers knew what we knew, they'd be in yere, turnin' the place over.'

'Are you *drunk*, man?'

Young Jane picks up the thread now. '*We* know you killed that old lady in New Radnor. You've probably killed, like, *loads* of people. You're probably like that Dr Shipman.'

'All right!' Dr Coll turning nasty at last. 'I haven't got all night to listen to a lot of ludicrous nonsense. Out of here, the pair of you!'

Gomer shoves himself back against the door. Dr Coll's eight, maybe ten years younger than him. And taller, but then most blokes are. Don't make no odds when you're madder than what they are, and Gomer is sorely mad now.

'Guess who just got dug up, Doc.'

Dr Coll tries to grab the door handle, but Gomer knocks his wrist away with his own wrist, which hurts like buggery. Gomer grits his teeth.

'Remember Barbara Thomas? Come to see you the other week, 'bout her sister, Menna? Likely you're one o' the last people poor ole Barbara talked to 'fore some bugger ripped the face off her then planted her in Prosser's bottom field, down where the harchaeologists was.'

Colour drains out of the doc's face something beautiful. Gomer's well heartened by this.

'Course, the cops don't know Barbara seen *you* 'fore she got done. Cops don't know nothin' about you an' Weal, the bloody

Hindwell Trust, all the doolally patients you recommended to Weal for sortin' their wills . . .'

'You're making no sense to me.' Dr Coll coming over with all the conviction of a bloke caught with a vanload of videos at two in the morning saying he's just been to a bloody car boot sale.

'Well, then.' Gomer folds his arms. 'I'll be straight with you, Dr Death. All we wants to know right now is where we finds the vicar. The lady vicar? We finds the vicar, we'll likely have that much to talk about, could be well into tomorrow 'fore we gets round to makin' police statements 'bout anythin' else – you gets my meanin'. Leavin' quite a bit o' time for a feller to pack his Range Rover with money and bugger off.'

'I've got a wife and family,' Dr Coll says. He blurts it out like he's just suddenly realized. Anybody else but a bloody doctor and Gomer could almost feel sorry for him.

'Where's my mum?' young Jane screams in his face.

A large chalice of red wine stood on the temple altar, with the scourge and the handbell, the wand for air, the sword for fire. Royally pissed off by now, sitting just inside the door, on the doormat for Chrissakes, Robin wanted to suggest they share it out or at least open another bottle.

Across the parlour, Betty sensed his impatience and sent him a small warning smile. The moment was close to intimate. Her face was warm and young and wonderful in the glow from the Tilley lamp which sat in the centre of the floor – what would have been the centre of the circle if they'd drawn one. But tonight's circle would be drawn outside.

If it ever happened, though they were robed and ready. Maybe this was no night for naked, and anyway Robin could appreciate the need for a sense of ceremony. He also loved to see Betty in the loose, green, medieval gown she'd made herself two, three years ago. Robin just wore this kind of grey woollen tunic; he didn't have anything more ceremonial. But then he would be peripheral tonight, an extra, a spear-carrier.

Ned Bain, in a long, black robe, sat on a bare flagstone below the window, opposite the hearth, where the heatless twig-fire burned. He was obviously listening, but Robin suspected he was not listening to Max.

In preparation, Max had led a meditation on the nature of the border, and read to them, in translation, an old Welsh poem about the death of Pwyll, son of Llywarch the Old, who sang, 'When my son was killed, his hair was bloody and flowed on both banks of the brook.' Robin had been painting it in his head – that long, bloodied hair was a gift to an illustrator. Wicca worked in strange ways; he himself might not be able to see spirits or know the future, but his imagination could be sent into instant freeflow by any image you cared to pitch him. Hell, that was *something*.

'On this holy Celtic night,' Max intoned, 'let us close our eyes and picture – all around us – the ghostly monuments of our ancestors. We are in a wide, silent valley, the stones in a grey mist around us. But over it soars Burfa Hill, and we can dimly make out the notch marking the rising of the sun at the equinox. In the black of the night is born the bright day, the new spring. And we, too, shall be born again into a new day, a new era.'

That was it. There was silence. The stones had loomed out of the mist for Robin, his soul reached for the new day, but he dispatched it back to his subconscious. He'd had enough. He shifted uncomfortably on his mat and, across the room, closest to the altar, Betty saw him and knew he was about to say something.

Instead, *she* did. But first, she smiled sadly in the lamplight, and it was for him, and Robin thought his heart would burst with love.

And then Betty said, very quietly, 'Once, not so very long ago, there were two stepbrothers . . .'

Jane and Gomer hurried across the street, making for the hall. It was, Jane thought, crazy to let the doctor just *go*, but Gomer said that if they didn't want to spend the rest of the night in some police station, they didn't have a choice.

The doctor had told them Mum had gone off with Father Ellis, and he knew Father Ellis was up in the hall, conducting a service. The doctor had then put his dignity back together, walked out across the yard, his medical bag swinging from his wrist, as if he was off on a house call.

Scumbag.

You couldn't miss the village hall, with that cross lit up on the roof. As soon as you turned up the track to the steps, you could hear the singing. A song which had no tune but lots of tunes, and endless words but no sense.

Jane started racing up the steps, saw that the hall was blazing with light. But, at the same time, she became aware that Gomer, behind her, was panting quite painfully. It had been a gruelling night and you tended to forget how old he was and how many roll-ups he smoked. She stopped halfway up and waited for him to catch up.

She reckoned afterwards, after the glass in the porch burst and the flames came out in a great gouging *whooomp* of heat, that Gomer's lungs had probably saved their lives.

FIFTY-ONE

Laid to Unrest

The laurel alley.

Later, its leaves would be crisp with frost. Merrily could see only the alley's outline, rippling black walls under the worn pebble moon.

'We could use a torch.'

'Amply bright enough,' Judith said, 'if you know the way.'

Which she, of course, did. She took Merrily's arm, leading her down to the fork in the drive. 'Mind the step, now.' Merrily remembered Marianne's hand on her arm, as the police burst through. *Things you oughta know.'* Judith's grip was firmer. Judith was without trepidation. What did Judith believe in? Not ghosts, perhaps not even God – except maybe some strictly local deity, the guardian spirit of Old Hindwell.

At the corner of the rectory, where the drive split, Merrily looked for a car, but there was just an empty space. J.W. Weal had gone to don his Masonic apron. It must look like a postage stamp on him. Lodge night: a crude ritual structure to further stiffen his already rigid life.

The police had gone, too, now. There seemed to have been a winding-down of the action at the gates of St Michael's. Nothing to see or hear when Merrily and Judith had walked past the farm entrance.

They dropped down to the tarmac and then the crazy paving to the lawn. Sharp conifers were all around, pricking stars. Merrily glanced back once at the grey-stone rectory, at the angular bulge of

421

the bay window: lightless, no magisterial shadows of furniture, no frenetic flickering, crackling . . .

Stop it!

'Something bothering you, Mrs Watkins?'

'Nothing at all, Mrs Prosser.'

At the end of the lawn, pale grey and shining slightly, was the squat conical building, the wine store . . . ice house . . . now tomb. Merrily stumbled on a lump in the lawn; Judith's arm easily found her waist, helped her up. Merrily tightened inside. It was about here that Weal had wrapped his arms around her, lifting her, whirling her around. *'Men-na.'*

Merrily shivered suddenly, and Judith knew.

'You're frightened.'

'I'm cold.' She clutched her blue airline bag to her side.

'As you wish.' Judith bit the end of one of her leather gloves to pull it off and produced from a pocket something that jingled: the keys to the mausoleum. 'But it will, I'm afraid, be even colder in here.'

When Betty had been talking for a while – calm, succinct, devastating – someone actually got up, went over and switched on all the lights. Hard reality time.

It was a starkly meaningful moment. Robin stared in cold dismay around the parlour, with its damp patches, its dull fire of smoky, sizzling green twigs, its sad assembly of robed witches and the crown of lights on the floor like some unfinished product of a kids' handicraft class left behind at the end of the semester.

It all looked like some half-assed fancy dress party that never quite took off. The air was sick with confusion, incomprehension, embarrassment – affecting everyone here, except for Ned Bain, who was still entirely relaxed in the lotus position, his butt on the stone-flag floor.

And Betty, in her green medieval robe, remained expressionless, having come out with stuff about Ned that Robin, with his famously huge imagination, couldn't begin to fathom how she'd gotten hold of. Was that where she'd been last night – obtaining Ned Bain's life story? And never saying a word to Robin because he was this big-mouthed asshole whom all subtlety deserted the second he put away his paints.

He felt royally betrayed, shafted up the ass, by everyone. Like, how many of them already knew this? How many knew that Nicholas Ellis was Bain's stepbrother, who covered up for his old lady after she stabbed Bain's father to death? Was this some British Wiccan conspiracy, to which only he was denied access?

But Robin only had to look at Vivvie's pinched and frozen face to be pretty damn sure that few, if any, of them had been aware of it all. They might've known about Ned's father and the lingering bitterness over his killing, but not about the real identity of the saintly Nick Ellis.

'Ned . . .' Max came to his feet, nervously massaging his massive beard. 'I do rather think we're due an explanation.'

All of them, except for Betty, were now looking over at black-robed Ned Bain, still relaxed, but moody now, kind of saturnine. Betty, having rolled a grenade into the room, just gazed down into her lap.

Ned brought his hands together, elbows tucked inside his knees, the sleeves of his robe falling back. He smiled ruefully, slowly shaking his head. Then, in the face of Max's evident disapproval, he brought out a packet of cigarettes and a small lighter, and they had to wait while he organized himself a smoke.

'First of all, what Betty says is broadly correct.' He sounded kind of detached, like it was dope he was smoking. 'My father married Frances Wesson, and our intelligent, free-thinking, liberal household changed almost overnight into a strict Christian, grace-at-mealtimes, church-twice-on-Sunday bloody purgatory. Icons on every wall, religious tracts on every flat surface . . . and the beatific face of my smug, pious little stepbrother. Well, of course I hated him. I hated him long before he lied to the police.'

There was another smoky silence.

'So Simon Wesson . . . changed his name?' Max prompted.

'I believe Ellis was Frances's maiden name. She'd already met the appalling Marshall McAllman during one of his early missions to the UK, but this only became evident later.'

'In other words,' said Max, too obviously anxious to help Ned clear up this little misunderstanding, 'with the promise of American nouveaux riches, your father had somewhat outlived his usefulness.'

'Oh, I've conjured a number of scenarios, Max, in the years since – none of which allows for the possibility of my father's death being self-defence. Simon knows the truth. I realized part of my destiny was to make him bloody well confess it. It became a focus for me, led me into areas I might never have entered. Into Wicca.'

Robin saw Betty look up, her green eyes hard, but lit with intelligence and insight. There would be no get-outs, no short cuts. Ned Bain took another drag at his cigarette.

'I'd tried to be a simple iconoclast at first, telling myself I was an atheist. Then, for a while – I'd be about nineteen – I was into ceremonial magic. Until I realized that was as cramped and pompous as Frances's High Church Christianity. Only paganism appeared free of such crap, and there was a great sense of release. Naked, elemental, no hierarchy – it was what I needed.'

Betty said, without looking up, 'How long have you known about this place?'

'Oh, only since Simon arrived here. Since he took over the church hall. Since he became "Father Ellis". When he first came back to Britain, he was a curate in the North-East, but that was no use to me. He wasn't doing anything that left him . . . open. I'd had people watching him in America for years – there's an enormous pagan network over there now, happy to be accessed. And other links too.'

'Like Kali Three?' Betty said.

Robin saw Bain throw her a short, knife-like glance; she didn't even react. 'I used several agencies.' He turned away, like this was an irrelevance. 'And then, when "Father Ellis" began to make waves on the Welsh border, I came down to take a look for myself. Fell rather in love with the place.'

Bain then talked of how the archaeological excavation was under way at the time, just across the brook from the church; how the immense importance of the site as a place of ancient worship was becoming apparent. 'One of the archaeologists told me he'd dearly love to know what lay under that church. Circular churchyard, pre-Christian site. I took a walk over there myself, and met some eagle-eyed old boy who told me he'd just bought it.'

'Major Wilshire,' Robin said. He couldn't believe how this was shaping up.

'Something like that. I didn't pay too much attention to him, as l was being knocked sideways by the ambience. It was while I was talking to this guy that I had . . . the vision, I suppose. A moment beyond inspiration, when past and future collided in the present. *Boom*. I became aware how wonderful and apt it would be if the power of this place could be channelled. If this church was to become a temple again.'

'Under the very nose of your fundamentalist Christian brother,' Betty said quietly.

'In fact' – Bain raised his voice, irritated – 'it was rather the other way round. For the first time I was almost grateful to Simon, for bringing me here. Ironic, really. But the church had now been sold, and that was that. I went home to London. You can imagine my reaction when, just a few months later, I learned that St Michael's Farm and Old Hindwell Church were on the market again.'

'No,' Betty said coldly. 'What exactly *was* your reaction?'

'Betty,' said Max, 'I really don't think we should prejudge this.'

Ned said, 'Simply that I wanted it to be bought by someone sympathetic to the pagan cause.'

Bulbs finally started flashing big time inside Robin's head.

MENNA WEAL

The actual tomb was bigger than Merrily had expected: perhaps seven feet long, close to three feet wide, more than three feet deep. From outside, with the funeral party of Prossers, Dr Coll and Nick Ellis grouped around it, it had resembled a stone horse trough. Now, under the cream light from the wrought-iron electric lanterns hanging above the head and the foot of the tomb, she could see that it was far more ornate. A complex design of linked crosses had been carved out of the side panels. The lid was not stone, but perhaps as good as: an oak slab four inches thick. The great tomb had been concreted into its stone plinth.

'All *local* stone,' Judith said proudly. 'From the quarry.'

'Got that done quickly, didn't he?'

Judith closed the oak door, so their voices were sharpened by the walls of the mausoleum, which were solid concrete, inches thick. The chamber was about twenty feet square, nothing in it but the tomb, and the two of them, and dead Menna.

Judith said, 'Mal Walters, the monumental mason, is a long-established client of J.W. Mal worked through the night.'

'Right.'

Judith Prosser stood by the head of the tomb, disquietingly priest-like in her tubular black quilted coat – not quite cassock-length, but close. Her short, strong hair had been bleached, her pewter-coloured earrings were thin, metal pyramids. She was waiting, behind the shade of a sardonic smile.

'I thought . . .' Merrily put down the airline bag she'd brought from the car. The junior exorcist's starter kit. 'I thought I'd keep it simple.'

But should she even be doing it here, rather than in that big room behind the bay window, where the 'baptism' had taken place?

Yes, she should. She didn't want the complication of having to try to restore peace to a room where the atmosphere had apparently been ravaged by another priest. Also, she had been asked by Menna's next of kin to calm the spirit. No one had invited her to deal with that room, least of all Weal. She didn't want to go in there, didn't want to enter his actual house in his absence. She really needed guidance. If she'd predicted this situation might develop, she'd have rung her spiritual adviser, Huw Owen, in advance. But there'd been no time for that.

Judith moved to a double switch on the wall, and the lantern at the head of the tomb went out, leaving Menna's concrete cell softly lit, like a drawing room.

'Are you a Christian, Mrs Prosser?'

'That's a funny question.'

'I know you go to church. I know you support Father Ellis. I don't really know what you believe.'

'Nor will you ever,' Judith said tartly. 'What's your point? What are you getting at?'

'Do you *believe* in the unquiet dead?'

Judith Prosser regarded Merrily across the tomb, her eyes half closed. 'The dead are always quiet, Mrs Watkins. The dead are dead, and only the weak-minded are afraid of them. They cannot touch us. Nor, I assume . . .' She laid a forefinger gently on Menna's small inscription. ' . . . can we touch them.'

'Meaning Mr Weal.'

'Mr Weal's a tragic figure, isn't it? He wanted what he *thought* Menna was. He liked it that she was quiet. He liked it that she was polite to her father and did not go with boys. A real, three-dimensional woman was far too complicated for J.W. He wanted, I suppose, a shadow of a woman.'

Oh my God.

Merrily said, 'You have to tell me this. If not you yourself, then has anyone else seen the . . . spirit of Menna Weal?'

Judith made a scornful *pfft* noise. She half turned and began to unbutton her coat. 'Anyway . . .' Sweeping the coat back to place her hands on her hips, turning to face Merrily. 'Time is getting on. What do you propose to do here, my girl?'

'Well . . . I'm going to say some prayers. What I really should be doing – I mean to be halfway sure of this – is holding a Requiem Eucharist. And for that there really ought to be a few of us. Like I said this morning, it would be better if we'd had Mr Weal with us. I mean *with* us.'

'And as *I* said, that would be imposs—'

'Or even Barbara. If Barbara were here, it—'

Merrily heard her own words rebound from the concrete walls. She lurched away from the tomb, as if it were mined.

Such a vast tomb for one small body.

Judith looked mildly curious. 'Someone walk over your grave, Mrs Watkins?'

Merrily knew she'd gone pale. 'Judith . . .?'

'Go ahead,' said Mrs Prosser. 'We're quite alone, almost.'

Merrily swallowed. The scarf felt tight around her throat.

'What do you think J.W. Weal would have done if he'd discovered that Barbara Buckingham had found out about Father Ellis's exorcism of Menna, performed at his behest?'

Judith's eyes were not laughing. 'What on *earth* am I supposed to say to that?' She stepped back.

Now they were both looking at the tomb.

'Oh, I *see*,' Judith said.

Merrily said nothing.

'You mean, after he dumped the *car* in the Claerwen Reservoir, what, precisely, did he do with the body?'

Merrily said nothing.

'Does Barbara perhaps lie below her poor sister? Were her remains, in those fine English clothes, already set in concrete when Menna's coffin was laid to . . . unrest?'

Merrily bit her lip.

'Come on, woman! Is that what you meant?'

'It looks very deep,' Merrily said. 'And . . . as you said, the monumental mason worked all night.'

'All right!' Judith's voice rang with challenge. 'Then let's find out, shall we?'

Merrily found she'd backed against the door.

'Oh, Mrs Watkins, did you think poor J.W. could bring himself to say such a *final* farewell to his beloved? What other reason would a man like him *have* for going to all this trouble?' She pointed.

From back here, Merrily didn't even have to bend down to see that the tomb's handsome oakwood lid was hinged.

'It's very heavy, all the same,' Judith said. 'You may have to help me.'

Merrily remembered, when she was a little kid, being towed along by her mother to make the arrangements for her gran's funeral, and how the undertaker's inner door had been left open. Merrily's mother thinking she was too young to understand. But not too young to absorb the smell of formaldehyde from the embalming room.

She'd been four years old, the formaldehyde alternating with the equally piercing tang of furniture polish, making her afraid to go to sleep that night, and she didn't know why. There was only this grim, opaque fear, the sense of a deep, unpleasant mystery.

Which returned when Judith threw back the solid oak lid of the tomb. Judith hadn't needed help with it after all. She looked down into the tomb and smiled.

'The dead are always quiet, Mrs Watkins. The dead are dead, and only the weak-minded are afraid of them.'

But Merrily who, since ordination, had seen any number of laid-out bodies *was* afraid. The same grim opaque fear, and she didn't know why.

What would be the point, anyway? Judith had only done this for effect, to put herself in control from the start. And if the body of Barbara Buckingham was in there too, it would be in the base, set in concrete, never to be discovered, certainly not in J.W. Weal's lifetime.

Menna, though – Menna was readily accessible. It was clear that Judith was not now looking down on merely a coffin lid.

'Close it, please,' Merrily said.

'How do you know it isn't Barbara? Come on, see for yourself.'

'This is intrusion,' Merrily said.

'It was always intrusion, Mrs Watkins.'

'Then close the lid and I'll say some prayers and we'll go.'

'If I close the lid,' Judith said, 'she won't be able to hear you, will she?'

The whole mausoleum stank of embalming fluid. Merrily needed air, a fortifying cigarette. She went back to the door.

'Don't open it, you silly girl. The light!' Judith let go of the lid and it hung for a moment and then fell against the stone side of the tomb with a shuddering crash, leaving the interior fully exposed. The single lantern, over the foot of the tomb, swung slightly, and Merrily saw a quiver of parchment-coloured lace from inside.

'Come over yere, Mrs Watkins,' Judith said.

'This is wrong.' Merrily's hand went to the centre of her breast where, under her coat, under her jumper, the pectoral cross lay. *Christ be with me, Christ within me, Christ behind me . . .*

'Come and see how peaceful she looks. It'll make you feel better. Then we'll say goodnight to her. Come yere.'

. . . *Christ before me.* Merrily walked into the centre of the mausoleum. If necessary, she'd close the lid herself.

'You *silly* girl.' Judith reached out suddenly and grabbed her by the arm, pulled her close. 'Don't be afraid. I'll look after you.'

I don't think so. As the formaldehyde seared the back of Merrily's throat, the lantern swung again at the sudden movement and shot spears of light and shadow from Menna's swaddled feet to Menna's exposed face.

'See how peaceful she looks.'

No.

That night in the hospital, with the freshly applied water on her brow, Menna had appeared simply and calmly dead. The body hadn't, from a distance, seemed much different during her funeral. Now, embalmed, only days later, her face was pinched and rigid, her mouth downturned, lips slightly parted to reveal the teeth . . . and that particularly, Merrily thought in revulsion, was surely not the work of the embalmer.

She recoiled slightly. Judith's arm was around her, gently squeezing.

'Thank you,' Merrily said. 'Now I know it isn't Barbara.'

'You're trembling.' Merrily felt Judith's breath on her face.

'Don't,' she said mildly.

'Things you oughta know,' Marianne had said. And earlier: *'That Judy. She took you outside, din't she? I was glad when she did that.'*

'It's been hard for you, Merrily, hasn't it?' Judith said, quite tenderly. 'All the pressures. All the things you didn't understand.'

'I'm getting there.' Marianne had been in shock. Marianne needed help. Marianne, who sometimes preyed on men, had herself become vulnerable, pitiable, accessible.

'Yes, I believe you are,' Judith said tonelessly.

FIFTY-TWO

Beast is Come

Jane watched, eaten up with dread, as the multitude assembled where two lanes in the village converged. The uniformed chief inspector in charge tried to organize some kind of roll-call, but it wasn't going to be easy. Only two people known to be missing, and one of them was Mum.

Once the fire brigade was in – four machines, two Welsh, two English – the police had sealed off Old Hindwell. Firefighters with breathing apparatus tried to get into the village hall but were eventually ordered out for their own safety. Jane was there when the order was given, and that was when she began to sob.

When – soon after the brigade got there – the porch's wooden roof had collapsed, lighting up the night and several Sitka spruce, many people fell down on their knees and prayed to the violent, orange sky. Jane was frantic and clung to Eirion, by the side of the police Transit in the filthy, choking air. She didn't remember when Eirion had appeared, or where he'd appeared from. Sophie was here too, now, and many local people had come out of their homes.

And Gomer . . . Gomer was a deeply reluctant hero. The media kept wanting to talk to him. They wanted to hear him describe how he'd spotted the flames and gone round to the rear entrance and opened it up and guided 350 Christians to safety. Gomer kept saying, 'Later, boys, all right?' But later he was muttering, '*Bugger off*,' as the firefighters went on blasting thousands of gallons into the roaring hall.

And still they hadn't found Mum.

Jane, by now hyperactive with fear, had dragged Eirion into the middle of the milling people, and she kept shouting through her tears, 'Small, dark woman in a tatty duffel coat, anybody? *Anybody!*'

But nobody had seen her. *Nobody.*

Though a number elected to pray for her.

Not nearly as many, however, as were praying for Father Ellis, last seen, apparently, stepping from the stage to sing with the crowd. Nobody, at that time, had been aware of the fire in the porch because of the fire doors, and nobody had heard it because of the glorious exultation of the Holy Spirit amplified through their hearts and lungs.

Nobody had known a thing, in fact, until a skinny little man with wild white hair and thick glasses had appeared at the bottom of the hall and had begun bawling at them to bloody well shut up and follow him. By then the fire doors were surrounded by flame and the air was turning brown and the tongues were torn with coughing.

Now Jane's arms were gripped firmly. Sophie said incisively into her ear, 'Jane, she is not *in* there, do you understand? She cannot *possibly* be in there.' Jane opened her mouth to protest and took in a wad of smoke, and was bent double with the coughing, and heard a man shouting in rage.

'They've found a petrol can!'

Obvious what this meant. Jane straightened up, eyes streaming.

A senior-looking policeman was saying, 'We don't know anything yet, so don't anybody go jumping to conclusions.' But he was wasting his breath, because everybody knew what the petrol can meant.

And then, suddenly, the white monk was there.

He was just suddenly *there*, about thirty yards away from the crowd, up against the schoolyard wall.

Jane's feeling was that he'd been sitting quietly in one of the cars or something, staying well out of it, and had come out casually when everyone's attention was diverted by the sound of the porch crashing down or something. Two women in their thirties noticed him first, and it was like Mary Magdalene and the other woman finding an empty tomb and then turning around and there He was. They ran towards him, shouting, 'Thank God, thank God, thank *God.*'

And it just kind of escalated like that. Jane saw all these people falling down on their knees at his feet and all shouting, 'Praise God,' and, 'Thank you, God,' and some of them even looked like local people. Jane heard a tut of disdain from Sophie, and, for the first time, felt something approaching genuine affection for the cool cathedral woman in the wreckage of her camel coat.

There wasn't a mark on the white monk.

'Please,' he was saying, 'don't you worry about me. I'm fine.' He bent to one of the women. 'Stand up, please.' He raised her up and hugged her and then he walked away from the wall. And his arms were raised, palms towards the crowd, fingers splayed. 'Stand up, everyone –

'Stand up and smell the foetid stench of Satan!'

There was this shattering hush.

'Feel the heat of the dragon's breath!'

A woman moaned.

'And know that the beast is come!'

'It was *you?*' In the dingy parlour-turned-temple, Robin stared at Ned Bain; Bain didn't look at Robin. '*You* had the estate agents send us the stuff?'

'Not . . . directly.' For the first time, the guy was showing some discomfort. 'We put out feelers through the Pagan Federation to see if anyone might be interested.'

'We?' Betty said.

'I did.'

'But, like, how come you didn't just buy this place yourself?' Robin was still only half getting this.

'And reveal himself to Ellis?' Betty said. 'Before he could get his plans in hand?'

'Coulda bought it through a third party.'

'He has,' Betty said acidly.

'I don't think that's quite fair,' said Max. 'There was hardly time for *plans* – except, perhaps, in spheres beyond our own. I'm inclined to believe this came about as a spontaneous response to what one might call serendipitous circumstance.'

'Max.' Betty was laying on that heavy patience Robin knew too well. 'Do you think, for one minute, that we'd all be here today, trying to pull something together at the eleventh hour, if Vivvie hadn't crassly shot her mouth off on a piece of late-night trash television and alerted Ellis to what he immediately perceived as the Devil on his doorstep? No, Ned would have waited for Beltane, Lammas, Samhain . . . and got it all nicely set up for maximum impact.'

Max started to speak, then his beard knitted back together.

George was up now – squat, stubbly George, partner of Vivvie.

'Look, people, I think . . . that however this all came about, we've got to put it behind us for tonight. If we allow it to destroy this seminal sabbat, under the spotlight of the entire pagan world, we are going to regret it for the rest of our lives, man. I agree that maybe Ned's not been as up-front as he might've been. I know we could start to accuse him of only setting this thing up to have this Ellis man go down in history totally humiliated, as the priest who lost his church to the Old Religion, but . . .'

'It's more than that,' Betty said. 'For a start, he set *us* up. And in a place which none of us—'

'It doesn't *matter*, Betty. We cannot let personal issues fuck up a seminal event. We have to hold the sabbat, we have to reconsecrate this church in the names of Manon and Brigid and . . .'

George stopped. Betty had stood up. In this damp, chilly room she was a heat source: the only one here who didn't look kind of tawdry. She looked like a goddess.

'Ask him what he's waiting for,' she demanded.

'Please . . .' George wilted back. 'Just leave it.'

Ned Bain didn't move.

'He's waiting for his stepbrother,' Betty said. 'He's waiting for the hymns to start up, only louder. He's waiting for his stepbrother to lead the enemy to the gate.'

'But, Betty, we *need* that tension,' George said. 'That's what this is about – the changeover. In the dawn of the year, the dawn of a millennium, a pretender is banished.'

'Christ, you mean?'

'If you like. I prefer to think in terms of the warlike Michael. I've

434

got nothing against Christ, but he was, at best, an irrelevance. Yeah, Christ, if you like.'

'I *don't* like,' Betty said. 'We're an alternative. We're not the opposition. I mean, *he* might be – he and Ellis both. Whatever else they are, whatever they claim to represent, it's completely soured by what lies between them. I don't want that. I don't want to go into that old, fouled place on the back of twenty-five years of pent-up hatred. I suggest everybody gets changed and leaves now.'

Howls of protest and serious consternation at this, shared by Robin. In some ways, the recent revelations had made him feel better about the situation – the great Ned Bain brought down to human level.

'Bets, look,' he said hoarsely, 'you can't precisely say we were set up. *We* decided to go for this place. All the omens said it was right at the time. Plus, we had the promise of the Blackmore deal and all that it could bring. We were on a roll.'

'Ah, yes,' Betty said, 'the Blackmore deal.'

Ned Bain shifted. Robin felt a pulse of alarm. *'I still think Kirk could be persuaded to listen to reason.'* This was all gonna crash now, the rainbows in the puddles turning black.

'Robin, love . . .' Betty's eyes had misted, or was it his own? 'Kirk Blackmore's been working you like a puppet, hasn't he? All your highs and all your lows.'

'He was important, sure.' Robin looked at Ned. Ned was staring at the stone flags in the floor, elbow on knee and arm outstretched, cigarette loose between his fingers.

And suddenly Robin knew.

'I guess *you're* Kirk Blackmore, huh?'

Bain didn't reply. The room was silent.

Robin turned to Betty. 'How did you find that out?' Inside his rough woollen tunic he was starting to sweat like a hog.

'Some . . . friends of mine got some information from the Internet. Blackmore's this notorious recluse supposedly living on a Welsh mountain and communicating only by fax. People speculate endlessly on the Net about the true identities of authors. Publishers often write novels under pseudonyms: usually lurid, mass-market novels they might not want to be associated with. I'm really sorry, Robin.'

Ned's brow was suddenly a little shiny.

'But he could've bought this place out of his small change,' Betty continued.

'It was your destiny, not mine,' Bain said calmly. 'At the time.'

'Bullshit,' Robin said quietly.

'Any time you wanted to get out, I'd have taken it off your hands.'

'You mean like after we ran out of money? After we'd taken all the shit from the local people? After Ellis got safely kicked out on his ass by the Church? After our marriage got smashed up on the fucking rocks?'

'There was always this growing atmosphere of turbulence,' Betty said. 'We were made to feel insecure from the first. He wanted us to feel beleaguered, maybe a little scared.' She looked down at Bain. 'You *needed* this, didn't you? Were you working on it with your coven, Ned, or was it some magical construction of your own – long and intrictate, like one of your novels? Generating unrest – backed up by a campaign of mysterious letters and phone calls directed at Ellis. The dragon rising? Were you working towards some kind of cataclysm . . . only forestalled by stupid Vivvie giving it away – resulting in *this* farce.'

Vivvie snarled, 'What *are* you these days, Betty? Because you're not one of us any more.'

Bain said, 'If you really want to discuss this, I'm perfectly willing—'

'Did *you* buy the witch box from Major Wilshire? Did *you* have someone deliver it to us, place it on our doorstep?' Betty paused. 'And were you . . . were you *really* that surprised when Major Wilshire fell from his ladder?'

Ned Bain sprang up in a single movement. 'Don't you fucking *dare* . .'

His stiffened finger inches from Betty's soft cheek.

Which was enough.

Robin lurched across the room to the altar. George reached out to stop him, but Robin shook George savagely away. He felt the weight of his hair on his shoulders. He heard warbling sirens in the night. He saw through a deepening mist. He remembered the pit of desperation that swallowed him when Al Delaney, of Talisman, had called to say, *'He wants someone else to do it, Robin. He doesn't want you.'*

Robin wrenched from the altar the great ceremonial sword. No toy this, no lightweight replica, but three and a half feet of high-tensile steel.

Robin raised it in both hands, high above his head. He heard Vivvie screaming.

FIFTY-THREE

Snakeskin

Merrily said, 'You really did look after her, didn't you? You really took care of her.'

Judith Prosser adjusted a fold in the corpse's shroud. 'I was the only one *ever* took care of her.'

'Could we close the lid now?'

Judith didn't touch the lid. 'Why don't you conduct your ceremony, Merrily? Take off your coat, make yourself into a priest.'

Taking control again.

Merrily moved to the head of the coffin, looking down towards Menna's feet. Her airline bag, with the Bible, the prayer texts, the flask of holy water, stood by the door.

'Why don't you finally leave her alone? Why don't you just accept that maybe you've done enough harm?'

'Meaning *what* precisely, Mrs Watkins?' Judith said briskly. She went to stand at the foot of the coffin, from where she could observe the faces of both Merrily and Menna.

'You had her on the Pill from an early age. Dr Coll's good like that, isn't he? Ministering to the *real* needs of the local people? Dr Coll understands these things.'

'She'd have been pregnant by fourteen if we hadn't done something.'

'Mmm, her father really *was* abusing her, wasn't he? Maybe over quite a long period.'

Judith shrugged.

'And, of course, you knew that.'

'We didn't talk about such things then. Other people's domestic arrangements, that was their own affair.'

'Yeah, yeah, but also because . . . whenever it happened, she would come to you.'

'Oh, well, yes. Almost a mile.' Judith smiled. Incredibly, it looked like a smile of nostalgia. 'Almost a mile across the fields to our farm. To my parents' farm. In tears, usually – or you could see where the tears had dried in the wind.'

'And you would comfort her.'

Judith breathed in very slowly, her black coat flung back, breasts pushing out the rugby shirt. Merrily thought of her in the toilet at the village hall, tenderly ministering to Marianne. Always victims: always vulnerability, confusion, helplessness, terror, desperation. Like Menna, alone on that remote hill farm with her beast of a father.

'What a turn-on that must have been,' Merrily said.

Judith's face became granite. 'Don't overstep the mark, Mrs Watkins.'

'Why didn't you just take her to the police?'

'To give evidence against her own father? Apart from the fact that, as I say, such things were not *done* yere in those days, not talked about, how would she have managed on her own, with her father in prison? How would she have coped?'

'Probably have been taken into care. And that's probably the best thing that could have happened, in Menna's case.' Merrily paused. 'If not in yours.'

'You don't know *anything* about this area!' Judith snapped. 'Social services? *Pah!* We have always managed our own social services.'

'I'm sure. Especially after you got married and you were operating from the perfect, secure social platform.'

Marriage to Gareth Prosser. *'Councillor, magistrate, on this committee, that committee. Big man. Dull bugger, mind. Lucky he's got Judy to do his thinkin' for him.'*

A very satisfactory arrangement that, in almost all areas of life, Judith needed Gareth for the framework, the structure, the tradition: a facade, and a good one. What did sexual orientation have to do with

439

it? Fancy, meaningless phrase from Off. Self-sacrifice was sometimes necessary – for a while.

'The foundations of rural life,' Merrily said. 'A husband, a farm and sons – preferably two of them, in case something happens to one of them, or the other grows up strange and wants to live in Cardiff and be an interior designer.'

Judith smiled thinly. 'Oh, you're such a clever little bitch. What about *your* life, Mrs Watkins? They say your husband died some years ago. Does the love of God meet *all* your needs?'

Merrily let it go. 'When you're married to a man like Gareth, nothing needs to change. You go to Menna, she comes to you. And then, when her father dies, you have the contingency plan for her: Jeffery Weal. Good old J.W., the solid, silent family solicitor. A local man, and discreet.'

'He was too old for her, yes. Too rigid in his ways, perhaps. But it was what she was used to, isn't it? She was a flimsy, delicate thing. She would always need protection.'

What could be more perfect? His clothes smelling of mothballs, and little or no experience of women. And living just a few hundred yards down the hill from the Prosser farm.

'*You* arranged that ideal marriage, Judith. You probably coached Menna in what would be expected of her. But she was used to all that, anyway, poor kid. She'd always been a kid – a sad, pale little girl. He must have frightened her a bit, at first, the size of him. He frightens *me*. But that would be no bad thing either, for you, if she needed a lot more comforting.'

Judith's hands were on her hips. 'Now you *have* overstepped the mark.'

'And of course she must continue to take her Pill because children would not be a good thing *at all*. Having a child can make someone grow up awfully quickly.'

'She was not strong enough for children,' Judith said sullenly.

'Was that how Weal eventually found out about you and Menna? Because *he* wanted children – with the family business to pass on to them. "Pills – what pills are these, Menna?"' She put up a hand. 'No, all right. I reckon he did find out, though, didn't he?'

'You *reckon*,' Judith sneered, 'you *guess*, you *theorize*.'

'Is that why you wanted me to come here tonight? To find out what direction the speculation was taking? I'd guess the answer is that you don't really know for sure whether Weal knows about you and Menna, or not. But if he does, he wouldn't say a word to you. It's not the local way. Besides, I suppose you were useful to him. I expect there *were* aspects of Menna he couldn't deal with. Maybe she'd finally changed – becoming a woman.'

'You don't know what you're—'

'But that wouldn't be awfully good for you either, would it? To have Menna becoming a bit worldly-wise as she reached middle age? What actually *was* her mental state? I wouldn't know but, my God' – Merrily pointed into the tomb – 'look at her now. Look at her face. It's all coming out now, isn't it, in that face? God Almighty, Judith, it's almost turning into *your* face.'

Judith Prosser stood very still, seemed hardly to be breathing. Merrily moved away, back towards the door.

'You know what I think? What I'd bet big money on?' She was aware of her voice rising in pitch, more than a bit scared now of where this was inexorably leading. 'When Weal had Ellis exorcize his wife, that was nothing to do with her father at all. Ellis seemed to be able to demonize *anything* and then get rid of it. He stopped your boy from nicking cars, didn't he? So maybe Weal thought that Nicholas Ellis could purge Menna of the demon . . . the demon that was *you.*'

Merrily was shattered. She hadn't quite realized what she had been about to say. But the evident truth of it was explosive.

Judith took a swift step towards her, then stopped, and said brightly, too brightly, 'You are off your head, Mrs Watkins. You do *know* that?' She laughed, her eyes glittering with rage.

'That was only the half of it, though,' Merrily said, to defuse things a little. 'The next part would be the baptism of the two of them, in the same little bowl of holy water, I guess. Something medieval going on there: the fusion of two souls?'

Merrily stared down at the soured face in the tomb. In the medieval church, baptism *was* exorcism. Exorcism charms had been included in marriage services, or blessing of the sick. Pregnant women were exorcized too. In those days, demons were getting expelled from people like tapeworms.

A scenario: late afternoon, the sky like sheet metal. The bay-windowed room north-facing, so not much of the sunset visible. A cold room and a cold time of day. Menna standing there like some white slave, her skin waxy, her arms like straws. Perhaps a bruise forming blue where Ellis had gripped her roughly – in his mind gripping not her but *it*. Perhaps she was wrapping her arms around herself and shivering. Or was she entirely unmoved? Compliant? Accepting this ritual as just another of those things men liked to do to her.

'Do you embrace God?' Ellis's customizing of the rite.

J.W. Weal standing there, big as God.

Menna hesitating, perhaps a little worried by the word 'embrace' and thoughts of what else God might do to her after this.

'Do you embrace Him?'

'I . . . Yes . . . Yes.'

Around the high, white room, dark oak chairs with long pointed spines, standing like judge and jury.

'Do you renounce the evil which corrupts that which God has created? And the sick and sinful, perverted desires which draw you away from the love of God?'

Menna beginning to cry again.

'Say it!'

Her head going back. A sniff.

'Say, "I so renounce them"!'

'I s . . . so . . . renounce them.'

'I can't begin to know where Ellis derived that rite from,' Merrily said. 'Or if he made it up. But there's an awfully long tradition of bodged religion around the Forest, isn't there?'

'I don't know what you mean,' Judith Prosser said sulkily.

'Like, what's the good of religion if it isn't *practical*? Whatever he did, it was nasty and unhealthy and yet . . . and yet somehow it worked, Judith. In some horrible, insidious way, it bloody well *worked*.

And he has her now.' Merrily felt she was drifting away on a formaldehyde fog, sailing so far from the land of normality that she was afraid of never getting back there. 'Got her to himself. At least part of her. Part of *something*. Something half realized, fluttering after him like a crippled bird. It's obscene.'

There was a slithering sound. Judith was shedding her long, black, quilted coat, like a snakeskin.

FIFTY-FOUR

No God's Land

Even Jane could see the police didn't quite know how to handle this any more. A routine peacekeeping assignment had turned into a confusion of arson and murder. They'd taken over the doctor's surgery as an incident room, for two separate investigations which might be totally unconnected.

Jane and Gomer were keeping well back from it all. They stood with Sophie and Eirion in the shadow of the rear entry to the pub yard. Gomer had a ciggy going, and looked more his old self. Jane, too, felt more in control since Sophie had taken her to the chief fire officer, and he'd confirmed that they'd now managed to get inside the hall and had found no bodies there.

But the police had a body: a body with no face, dug out of the mud. And now that the immediate fire crisis was over, this had become their priority again, and they wanted very much to talk to Gomer. Wanted to know why he'd been so sure that something was buried in the old archaeological site that he'd gone up there with a digger, at night. Sophie, her white hair in almost hag-like disarray, was trying to explain to him that all they wanted was a statement, to allay their suspicions.

Gomer didn't want to know, though. It was a plant hire thing that it would take too long to explain; Jane understood this. 'It's stupid. Why would Gomer have sent you to tell the police if *he* had something to do with it?'

Eirion said to Gomer, 'I think what Mrs Hill's trying to say is it would be better if *you* approached *them*, rather than have them come find you.'

'Eirion, what can I tell 'em that's gonner be any help?' Gomer growled. 'I'll talk to the buggers tomorrow, ennit?'

And Jane realized that he was worrying about Mum.

She looked out of the entry to the street, where a sombre assembly had formed around two priests – or, at least, two men in dog collars. One of them was raising his hands as if holding up a huge rock he was about to smash down on something. Jane just knew that some crazy scenario was being manufactured around the village hall fire, involving not a furtive little green-haired plonker with a can of petrol and a grudge, but some great satanic panoply clanking through the night. They'd asked Father Ellis what he wanted them to do, but Ellis had said, cleverly, 'I'm not your leader. Listen to your hearts and let the Holy Spirit move within you.' And he had walked away, leaving bitter, apocalyptic stuff on the air amidst the hellfire fumes. He knew what they'd do. He just wasn't going to be seen to instigate it.

Watching this, Gomer had nodded knowingly. 'Truly a local man at last,' he'd said – which Jane didn't really understand.

Sophie appeared at her shoulder. 'There's one place we haven't tried,' Jane said.

'The church, I suppose,' Sophie said. 'She had a loose arrangement with that young pagan woman, didn't she? To do some sort of Deliverance work? You're probably right. If you and Gomer want to go down there, Eirion and I will stay here, in case she shows up.'

Gomer nodded. He never liked to stand still for very long. 'Thank you, Sophie,' Jane said. 'You've been—'

'Shut up, Jane,' Sophie said wearily. 'Just go. And perhaps you could warn them over at the church' – she nodded towards the assembly on the streets – 'about *that*.'

Robin and Betty were holding one another in some kind of sweet desperation. Everything seemed lost: Robin's work, the house, their friends, their religion, their future here. Everything smashed in an act of sacrilege so gross it was worthy of a Christian. The candle chopped in half, the scourge handle snapped, the pentacle sent skimming like a frisbee into the wall. The chalice of red wine draining into the rug.

Finally the one-time studio table hauled from its trestles, flung onto its side. Max's wife Bella screaming, Vivvie raging, calling down the vengeance of the gods, or some shit like that. This was before Ned Bain had come and stood, unflinching, in front of Robin, who still held the sword. Robin had felt like decapitating the bastard, but Ned Bain had remained impressively cool. That quiet power, even Robin felt it.

'Before I leave,' Bain said, 'I want to make it clear that no one else here was involved, no one conspired. No one else deserves to suffer.'

And then he turned and gathered his robe and walked out without another word.

There'd been a long period of quiet then, broken only by some weeping. Betty leaned against a wall, drained. Vivvie had her head in her hands. Even Max had nothing to say. His kids hovered in the doorway, the fiendish Hermes looking satisfyingly scared. The pregnant witch, whose name Robin couldn't recall, had left the room with her partner. Robin only hoped she was OK. He was starting to feel sick and cold. The twig-fire hissed. A thick piece of altar candle rolled into a corner.

Alexandra, who'd been sitting calmly, with the crown of lights on her knees to protect it, was the first to speak. 'I think we should all leave Betty and Robin alone for a while.'

And so Robin and Betty, covenless, had rediscovered one another. *I take thee to my hand, my heart and my spirit at the setting of the sun and rising of the stars.* Robin started to weep again and buried his face in her hair. Clinging together in their stupid robes, in the wreckage of the altar.

They went hand in hand to the door, and looked out at Winnebagos, the barn and puddles. Robin watched the moon in the puddles, icing over. You could almost get sentimental about those puddles. But not quite.

'We should get outa here tomorrow. Go check into a hotel someplace. Think things over. I love you.'

Betty had her red ski jacket around her shoulders. 'And I love you,' she said. 'But Robin, honey . . .'

Betty fell silent. He hated when Betty became silent.

'OK, what?' he said.

She held his hand to the centre of her breast, her emotional centre.

'We can't just leave it.'

'Watch me,' Robin said.

But his spirit took a dive. She'd already explained how she'd spent the night at a Christian priest's house. A woman priest, who was also the county exorcist or some such, and knew a lot of stuff. He had the idea it had all come about through Betty's meeting with Juliet Pottinger. A part of him still didn't want to know about any of this.

He thought he could hear distant voices, beyond the trees. Like from a barbecue. Or maybe he just thought barbecue on account of the red glow in the sky. Perhaps a glimmering of Imbolc.

'There's a fire somewhere,' Betty said. 'Can't you smell it? Didn't you hear the sirens?'

'I was maybe smashing things at the time. Coming on like the Reverend Penney.'

'Let me tell you the truth about Penney,' Betty said. 'He had a bad time in Old Hindwell Church. I think he was basically a very good man, probably determined to make a success of his ministry. But I think there were some aspects of what he found here that he couldn't handle. Began taking all kinds of drugs.'

'Didn't the Pottinger woman say, in her letter to the Major, she *didn't* think he was doing drugs?'

'She was wrong. He seems to have had a vision, or a hallucination . . . of a dragon . . . Satan . . . in the church. And he seems to have thought that by discontinuing active worship there, it would . . . make it go away.'

Nothing very new there. 'But?' Robin said.

'But I *don't* think what he experienced was anything to do with the Old Religion or the rise of the new paganism. I think he became aware of the dualistic nature of religion as it already existed in this area; that there *is* a paganism here, but it's all mixed in with Christ-

447

ianity. A kind of residual medieval Christianity – when magic was very much a part of the whole thing. When prayer was seen as a tool to get things done. It's practical. It suits the area. Marginal land. Hand to mouth.'

Robin thought of the witch box, the charm. Christian, but not entirely Christian. Those astrological symbols, and some of the words – using witchcraft against witchcraft.

'There are five St Michael churches,' Betty said. 'A pentagram of churches, apparently to confine the dragon. But it's an *inverted* pentagram, right?'

'That . . . doesn't sound good.'

'Perhaps,' Betty said, 'it was accepted that, at some time, they might need to *invoke* the dragon. It's border mentality. I met a bloke called Gomer Parry. Radnorshire born and bred. He'll tell you this place took a lot of hammering from both the English and the Welsh and survived, he reckons, by knowing when to sit on the fence and which side to come down on.'

Robin took some time to absorb this. He could smell those bonfire fumes on the air now. It was, in some ways, a sharp and exciting smell carrying the essence of paganism.

He said, 'You mean they're . . . I don't know this stuff, the Book of Revelations and all . . .'

'Sitting on the fence while the war in heaven rages,' Betty said. 'Five little old churches in a depopulated area with a rock-bottom economy. No-man's-land.'

'No-god's-land?' Robin said, awed. 'But, like . . . way back . . . way, *way* back . . . this place *was* something . . . the archaeology shows that.'

'Maybe that accounts for its inner strength. I don't know. We don't know what we're standing in front of. We don't know the full nature of what lies the other side of that barn.'

'Does Ellis?'

'I don't know.'

'Or Bain?'

'Partly. Maybe.'

'But Bain's big thing was personal. That's dark magic. *Low* magic.'

448

'There are people round here who would understand it. It's notorious for feuds lasting from generation to generation.'

Robin said, 'I wonder, how did Ned Bain get the box from the Major? He buy it? Or just push the old guy off of his ladder and steal it?'

'I don't think he'd push the Major off the ladder. But I don't think he'd have been averse to posting his name on the Kali Three web site.'

'What is that, anyway?'

'You don't want to know,' Betty said.

'Don't wanna dump on my idyll, huh? There's no idyll, babes. No more idyll. Where's that leave us?'

'Leaves us with eleven disappointed witches,' Betty said. 'And a contaminated church.'

Robin breathed in the distant smoke. 'What do we do?'

'I was expecting somebody. I thought she'd have come by now.'

'The woman priest? The Christian priest?'

'She's also an exorcist.'

'Excuse me,' Robin said, 'but didn't we pass this way before?'

'It would've been very wrong to let Ellis do it. You were right about that. From the start.'

'Don't try and get me on your side.'

'OK.'

They looked out over the freezing puddles to the barn on the other side of which the Church of St Michael overhung the restless Hindwell Brook, probably the very same brook into which that guy's son's blood flowed from his hair, in the old Welsh poem Max had read out.

'On account of you know you never need to,' Robin said eventually. 'You know that whatever shit comes down, I am on your side. Do what you think is best.'

He felt like crying. He wished for subsidence, an earthquake. He wished the freaking church would fall into that freaking brook.

Presently, Alexandra stood on the edge of one of the puddles, her long, grey hair loose, a thick woollen shawl wrapped around her.

The emissary. The negotiator. The one they were most likely to talk to.

'It has to be your decision,' Alexandra told them.

'I don't know what to say,' Betty said.

'Babes,' Robin said gently, 'it's getting late. And the priest isn't here. If she was ever gonna come at all.'

'We don't know what that place is really about.' Betty looked out into the night, in the direction of the church. 'We don't know what rituals they were performing, what kind of magic they were trying to arouse or for what purpose. All those millennia ago.'

'Bets,' Robin said, pained, 'the ancient powers locked into the land? The magic of the Old Ones? This is Blackmore shit.'

She looked at him, puzzled. She was probably thinking of him standing watching the water rushing below the church and ranting about the cool energy, him and George with their dowsing rods working out how many old, old bodies were under there, where the energy lines converged. She didn't understand – as Robin now did – that to do his paintings, to be what he was, a true creative artist, he just had to *live* the legend. That was all. That was as deep as it went.

Alexandra said hesitantly, 'May I make a suggestion?'

'Please,' said Robin.

'We abandon all reconsecration plans. That's been tainted now, anyway, because of Ned. And Ned's gone, and we talked about that and we were all relieved, even George, because Ned's . . . Ned's a little bit dark.'

'Fucker,' Robin said.

'So we forget all that. We forget the politics.'

'Even Vivvie?'

Alexandra glanced behind her. Robin saw the whole coven in the shadows.

Vivvie came forward, looking like some rescued urchin. She stood beside Alexandra. 'Whatever,' she said.

'My suggestion,' Alexandra said, 'is that we simply enact the Imbolc rite.'

'Who'd be the high priest?' Robin said.

'It should be you.'

Robin knew this was a major concession, with George and Max

out there. Although he'd been through second-degree initiation, he'd never led a coven.

'And when we come to the Great Rite,' Alexandra said, 'we'll leave so that you can complete it.'

For Robin, the cold February night began to acquire luminosity.

Alexandra smiled. 'You've both had a bad time. We want this night to be yours.'

Robin tingled. He did not dare look at Betty.

FIFTY-FIVE

Grey, Lightless

Only a dead body.

Whatever else remained was not here; it was probably earthbound in that back room, where a medieval exorcism replayed itself again and again, until the spirit was flailing and crackling and beating at the glass. The grey and lightless thing that J.W. Weal brought home from Hereford County Hospital.

'Look at her . . .' said Merrily, in whom guilt constantly dwelt, like an old schoolmistress. 'That's what you all did. That's what you left behind. Take a proper look at her face. Go *on*.'

But Judith Prosser looked only at Merrily. And there was no guilt. Practical Judith in her tight blue jeans, the sleeves of her shirt pushed up to the elbows, her black coat in a heap on the floor. Practical Judith Prosser, ready to act, thinking what to do next, how to make her move. A smart woman, a hard woman, a survivor.

But Merrily, perhaps taking on the guilt that Judith would never feel, pushed harder.

'Maybe that's why J.W. invited you to the interment – you and Gareth and the good Dr Coll. Did Dr Coll, by the way, prescribe Valium to keep Menna afloat, keep her quiet when she threatened to be an embarrassment? Was there medication for Marianne, too? I thought Marianne seemed *awfully* compliant during her cleansing.'

'You have it all worked out, Mrs Watkins,' Judith said.

'Yeah,' Merrily said. 'I finally think I do. It stinks worse than this embalming stuff.'

'And what will you do with it all? Will you go to the police and make accusations against Dr Collard Banks-Morgan and Mr Weal, the solicitor, and Mrs Councillor Prosser?'

'It would help,' Merrily conceded, 'if Barbara Buckingham's body *was* in here.'

'So why don't you come back here with a pickaxe? Or with your good friend Gomer Parry and one of his road-breakers?'

It wasn't going to be there, was it? There was no one under Menna. Yet Merrily was sure now that Barbara Buckingham was dead.

'*Did* Barbara find out about the exorcism?'

Judith slowly shook her head, smiling her pasted-on smile, back on top of the situation, giving nothing away.

'Still,' Merrily said, '*Menna's* here. For any time you want to look at her and remember the old days before she turned into a woman and became less malleable. And J.W.'s left you with a key. So you can come in any time and watch what you once had . . . see what you did. Watch it slowly decaying before your—'

Merrily sank to her knees.

She'd been expecting, if anything, a shriek of outrage and clawing hands. She hadn't seen this coming. Judith Prosser didn't seem to be close enough. Now Merrily was on her knees, with the flash memory of a fist out of nowhere, hard as a kitchen pestle. On a cheekbone.

She had never been hit like this before. It was shattering, like a car crash. She cried out in shock and agony.

Judith Prosser bent with a hand out as if to help her, and then hit her again with the heel of it, full in the eye. Merrily even saw it, as if in slow motion, but still couldn't move. It drove her back into the wall, her head connecting with the concrete, her left eye closing.

'You can tell the police about that, too, Mrs Watkins.' Judith was panting with satisfaction. 'And see who they believe – a hysterical little pretend-priest from Off, or Mrs Councillor Prosser. Ah . . .'

One hand over her weeping eye, Merrily saw through the other one that the door had swung open. And the doorway was filled. Really filled.

'Good evening, Jeffery,' Judith said.

'You have me, Judith, as a witness that she hit you first.' Weal's voice was colourless and flat as card. 'But only if you make no further mess of her than that, or it would not be a reasonable defence.'

He was carrying what looked like a kind of garden implement. He came in and gently closed the door of the mausoleum behind him. He was wearing a charcoal grey three-piece suit and a white shirt, and a black tie to show he was still in mourning. His face was pouchy, red veins prominent in his grey cheeks.

He propped the garden implement against the door. Merrily saw that it was a double-barrelled twelve-bore shotgun.

'Thought it was the hippies, see.' He nodded at the twelve-bore. 'Some satanist hippies are parked up in the clearing by the Fedw Dingle. Father Ellis phoned to warn me. They break in anywhere.'

'Isn't loaded, is it, Jeffery?' Judith said.

'It's always loaded. There are foxes about. And feral cats. I hate cats, as you know.'

'Not going to the Masonic?'

'I *was* going, Judith, till I saw all those troublemakers in the village. Can't leave your house unguarded, all this going on, can you?'

Talking politely, like neighbours over the wall, people who knew each other but not that well.

They must have known one another for most of their lives.

Merrily didn't try to move. Judith looked down at her.

'Recognize this one, do you, Jeffery? Came to see me this morning. Asking all kinds of questions about Father Ellis. And about you, and Menna. When she left, I saw that the keys . . . You know where I keep your keys, on the hook beside the door? Stupid of me, I know, but I trust people, see, and we've never had anything stolen before. But when she left I seen the keys were gone.'

Weal stood over Merrily. 'Called the police?'

'Well, next thing, there she is coming down the lane tonight. I thought, I'll follow her, I will, and sure enough, up the drive she goes, lets herself in and when I came *in* here, she'd already done *that.*' They both looked at the open tomb. 'Disgusting little bitch. I shouldn't have touched her but, as you say, she went for me. Like a cat.'

'*I hate cats, as you know.*' How instinctive she was.

Merrily was able to open her swelling eye, just a little. She looked up at Weal. It was like standing under some weathered civic monu-

454

ment. She didn't think there was any point at all in telling him that Judith had lured her here, picking up, with psychopathic acumen, Merrily's guilt, her sense of responsibility for Barbara Buckingham.

'Why did you do this? Why do you keep coming here? Why do you keep wanting to see my wife?'

J.W. Weal gazing down at her sorrowfully, giving Merrily the first real indication that there was something wrong with him. His speech was slow, his voice was dry.

'The truth of it is,' Judith said, 'that she seems to have a vendetta against Father Ellis.'

'Father Ellis is . . . a good man,' Weal said calmly.

No, it wasn't calmness so much as depletion. Something missing – almost as if he was drugged, not fully here. As if part of him existed on some intermediate plane, at grey-and-lightless level. Lying there in a cocoon of pain, detached, Merrily felt her senses heightened, her objectivity sharpened.

'Supposed to be the exorcist for the Hereford Diocese, she is,' Judith told Weal. 'Doesn't like him working in her back yard – a priest whose feet she is not fit to wash. What good would a woman like *this* be at what he does?'

Merrily tried to stand. Judith immediately pushed her down again and she slid into the corner by the door. Judith was wearing her leather gloves again, perhaps to cover up any slight abrasions or bruising from the punches. Merrily's face felt numb and twisted. She wondered if her cheekbone was broken. She wondered where this would end. The way these two were talking to each other, it was like a bad play.

'Gave me some nonsense story,' Judith Prosser said. 'About Barbara Buckingham being murdered and buried in there.' Another nod to the open tomb.

Why, in God's name, didn't one of them close it?

'Buckingham?' Weal said vaguely. What was *wrong* with him?

'Barbara *Thomas*.'

'Murdered?'

'*She* thinks Barbara was murdered.' A gleeful, almost girlish lilt now. 'Thinks you did it, Jeffery.'

Merrily didn't look at him. She could almost hear his mind trying to make sense of it.

'Because . . . Barbara Thomas . . . came to see me, is it?' His voice thin and stretched, as though he was trying to remember something. 'Because she . . . accused me?'

'Did she?' Merrily said.

'Shut up!' Judith moved towards her. Merrily shrank back into the corner. If she could just get to her feet, she might . . . but then there was Weal.

'If you grievously injure her,' he told Judith earnestly, 'you know I may not be able to help you.'

Merrily shut her eyes. *Think!* Barbara believes Weal was responsible for Menna's death, so she goes to see Weal and accuses him of bringing about Menna's death by subjecting her to Ellis's perverse ritual. What does Weal do then? What does he do to Barbara?

Nothing.

The way he was talking now, viewing the situation, almost naively, from a pedantic legal perspective, made one thing clear: whatever else he was, this man was not a killer.

There's only one killer.

'J.W.,' Merrily said. 'When Barbara came to see you . . . when she went a little crazy and started accusing you of . . . things, did you . . .' She could hear the acceleration of Judith's breathing, but she didn't look at her; she was going to get this out if she was beaten into the ground for it. 'Did you send her to see Judith?'

Weal didn't answer. He glanced briefly at Judith, then down at Merrily. The question had thrown him. He looked at Judith again, his jaw moving uncertainly, as if he was trying to remember why it was that he hated her so much.

Merrily could suddenly see Weal and Barbara in the old rectory, Weal red-faced and anguished. *Why are you plaguing me, you stupid, tiresome woman? Why don't you talk to the one person who, for twenty-five years, has been . . . ?*

Judith said, 'Jeffery, you're tired.'

'Yes,' he said. 'I'm always tired these days.'

'Why don't you go back to the house now?' Judith said kindly. 'I'll sort this out.'

He put his fingers vaguely to his forehead. 'You won't go doing anything stupid, will you, Judith? We are entitled to protect our property, but only . . .'

'Don't worry about me. I have never been a stupid woman. I was just carried away, see. Just carried away, Jeffery.'

He nodded.

'Here,' Judith picked up his shotgun. 'Take this with you and lock it away. No one will try to get in now.'

She held the gun upright and handed it to him. Weal accepted it, holding the barrel loosely.

'Right,' he said. 'Thank you, Judith.'

When Judith's gloved hand slid gracefully down the barrel, down the stock, the blast was like the end of the world. Merrily, shrinking into her corner, into herself, saw J.W. Weal's head burst like a melon in a rising red spray.

Felt it come down again, a warm hail.

FIFTY-SIX

Each of my Dyings

Judith still held the shotgun, her face creased in concern.

'Poor man,' she said. 'But, see, what did he have to live for now?'

Judith held the gun with both gloved hands, the stock under her arm.

'Not much,' she added. 'Not much at all.'

Weal's great body blocked the door. His blood and flesh and bone and brain blotched the walls, but most of the mess, still dripping, was on the ceiling. Merrily, sobbing, was still hearing the sound of Weal's head hitting the ceiling. Would hear it for ever.

'A terrible accident,' Judith said.

Two smells now: the embalming room and the slaughterhouse. Merrily hung her head. She felt very cold. She heard something sliding stickily down the wall behind and above her.

'An accident, Mrs Watkins. A *terrible* accident.'

'Yes,' Merrily croaked.

'Or perhaps he meant to do it, do you think? You saw me handing it to him. Such a tall man, it was pointing directly under his chin.' She laughed shrilly. 'Such a big man. They calls him Big Weal in Kington and around. *Big Weal – The Big Wheel.*'

'That's very good,' Merrily said.

Judith said flatly, 'I'm making excuses, isn't it?'

Merrily felt something warm on her forehead, wiped it roughly away with her sleeve. She thought that maybe being squashed into a corner had protected her from most of the carnage. She remembered

Judith jumping quickly back, snatching the gun away too. Not a speck on Judith.

She heard herself say, 'These things happen,' and felt a bubble of hysteria. She began to get up, levering herself, hands flat behind her pushing against the floor, her bottom against the wall. Now she could see J.W. Weal's huge shoes, shining in the lantern light, his legs . . .

'Oh no, you don't!' Judith swung round, the stock hard against her shoulder. 'You'll stay there while I think, or you'll have the other barrel.'

Merrily froze. Judith's eyes were pale – but not distant like J.W.'s had been. Her gaze was fixed hard on Merrily.

'*You* made me do that. It's *your* fault. You suggested to J.W. that he must've sent Barbara Thomas to me. He never did. He wouldn't do that.'

'Didn't she . . . tell you?' Merrily's gaze turned to the river of blood that had pumped from J.W. Weal's collar. She gagged.

'She was off her head, that woman,' Judith said. '*Off her head!* Screaming at me. Standing there, screaming at *me*, in her fancy clothes. How dare she run away, go *from* here, spend her life in cushy . . . where was it? Where *was* it?'

'Ham . . . Hampshire.'

'*Hampshire*. Soft, cushy place that is. How dare she come back from Hampshire, start screaming at me – *me* who's had it hard all my life. They comes here, the English, think they can say what they like.'

Half a mile over the border – just half a mile – and this myth of the English having it so good.

Judith's accent seemed to deepen as she remembered the encounter. 'But a scrawny neck, she had, like an old bird. Trying to hide her scrawny neck with a fancy, silk scarf. But I found it, Mrs Watkins.'

Oh God. Merrily stiffened in her half-crouch against the wall. Sinewy hands around a scrawny neck. Maybe a silk scarf pulled tight.

'Going to tell everybody, she was, that bitch! *Everybody!* Going to shout it all over Radnorshire that Mrs Councillor Prosser was a lesbian! How *dare* the bitch call me a lesbian? "I'll sue you!" I said to her. "I'll hire *J.W.* to sue you. See how long your English money lasts you then!"'

Merrily retched again.

'Never seen blood before, Mrs Watkins? Used to kill all our own pigs, we did, when I was a girl. And whatever else we wanted to, until the regulations. Regulations about this and that . . . Regulations, it is, killing country life.' She calmed down, sighed. 'Poor Jeffery – it's just like putting down an old horse.'

'What was . . . the matter with him?'

'It was since she died.' A toss of her head towards the tomb. 'He was hardly awake since. Couldn't face being awake.'

'Was he . . . on medication? From Dr Coll?'

'Wouldn't have it. Said it was the mourning took his energy, eating him up inside.'

Took his energy?

Menna.

'Do you know what I think?' Judith said, brightening. 'I think he ought to have killed you, Mrs Watkins.'

Merrily felt the first spasm of a cramp in her right leg. She had to move.

'That's what I think. Meddling little bitch, you are, come to spy on Father Ellis.'

Merrily braced herself against the wall, straightened the leg in front of her, looking up. Into the black, metal-smelling barrels of the twelve-bore hovering six inches from her face.

Judith said, 'Perhaps he *did* shoot you.' She raised a hand to her head for a moment, horribly childlike, as if putting something together in her mind. 'Likely he shot you before he killed himself. Blew your little head off with the one barrel, saved the other for himself. He was a solicitor. A logical man, see.'

She looked delighted – the woman was mad.

Merrily looked along the barrel of the great gun towards the stock. She saw two triggers, one slightly in front of the other, Judith's finger around the second one. The speed she'd managed it last time, there must be hardly any tension in those triggers.

Merrily jerked her head to one side, but the two holes followed her.

Judith was a practical woman.

'First used one of these when I was nine year old,' she said proudly, 'when I could hardly lift it. Saw my father shooting crows.' She smiled happily. 'Country girl, see, always the tomboy. Always a better shot than Councillor Prosser.'

The trigger finger relaxed. Merrily still held her breath. Could she summon the strength to throw herself from the wall, knock the barrel aside? As if she'd picked up the thought, Judith backed away smartly, smiling.

'Jeffery thought you were one of the hippies broken in. Thought you were a hippy, and you went for him and his gun went off. That's what they'll say, isn't it? Then, when he saw what he'd done, he turned the gun on himself. Suicide while the balance of mind was disturbed. Went to an inquest two year ago, we did, Councillor Prosser and I. One of our old neighbours hanged himself – verdict of suicide while the balance of mind was disturbed. Everyone here knew J.W.'s balance of mind was gone.'

Merrily shook her head helplessly.

Judith waggled her fingers to show she was still wearing gloves. 'Dropped the gun as he died. Two of you dead.' She glanced at the open tomb. 'Went to say goodbye to his wife, before he killed himself. Poor Jeffery, he's with her now – is that what you think, Mrs Watkins?'

'Yes.'

Judith's face turned red. 'Rubbish! Nonsense! How can a *woman* be so stupid. There is nothing after death! Menna waiting in the clouds with her arms open, waiting for her J.W. with no head? Is that what you would tell them in your church, Mrs Watkins?'

'Is that what you say to Father Ellis?'

The barrel moved down to Merrily's chest. At this range, the blast would cut her in half, and it could happen any time. If she moved too quickly, Judith would blow her apart. She wouldn't feel anything. She wouldn't even hear the shot. Her last moment would be a moment just like this.

'We could have been friends, you and I, Merrily Watkins.'

'I'm not sure that we could,' Merrily said honestly.

'I'm not a lesbian, you know. Are you calling me a lesbian?'

Merrily thought of Jane, glad that Gomer was with her. Would the kid later remember hearing a distant explosion from the village, hear it echoing down her life. Pray that these concrete walls were too thick. Pray: *Please, God, Oh God. Please, Jesus, hold me safe from the forces of evil. On each of my dyings shed your light and your love.* Would she die wearing Jane's coat? She saw not her own life flashing before her, but Jane's. Jane aged three on the beach in Pembrokeshire, following a ball, tripping over it, starting to cry because she thought she should, and then bursting into wild laughter, rolling over and over like a kitten.

Merrily tore herself wretchedly back into the present.

'Frankly, Judith, I couldn't care less where you stand sexually. It's insignificant.'

'Not to me, Mrs Watkins. Not to my reputation.'

'The real point is, you're a monster. A monster that feeds on the vulnerable. Anything that brings out pity in the rest of us, it just makes you more excited. Tears turn you on. You were probably everything to Menna – all she had sometimes. But she was nothing to you, no more than a slim, white, trembling body to play with.'

She stood up, looked at Judith and shrugged.

'You may close your eyes, if you wish,' Judith said coldly, but she'd squeezed the second trigger before Merrily even had time to decide.

Betty and the stately Alexandra drifted about the ruins like mother and daughter ghosts, moving things around while Robin watched and held the lamp.

The fat candles mostly stayed: on sills and ledges, and in glass lanterns on the top of the tower.

The altar got moved. This was an old workbench from the barn, with a wood vice still clamped on the side. Robin helped Alexandra carry it from the north wall to a place in the middle of the nave, opposite the tower but facing where Betty figured the chancel had been. East-facing, like a Christian altar, in case this Merrily Watkins turned up.

The ruins hung around them like old and tattered drapes, moonlight showing up all the moth-holes. The moon was real white now, like a slice of Philadelphia cheese over the tower. Robin thought he saw a movement up there. An owl, maybe.

Across the roofless nave, Betty was taking some crystals from a drawstring bag. She kept her eyes down.

When it was all ready, the coven was summoned in, and Alexandra said to Betty, 'Will it be?'

Robin looked at Betty, and he knew she had at last accepted that the Christian priest would not come.

Betty nodded.

Tapers and matches were handed out. The coven moved like shadows, dipping and bending, and when each one rose there was a new glimmering.

Max's wife Bella did the tower. 'Creepy,' she said when she came down. 'Felt I was being watched.'

In the end, there must have been seventy or eighty candles alight. Lined up in every jagged, glassless window. Along the walls of the roofless nave. In the arrow-cracks of the tower. On top of the cold battlements, in glass lanterns.

St Michael's, Old Hindwell, was ethereal, unearthly, shivering with lights, and the display reflected, crystallized, in the Hindwell Brook.

FIFTY-SEVEN

In Shock

Never had a gun, never wanted one, but Gomer knew about gun-shots, how loud they could be at night, how the sound would carry miles, and he'd figured out roughly where this one had come from, and it wasn't likely to be poachers or lampers of hares – not tonight with all these coppers on the loose.

'The church?' young Jane said, scared.

'Further on, more like.'

He wasn't gonner say it was the ole rectory yet, but he was gonner check it out.

As they reached Prossers' farm, a police van shot past them – far too fast, in Gomer's view, to be heading for the entrance to the ole church. They wouldn't've heard the shot. Most likely they was heading for the camp the coppers would've now set up where they'd dug up Barbara Thomas.

Gomer had been worried they might get stopped. Under his bomber jacket, he had his sweatshirt on back to front, so it no longer said, 'Gomer Parry Plant Hire'.

Behind them, the fire was just fumes on the air, almost unnotice-able as they reached the St Michael's entrance. No protesters here yet. No coppers, neither. And no reporters. A woman's body and some bugger figuring to fry 300 people had to be more important than God and the Devil.

The five-bar gate was closed across the track, but the padlock hung loose from the hasp on a chain. Gomer was about to open it when Jane let out a gasp.

Two women were approaching up the road.

Jane hesitates a moment, then starts to run. Gomer levels his torch.

It lights up Judy Prosser. Also the vicar.

The kiddie runs to her mam and they starts hugging, but Gomer knows straight off this en't normal. He walks over, slowly.

''Ow're you, Judy?'

But he's looking at the vicar in the torchlight, where her eye's black and swelled-up, her face lopsided.

Jane's now spotted it, too. 'Mum, what have you—'

But Judy cuts in. 'Gomer, we're looking for the police, we are. Something terrible's happened.'

'What's that, Judy?'

'I have to report a suicide.' She's holding herself up straight in this long, black quilted coat. 'Mr Weal – he's shot himself, I'm afraid to say.'

'Big Weal?'

'Blew his head off with a shotgun. In his wife's tomb, this was, poor man. Turned his mind, isn't it? The grief. Tried to stop him, didn't I, Mrs Watkins? Tried to talk him out of it.'

The vicar says, in this clear voice, like in the pulpit, 'No one could have done more, Mrs Prosser.'

'You all right, vicar?'

'Yeah, I'm . . . fine. Apart from a few bruises where . . . Mr Weal hit me.'

'I warned her not to approach him,' said Mrs Prosser. 'Silly girl.'

'Yes, I've been a very silly girl.'

Judy says, 'We all were terrified that he might do something stupid. So, as a close neighbour, I was keeping an eye on him. I go there every night, I do, to check he's all right, and sometimes I finds him beside the tomb, with the top open, just staring at Menna's remains. Mrs Watkins said she did not think this was healthy and she asked me to take her to see Mr Weal, and we finds the poor man in there, with his wife on show and his twelve-bore in his hands. Mrs Watkins panics, see—'

'Gomer . . .?' the vicar says.

'Ar?'

'Are there any police around? I thought there'd be some here.'

'Over the harchaeologist site, vicar,' Gomer says warily. 'Any number o' the buggers.'

'Could you take Mrs Prosser. Ask for a senior officer, and tell them Mrs Prosser has a lot of . . . information.'

'You can tell them my husband's on the police committee,' Judy says. 'That should expedite matters. But surely you're coming, too, Mrs Watkins?'

'I have to take my child back to the vicarage, Mrs Prosser. She's too young to hear about this kind of thing.'

The vicar hugs young Jane very close for a few seconds.

'Say goodnight to Gomer, Jane,' the vicar says.

The kiddie comes over, puts her arms round Gomer's neck and hugs him real tight, and in his ear in this shocked, trembling whisper, her says,

'Mum says to tell the police not to let her go. She's killed twice.'

They followed the path to the old archaeological site. Some thirty yards away, they could see two police cars lined up, a radio crackling from one of them. They could see the low, white tent, the orange tape. The second car was parked on the edge of a small wood full of dead trees, white branches shining like bone. Jane had told her what was probably still lying under the tent.

'Are you sure?' the kid kept saying. 'Are you *sure?*'

'I promised.'

'But with everything that's . . . And look at you . . . *Look* at you. You need a doctor.'

'Dr Coll?' Merrily started to laugh, and the laughter wouldn't stop.

'Stop it!' Jane screamed. 'What's that on your hands?'

Merrily looked down, still laughing.

'Oh.'

Thock, she heard. *Thock*.

*

Seeing the ridiculous dismay on Judith's face . . . watching her step back, angrily breaking open the gun, and coming out with that brilliantly dry observation.

'Wouldn't you know it, Mrs Watkins? A Radnor man to the core. Never load two cartridges when you may not even need the one.'

The funniest line Merrily had heard in a long time. Possibly, at that moment, the funniest line being spoken in the whole, insane world. When she started to laugh, she was half expecting Judith to come at her with both fists or take a swing at her with the shotgun. But smart Judith, canny Judith . . . this was not how Judith reacted at all. She simply laid down the empty gun, a few inches away from the half-curled hand out of which she'd snatched it before the fingers could spasm around its barrel.

'The stupid man.' Voice flat, eyes flat like aluminium. 'What did he want to do that for? You saw it, Mrs Watkins, you saw how I tried to stop him.'

As if the previous minutes had never happened – as if editing her life like a videotape. Instinctively compiling the alternative version, with an efficient jump-cut from the second the gun went off. So practical, this Judith.

And Merrily had reacted quickly for once, getting it exactly right.

'You'd better tell the police what happened then, Mrs Prosser.'

'It's my duty, Mrs Watkins. Give me a hand here, will you?'

Both of them then pulling the body away from the door, as though it was a huge dead sheep, so they could squeeze outside.

This was how Merrily had got the blood on her hands.

To the left, she could hear the sound of the Hindwell Brook.

Jane said, 'She killed Barbara Buckingham, that woman?'

'Yes.' *Strangled her with her own silk scarf. Beat her up first, probably.* 'Perhaps when Barbara went to see her and challenged her over . . . certain things. I think Gomer said her husband owned a digger. I suppose one of them would've driven her car over to the Elan Valley, with the other following.'

'Who *is* she?'

467

'She's Mrs Councillor Prosser, flower – fortified by the local community: the doctor, the lawyer, the councillor . . . even the priest. Solid as a rock, she was, until someone from Off blew it all open. Someone who hadn't always been from Off, and realized what she was seeing here.'

And Merrily couldn't help wondering to herself, then, if anything had ever gone on, way back, between Judith and Barbara – something Barbara had suppressed, erased from her memory as simply as Judith Prosser had erased from her mental tape the murder of Weal and the attempted murder of Merrily.

Over her shoulder was slung her airline bag, bought because it was blue and gold. She'd brought it out of the tomb with her, but there was no blood on it, a small miracle. It contained the Bibles, prayers, altar wine and holy water. So medieval?

They stopped at the bridge, and there was the church across the water, and also reflected in the water. Betty's birthday cake.

'It's beautiful,' Jane breathed. 'It's . . . *son et lumière*. Without the *son*.'

Merrily smiled wildly. Less than an hour ago, she was staring into eternity down the barrels of a twelve-bore. Now she was back in airy-fairyland.

'Are you *sure* about this?' Jane said. Merrily squeezed her arm.

'Jane . . . look . . . I don't want to have to worry about you, OK? So I'd like you to stay out of the way. I know you're sixteen and everything . . .'

'You're in shock, aren't you? I mean, you've just seen something totally horrific. You've been through a really horrifying—'

'Yeah, I probably am in shock.'

'You could do this tomorrow.'

'I said I'd do it tonight.'

'We could explain to Betty . . .'

They were halfway across the footbridge now. The ruins shimmered in a hollow of silence.

Then a woman's voice rose up.

'Dread lord of Death and Resurrection
Of life and the Giver of life
Lord within ourselves, whose name is Mystery of Mysteries
    encourage our hearts
Let thy light crystallize itself in our blood . . .'

Merrily slumped over the rail of the bridge.
Too late.

FIFTY-EIGHT

The Woman Clothed with the Sun

His coven around him, Robin lifted the wand high, in his right hand, until it divided the moon.

The wand was a slender, foot-long piece of hazel wood, cut from the tree with a single stroke on a Wednesday, as laid down in the Book of Shadows. In his left hand Robin held the scourge, a mild token thing like a riding crop with silken cords.

Behind him were the crone – Alexandra – and a woman called Ilana, who was twenty-four but looked a lot younger and represented the maiden tonight.

The flames rose straight up out of the tight nest of stones in the centre of the nave as he brought down the wand in a long diagonal, right to left, then left to right in a forty-five-degree angle and straight back horizontally and down . . . and up.

To a point. One point.

The positive, invoking pentagram of Earth . . . drawn before his high priestess, whose hair shone brighter than the fire, whose eyes were deeper than crystals.

'*Blessed be*,' Robin whispered.

And never had meant it more.

Merrily followed Jane around the church tower. The kid had a small torch, borrowed from Gomer, but they didn't need it; the church cast its own light. When she looked up to the top of the tower, she could no longer see the candle-lanterns, only the highlighted stones.

She and Jane slipped – unseen, she assumed – from the tower, across a grassy, graveless churchyard, glittering with frost, to the side of what looked like a stone barn.

What to do? Watch and pray?

Christ be with us, Christ within us, Christ behind us.

They stood with their backs to the barn. From here, through an empty Gothic window in the nave, about twenty feet away, they could see the long candles on the altar, and they could see, by the fire and candlelight, Betty in her green robe. On one side of her was a girl of about eighteen, on the other a plump and placid woman, who looked like she ought to be running a day nursery. The girl was combing Betty's blond hair.

There was now music on the freezing air: vaguely Celtic, string and reed music from some boombox stereo concealed in the ruins. It all seemed gentle and poetic and harmless and not a lot, in Merrily's view, to do with religion.

The distance, the walls and the music allowed them to talk in low voices. Jane said, 'Doesn't look as if she's been, like, coerced, does it?'

Betty stood with her back to the altar, the other women on either side. The male witch, who looked like he should be playing bass with Primal Scream, appeared in the Gothic window.

'We saw him in the *Daily Mail*, right?' Merrily said.

'Yeah, I'm pretty sure that's Robin.'

'And is he the high priest? You know this stuff better than me.'

'Has to be.'

'Not Ned Bain, then.'

'Which is a mercy?' Jane said.

'Which has to be a mercy.'

A shadow moved beside her, as if off the barn. Any night but this, she might have cried out.

'A mercy, you think, then?' the shadow said.

'Hello, Ned,' said Merrily.

They'd customized the rite slightly, to allow for the place and the changed circumstances, but Robin thought it could still be OK. He

471

tried to concentrate on the meaning of the ritual – the birth of spring. And the purpose – the bringing of fresh light to an old, dark place. He wondered if Terry Penney could see them in some way and feel what was happening. For in the absence of the woman priest, Betty said, this rite must also be a form of exorcism, to convey Terry's spirit into a place of peace.

But Robin couldn't dispel the awareness that they were doing this in a *church*. He would close his eyes for a moment and try to bring down the walls until there was only a circle of stones around them, but he was finding he couldn't hold that image, and this *wasn't* Robin Thorogood, visionary, seducer of souls, guardian of the softly lit doorways. He found himself wishing they were someplace else, in a frosted glade or on some open moorland . . . and *that* wasn't Robin Thorogood, custodian of an ancient site which tonight was entering its third incarnation, quietly and harmoniously, without tension, without friction.

He laid the wand and scourge upon the altar and helped the maiden to arrange the shawl around the shoulders of the crone.

From a jam jar on the altar, he took a small bunch of snowdrops – the flowers of Imbolc – which Alexandra had found growing behind the barn and had bound together with some early catkins.

He presented this humble bouquet to Ilana, the maiden.

He lifted the crown of lights from the altar and waited while the three women arranged themselves.

He raised the crown of lights and placed it on Betty's head, and the maiden and the crone tucked and curled her golden hair becomingly around it.

'Merely spectators,' Ned Bain whispered, 'isn't it sad? Came for a baptism and they wouldn't even let us be godparents.'

Merrily said nothing, keeping her eyes on the Gothic window, full of moving lights.

'I've been barred,' he said. 'Might that be down to you?'

She flicked a glance at him. She hadn't seen him clearly, but he was not robed, like the others. He seemed to be wearing a jacket and jeans. She made sure she kept Jane on the other side of her.

'If you've been barred, why are you still here?'

'Because Simon will come,' Bain said. 'If he isn't here already.'

'Simon?'

'*You* know who I mean.'

'Maybe.'

'You really aren't on his side, are you, Merrily?'

'I'm not on anybody's side.' She was picking up a musky, sandy smell on him. It reminded her, for just a moment, of Sean. She made the sign of the cross and cloaked herself and Jane in the glow from the breastplate of St Patrick. The smell went away.

Bain said, 'Am I right in thinking Simon's offended you?'

'Am I supposed to think this is ESP, Ned? Your awesome powers at work?'

'Isn't Father Ellis performing exorcisms?'

'Is he?'

'Do they work?'

'Depends on what he intends them to do. That's where the problems arise.'

'Tell me.'

Jane touched her shoulder. 'Mum . . . I think they're coming.'

'If I tell you what he did,' Merrily said, 'will you bugger off?'

'OK.'

'He performed some kind of baptismal ritual which effectively bound together two people who never should have been brought together in the first place. And when the woman died, her . . . spirit would not leave the man. And instead of bringing him comfort, it oppressed him and sapped his energy, and turned him into . . . even less than he was before.'

'Mum . . .'

'Thank you,' Ned Bain said. 'What will you do about that?'

'I don't know that I can do anything.'

She moved behind Jane to the corner of the barn, looked out across a yard, past the farmhouse to where a track was marked out by a line of swinging torches and lamps.

She heard singing – inane, redneck gospel, with all the spirituality of a football chant.

'We shall raise the sword of Christ and strike the Devil down.'

'Sounds like your people, Merrily,' Ned Bain said. 'And my cue to disappear.'

In the night, with all the spearing torches, the hymn sounded dense and menacing. Merrily remembered the Christian biker with the dead dragon on his T-shirt.

'This is what you wanted, isn't it, Ned?'

'If I were you,' Ned Bain said, 'I'd stay well out of it. Call that a gentle warning. Call it a prophecy. Goodnight, Merrily.' He turned and merged with the shadows. 'There's blood on your hands. Why's that, I wonder?'

She didn't see how, in this light, he could possibly have seen her hands. And she'd got it all off, hadn't she?

In the shimmering silence of the open ruins, with the tower rearing behind his priestess, Robin brought a taper from the fire and lit the candles around the crown of lights. The little flames sprang brightly. Robin said,

> 'Behold the Three-formed Goddess,
> She who is ever Three
> Yet is she ever One.
> For without Spring there can be no Summer,
> Without Summer, no Winter.
> Without Winter, no new Spring.'

Tears in his eyes as he gazed on his goddess. She was everything he'd ever imagined, the beautiful book cover he'd painted so often in his head for the book which was too profound, too poetic, too resonant for anyone yet to have written. He looked into Betty's eyes and then up at the blurred moon.

'Listen to the words of the Great Mother – She who, of old, was also called among men Artemis, Astarte, Athene, Dion, Melusine, Aphrodite, Ceridwen, Dana, Arianrhod, Isis, Brigid and by many other names.'

And so it went on, and when it was over, the maid took up a broomstick and walked clockwise around the fire, followed by the mother and the crone, sweeping away the old, and Robin prayed to the moon for the badness and torment in this place to be swept away for ever.

When the torch and lamp lights were enlarged, beams crossing in the air, and the hymn behind her began to sound like the baying of wolves, Merrily looked up and saw him.

Just a shadow against the stars, then faintly lit by the lanterns on the battlements. He was not in his white robes, which would have been too conspicuous; someone would have seen him getting into the tower.

'Oh Christ,' Merrily said. She turned to Jane. 'Stay there.'

'No chance,' Jane muttered, and followed her towards the church.

They kept close to the walls so they couldn't be seen from the tower itself, passed by the Gothic window full of lights, edged around the building to the opening, where the south porch had been. Merrily began to pray softly and realized, with horror, that she was praying to God for protection against His servants at the gate.

She was very anxious now.

Robin picked up, from outside the ring of stones surrounding the fire, two twigs of holly he'd cut a week ago and hung over the back door, so that they were now nicely brittle.

The coven gathered around him. He knelt before the fire and set light to each twig in turn and held it up for them all to see. Then he tossed each of the twigs into the flames. And the coven chanted with him, in what ought to have been joy and optimism but sounded scarily flat and formulaic,

'Thus we banish Winter,
Thus we welcome Spring,
Say farewell to what is dead
And greet each living thing.
Thus we banish winter,
Thus we welcome Spring.'

Then the coven melted away, into the shadows and out of the church, Max patting Robin on the shoulder as he passed. 'Well done, mate,' Max whispered.

All over.

All over, but for the Great Rite.

A double sleeping bag lay directly under the tower, protected from the wind, a candle-lantern quietly alight at either end.

Robin stood by the fire. Betty walked away toward the base of the tower and when she reached it, she turned around, all aglow in her nest of candles. But the glow came from more than the candles, and there was a strange moment of fusion, as if the whole church was a crown of lights around them both, and Betty's gown slipped down with a silken rustling, and Robin's heart leapt like a fawn and he moved toward her along the open nave.

And then he heard a voice, cold and strident on the night.

'Foul serpent!'

Robin looked up and saw the spectre on the battlements, its arms raised like the twin points of a pentagram upside down.

'O most glorious leader of the heavenly armies, defend us in our war against the dark spirits which rule this world and the spirits of wickedness in the high places. For the Holy Church venerates you as her guardian and the Lord has entrusted to You the souls of the redeemed, to be led into heaven.'

'St Michael,' Merrily explained. 'He's invoking St Michael. It's his exorcism.'

She stood in the entrance, with Jane.

'You've got to do something,' Jane said.

A bright light lanced over the kid's shoulder. A TV cameraman was moving up behind her. They were all piling in now, whether they'd come over the gate or across the bridge, forming a big circle around the ruins. But it had been a small church and she and Jane were blocking the narrow entrance. People began to push at her back.

'Make them go away!' A woman's voice she'd heard somewhere

before . . . *I can show you a church with a tower and graves and everything* . . . 'This is sacrilege!'

Merrily put an arm around Jane and didn't move.

Ellis boomed from the tower, his voice like a klaxon in the still, freezing air. *'In the name of Jesus Christ, our Lord, and of Michael, the Archangel, we confidently undertake to repulse the deceits of Satan!'*

Merrily was furious. He was not entitled. He was not *entitled* to wield the name of Christ like an axe . . . or the cross of Christ like a dildo . . .

Robin Thorogood couldn't seem to move. He stood in the nave, staring up, as if his blood had turned to ice. Impaled by TV lights, he looked like a prisoner caught in the searchlights escaping from some concentration camp. Merrily couldn't see Betty.

From the tower, in the haze of the lanterns, Ellis cried, *'God arises! His enemies are dissembled, and those who hate Him shall fall down before him. Just as the smoke of hellfire is driven away, so are they driven. Just as wax melts before the fire, so shall the wicked perish before the presence of God. Behold—'*

He stopped. Betty had walked out. She was robed again. She looked terrified, but she didn't look up, not once.

She was somehow still wearing the crown of lights.

And Merrily, in a vibrantly dark moment, was already hearing the verse from Revelations when he started to broadcast the words.

'Now a great sign appeared in heaven . . . a woman clothed with the sun, with the moon under her feet . . . and on her head . . . a garland of twelve stars . . .!'

Robin Thorogood shouted, 'No . . . that's not . . .' Throwing out his arms in protest.

'Serpent!'

Merrily saw what she knew that Ellis was seeing. She saw the picture in his war room, the one by William Blake, and it turned Robin's arms into great webbed, leathery wings the colours of a freshly dug worm, and his wild hair into a ram's curling horns. She saw the Woman Clothed with the Sun, stars around her head, a twinkling lure for the Great Red Dragon.

Merrily at last gave way to the prods and thrusts at her back.

*

Robin saw the small, dark-haired woman running into the nave.

'*No* . . .' she was yelling. '*Please God, no.*'

And when he heard, from above, this sickening, crumbling, creaking, cracking sound, he realized he was screaming too as he hurled himself towards Betty, threw his arms around her and bore her to the ground, covering her with his body and closing his eyes as the first stone came out of the sky.

He didn't feel it. He couldn't feel anything. But he could hear other people's screams and, above them all, Ellis's bellow.

'*And there was war in heaven!*'

Robin just lay across his goddess on the sleeping bag, unmoving as the black sky tumbled.

He opened his eyes just once, to watch the crown of lights rolling away like a cheap Catherine wheel, the birthday candles going out one by one.

There were many other lights, too, but he closed his eyes on them; many other sounds, but he didn't listen to them. He heard only the heart of his goddess, and his own voice whispering the words which moved him beyond all others.

'*In the fullness of time we shall be born again, at the same time and in the same place as each other, and we shall meet and know and remember . . . and love again . . .*'

FIFTY-NINE

Damage

He was a tall, stooping man with a mournful, half-moon kind of face, a heavy grey moustache. He was the recently appointed head of Dyfed-Powys CID, a mere caretaker role, he said, before retirement. His name was Gwyn Arthur Jones, detective superintendent. Gomer Parry knew him from way back, which saved them some time.

But it was still close to 3 a.m. before they left the incident room – Dr Coll's waiting room – for the comparative privacy of Dr Coll's surgery. The door was closed, and a metal Anglepoise burned on a desk swept clean of all papers.

Formal statements had been taken and signed. Jane was asleep on Dr Coll's couch. Sophie had taken Eirion back to Hereford and his stepmother's car.

Detective Superintendent Gwyn Arthur Jones had brought out his pipe and discovered a bottle of single malt in Dr Coll's filing cabinet.

'Kept naggin' at me, see,' Gomer said, 'that piece o' ground. Amateur job, stood out a mile. Why would bloody Gareth dig it up again and put it back, 'less he was lookin' for treasure, and Gareth wouldn't know treasure 'less it come in a bloody brass-bound chest with "Treasure" wrote on it.'

'And Mrs Prosser?' The superintendent's accent was West Wales, quite soft, a first-language Welsh-speaker's voice. 'Did no one *ever* nurture uncharitable suspicions about her?'

'Judy?' Gomer shook his head as though he would go on shaking it for ever. 'Not me.' Least nothin' I could get a ring-spanner to. But

479

her kept croppin' up, ennit? I kept sayin' to the vicar, didn't I, vicar, you wanner talk to Judy . . . Judy's smart . . . Judy *knows*. Bloody hell, Gwyn, I never guessed Judy knowed it all.'

'And still holding out on us.' Gwyn Arthur sipped Dr Coll's whisky. Merrily had noticed that when he'd taken the bottle from the drawer he'd replaced it with a twenty-pound note. 'I don't somehow think she will ever do otherwise. "Mrs Councillor Prosser, wife of a former chairman of the police committee" – time and time again, like name, rank and number.'

'Local credentials,' Gomer said. 'Means everythin' here.'

'And Dr Collard Banks-Morgan, former acting police surgeon – the allegations about *him*, he tells us, are quite risible. As we would have been further assured by Mr Weal, had the poor man not taken his own life. I suspect people cleverer than me will have to spend many days among Mr Weal's files.'

Gwyn Arthur poured further measures of whisky into those little plastic measuring vessels you got with your medicine.

'All in all,' he said, 'never, in my experience, have so many eminently respectable, conspicuously guilty people lied so consistently through their teeth. I'm awfully afraid, Mrs Watkins, that you are destined for a considerable period in the witness box.'

'What will you do with Ellis?' Merrily asked.

'We'll hold him until the morning, then we shall have to think in terms of charges, and I'm very much afraid that my imagination, at present, will not stretch a great deal further than wilful damage – if that – regardless of the tragic consequences. He didn't even have to break into the tower. Just bolted himself in from the inside. What happened later was, he insists, an unfortunate accident. He hasn't even described it as the will of God. The tower parapet, as the late Major Wilshire discovered to his ultimate cost, was horribly unstable. He did not mean for all those stones to fall.'

'What about the TV pictures?'

'Almost gratuitously graphic when it comes to portraying the results. But the lights on the cameras were insufficiently powerful to reach the top of the tower – or to illuminate Ellis's movements in the moments before the stones were dislodged. I would give anything for it to be otherwise, but there we are.'

Merrily lit a cigarette with fingers which still would not stay steady. 'I'm not giving up on that bastard. Expect me at the station later today, with a Mrs Starkey, if I've got to drag her. But I don't think it'll come to that. Not now.'

'Yes, indecent assault is a better beginning.' Gwyn Arthur Jones drained his medicine measure and went to stand at the window. The only vehicles left on view in the village were the police cars and vans, Merrily's Volvo, Gomer's Land Rover and Nev's truck with the digger on the back. Gwyn Arthur came back and sat down and contemplated Merrily. 'And what else? What else, in your wildest imaginings, Merrily, would you think Ellis might have done?'

She took a tiny sip of Scotch. 'Well . . . have you got anybody yet for the village hall?'

'Interesting,' Gwyn Arthur said, 'but no we haven't. The travellers we brought in were *most* indignant.'

'I mean, it was all getting a bit tame, wasn't it? A few hymns, a little placard-waving. He'd had his chance to convince 300 fundamentalist Christians that Satan was in residence in Old Hindwell, and he hadn't *really* pulled it off, had he?'

'You think he planned to inflame these people, as it were, with the thought that the pagans wanted to burn them alive? Maybe to drive them to excesses?'

'Knowing full well he'd have been able to lead them to safety out of the rear entrance, even if Gomer hadn't turned up and received the credit? I think that's very much on the cards.'

'Hmm,' said the superintendent. 'Certainly, emotions among those decent, church-going Christians were running at a level possibly unparalleled since the days of the witch-hunts. There's no question in my mind that it *could* have become extremely nasty . . . if, ironically enough, those stones had not fallen when – and where – they did.'

'You could always check out his robe for petrol traces or something.'

'No one as yet, has been able to *find* his robe,' said Gwyn Arthur Jones regretfully. 'He doesn't remember where he left it. Unlike Mrs Prosser, he's being entirely cooperative. He tells us he chose to go alone to the church, one man against a horde of heathens, precisely because he did not want his legitimate Christian protest against the desecration of the house of God to become a bloodbath. Several witnesses confirm that he tried to stop them.'

Merrily closed her eyes. 'He doesn't *like* churches. Churches are disposable. Instead, he set up in this village hall because it was close to Old Hindwell Church . . . the battleground. He claimed he'd been getting anonymous letters, phone calls . . . signs on the Internet.' She sighed. 'Do you know the Book of Revelations at all? The paintings of William Blake?'

Betty stared down into the near-black water. She said slowly, 'O Lord, Jesus Christ, Saviour Salvator, I beseech the salvation of all who dwell within from witchcraft and from the power of all evil men or women or spirits or wizards or hardness of heart. Amen Amen Amen.'

An ambulance warbled across the city. Maybe the one which had brought her here several hours ago.

From the viewing platform above Victoria Bridge, the suspension footbridge over the Wye, bushes hid the sprawl of Hereford County Hospital.

It was dawn, that coldest time, with only a few lights across the river, shining through the bare, grey trees.

'Either the charm didn't work,' she said, 'or it worked all too well.'

'Get rid of it,' Merrily said.

Half an hour ago, she'd been waiting with Betty when the ortho-paedic surgeon, who was called Frank, had explained that Robin's pelvis was smashed, and there was some spinal damage. 'Will he walk again?' Betty had asked. Frank couldn't answer that one, yet, but he said he was hopeful.

Merrily said bitterly, 'War in heaven, and all the casualties down here.'

'Don't you go losing your faith,' Betty said. 'It's only religion. Faith is faith, but religions are no better than the people who practise them.'

SIXTY

Lamplit

It was still only mid-morning when the bedside phone awoke her. She hadn't been in bed long enough for it to be a sleep of any depth – although the half-dreams were dark – and she was instantly focused and expecting the worst.

She didn't expect *him*.

'It all comes down to demonization, you see, Merrily,' he said, as if they'd been talking for hours. 'I was demonized from an early age – twelve, to be exact. He was the little Christ, and I was the Antichrist. He and his mother were always very efficient at the demonization of anything in their way. And he still is, of course.'

He sounded as if he'd been drinking. His voice was dark and smooth and intimate. Merrily sat up in bed, fumbling a cardigan around her shoulders.

'He wanted dragons, so I sent him dragons. I sent him serpents.'

'What do you mean?'

'It isn't *all* done by magic. The postal service can be equally effective, and now the Internet and email . . . almost as fast as one can transmit a thought. But then it's all electricity, isn't it? Everything's a form of electricity. Science is catching us up. Soon *everyone* will be doing magic. What a dispiriting thought.'

She heard the clink of a glass against his teeth.

'I've been a bad man, in my way. No worse, I would submit, than Simon, but bad enough. Sometimes I yearn for redemption. Is that possible, do you think, Merrily?'

'It's possible for everybody.'

The sunlight penetrated through the crack in the curtains and put a pale stripe down the bed. Celtic spring had come.

'I hoped you'd say that,' he said. 'So . . . will you help me? Will you help a poor sinner onto the . . . lamplit path?'

She froze. 'Who told you about that?'

He laughed. 'I know everything about you. You're in bed, aren't you?'

She felt his Sean-breath, the warm dusting, and she was afraid.

'I can just see you in bed,' he said, 'all rumpled, a little creased around the eyes. Rumpled and smelling of softness and sleep.'

She remembered the blood he could not have seen on her hands. She remembered the red and white lights on the motorway, false lights in a night of filth.

'Can we meet?' Ned Bain said. 'And discuss my redemption?'

'I don't think that's a good idea,' she said, and put down the phone and sat there in bed, shivering.

Notes and credits

Most of the stranger aspects of this novel are based (as closely as the law and the rules of fiction allow) on fact. The 'Abracadabra' charm can be seen at the charming Cascob Church; the Four Stones nestle behind their hedge off the Kinnerton road; and, although you may have difficulty finding Old Hindwell itself, the Hindwell Brook still meanders and sometimes rushes through the Radnor Valley. The area's huge importance in the Bronze Age was uncovered by the Clwyd-Powys Archaeological Trust and documented by Alex Gibson in *The Walton Basin Project*, published by the Council for British Archaeology.

My thanks to Glyn Morgan, who pointed me down the dark lane of border spirituality with a very timely photocopy of the witch charm, found in the wall of an old house in North Radnor.

The imperfect Radnor Pentagram also exists. It's true that only four churches are listed in the official tourism brochure, but the pentagram can be completed by adding St Michael's, Discoed, an ancient church with an even more ancient yew tree in front. Thanks to Carol for first suggesting what proved to be more than an idea, and to the distinguished medieval historian, Alun Lenny, of Carmarthen, for completing the picture, with the help of Francis Payne's classic work on Radnorshire.

Pam Baker told me a hospital ghost story and explained about oestrogen, etc. Quentin Cooper discussed a few of the problems involved in owning a church, and extra details were filled in by Brian Chave, Steve Empson and Steve Jenkins at the Church of England.

Geoffrey Wansell and John Welch helped with the setting up of the *Livenight* programme.

Thanks also to Neil Bond, Sally Boyce, Jane Cook, Gina-Marie Douglas, Paul Gibbons, Gavin Hooson, Bob Jenkins, Dick Taylor and Ken Ratcliffe. And, for inspiration, to the white magic of XTC and 'Apple Venus'.

There was important help and fine-tuning from my editor at Macmillan, Peter Lavery, and my agents, Andrew Hewson and Elizabeth Fairbairn. And, of course, the thing would never have come together at all without my ingenious wife, Carol, who plot-doctored, character-trimmed and edited for weeks, with her usual inimitable flair, ruthlessness and lateral thinking. You *can* do it alone, but it's never as good.